THE

Lassoed by

MARRIAGE

ROMANCE COLLECTION

9 Historical Romances Begin After Saying "I Do"

THE
Lassoed by
MARRIAGE
ROMANCE COLLECTION

Mary Connealy
Angela Bell, Angela Breidenbach, Lisa Carter,
Rebecca Jepson, Amy Lillard, Gina Welborn,
Kathleen Y'Barbo, Rose Ross Zediker

BARBOUR BOOKS
An Imprint of Barbour Publishing, Inc.

Print ISBN 978-1-63409-120-6

eBook Editions:
Adobe Digital Edition (.epub) 978-1-60742-572-4
Kindle and MobiPocket Edition (.prc) 978-1-60742-573-1

Published by Barbour Books, an imprint of Barbour Publishing, Inc., P.O. Box 719, Uhrichsville, Ohio 44683, www.barbourbooks.com

Our mission is to publish and distribute inspirational products offering exceptional value and biblical encouragement to the masses.

Member of the
Evangelical Christian
Publishers Association

Printed in Canada.

Contents

The Substitute Bride by Angela Bell 7
Bridal Whispers by Angela Breidenbach 49
Mule Dazed by Lisa Carter 101
The Sweetwater Bride by Mary Connealy 149
A Highbrow Hoodwink by Rebecca Jepson 197
Not So Pretty Penny by Amy Lillard 253
All's Fair by Gina Welborn 291
The Colorado Coincidence by Kathleen Y'Barbo 349
Railroaded into Love by Rose Ross Zediker 403

The Substitute Bride

by Angela Bell

Chapter 1

London, England
On a Sunday in June of 1865

Gwen's husband suffered quite the shock upon lifting her Brussels lace veil at the conclusion of their wedding ceremony. A most natural response, when taking into consideration that Lord Carlyle had rather expected to see her sister.

Cynthia, his betrothed.

Poised at the altar of St. James's Church, dressed in a gown of white and a veil of falsehood, Gwen held her breath. Lord Carlyle's complexion dulled. Mouth agape, his brown eyes gawked at her as if he had unveiled a diseased hag, not a bespectacled spinster. She clutched her white rose bouquet, hands trembling. *Please God, don't let there be a scene.*

Clearing his throat, the bald vicar repeated himself. "I have pronounced thee man and wife, Lord Carlyle. God will not take offense if you kiss your bride."

Gwen's cheeks flamed under expectant gazes. God might not object to such a display of affection, but Lord Carlyle appeared to object more than she had feared. A furrow entrenched along his brow, deepening by the second. She never should have allowed Mamma to push her into this scheme. Yet now it was too late. Here she stood, before a hundred guests, at the mercy of a man whom she'd met but twice and never shared a word.

Would Lord Carlyle expose her sham?

With visible effort, Lord Carlyle closed his mouth into a firm line. He thrust a rigid elbow in her direction. Gwen's head lowered as she slipped an arm through Lord Carlyle's. There would be no kiss. Not today, not ever. In silence he led her up the church's middle aisle bookended with smiling faces, feathered bonnets, and wildflower garlands.

Once concealed in the vestry, Lord Carlyle broke free of her arm and paced the diminutive room. He seemed to have forgotten Gwen's presence—not speaking, avoiding eye contact and physical touch. Nothing she wasn't already accustomed to after seven seasons in London society. After all, why would anyone notice her while stunning young Cynthia flitted about on a cloud of mirth and light?

Heaving a sigh, Lord Carlyle leaned against the wood-paneled wall. Gwen pursed her lips. The poor man seemed so distressed, so utterly disappointed. She ought to say something. Some sort of apology. He deserved better than this, better than her.

Before Gwen could muster the courage to speak, the vicar entered, accompanied by her twittering mother, beaming father, and Lord Carlyle's esteemed aunt, Lady Agatha Carlyle, social pillar of the ton. The clergyman handed Gwen a quill, issuing orders as to where she ought to sign the register. After writing her name, she offered the pen to Lord Carlyle.

For a moment Lord Carlyle remained still. Gwen swallowed. What would she do if he refused to sign? *Please, please, just end this.*

Lord Carlyle snatched the quill, plunged it into the inkwell, and hastily scrawled his name. Dropping the pen upon the register, he struck her with a glare and strode out of the vestry. Gwen's shoulders drooped, the surrounding voices fading into a droll hum. What must he think her? A fortune hunter? Conniving social climber?

If only she could tell him the truth, that she had never wanted this. She'd only wanted to fulfill her duty as a daughter by making a good match and save her family further embarrassment. With a gloved finger, Gwen pushed her wire frames up the bridge of her nose. Lord Carlyle wouldn't believe anything she said. Not while blinded with love for Cynthia—an infectious malady caught by every man in her younger sister's sphere, which resulted in the illusion of reciprocated feelings. None of them knew that only Cynthia's mirror enjoyed her affections.

"Gwendolyn." Mamma's high-pitched voice shattered all thought. "How wonderful it is to see you rescued from the shelf. I thought the day would never come. But here you are. A bride." Sighing, Mamma clasped her hands together. "Finally."

"Yes, Mamma." Finally married—to a man who despised her. Every girl's dream.

Papa caught her up in an embrace warmed by the aromas of sandalwood, turmeric, and cinnamon. The spices of his merchant trade. "I'm glad to have found a smart chap who appreciates my special girl."

Tears burned Gwen's eyes, fogging her spectacles. How pained dear Papa would be to know that wasn't true. Keeping him in the dark was the worst part of Mamma's plot, one for which she would never forgive herself.

Shortly, a stoic Lord Carlyle returned to half-escort, half-drag Gwen to his waiting carriage. After assisting her inside, he seized a place on the opposite seat. In the farthest corner possible. As the carriage tottered over cobblestone, Lord Carlyle's gaze stayed fixed out the open window. Burdened by the oppressive silence, Gwen bowed her head.

This, then, was her future.

Thank God for the serving of cake. If Elliott had been forced to endure another lengthy congratulatory toast, his ego would've spontaneously combusted.

While the quiet bride studied her frock and her conniving parents made small talk with the guests in their home's front parlor, Elliott managed to escape to an unoccupied corridor. With both hands, he raked fingers across his scalp. How he wanted to shout. Stride up to Mr. and Mrs. Bradbury and demand an explanation. But he couldn't afford to ignite a boisterous row, not with Aunt Agatha and all the cousins here. Such a spectacle would only alert the family to his stupidity. Besides, no explanation was actually required. It was quite clear.

He'd been duped into marrying a spinster. His entire engagement to Cynthia had been nothing but a ruse. A ploy by the Bradburys to rid their nest of an elder daughter whom no one wanted. All the while Cynthia. . .

Oh, dear Cynthia. Elliott's hands sank back down over his face. His sweet, angelic Cynthia. What agony she must feel at their permanent separation. The betrayal he felt could be slight in comparison to the pain she'd suffered at the hands of her own family. He had to speak with her. Alone. And find out what in blazes had happened while he'd been away from London.

Elliott strived to regain a look of composure, tugging at his waistcoat and smoothing his hair. The Bradburys had kept Cynthia out of sight during the wedding, but she must be in or near the house someplace. Maybe consoling herself in the garden? She did so love flowers. With determined steps, he marched toward the front door.

Aunt Agatha's bejeweled person barred his path. *Blast.*

"There you are, Elliott. How marriage suits you." Aunt Agatha stretched her short height to give him a wispy peck on either cheek. "I admit, upon first meeting the Miss Bradburys, I was a trifle shocked you'd chosen the plainer of the two."

Elliott bit his tongue. Not as shocked as he.

"However, I'm sure she will make a fine wife." Waving a fan before her line-etched face, Aunt Agatha continued in her dry manner. "In fact, I believe it will be good for you to have a stabilizer, something grounding you to reality. Now your time can be more appropriately utilized, instead of frittered away on those silly contraptions."

"Automata," he corrected, jaw tensing.

Aunt Agatha flicked the annoying word away with her fan. "The point is, now you can put aside your little hobby and focus on the responsibilities of family life. Producing an heir for the barony. Overseeing the running of the estate with greater involvement. Along with other serious matters more deserving of a true nobleman's attention."

While Aunt Agatha droned, Elliott nodded curtly. He'd heard many variations of this speech over the years. A true nobleman hunts game outdoors, discusses business with his land steward, etcetera. He does not stay cooped up in a workshop and tinker with clockwork automaton figures. That makes a man an absurd joke. Elliott bit his inner cheek. This marriage was meant to elevate him in the family's esteem. Rob them of their punch line.

Instead it had only proven them right.

A familiar tinkling laughter wafted from outside, penetrating Aunt Agatha's musings. *Cynthia.* Elliott sidestepped his aunt. "Beg pardon. I need some air."

He rushed outside as a footman aided Cynthia's graceful descent from a newly arrived carriage. Blond ringlets framed her fair face, bouncing as she moved. Elliott clasped her gloved hands. "Darling, where did your parents have you cloistered? Which one arranged this outrageous switch?"

Cynthia's blue eyes captured the sunlight, improving upon its rays. "Mamma, of course. She always has the most brilliant ideas, and I believe this is her greatest accomplishment, for it works to the advantage of all concerned."

Advantage? Of whom? Elliott swallowed. "My love, what do you mean?"

Coral lips forming a smile, Cynthia beckoned over her shoulder. "Do come out, beloved. You know I simply wither away when deprived of you too long."

"Coming, my pet."

A broad-shouldered man exited the carriage. Cynthia ripped her hands from Elliott's touch and practically threw herself at the other gentleman, latching on to his thick arm. A new kind of glow illuminated her delicate features. "Lord Carlyle, allow me to introduce my fiancé. Lord Algernon Mountbatten, Marquis of Glendover."

Fiancé? Elliott's heart caught and sputtered like jammed gears. As their carriage left for the stables, he struggled to find words. "When. . .did this. . .joyful event occur?"

Cynthia rested her head upon Mountbatten's shoulder. "After my family had the pleasure of seeing you off on the morning train to Essex, concluding your stay in London. Only an hour later, Algernon paid call and proposed in our front parlor. It was quite romantic."

He took in a slow, deliberate breath. An hour later, the morning he'd departed from London. Meaning after she had already accepted his proposal.

"It was a blissful day for the whole family," Cynthia cooed. "For after Algernon departed, who should arrive but Lady Agatha to begin preparations for your union to Gwen. Imagine, two sisters engaged in the same season. It's marvelous. We've just returned from delivering our engagement announcement to the *Times*. Isn't it exciting?"

This final proclamation knocked out the breath Elliott had forgotten to exhale. His lips fumbled, attempting to fasten words into a reply but failed. Cynthia, his dear Cynthia, wasn't the least despondent. It was like she'd never met him. Never giggled at his jokes, never danced in his arms.

"I've had so many decisions to make." Cynthia's hand flitted about, flashing a lavish engagement ring. "Wedding date, gown selection. Not to mention the matter of where to set up house. At first, I couldn't settle on which of Algernon's exquisite country manors would suit me best, but then I decided on his house in Berkeley Square. I've always preferred living in town."

"I see." His single country house must've been most unsuitable to her tastes. Just like his lower-ranking title.

Mountbatten patted Cynthia's hand. "I'm quite lucky she said yes."

Playfully swatting Mountbatten's arm, Cynthia giggled. "I'd have said yes much, much sooner had you made your intentions known. Fool."

Elliott's heart ground to a painful halt. *Much, much sooner.* How could he have been so deceived? Cynthia partnered in her mother's plan from the start. His love had been nothing more to her than a trivial consolation prize when Mountbatten had yet to propose and a hindrance once he had. He was the fool.

At that moment his carriage rolled up as Mrs. Bradbury led his bride from the house. Mrs. Bradbury's shrill tone quipped sharp as her angular features. "Time to leave for the wedding tour."

A footman produced Elliott's hat and kid gloves. *Time to leave, indeed.* One last time, he searched Cynthia's face for a remnant of the sweet girl he'd known, but found none. It had all been smoke and mirrors, a sparkling facade. A game. The Cynthia he knew had never existed.

Without a single remark or good-bye, Elliott climbed into the carriage and rode away with his substitute bride.

Chapter 2

Gwen crossed the threshold of Briarcliff Park on her own two feet, her husband having fled the carriage—and her presence—immediately upon arrival.

An empty foyer constituted her welcoming party. Its dark woodwork and autumnal colors failed to warm the coldness of her first entrance into her new residence. Running her teeth along her bottom lip, she clutched the folds of her skirt with a gloved hand. She dared not move from the vestibule. Not without specific instruction. Would Lord Carlyle reappear long enough to escort her to her new living quarters? Her gaze lowered to the floor.

After what she'd put him through, she deserved no such courtesy.

The *click-clack* of heeled shoes lifted Gwen's gaze to the main staircase. A woman thin as the spine of a children's book took each of the steps at a brisk pace. Strands of thread, in a wide array of outlandish colors, hung out of every single pocket in the woman's black uniform and white apron. Such a sight could not be found in London.

"Apologies for the postponement of politeness, dearie." Now standing before her, the tall woman bobbed a crooked curtsy. "I'm Mrs. Nesbitt, head of housekeeping. Welcome to Briarcliff, Lady Carlyle."

A sinking feeling tugged at Gwen's stomach. That honored name had never been offered her, and she could not bring herself to don it now. Not in the house of the man she'd deceived. "Please, Mrs. Nesbitt, call me Gwen."

"Very well, m'lady." Mrs. Nesbitt withdrew a fuchsia thread from a pocket and expertly tied it in a bow around her left ring finger, her only digit not festooned in a rainbow of string. Having done this, she bestowed on Gwen a crinkled smile. "Let me see now. . . ." Her fingertips danced up and down the bows, landing on a teal string looped about a knuckle. "Ah, yes. I'm to convey you to your quaint quarters. Follow me, Lady Gwen, if you please."

As Mrs. Nesbitt started back up the staircase, Gwen trailed closely behind. What would the situating of rooms be like? Would she and Lord Carlyle. . .share a chamber? Flaming heat washed over her cheeks, and her empty stomach rolled. *Please, let that not be the case.* Not so soon, at any rate.

She placed a hand upon her traveling dress's tight bodice, willing her uneasy stomach to be tranquil. Indulging worry was useless. Besides, if one judged things by the speed of Lord Carlyle's escape from the carriage, a shared chamber seemed rather improbable. Adjoining rooms, like Papa and Mamma had in their London town house, would be a more likely and desirable scenario. In such an arrangement, things could be taken slowly. Develop gradually. While a connecting door retained a hopeful prospect.

Assuming, of course, that Lord Carlyle didn't keep the door forever bolted.

At the top of the stairs, a long corridor branched out in two separate directions. Mrs. Nesbitt guided her down its right end and opened the final door of the same side. "Here we are, dearie." She removed the teal string from her finger, tucking it into a pocket. "Hope everything is to your liking."

Gwen took a turn about and studied the room. Small but not cramped. Comfortably furnished with the necessities—bed with nice linens, washbasin atop a stand, and a desk. Her new quarters appeared to have everything important except books and. . .a second door.

This was not a grand master's suite, nor was it an adjoining couple's quarters.

In what kind of room had Lord Carlyle placed her?

All previous blushing worries diminished under a frosty wind of suspicion. Gwen inhaled a deep breath and faced the doorway where Mrs. Nesbitt stood. "The master of the house. . .Where is his room located?"

"His room?" Mrs. Nesbitt's decorated fingers twiddled with her apron hem, and her gaze flitted down the other end of the corridor.

Gwen exhaled as her suspicion froze over, heavy and cold. It was true, then. The Carlyle family quarters, including the master's suite, were situated on the opposite wing of the house. Lord Carlyle had run ahead of her to ensure she never drew near that wing. By his order, a teal-colored string had hastened to prepare a far-off guest room and convey her to its door. Like an unwanted visitor.

Latching on to a yellow bow around her thumb, Mrs. Nesbitt blurted, "You must be fairly famished after your travels. Could I bring you some luncheon?"

Nothing could entice her to eat at the moment. Gwen turned away, pushing her spectacles up the bridge of her nose. *Breathe, just breathe.* "Thank you, but I. . .I don't wish to be a bother."

"You're no bother, Lady Gwen."

"Only one person has ever shared that sentiment, and I doubt more will be added to your number. Nobody desires an ink blot on their page." The sinking feeling tugged at Gwen once more. How could she endure this without Papa? She made to sit on the bed but couldn't. This wasn't her home. She was no bride, but a trespasser. How could she find peace here, where not one soul wished to see her face or bid her good morning? What was she to do with her days?

"Please don't fret, dearie." Mrs. Nesbitt tailored her tone in an attempt to soothe. "I know things have been. . .trying, but I promise to make you as content and comfortable as I'm capable. Anything you need. Anything."

What she needed was for an author to lean over her story, rip out the last few pages, and pen a new ending. Alas, "happily ever afters" existed but in fairy tales. Gwen wrapped her arms across her chest. "Are there any books in the house I may read? My own will not arrive from London for some time."

"We've boundless books on the ground floor. You're welcome down there. Why don't I fetch you some tea and then lead you to the library's location, eh?"

Gwen nodded.

Tying a plum-hued string on her pointer finger, Mrs. Nesbitt left to execute her task.

Now alone, Gwen settled onto the chair at her new desk. With access to a library, she might just be able to bear living at Briarcliff Park. She'd simply do as Lord Carlyle wished—stay out of his sight and allow him to forget that she existed. Spend her time in her room and in the library, reading. Characters in novels would keep her company as they had in London, and their companionship would have to be enough.

Since God also seemed to have wiped her existence from His memory.

⁓

Gear. Cogs. Axels. These things made sense.

These things were safe.

Tucked away in his workshop and hunched over a scarred wooden desk, Elliott tinkered with the mechanism inside an automaton frog's throat. It had yet to produce the desired croaking sound. Just as its legs had yet to carry it across the desk with a hop, hop, hop. But it would work. He would make it work. This he could actually fix. Here, in this workshop, he could fix anything. Build anything. Here, there was an understandable and rational order. Peace.

Everything London lacked.

The automaton frog and the pliers slipped from his hands and clattered onto the desk. *Blast.* A groan rumbled from Elliott's throat. Must everything he tried to do fall apart? He attacked the buttons on his waistcoat and tossed it across the room, giving no heed to whether it had landed in the same location as his already shed overcoat.

Never, he'd said. Never would he let Aunt Agatha pressure him back into the London scene. The buttons on his cuffs received the next assault. Why hadn't he held firm? He should've stood his ground. One cuff fell open then the other. Each defeated. Like him. He shoved both sleeves up to his elbows. No. He had to cave under an old woman's nagging criticism and return to the city with its pretention and crowds and flaxen-haired deceivers.

Cynthia's laughter scratched across his mind like so many nails on a blackboard. Slumping in his chair, Elliott sighed. How could he have been such a fool?

The workshop door creaked open and whined shut. Must be luncheon hour.

Harrison's familiar hands set a tray of food on the desk, right atop the mass of parts and tools. "Time to eat, sir."

"Not. Hungry."

"You never are when you're working. Nevertheless, eat you must."

Elliott looked up at his persistent butler. "Make me, old man."

Every line on Harrison's face solidified into a scowl. "I feared it would come to that." With a deft move, he withdrew a silver spoon from the inside pocket of his immaculately pressed black jacket. "Thus, the reason I came prepared." A fissure of a smirk cracked through his frown.

Elliott chuckled, despite himself. "I must look bad form. You haven't threatened me with that in years."

"Not since you were in nursery and drove poor Nanny Alice downstairs in search of reinforcements over a plate of brussels sprouts." Harrison put away the spoon, his features taking on a softer form of severity. "I know you are suffering, my lord, but I must urge you to move beyond that distress in order to make our new resident more comfortable. From Mrs. Nesbitt's report, the girl is quite miserable."

Elliott's gaze dropped to the food. She wasn't the only one. "Is she now?"

"Yes, and more than a little afraid. Contrary to the way things seem, I'm not certain the present circumstances are her doing. At least, not entirely. Reach out to her, my lord. You might discover her to be a pleasant young lady, and perhaps in time, the situation can yet be redeemed."

"Redeemed?" Elliott scoffed, face hardening. "I don't think so, Harrison. There isn't enough time in eternity for that." Nothing could redeem this situation. Not time, not God.

"Be that as it may, here she is and here will she stay as Lady Carlyle."

Elliott's teeth clamped together, clenching tighter and tighter until the mounted pressure birthed a throbbing pain along his rigid jaw. The servants might address his bride by that usurped title, as could the family in London, the villagers of the county, and society at large.

But he would not.

"You can't just cast the girl aside, my lord."

Leaning an elbow on the desk, Elliott wiped a hand over his face and gripped his chin. What was he to do about his substitute bride, then? Befriend her? Dig a grave for his feelings and produce the heir the family wanted? Have a marriage that was all show and nothing more? No. That he would not do. Deception might have arranged this marriage, but he refused to live a lie.

He straightened, pushed aside the tray of food, and set back to work on the clockwork frog. "I'll see to it that Miss Bradbury's needs are provided. I can offer her nothing more."

Chapter 3

H ow slowly the time passes here, encompassed as I am by frost and snow!"
Gwen's gaze lifted once again from the page of Mary Shelley's *Frankenstein* and sought out the library door handle. Still in place, still not touched. Gripping tighter onto her novel, she nestled against the library's lone chair. She rubbed her temple with the middle finger of her free hand. Why she insisted upon torturing herself with fleeting glances at the door, she did not know. Many weeks had transpired since she'd last seen Lord Carlyle. Like characters from different books, they carried on completely separate lives. Separate stories. Although they lived under the same roof, shared the same library, one had nothing to do with the other.

There was no fear of Lord Carlyle seeking her out.

Why, then, did she not feel relieved?

Gwen shook her head and forced herself to exhale. *Breathe. Go back into the story.* She read on, turning to a new page. *"I have one want which I have never yet been able to satisfy, and the absence of the object of which I now feel as a most severe evil, I have no friend, Margaret: when I am glowing with the enthusiasm of success, there will be none to participate my joy; if I am assailed by disappointment, no one will endeavor to sustain me in dejection."*

A twinge constricted Gwen's heart. *"I haven't any friends, Papa, and these horrid spectacles will only make matters worse."* She shut the book. Light streaming through the window behind her chair glistened on the marbled leather binding. Perhaps *Frankenstein* had best be saved for another day. While she appreciated novels that resonated with the heart and stirred the mind to thought, for now, she wished neither to think nor feel.

Gwen stood and returned the book to the exact spot from whence it had come—second bookcase from the left, third shelf down, seventh volume over, adjacent to the metal figurine of an owl. Every book ought to have its designated place on the shelf, and she always desired to respect that order whether or not it be of her own design. Besides, she did not want to break any rule that might upset Lord Carlyle or worse, draw his attention upon her. She'd been the object of people's disdain often enough.

Walking along the border of the library, she surveyed the dark wooden bookcases that stretched from floor to ceiling. Simply carved, yet possessing a certain grandeur, they lined every wall but the one at the library's center where the window and lone wingback chair had been situated in a reading nook. A perfectly quaint library, really. Not to mention fully stocked with a wide assortment of titles. She'd not yet been tempted to open her crate of books from London, although they'd arrived.

Gwen stopped before one of the rolling wrought-iron ladders attached on tracks to access the bookcase's highest shelves. She lifted her skirt and climbed to the second step. How she would love to give one great push and go flying across the room. Yet she dared not indulge such silliness. This house was not her own, and she'd yet to learn its regulations.

Leaning forward against the ladder, Gwen focused on the books at eye level. The majority of Lord Carlyle's collection consisted of various scientific texts, but a few fictional works could be found among them. On this particular shelf, a brass deer figurine with jade eyes watched over *The Hunchback of Notre-Dame* by Victor Hugo, *Robinson Crusoe* by Daniel Defoe, and *The Pilgrim's Progress* by John Bunyan, the latter of which appeared to be a first edition from 1678 in its original publisher's cloth. How rare to find a copy that had not been rebound in leather by the owner. She reached toward *Pilgrim* but hesitated. Better not disturb such a valuable book.

Nearby, a cobalt volume with a well-creased spine beckoned to be held. Despite being unfamiliar with the author, she obeyed its call. The cobalt continued around the front in a beautiful Cosway-style binding, framing at its center an embedded image of a seated woman with a bird perched upon her finger. *Britannia Ornithology: A Study of England's Native Birds* scrolled along the top in gold embossed lettering. A textbook. Explanation for her failure to recognize the author. She rubbed a finger along the damaged spine. It had obviously been read a number of times, enough to loosen a few of the pages from the binding. Perhaps, through Mrs. Nesbitt, she might request permission to mend it? The task should be easy enough as she'd repaired books in worse state.

Gwen descended the ladder and returned to the reading nook, pausing for a moment to admire the window's view of a magnificent tree situated on a blanket of green. *Absolutely charming.* Later in the afternoon, perhaps she might take one of her own books outdoors to read under the shade of its stately branches.

Seated again on the singular leather chair, she opened the ornithology book and discovered not loose pages but sketches of birds that had been tucked into the textbook beside the descriptions of their namesakes. She picked up a sketch of an owl. Detailed and intricate, it appeared identical to the metal owl on the shelf beside *Frankenstein*. Every sketch, in fact, had a figurine counterpart within the library. Incredible. Who was behind these masterful creations? Had Lord Carlyle purchased the figurines and text from an artist in London? Perhaps Lord

Carlyle served as the artist's patron.

Footsteps announced someone's arrival.

Gwen's gaze leaped to the door as a disheveled Lord Carlyle strode into the library. Her breath stalled. Lord Carlyle's eyes latched on to her own, and the abrupt contact brought him to a halt. His countenance stiffened.

Neither of them said a word. Neither of them looked away.

She dared not be the first to speak, nor could she leave the room without being dismissed by her husband. Lord Carlyle had her trapped as she had trapped him. *How painfully fitting.* Remaining perfectly still, Gwen waited. When he spoke, what would Lord Carlyle say? Would he be angered at her presence in the library or simply at the reminder of their cohabitation?

Like one doomed to face the guillotine, Lord Carlyle at last strode toward her with a look of grave resignation. "I came in search of a text required for a project. *Britannia Ornithology.*"

Her gaze dropped to the book in her hand, the book Lord Carlyle sought. Gwen stood and hastily surrendered it to his keeping. "Here. I apologize. I should not have read one of your books without first gaining your consent."

Lord Carlyle's expression softened a little beneath several days' accumulation of stubble, although his tone and posture remained rigid. "No fear. If you overstepped any rule, it's one of propriety's. Not mine."

He acted as though propriety's laws were a matter of little importance. Perhaps she adhered to that unwritten rule book too closely?

"So." Opening the book, Lord Carlyle fanned through the pages. "What do you think, then?"

She stared at him, unable to produce a single syllable. Had Lord Carlyle just inquired for an opinion? Her opinion? No man of her acquaintance had ever cared to do so. "Excuse me?"

"The sketches." Tension clipped his words short and brusque. "I'd like to know what you think of my sketches."

Lord Carlyle had drawn the sketches? Then the metal figurines must also be his work. She'd never imagined him to be so inventive. Gwen slid her glasses farther up the bridge of her nose. "Well, I. . .I think your sketches are. . .beautiful. Gifted."

The tension holding Lord Carlyle's countenance in its grasp released him, and his jaw slackened. He eyed her with the conflicted expression of one who wishes to believe something very much and yet expects a falsehood to be lying in wait. "Gifted, hmm?" He studied the sketches in his hand. "Of all the words used to describe my work, I've yet to hear that one."

Why ever not? Lord Carlyle's creative works deserved praise. Perhaps. . .perhaps she might tell him as much? Protocol dictated that wives seldom speak and avoid having opinions, but Lord Carlyle didn't seem to care about society's rules. Gwen pursed her quivering lips. If she wanted things between them to improve, she must take advantage of this opportunity to connect their stories. *Courage now.* "Perhaps the previous viewers of your sketches possessed a limited vocabulary."

Gaze still attached to his book, a smile came and went on his face. "Perhaps."

Faint warmth bloomed on her cheeks. That was the first time Lord Carlyle had ever smiled in her presence without Cynthia being in the room. Granted, it hadn't been directed her way. But still, he'd smiled. *Say something else.* "May I be so bold as to inquire why you craft your figurines from metal instead of traditional mediums such as porcelain or bronze?"

Lord Carlyle met her gaze, a new lightness in his eyes and demeanor. "Because they're not mere figurines or statues meant to remain immobile. They are automata, machines designed to move, each in their own way."

"That's incredible." Almost as incredible as him conversing with her now, engaged and responsive. Perhaps their situation wasn't entirely without hope. "What different things can your machines do?"

With his free hand, he indicated the bookcases across the room. "The owl there can turn his head in a full rotation. A frog I recently finished can hop and croak, and my current design, a wren, will preen its feathers once completed. Automata are as much or more science than art."

A slight smile lifted Gwen's lips. "How fanciful."

Tension reclaimed its hold over Lord Carlyle's demeanor, hardening his eyes and straightening his posture. "I must return to work." He again opened *Britannia Ornithology*, directing his gaze to the words therein. "If you will excuse me."

The phrase was not so much a begging of pardon as a command to leave. A command Gwen heard all too clearly. She should've held her tongue. Bowing her head, she skirted around Lord Carlyle and exited the library in all haste. Once the door shut behind her, she found herself in the corridor and quite alone. Exactly how she'd wished to be this morning.

Yet now she found herself wishing Lord Carlyle had asked her to stay.

Chapter 4

Although days had passed, although the doors of his workshop guarded against everything contrary to logic and reason and knowledge, Elliott could not free his mind from one barbed word and its invisible film of patronizing poison. The one Miss Bradbury had flung at him so casually, so carelessly. *Fanciful.* A very pretty term for imaginative foolishness.

Grinding his teeth, Elliott begged all his concentration to focus on the task at hand—increasing the mobility of the automaton wren's neck. He examined the parts of gleaming brass. Tighten this here. Loosen this there. Another day's work and he should have the mechanics of the preening action smoothed out and the wren completed. Then he could add it to his useless collection of mechanical accomplishments that remained unseen and unappreciated.

"Nephew, your little hobby is fanciful, not scientific."

Elliott slammed his pliers on the desk. There was that word again. Sinking against the back of his chair, he cupped both hands over his chin and mouth. Miss Gwendolyn Bradbury was quite the play actress. For a few brief moments, she'd actually made him believe that she respected his work. That she cared enough to learn more about automata. That she was different than snide, belittling Aunt Agatha. Yet it was nothing but another veil. Another show that concluded in his humiliation.

Snatching up the rivet-extracting pliers again, Elliott delved into the wren's neck. Work. That would clear his head. Pushing forward to new inventions, scientific advances, and discoveries. That was all that mattered. It certainly mattered more than Miss Bradbury's estimation of him. Let the pretender think what she would. He did not care. He didn't.

A crash resounded out in the hallway. Elliott's gaze flew toward the door. Had Harrison dropped his dinner tray? Unlikely; it was early yet for dinner. Maybe Mrs. Nesbitt had taken a stumble? He strode across the workshop, flung open the door, and stepped into the hall. A hard object jabbed the instep of his slipper. *Blast.* Yanking away his foot, he discovered a fork from the tray he'd set in the corridor after luncheon. His plate, teacup, and the tray's other contents also lay scattered about the floor along with a book and puddle of the remaining cream he'd not poured in his tea. What had happened here?

Young Molly from the kitchens returned the assaulting fork to the tray while a second woman assisted by mopping up the cream.

Miss Bradbury.

Elliott took a slow step backward. Kneeling on the carpeted runner, Miss Bradbury worked in all diligence with no apparent concern about soiling her dress. No concern about doing a menial task. She did not even seem bothered to be working alongside a kitchen maid. She was simply helping. Would Cynthia have done likewise?

Looking up from her task, Molly caught sight of him. A weak smile propped itself on her face with a crutch. "'ello, Lord Carlyle."

One mention of his name and Miss Bradbury shot to her feet. "Lord Carlyle." Her eyes widened to fill the circumference of her rounded spectacles. She motioned the damp rag in her hand toward the floor. "I take sole responsibility for this mess. If I'd possessed better sense than to have my face in a book while walking down the corridor, we wouldn't have collided into each other. Please. . .do not punish Molly."

Elliott scratched the nape of his neck. Never had he seen someone raised in the upper-class London scene demonstrate such concern for a servant's welfare. Not even his sweet Cynthia. He looked at Molly then to the cracked teacup on the tray. Cynthia's smile seemed to appear on the fractured porcelain, taut and disparaging. *I said Assam, not Darjeeling. The kitchen maid shouldn't be so stupid as to confuse the two. Take this back immediately, and have someone competent brew a fresh pot.* His jaw tightened.

How wrong he'd been about his sweet Cynthia even then.

"You all right, Lord Carlyle?" Molly hoisted the tray onto her hip. "I'll 'ave this cleaned oop soon."

Miss Bradbury nodded. "Indeed, we will, and again I must ask that any chastisement be directed toward myself, as the mess resulted solely from my clumsiness."

Why did Miss Bradbury feel the need to beg for mercy? Did she think him so unfeeling? "There will be no punishment. It was obviously an accident, not an act of malice. As for chastisement, a simple 'watch your footing' is all I think necessary." Elliott turned his gaze to Molly. "You were not hurt, I hope?"

"No, m'lord."

"Good. Then you best take the debris to the kitchen and ask Mrs. Nesbitt what can be done about the carpet."

Nodding, Molly took her leave. Now with he and Miss Bradbury alone, the climate in the corridor altered, mimicking the environmental traits found at the peak of a mountain range—thin air, bitter cold, and overwhelming silence. Miss Bradbury stood, gaze darting about as if unsure where it belonged. Tension pulled the muscles in Elliott's neck and shoulders. Should he say something? Take his leave to the safety of the workshop? The latter idea held far more appeal.

Harrison's voice haunted his mind like a specter. *"You can't just cast the girl aside."*

Elliott sighed through clenched teeth. *Blast, that Harrison.* Fine, he would reach out. After all, Miss Bradbury had shown kindness in assisting Molly. But he refused to lower his guard. Her devious nature might reassert itself, accepting his offered hand only to yank him down from the precipice's edge.

Clasping both hands behind his back, Elliott cleared his throat. "I hope you're also unharmed. No injuries?"

Miss Bradbury's jaw slackened. She fiddled with her glasses and averted her gaze to the cream-saturated carpet. "I'm fine. Thank you."

The intense silence resumed, and his posture suffered under its oppressive weight. She *did* think him unfeeling. Is that how he came across? As a coldhearted louse who cared not if a lady was injured?

As if in answer, Miss Bradbury's gaze remained fixed to the floor.

The burden for further conversation apparently rested on his incapable shoulders. What more could he say? He'd never possessed a talent for small talk. Should he do something, offer her tea?

Miss Bradbury shifted on her feet as if eager to flee.

Whatever Harrison said, the young lady before him did not desire his attentions. Nor did she hold him in very high regard. Not that her good opinion carried any value or importance. That fact had already been established. Hadn't it?

Shaking his head, Elliott allowed his arms to fall relaxed at his sides. Of course it had. Now, better release Miss Bradbury from his company lest she suffer greater distress. And he, greater embarrassment. "You may leave the rag here and return to your book. Mrs. Nesbitt will tend to the carpet."

Without a word or glance his way, Miss Bradbury placed the cloth on the floor, secured her fallen book, and escaped down the hallway. Posthaste.

Chapter 5

Warm light brushed against Elliott's eyelids, inviting him to awaken and greet the day. An invitation that was becoming increasingly irritating. He must ask Mrs. Nesbitt to acquire curtains for the workshop window. With a groan, he opened his eyes and lifted his head off the worktable. Pain wrenched his neck, tightening the muscles. He rubbed a hand along his nape and arched in a stretch. Maybe he should request that a cot be brought into the workshop as well. He was sleeping here every night anyway. Might as well be comfortable.

Elliott rose to his feet and ambled over to the window. Instead of the usual dusting of dew, vast puddles of water had formed overnight in low-lying areas. Leaves and snapped branches of varying size and thickness littered the grounds. Had there been a storm?

A yawn escaped his lips. Yes, he vaguely recalled hearing the presence of a strong gale. Rumbling thunder. Howling wind. The slapping of rain against the window. Yet there'd been another sound as well. A crash? The wind must have hurled a stray branch through a window. Hopefully that was the extent of the damage.

Elliott rubbed sleep from his eyes. Although, come to think of it, the clatter had sounded quite severe. Loud enough to rouse him from a sound slumber, which was no small accomplishment. He'd best locate Harrison and the groundskeeper to launch an investigation and evaluation of the damages.

After straightening his rumpled shirt and slipping on a waistcoat, Elliott ventured out into the corridor. Not long into his search he came upon a quick-striding Harrison. "I'm glad you've awakened, Lord Carlyle. You're needed in the library."

Blast, not the library. Of all the rooms to be damaged. . . "How bad?"

"Oftentimes things are not as bad as they seem." Gray brows furrowing, Harrison embodied the definition of *grave.* "I'm afraid this is not one of those times."

A sinking feeling weighted Elliott's heart. *The books.* Sidestepping around Harrison, he rushed toward the library and then skidded to a halt in the open doorway. A tree. There was a tree in his library. In the midst of the storm, the giant tree he'd climbed on as a boy had sought shelter in his favorite chair—by toppling leaves-first straight through the window.

Elliott blinked.

The tree and destruction remained.

He staggered into the library, struggling to absorb the surrounding chaos. Broken glass crunched underfoot. Smashed table and chair legs poked out amid the fallen tree's mangled branches. Leaves skittered about the room chased by an invading breeze while water dripped from the bookcases nearest the window and gathered in puddles. And the books. . .

The important knowledge he'd collected and preserved, now strewn. Everywhere.

On the glass shards that cut through pages.

In the water that bled ink.

Everywhere.

Elliott crouched and picked up a sodden book, one of the few educational volumes written about automation and printed in an extremely limited quantity. Could it be repaired? Could any of them be repaired? He stood and took in the damage once more. How was he going to salvage everything? His sweeping gaze settled on the automation book—damp pages sticking, melding together; black ink bleeding, seeping into margins; words disappearing, erasing precious knowledge. *Ruined.*

Exhaling a long breath, he released the volume and let it fall to the floor. He couldn't salvage everything. All he could do was refocus, rebuild, and replace the titles that weren't one of a kind. Anything irreplaceable and beyond mending must be considered a loss.

"Harrison." Elliott massaged his brow with all ten fingers, willing away the looming shadow of a migraine. He needed to think, clearly and quickly. They must waste no time. Options must be discussed, servants organized.

Harrison appeared to the right in his peripheral vision. "Ready to assist, my lord. How would you like us to begin?"

"Priority number one is to move all the volumes into another room. Select whichever room you deem suitable. Then instruct the servants to box up the books that are unscathed and set aside the ones in need of repair. Any with water damage must be tended to immed—"

Crunching glass drew Elliott's gaze to the door where Miss Bradbury stood, mouth agape. He held back a groan. *Blast and blazes.* After weeks of successful avoidance, she would appear now. At the very moment when he most needed to be free of the mind-fogging emotions she dredged up. The migraine broke from the shadows and pulsed in his temples. He simply couldn't deal with her now. Could. Not.

"Excuse me, Harrison." Elliott marched in the direction of Miss Bradbury.

Were those tears in her eyes or simply the light glaring off her spectacles? "I must ask that—"

"Anything. I'm ready to do whatever is needed." An odd waver affected Miss Bradbury's diction. "Simply tell me how I can be of service."

Elliott's headache worsened by the second. Normally he would welcome another pair of hands, but having Miss Bradbury working alongside would be more hindrance than help. A painful distraction. One he couldn't afford to entertain. "Your assistance isn't required. Please vacate the premises, and for the duration of reconstruction, stay out of the way."

In the vacant corridor, Gwen leaned her back against the wall. Despite having seen the devastated library, her mind and senses still wrestled to process the sight. The library was destroyed. Her haven ruined. What was she to do with herself now? Without the reading nook, the books, she had nothing here. Nothing.

The brimming tears she'd suppressed in front of Lord Carlyle spilled over, one by one, first misting then completely fogging her spectacles. Why couldn't Lord Carlyle refrain from pushing her away, just this once? She neither asked for, nor expected, his affections. She only desired to assist in minimizing the damage and make repairs to her—his—books. Something she was quite capable of doing. Even Mamma had acknowledged her ability. *"You are quite skilled, my dear. Pity you're not a son, for then it might be useful."* True, it wasn't a compliment by any stretch of the definition, but for Mamma it was near enough.

Gwen sighed. If Lord Carlyle could only be made to listen. It might take days to get a professional bookbinder from London out to Briarcliff Park, which would be much too late for many of the waterlogged volumes. She could help now. Ought she to say something or do as she'd been told and *stay out of the way?*

Gwen took off her glasses and squinted in the direction of the library door. Although she had no desire for confrontation, if she was to have any happiness in this house, she needed the library and its books repaired as soon as yesterday. A deadline that required immediate action.

Withdrawing a handkerchief from her skirt pocket, Gwen cleaned the tear spots off her spectacles and then wiped the white linen over her face, drying each eye. Now somewhat presentable, she returned the spectacles and handkerchief to their former place. She faced the library and took a deep breath. *Courage.*

Gwen opened the door.

Near the shattered window, Lord Carlyle and Harrison stood together, conversing. She walked straight to their sides and spoke without introduction. "Lord Carlyle, I don't wish to blatantly defy your orders, but I must insist that I be allowed to utilize my skill and tend to the damaged books before they are lost."

Lord Carlyle raised an eyebrow. "Skill?"

"Yes, skill." Burning under his and Harrison's fixed gazes, Gwen forced herself not to look away or look down. She had better push through without pause lest she be interrupted or worse: lose her nerve. "As a child, I taught myself the trade of bookbinding by reading copious instructional texts and asking questions of bookbinders in Papa's employ. Eventually, Papa dispensed with sending for professionals and began coming to me for binding and repair work. Loose pages resewn onto bands, torn ones pasted, et cetera. Point being that whether or not you require my capable assistance, the damaged books here do."

Harrison smirked as if impressed.

Meanwhile Lord Carlyle eyed her with an illegible expression.

She waited, breath held. *Please, please, say yes.*

After exhaling a long, slow breath, Lord Carlyle nodded in consent.

For once, allowing her to stay.

Chapter 6

L emuel Gulliver would live to see another day.

Tucked in a dry corner of the library, far from the devastated window, Gwen mended a copy of *Gulliver's Travels*. More books lay on a table before her in neat rows. A sliver of bare space divided the books into two sections—the right section needing light, eventual repair and the left needing significant, immediate repair. She still couldn't believe Lord Carlyle had granted her request to station a literary triage in the library. From here she could reach and treat her paper patients faster. As well as keep an eye on the library's reconstruction.

Across the way, Lord Carlyle attended to his automaton inventions while male servants removed debris. Three days now and still they worked. Hauling away furniture and branches. Sweeping up tricky glass shards that hid in plain sight. Cutting the tree into smaller pieces to be removed, stored, and used for firewood. She shook her head. Who knew one storm could wreak so much havoc?

A young footman approached, carrying a book in each hand. "Here you go, Lady Carlyle."

Gwen forced herself not to cringe as she received the volumes. Would she ever be able to hear that name without envisioning Cynthia? "Thank you, Tomlin. These books on the right may join the other lightly battered volumes in the dining room. Gently, now."

With a nod, Tomlin gathered the indicated books and departed. Gwen turned her attention to the new finds in her hands. *Let's see.* A text entitled *The Mechanics of Clockworks*, suffering a broken spine and complete page detachment. This would require urgent pasting lest any pages be lost amid the shuffle of workers. She placed it on the left side of the table. Next to the copy of *Pilgrim's Progress*, which was in fact a first printing and, thankfully, still in near-mint condition. One of the few that had managed to come through the gale unscathed. She placed the book in a crate beside the table and then wiped her hands on her apron. Now back to Gulliver.

As Gwen worked, a faint *clank* alerted her that Lord Carlyle had placed yet another invention on the table situated to her left, his automata triage. The whole morning long he had gone by her, back and forth. First, gathering his inventions on the table and assessing the damage. Then transporting the ones in need of repair to his workshop and boxing the remainder to be stored until the library's restoration. All in complete silence.

Lord Carlyle had yet to grace her with even a glance since she had marched in the other day proclaiming her skill and demanding to help. A reaction she'd quite expected. After all, working in the same room did not equate working together.

A lowering crate entered Gwen's line of view as it touched the floor in front of the table. More patients, no doubt. "Thank you, Tomlin." She raised her head. "I will see to those—"

Lord Carlyle stood behind the crate, staring at her dead-on.

"I. . .I th–thought you were Tomlin." Her cheeks warmed to a scalding temperature. *Brilliant, Gwen. Care to mumble any more statements of the obvious?*

A small smile broke through the corner of Lord Carlyle's mouth but was quickly boarded over and secured with the cold spikes of indifference. He began to open the crate. "These are the books Mr. Bradbury sent from London. I want to inspect them myself, so you may be properly compensated for any damage."

An almost sweet notion, if it hadn't been voiced like an estate agent or solicitor.

Lord Carlyle at last succeeded in prying open the crate. Reaching inside, he selected one of her books and started his examination, slow and thorough. Almost every single page of the paneled leather-bound text received his careful scrutiny. Gwen's head tilted to the side. He did seem legitimately concerned about the welfare of her personal collection. A greater tenderness than she ever expected to receive from him.

Perhaps she ought to return his kindness in like by offering an update on the status of his books? Gwen lightly cleared her throat. "Y–your books are pulling through nicely. Overall."

This failed to evoke from him a glance. "Really?"

"Indeed. I've been pleasantly surprised at the number of volumes that incurred no scars whatsoever. A few books more and this crate can be closed. It will be the fifth box of undamaged volumes to go into storage. Also, all the books in the dining room promise to make a full recovery with a little effort and. . ." Gwen let the sentence drift off and hang, incomplete. Why was she rambling on so? Lord Carlyle obviously had no interest in listening to her speak.

Stay out of the way. Keep silent. Lowering her gaze to the worktable, Gwen beseeched her attention to return to her previous task.

"What is your middle name?" Lord Carlyle's smooth voice erased all thought of work.

Why would he suddenly make such an inquiry? Gwen elevated her gaze only slightly, peering at Lord Carlyle over the rim of her spectacles. "Louisa."

A spark of interest brightened Lord Carlyle's eyes. Lifting the book in his hand, he indicated the cover with a pointed finger. "By G. L. Bradbury. Did you write this novel?"

Gwen's stomach leaped to her throat and then plummeted. Every word on all three hundred and fifty pages. And she did not wish Lord Carlyle to be her first reader. She straightened and adjusted her lowered spectacles. "That? It—it's nothing. Mere coincidence."

"Coincidence is ruled by chance, and I don't put stock in chance. It's a simple word utilized by simple men to label a truth they don't like, a miracle they refuse to credit to the Divine, or facts they can't explain away with their finite reason." Lord Carlyle smiled again, broader, fuller. "The facts here are quite easy to explain."

Yes, but she'd rather he avoid such enlightenment regarding her writings. Gwen placed a shaking hand on the table. "Shouldn't we get back to work? There is still much to be d—"

"Fact one." Lord Carlyle opened the cover of her novel. "The book's author shares your initials. Fact two, it was in your possession. Fact three, you have the needed skill to bind a book yourself. And lastly. . ." He turned to the first page and met her gaze. "You have every symptom of a nervous novelist who has yet to share their work with another."

A deflating sigh escaped from Gwen. She didn't know whether to be irritated by his insistence or flattered that he'd referred to her as a novelist.

Lord Carlyle cradled her novel in the palm of one hand. "May I?"

Had he truly just asked for her permission? And in all politeness? Gwen pursed her lips. How could she refuse his request when it was made with such courtesy? She nodded.

An air of seeming pleasure brightened Lord Carlyle's countenance as he began to read over her first page. Then the second page, the third. Gwen's heart beat painfully slow, and she twisted her apron string round and round with her finger. What was he thinking? Did she want to know what he was thinking?

Well into the first chapter, Lord Carlyle finally lifted his gaze and fixed it on her, really and truly. Not in a glance but in a steady manner that would not waver. "It's. . .very good."

Good. Gwen released the mangled apron string and indulged in a smile. He'd said it was good. Very good, no less! Before responding, she took a calming breath and clasped her hands before her skirt. "Thank you."

"Whatever possessed you to write a novel?" His eye contact remained steady.

"It began as a way to pass the time, but the more I wrote, the more I desired to create something that conveyed hope. Something that might cheer another through the written word as I have been countless times." Gwen's gaze faltered, dropping for a moment to the book-laden table. She couldn't believe she had just confided such feelings to Lord Carlyle of all people. Not even Papa knew about her novel or daydreams.

"Sounds like a noble ambition. You ever attempt to have it published?"

"N–no. I never felt it was ready. Besides, I knew Mamma wouldn't approve."

"Nonsense. You should begin inquiring among the London publishers. Try to generate interest. Perhaps transcribe a sample chapter for submission." Lord Carlyle passed her the novel over the table. "Dreams are vital to life and should be fed, not starved."

There was a story hidden behind that statement, one she very much longed to read. Gwen accepted the book, holding it against her chest. "Do you have a dream?" Something to do with automata, perhaps? His inventions were lengths more creative than her writing. The world should know of them.

Lord Carlyle's posture resumed its former rigidity, every spark and smile packed into storage and boarded once more. "You were quite right before. There is much work to be done."

⌀

Later in the evening, Gwen sat at the desk in her chamber and composed a letter for Papa.

> Dearest Papa,
> I am sorry you learned of the swap scheme from Cynthia's slip of the tongue. I should have told you long before. Yet I beseech you not to grieve for me. Neither let your fear run wild. I admit that my circumstances have not been comfortable or ideal. Yet I'm beginning to develop newfound hope that, one day, Lord Carlyle might think of me fondly.

Gwen's pen hovered above the page. Perhaps God saw her plight, after all.

Chapter 7

Finally, after four and twenty days, the library no longer resembled a greenhouse.

Blueprint in hand, Elliott surveyed the laborers constructing the new window frame. A quartet of pounding hammers struck nails to differing rhythms as they secured the hand-carved wooden molding. Now they were making progress. Removal of that infernal tree, done. Relocation and temporary storage of the salvageable furnishings and books, done. Reconstruction of the window frame and exterior of the house, nearly done. He consulted the blueprint and nodded. *Excellent.* Once the glass he had ordered arrived from London and was installed, nature would be put back in its rightful place—outside.

Now he could shift his attention to another matter.

Miss Bradbury.

Elliott cast a glance at his bride in the far corner where she worked, repairing books. Tirelessly, as she had for days on end. At the onset, he'd harbored reservations about the quality of her workmanship, but he could not criticize the results. She lacked neither intelligence nor diligence. In fact, her work was comparable to that of any professional bookbinders, except it hadn't cost him a halfpenny. By defying his order to keep back, Miss Bradbury had actually done him a service. A kindness. One characteristic he'd not have wagered her to possess at their wedding.

Yet, as days had accumulated into weeks, she had proven his initial estimation of her to be faulty. While they'd worked in the library, he had not once seen her speak an unkind, harsh, or belittling word to anyone. Not even the servants. Each person received her respect whether they worked upstairs or down. Elliott snuck another glimpse of the literary triage. Miss Gwendolyn Bradbury was not the deceptive, diabolical person he'd imagined. Perhaps Harrison was right. Maybe he ought not cast her aside.

Maybe he ought to give God the opportunity to redeem their marriage.

Rolling up the blueprint and tucking it in his waistcoat's inner pocket, Elliott dismissed the workers for the day and then rang for Mrs. Nesbitt. Upon her arrival, he asked that tea be brought to the library. And that it be made for two. Mrs. Nesbitt tied a new string about her thumb and hastened from the room to carry out her task.

Elliott followed her departure as far as the hallway and then waited in the vacant passage, shoe tapping the floor. *All right then.* He was going to do it. He was going to give Miss Bradbury a chance. Probably the most dangerous experiment he'd ever undertaken.

A few moments later, Harrison walked toward him harboring a stowaway grin beneath his lips and firm jawline. No unusual inflections altered his voice. "I heard you've ordered tea, my lord."

"Indeed."

"I also heard that the tea is to be arranged for two."

Blast. He should've known his request would ignite a gossip fire in the kitchens. The knowledge of such a blaze elevated his body temperature and scorched through his cheeks. "And?"

"And Mrs. Nesbitt and Cook were perplexed as to why you'd request to have it served in the library. They suggested that the parlor would be more suitable for entertaining a guest." Harrison's eyes glinted, asking a question for which he already knew the answer.

Elliott huffed out a sigh. "The tea is for myself and Miss Bradbury. And I suggest, Harrison, that you take off that smug expression and swallow it along with the forthcoming 'I told you so.' I may be taking your advice, but you've yet to be proven right. This experimentation could explode in my face and make matters worse."

"Lady Gwen is a young woman, not a test subject. And you are going in there, not as a mad scientist, but as her husband. Best look the part." One by one, Harrison unrolled Elliott's scrunched, wrinkled sleeves and buttoned them at the wrists. Then he withdrew a fine-tooth comb from his black jacket's inner pocket and attempted to tame Elliott's unkempt hair.

Mrs. Nesbitt arrived with the loaded tea tray. "Here you are, Lord Carlyle."

Waving off Harrison's attempts to preen him, Elliott seized the tea tray. "Thank you. I'm quite capable of taking it from here. It's only tea." He strode up to the library's open door, but his feet refused to convey him farther. What was he thinking? He'd never been capable of carrying on idle teatime chatter. Nor had he ever been skilled at conversing with young ladies. In their brief courtship, Cynthia had always maintained—dominated—the conversation, which had suited him just fine. But Gwendolyn was so much quieter, so reserved. Would he have to carry all of the talking? What if he said the wrong thing?

"It's only tea, my lord." Harrison's voice drew his gaze back into the hall.

Mrs. Nesbitt took a red string from out of her pocket, tied it in a bow around Elliott's thumb, and gave it a gentle tug. "Breathe. You'll be all right."

"Right." Elliott inhaled a deep breath and walked into the library.

All too soon he found himself facing Miss Bradbury with a tea tray in his hands, a table spread with books between them. Miss Bradbury looked up from the volume she was rebinding, and her spectacle-framed eyes widened, though she said not a word. Elliott's stomach took a tumble. *Say something, fool.* "Good afternoon."

Miss Bradbury remained frozen in place. "Good afternoon."

Blast, his turn again already. How should he proceed? Which method of social convention would be appropriate for this scenario? For a second, his gaze dropped to the tray and the red string on his thumb. *Breathe.* Elliott cleared his throat. "You—and I—w—we, rather, have been working hard. Long hours and so forth. I thought we'd more than earned a break from our labor." He lifted the tray, rattling the cups on their saucers. "For tea."

Miss Bradbury set aside her task and pushed her spectacles up her nose. "Sounds delightful. Shall we go into the parlor?"

"Actually, I thought we might take tea here. And admire our progress. On the renovations, that is." How many ways could he butcher a sentence?

"Where are we to sit?"

Sit? Elliott looked over his shoulder. Not one stick of furniture remained in the library except for Miss Bradbury's worktable and the large bookcases, which had been covered with tarpaulin. More of the same waterproof canvas covered the floor near the window. *Dash it all.* He should've thought to provide proper seating. Perhaps he should escort her to the parlor? But there he would feel stiff as the formal, uncomfortable furnishings. It was almost as bad as being in London. Here, he could relax. Here, he and Miss Bradbury had common ground.

Come on, man, think. He rotated in place, searching for a swift and tangible solution. Someone had placed a few clean tarps beside the doors, folded and forgotten. It would have to do. Spinning back around, Elliott extended the tray toward Miss Bradbury. "Would you hold this for one moment? I'll be right back."

Without a word, Miss Bradbury accepted the tray, her expression heavily burdened with unasked questions. Elliott hurried to the door and acquired one of the tarps. Unfolding the canvas, he laid it out in a place warmed by the afternoon sun, yet not in direct light. Once satisfied with its appearance, he returned to Miss Bradbury and reclaimed the tray.

Elliott motioned his head toward the tarp and offered her the use of his elbow. "Care to join me for an indoor picnic?"

A slight, unsure smile lifted Miss Bradbury's countenance. She came round the table and placed her hand within the crook of his elbow. Elliott guided her to the tarp where he then put down the tray and assisted Miss Bradbury in lowering herself upon their makeshift picnic blanket. After she seemed comfortable, he sat on the opposite corner and began to serve tea.

Miss Bradbury sipped from her cup. "This is lovely. I haven't been on a picnic in years."

"Neither have I, actually."

They exchanged a smile over this commonality and then fell once more into an uncomfortable silence. Miss Bradbury took her tea, rarely making eye contact. Sweat beaded on Elliott's brow while his stomach engaged in more acrobatics. As he suspected, she was waiting for him to lead the conversation. What could they talk about? Perhaps he could inquire about her writing? He would like to know more about her process.

"At what age did you begin writing your novel?"

"Eighteen."

Quite impressive. "How long did it take to complete?"

"Two years."

Elliott swigged the remaining tea in his cup like a draught of cognac. This wasn't working. Surely she wasn't so painfully shy? She had spoken more freely than this on previous occasions. Something must be wrong. Otherwise, why would she suddenly be unwilling to supply more than curt answers? Maybe. . .maybe it was because he had refused to answer the one question she had asked of him?

He sighed. He wasn't being fair. When he'd prodded, she had told him about her novel, her dream. How could he ask more from her unless he was willing to do as much?

Slowly Elliott placed his empty cup and saucer upon the tarpaulin. *Breathe.* "Miss Bradbury, I must offer you an apology for leaving your question so rudely unanswered the other day. If you still wish, I'd like to answer it now."

Miss Bradbury's gaze rose and stayed firmly upon him, waiting.

"I tend to be. . .hesitant when asked about my work or my ambitions. You see, unlike yourself, I have attempted to pursue my dream. And it ended badly." Elliott shifted, sank, anchoring a palm on the canvas and allowing it to bear his weight. Why was he doing this? This whole thing was a bad idea.

"Please, go on." Miss Bradbury's tone contained not a tinge of patronization.

Too late to back out now, chap. Inhaling a breath, he met her eyes. "Knowledge is very important to me. The gaining of new knowledge, the sharing of that knowledge with others. If my pursuit of knowledge had led me in a traditional direction, I might have garnered praise from my peers and esteem from my family. Unfortunately, to the dismay of both parties, my pursuit led me to automata."

"I fail to see the problem."

"The problem is that automation has yet to be accredited as a valid science. It's a relatively new technology and, on the whole, unexplored apart from ambitious clock and watchmakers who wish to display their skill for wealthy clientele. Most in the scientific community believe it should remain relegated to that sphere— that it has no great benefits beyond artistic sensibility. Disagreeing with their scruples, I ventured to explore the frontier of automaton engineering and broaden its limitations. Then years ago, I petitioned to have my work featured in a display at my graduating university."

Her eyebrows raised. "And?"

And his former professors had laughed him out of the room. "My petition was declined." Solidifying all of his family's criticism and concerns in one fell swoop.

"Why? What was their reasoning?"

"They thought my inventions too. . .fanciful." He gently tossed the barbed word out there and let it fall where it may.

Miss Bradbury's teacup clattered against the saucer and settled down to her lap. "S–surely. . .they could not have meant that? Not in that way. Words have so many different facets, different meanings. And people aren't always capable of handling them properly, especially when not aided by a steady pen." She glanced at her cup before returning her gaze to him, accented with a furrowed brow. "One can quite easily be misunderstood."

Misunderstood. She hadn't known the barb existed, then? The word had never been crafted as an insult. She might even have been paying him a compliment. Elliott straightened his posture. "Words are tricky devices. I think, in such cases of their misinterpretation, it's best to place blame on the language's complexity. Not on the speaker."

A faint smile smoothed the furrow from Miss Bradbury's brow.

"However, in the case of my professors, I'm certain they meant their every word."

She shook her head. "I cannot believe they would be so dull witted. I agree your inventions possess an artistic quality, but even I know there's more to them than that. Much more. How could they look at one of your inventions and doubt that intelligence and scientific ingenuity went into its making?"

Scientific ingenuity, eh? She seemed even more passionate about his work than he. "Perhaps you should write them a letter, or better still, write Aunt Agatha." He chuckled.

"I very well might." Miss Bradbury set her cup aside on the tarp, eyeing him with an expression that appeared to be concern. "I hope you're not going to allow one group of shortsighted men to dissuade you from pursuing your dream."

"I am not. I have simply chosen to bide my time and change my strategy. Since the universities will not acknowledge my work, I have decided to go elsewhere. I'm currently petitioning various museums throughout London for my work to be featured in an exhibition. If I can gain enough public esteem, I might receive invitations to lecture about my automation research." A chance to share his knowledge.

"That sounds like a fine plan." Miss Bradbury poured them each another cup

37

of tea, apparently having taken notice of his preference for sugar and no cream. "Your inventions are brilliant, Lord Carlyle, too brilliant to be hidden away in a country manor."

"Please, stop with the Lord Carlyle nonsense. Call me Elliott."

"Only if you will call me Gwen." With an uncanny amount of grace, she lifted her cup and saucer, concealing behind it all facial features but her eyes, which peered at him above the porcelain rim.

"As you wish." Elliott did not reach for his tea, too absorbed in study of those eyes. For now, under closer observation, the spectacles seemed not a ghastly obstruction or foreign object but a well-suited setting for two lovely examples of shining amber. Cynthia's eyes had never possessed such an intense depth and color, nor had she ever shown any interest in his work or anything other than herself. She had talked, taken the burden of conversation, yes. But she'd never truly listened. Never truly cared.

Not like Gwen.

How blinded he'd been by infatuation.

Elliott shook his head. "You really are nothing like Cynthia."

A shadow fell across Gwen's face, dimming the light in her amber eyes before they once again lowered and cut him from view.

Chapter 8

Hello again." Gwen knelt beside the crate of her books from London, the only books still in the library. Now that she had seen to all of the emergency cases, she could attend to the remaining damaged books at a more leisurely pace. Thus, freeing a portion of her time to become reacquainted with dearly missed friends and make decisions about their lodgings.

Gwen selected a volume bound in straight-grain treated Moroccan leather tinted a dark shade of evergreen. *Jane Eyre*, the unfortunate soul. After enduring so much heartache, poor Jane especially deserved to be settled someplace quaint and safe. Facing the boxes arranged on her left, Gwen's gaze shifted back and forth between the two. Where ought Jane to live? Here in the library or upstairs on her private shelves? Upstairs, for starters. Jane's tale warranted another read through. With great care, she placed the book in the box on the right.

Next Gwen assisted Jane Austen's children in stepping out of the crate, first Elizabeth and Jane, then Elinor and Marianne, and lastly black sheep Emma. The three volumes weighed Gwen's hands down to her lap, each one heavy, laden with words and memories.

Her memories.

Dreary afternoons plagued with silence, by the first line brightened with quadrille music and laughter no one could hear but herself. Long hours endured with not one soul for company, in the turn of a page rescued by this Austen sisterhood that welcomed her into their fictional family. That encouraged in the face of adversity, triumphed over hardship, and shared the joy of their happy endings with one bespectacled spinster who had very little happiness of her own.

A smile lifted Gwen's lips. Without a doubt, the sisterhood belonged upstairs as well. She placed the three volumes inside the right-hand box. Perhaps together, Austen's merry daughters could cheer up melancholy Jane Eyre.

The thought widened Gwen's smile, pulling her cheeks taut. She turned back to the crate. Next, good old *Silas Marner* emerged from the stack of books. Her gaze drifted to the left-hand box designated for the library. Perhaps she ought to give Lord Carlyle—Elliot—the opportunity to meet Silas. She had a feeling the two gentlemen would get along rather well.

She herself seemed to be faring better with Elliott. Their indoor picnic a few days prior had been lovely. For the most part. A swift nudge with Gwen's pointer finger prevented her sliding spectacles from furthering their descent. She could not expect things to be perfect in the course of a few days, if ever. Therefore, the awkward comment here and there must be tempered with the positives, counterbalanced. Ignored.

Perhaps by doing so, she might convince herself it had not hurt so much.

Renewing her focus on the present task, Gwen placed *Silas Marner* in the left-hand box and continued sorting through the crate. Alexander Dumas's bitter *Count of Monte Cristo*, upstairs. Elizabeth Barrett Browning's painfully romantic *Sonnets from the Portuguese*, buried in the library. The process rolled on in monotony for an hour or so, title by title. Until finally only one book remained at the bottom of the crate. One that she had forgotten about long ago.

The very one that had sparked her love of books.

Hans Christian Andersen's *The Ugly Duckling*.

Gwen withdrew *Duckling* from the crate, gently brushing her fingers across the worn calfskin binding and the painted Cosway-style cover illustration of a swan framed in flaking gold. How long had it been since she'd read *Duckling*? The number of years mattered not; she'd read it often enough as a child to know every word, sentence, and paragraph by heart.

"That summer the country was particularly beautiful, and it was glorious to be out in the green fields and meadows." Every time Gwen read that introductory line, she still heard it spoken in Papa's voice. Not a small wonder. After he had presented her with *Duckling*, she'd begged him to read it aloud at least five and twenty times in that one day's span.

The day she had first gotten spectacles.

Papa's voice warmed her faraway memory. *"You will always be my little swan, Gwen. People might not see it now, but one day they will."* A quiver unsettled Gwen's jaw and bottom lip. Except that one day had never come.

Because life off the storybook page was nothing like in fairy tales.

The ton in London never thought of her as a swan, only as a bespectacled spinster, a failure, a financial burden on the family. If they bothered to notice her at all. To most, she was nothing but a shadow in the foreground. The guest no one wanted to converse with but invited anyway to make an even party at a table.

In a way, Mamma's brutal honesty had been kinder than Papa's well-meant fairy stories. *"The swap is your only chance to get off the shelf, Gwendolyn. New young blooms are entering the marriage market every season, and you simply cannot compete. No man wants a wilting dandelion when they can have a rosebud like your sister."*

Gwen's head drooped as she bit her lower lip to contain a fresh tremor. No man wants an ugly duckling when he can have a swan.

"You really are nothing like Cynthia."

Once more Gwen's accursed spectacles slipped farther and farther down the bridge of her nose, yet this time she lifted not a finger to prevent their fall. However kind Elliott attempted to be now, it did not alter his true feelings. He had sought out Cynthia, courted and proposed to Cynthia. Without Mamma's interference, he would have happily married Cynthia because she was the one he had wanted.

Her glasses fell from her face and landed on *Duckling*'s faded cover with a wire rattle. Gwen inhaled a heavy breath as a single numbing tear trailed down her cheek. Nothing had changed to make her desirable to Elliott. Nor would such a change ever occur. She needed to cease believing the storybook notion that things could be otherwise. She would never be anyone's swan.

Rising to her feet, Gwen put her spectacles back in place, walked across the room, and turning her gaze away, dropped *Duckling* into the wastebasket.

Dashing here and there, Elliott stowed away tools, sorted clockwork parts into drawers, and attacked dust particle invaders with a rag and righteous indignation. Never again would he allow such a mess to accumulate. Never. Again. Of course, he'd sworn an identical solemn oath the last time he tidied the workshop—three years ago. Or was it five?

No matter. Today it would be spotless and in order. For now, that was all he required.

One day to set things in order. One day to set things right with Gwen.

"You called, m'lord?" Mrs. Nesbitt appeared in the doorway.

"Affirmative." Elliott paused from his work, one hand filled with jabbing springs and the other brass cogs. "Where is Gwen?"

"In the library I suspect, m'lord. You'd be hard pressed to find her anyplace else. The sweet, studious soul prefers books to air, I think."

Indeed, that was one of the reasons why he was beginning to like her so much and why nothing must go wrong today. Opening two more of the numerous tiny desk storage compartments with his knuckles, Elliott disposed of the springs and cogs. "This afternoon we—er, Gwen and I—will take lunch in the workshop. And, please, send it up with Harrison. I don't want any giggling maids or gabbing footmen eavesdropping at the door."

Mrs. Nesbitt curtsied, fiddling with the string on her apron pocket. "Yes, sir."

As the door closed, Elliott finished clearing his desk of all automaton projects and debris. He then scoured the wooden surface once more with the rag, allowing no oil smudge or speck of dirt to escape. This time must be perfect. Had he neglected to remember anything? Workshop tidied. Lunch ordered. Shirt and waistcoat freshly pressed. Nothing else remained on his mental list, except the notation written in bold red letters and repeatedly underlined.

Don't say anything stupid.

If need be, err on the side of silence and shut up.

Elliott tucked the rag in another drawer, arranged two chairs on either end of the desk, and then surveyed the results of his efforts. *Good, good.* After a nice lunch, he would take Gwen on the full, albeit brief, tour of the workshop. A tour Cynthia had never experienced, nor likely would have enjoyed. But he had a feeling, a hope rather, that Gwen just might.

Besides, here he'd be less inclined to make a verbal misstep while surrounded with safe subjects for conversation. Subjects he knew a great deal about and could discuss at length. Ones that would prevent him from looking foolish and hurting Gwen. Again. That was the working theory at any rate. Divine assistance might be required to put it in action.

Elliott consulted his pocket watch. *Time to go.*

Striding out the door and down the hall, he soon entered the library. Gwen sat in her usual spot, boxes and books arranged around her on all sides. He paused, dragging in a long breath. *Don't say anything stupid.* He exhaled and headed toward Gwen's corner.

As he crossed the library, his foot collided with something hard. *Blast.* Gwen did not lift her gaze. Too absorbed in her book, thank heaven. Kneeling down, Elliott found the trash bin on its side and its contents spewing out. Contents that included one worn copy of *The Ugly Duckling.* Odd. Why would it have been discarded? It wasn't that bad off.

Elliott put the book under his arm, shoved the litter back into the bin, and set it at an upright position. With a few more steps, he closed the distance between himself and Gwen. Her gaze still did not rise. The book must be very intriguing, indeed. "Gwen, do you know why this book was thrown out?"

Gwen looked up at him yet said nothing.

Maybe she hadn't heard his question clearly while engrossed in her story. Elliott bent at the torso in a partial bow. "Sorry to intrude upon your reading. I was just wondering if you knew the reason this book had been discarded." He withdrew the book from under his arm and held it up for assessment.

Her eyes lowered, not once examining the volume in question. In fact, she seemed to be doing her best to avoid looking at the book entirely. Elliott glanced at the apparently offensive fairy tale and then back at the downcast girl before him. *Gwen evading, ignoring, a book. Unimaginable.* And were those tears in her eyes? "Gwen, I—"

"The book is mine, and I have no further need of it." Haste rendered her words brittle, jagged-edged.

Gwen had thrown it away? None of this made sense. Not one word. "But why toss it in the bin?"

She rose slowly but refused to meet his gaze. "Because, Lord Carlyle, I stopped believing in fairy tales long ago." With that she walked away, leaving the pile of books on the floor, leaving the library, leaving him.

Elliott stared at the library door as it swung shut. What now? Should he go after her? *Think, man, think.* He paced, started for the door, turned round and paced again, wasting precious moments. *Blast.* Following after Gwen now would only make things worse. In his muddled state, he'd, without question, say the wrong thing. Blunder himself into a tighter corner. Cause her greater pain. *Err on the side of silence. Shut up. And think.*

Chapter 9

The ominous day Gwen had dreaded throughout her month long, self-sentenced incarceration had finally come—she had run out of books.

Arms wrapped around her person, Gwen took yet another turn about her room, which seemed to be dwindling in size by the minute. What was she to do now? She had already read through the small assortment of books she'd conveyed to her bedchamber last week, some of them twice. Reading them through a third time would serve only as a tedious aggravation. She needed a new book, something fresh, something she had not read recently. Without a volume of undiscovered words, her mind had no sanctuary from thought, no haven of comfort, no distraction.

Nowhere left to hide.

Gwen cast a glance at her newly acquired bookcase whose sad, empty shelves outnumbered those occupied. Somehow hiding among fictional friends no longer provided an escape from the ever-creeping loneliness and failed to blot out the harsh reality that hummed in the silence. A stark, oppressive quiet that seemingly confirmed Elliott's lack of affection. In all this time, why had he not once sent her word or sought her out? Gripping the back of her desk chair, she sank into its hard wooden seat. Had she lost his attentive friendship forever?

The continued silence provided her answer.

Gwen propped an elbow upon the desk, leaning her brow against her hand, and massaged away the residing tension. She could not continue on in this manner. When Mrs. Nesbitt arrived with luncheon, she must ask the housekeeper to retrieve her box of books from the—

A knock shattered the stillness. Gwen spun round in the chair and latched her gaze on to the door as another more timid knock rapped against the wood. Who could that be? It wasn't yet time for lunch. She stood, calling out to the unknown visitor. "You may enter."

The brass knob turned and the door swung inward, revealing Elliott standing in the doorway, face clean shaven, shirt and waistcoat pressed, and every button secured in place.

Gwen's breath caught. He'd come, he'd actually come.

When she failed to speak within the socially acceptable time frame for staring at another person in silence, Elliott presented an informal but stiff bow. "Good morning."

She nodded in reply, words being too difficult to form.

Elliott cleared his throat and spoke in a matter-of-fact nature. "I thought you'd like to know that the library's reconstruction has been completed."

The library. He'd only come to tell her of the library. The breath Gwen had been holding dissipated from her in a muted sigh. "Oh, that. . .that is good news."

"Indeed, and I would like for you to inspect the results. If you want to, that is." Retreating a step, Elliott made another bow. "I'll be in the library, if you should care to join me." With that, he walked away and left the door open.

Did she care to join him? Gwen pursed her lips, not moving a fraction from where she stood. The horrible awkwardness had returned to their interactions, but now such an exchange felt worse still when compared to the memory of their more relaxed conversations. Could she bear to be in the same room with Elliott under this renewed discomfort? Perhaps, perhaps not. Either way, she could not go another day without a new book to occupy her mind, and she did so want to see the library restored.

Venturing into the corridor, Gwen crept downstairs, passed Elliott's workshop, to where the library's huge double doors stood closed. She took a deep breath and pushed them open.

Warm sunlight greeted her upon entry, streaming through the new window, which featured a border of rectangular panes stained in an alternating pattern of red and gold. On either side of this, all the books she had repaired lined the shelves of the ceiling-high cases. Elliott's automaton inventions stood among them, here and there, as if on sentry duty, guarding precious treasure—the literary gems rescued from a midnight tempest. Gwen approached one of the bookcases and stroked a hand across the freshly polished, gleaming mahogany. They had truly done it; they'd saved the library.

Walking beside the wall of bookcases, Gwen soon neared the center of the library, the sun's gentle rays now close enough to warm her skin. Her gaze traveled away from the books, toward the source of warmth, and she paused mid-step. Before the window, two wingback chairs now sat, angled toward each other with a table between. Her breath slowed along with the beating of her heart. *Two chairs.* One for Elliott, and one. . .for her?

With tentative steps, Gwen drew closer to the seating arrangement. Instead of the previous masculine leather, toile fabric displaying various scenes of birds among flowers and trees covered the set of tufted chairs, soft and lovely. Had Elliott picked that fabric with her in mind? Gwen's fingers glided over one of the plush chair arms. How she wished to nestle in this perfect spot, lounge there with a book for hours and hours until night brought need of a candle's flame. Her gaze wandered to the table between the chairs, searching for a candlestick for such purpose. Yet she found none. Only one item occupied the tabletop.

45

A beautiful automaton swan.

Gwen's chest tightened, breath stalled. *A swan.* Not in all her time at Briarcliff had she seen a swan among Elliott's inventions. This was a recent endeavor. A new creation. Wings folded against its body, the swan rested on a wooden base, which featured a brass plate bearing an inscription. She knelt, peering at the tiny engraved letters.

For the first time he saw himself as he really was.

A line from the conclusion of *The Ugly Duckling*.

Straightening, Gwen placed a hand over her trembling lips. Had Elliott designed, crafted, and inscribed this swan. . .for her? No, it could not be. There must be another reason behind its creation. Although, none came to mind. Her lips stilled, but the trembling reemerged in her stomach as an incessant flutter. A swan, bearing a line from her book. Perhaps it had been made for her. Yet, why would Elliott go to such trouble for her, unless. . .

"This swan has a secret, you know." Off to her right, Elliott looked at her from the corner of his eye.

Gwen's heart skipped over a beat. How long had he been standing there?

Without waiting for an inquiry, Elliott leaned forward and turned a small knob on the side of the swan's wooden base. A faint metallic clicking ignited. Seconds later the swan arched its long, graceful neck back toward its body as its wings unfurled, lifting to the sky. A scene from Duckling's tale, the very one from which the inscription derived. The moment when Duckling saw himself as he really was, a beautiful swan.

The metallic sounds clinked until the automaton swan returned to its original position, eyes of amber gleaming.

Gwen stood in silence, knowing neither how to react nor what to say. Other than Papa, no one had ever presented her with such a special gift. No one had ever cared.

"What do you think?" Something akin to hope breathed life into Elliott's usual mechanical tone. "Do you like it?"

She turned to face him. Arms tucked behind his back, he waited with an expression on his face of restrained eagerness. He really did care, didn't he? "I believe it is the most wonderful thing I have ever seen in my life."

"Good." Elliott's voice thrummed so much feeling into the word one might have thought he had jumped up and cheered. Bringing his arms out of hiding, he produced her old copy of *The Ugly Duckling*. "I have read this many times over the last few days, but I'd enjoy it very much if you would read it to me. Please?"

As Elliott held the book outstretched, a shadow fell across them both. The sun's warmth receded from the library. Gwen swathed her chest with both arms and turned her gaze out the window where a cluster of clouds held the sun captive. She sighed. Another debilitating shadow still lingered over Briarcliff and it must be addressed lest it haunt her forever.

Gwen met Elliott's gaze and then glanced at the offered book. "Wouldn't you prefer someone else read to you? One of the servants." *Cynthia?*

Taking a step forward, Elliott shortened the distance between them. His brown-eyed gaze held on to her own. His words flowed smooth and sure. "No. I would not prefer one of the servants. Nor anyone else you could name here, in London, or beyond." Once again he held out the book. "Now, will you read to me, dear Lady Carlyle?"

Although the clouds outside did not stir, Gwen no longer felt chilled. *Lady Carlyle.* She smiled. That honored name was hers now, really and truly. Not because of a scheme, but because Elliott had given it to her, freely and willingly. For the first time in her life, she had been chosen.

For the first time, she felt like a bride.

A tear escaped Gwen's eye. "It would be my pleasure to read you this tale, Elliott. As many times as you'd like." She reached to accept the book from him, and their bare fingers touched for the briefest of moments. Heat radiated through her cheeks.

A grin appeared on his face and then ducked behind a creased brow. "I'm sorry it took so long for me to figure things out. Make things right. I should have come to you sooner." Elliott shook his head, voice and gaze falling. "I'm such a fool."

"You are no more a fool than I am a duckling." A statement she could neither have uttered nor believed, before today.

Elliott lifted his head, a new glow illuminating and softening his entire countenance. He indicated the chairs with a sideways glance and extended his hand toward her. "Shall we begin?"

"We shall." Accepting Elliott's hand, Gwen followed his escort to the reading nook, where they sat side by side to begin the first chapter of their ever after.

Novelist **Angela Bell** is a 21st century lady with 19th century sensibilities. Her activities consist of reading voraciously, drinking copious amounts of tea, and writing letters with a fountain pen. She currently resides in the southern most region of Texas with pup Mr. Darcy and kitty Lizzie Bennett. One might describe Angela's fictional scribblings as Historical Romance or as Victorian History and Steampunk Whimsy in a Romantic Blend. Whenever you need a respite from the 21st century hustle, please visit her cyber-space parlor www.AuthorAngelaBell.com where she can be found waiting with a pot of English tea and some Victorian cordiality.

Bridal Whispers

by Angela Breidenbach

Dedication

In memory of my amazing grandparents, Maybelle and Birchard Nelson.
Your fifty-four years of marriage taught me love can last.
I look forward to seeing you in paradise.

Hope deferred makes the hear sick, but a longing fulfilled is a tree of life.
PROVERBS 13:12

Chapter 1

Maila fingered the lavender grape clusters on her necklace. With every bag stuffed and every pocket full of her things, she'd decided to wear her favorite bauble even if she didn't have the matching earrings anymore. Surely he'd be a gentleman and return them?

The earbobs had grown heavy and pinched on their walk home from the Saint Paul theater last week, and Benjamin offered to hold them. Maila sighed, remembering the romantic moment when he'd pocketed them with a twinkle in his eye and then promised to wrest an important answer from her as payment for returning the earbobs at dinner tonight. But instead of sitting in the soft glow of candlelight with Benjamin, here she sat, alone, on a train, headed home to Fergus Falls. She'd be there in time for a late supper. Would Benjamin think she'd stood him up? Hopefully the message arrived before he left to collect her.

"Miss?"

Maila turned from the window, startled. "Yes?" The early morning hadn't yet released the sun. But the Pullman lanterns shed plenty of light in the car.

"May I sit with you?" The woman indicated the full car around them. Lost in thought, Maila hadn't noticed other passengers.

"Oh dear, forgive me." Standing to make way, Maila asked, "Would you like the window?"

"How kind." The woman scooted in. "Your necklace, it's lovely." She smiled as she dropped a bundle on the bench to offer her hand. "I'm Jenny Ault. Please call me Jenny."

"Thank you, Jenny." Maila accepted the greeting and smiled at the friendliness extended to her. "Maila Holmes."

"Did you get that from your beau?" Jenny pushed and prodded the bulging bags around her feet as she squeezed into the window seat.

Jenny didn't appear to have any qualms with personal matters. Maila touched the hollow of her throat. "I bought it to celebrate becoming a nurse."

Jenny's eyes flickered in surprised glee. "Now, that's something special." She plunked down in the seat finally cleared of travel paraphernalia. "Go ahead, sit back down. I won't be a bother."

Cautious of flying elbows as the young lady ducked down, prodding the bulging belongings and battling for foot space, Maila took the aisle and offered her arms to hold packages as Jenny rearranged. "You're no bother. It's lovely to have someone to share the ride with me."

"I'm going to Seattle. I've a new position as a nanny." Peering up at Maila, she asked, "Where are you headed?"

Away from the life I had to build when no one wanted me. Away from the man I think I love. "Home." Maila stared at her folded hands. Hands that held value because they could work—not because she was loved.

"Have you been away long?" Jenny resettled with foot space conquered. She'd turned the bundles into a footstool.

Jenny's gregarious personality would be a welcome addition to a long ride in a day car. How did people find it so easy to talk to strangers? "Nine years, minus an occasional holiday." In those years she'd earned enough money waitressing to attend school in Saint Paul, found gainful employment nursing, and built a life in a nice apartment. Not the scratching at the ground her family did that made strong boys so valuable and girls—

"You must be so excited to be going home, then."

The whistle blew their departure, and the train chugged through the breaking dawn ahead of the waking sun.

"We've kept up through letters." Maila pretended to look around the train car. No reason to share such tragedy with this happy girl. Maila kept the loss of her favorite cousin, and the other loved ones the flu epidemic stole, private. It would be a very long train ride if her seatmate felt uncomfortable for the next thirteen hours. "It'll be *goot*"—she cleared her throat—"I mean, good to see my family."

Why did her Swedish accent still show when she was stressed? The tutoring to learn to speak more like an American, with less of an accent, had paid off with better employment. But she missed the musicality and freedom of her native language. She didn't like talking much in either English or Swedish. Where had it ever gotten her but into trouble? Especially at home. But it was nice to know she said exactly what she meant. One-on-one, like with this girl, a conversation could be fun. But she let Jenny do most of the conversing.

Jenny didn't seem to notice one whit that her travel partner barely spoke as she prattled away the train stops from Saint Paul, across Minnesota, until finally, she slept.

Maila missed the congeniality the last little bit, unable to sleep away the miles. She pointed Jenny out to the conductor. "Would you keep my friend safe? She's traveling alone to become a nanny." He agreed to keep an eye out for the girl, giving Maila a sense of relief. It was one thing to travel for a day. Completely another to go off on a lengthy trip, as a lone woman, with all the train robberies lately. At least one person knew to offer assistance should Jenny need it.

Maila tipped the man and left a courteous good-bye note for Jenny with him for when she woke. She slipped off the train onto the new Fergus Falls platform at Vine and Laurel.

Assured Jenny would get the note, Maila worried whether Benjamin would get the message she'd sent from the train depot before their appointed dinner. He'd understand she left in a hurry for her family's sake, wouldn't he?

∽

Burton caught sight of a brown figure—all brown, from the plain hat to hair to coat to boots—framed from behind by the cream exterior of the depot like a shadow in the waning sun. An overwhelming sense of unadorned simplicity, like a plain winter thistle. Even her assorted bags poking out around her, hooked on elbows, and held in a hug had to be the least assuming, practical carryall choices possible.

Rose had loved to wear sky blue, yellow, and green. Colors of spring that set off her sparkling blue eyes and silky blond hair. Burton longed to be collecting his pretty Rose instead of her shy, prickly cousin. He remembered a chubby little girl who'd rather sass off than curb her tongue—when she chose to communicate. Perhaps she'd changed in the years she'd been away? Her letters during the last couple of months were short, but comforting, memories of his wife. Perhaps that sweetness came from maturity.

"Maila?" he called over the March gust. "Is that you?"

She turned and flapped an elbow under her load. "*Ja*, sure it is."

He swung off the sleigh and looped the reins around the hitching post. "Let me help." He avoided a direct look at Maila. Cousins tended to have a family resemblance. Could he look on a familial face and not see his dead wife in it? Blue eyes would be his undoing. Ten weeks ago he'd closed Rose's blue eyes on Christmas Day, but not before the sparkle dulled as she stared over his shoulder at the ceiling corner. The happiness had bled from his being as he held that vigil. And then she was gone. One day fine, the next gone.

Fifteen years. Burton pressed his lips together. Not fifty like she'd promised. Not long enough. Rose couldn't celebrate the turn of the century. No dance and kiss at midnight. The new blue gown meant for the New Year gala worn for her funeral instead. And no little ones to tell stories about her, since Rose hadn't been able to bear children. He had nothing but a portrait to remember her beauty and grace.

"It's good to see you again, Burton. I'm so sad for your loss."

He couldn't avoid responding, but he still didn't have to see her face. The girl had traveled across the state to come back and help him pick up the pieces of their combined family. She'd shared beautiful memories of his precious Rose. Memories he cherished.

Burton cleared his throat. "Thank you—and for the thoughtful letters." He chanced a glance. Maila's travel bonnet shadowed her features enough in the growing twilight. He didn't have to connect with the soft blue eyes all of Rose's family inherited. He didn't have to wish Rose's eyes read the love in his. He didn't have to feel the lurch stop his heart like an ax splitting wood. .

"Thank you for writing back. I wouldn't have known—" Maila's throat closed. "I don't know what would have happened if you hadn't helped Mama through it all."

"Your mama sent some food with me. I'm to get you settled in the rooms above the store, feed you, and let you rest from the trip. It's too cold tonight with the storm rolling in to go all the way out to the farm."

Maila regarded the heavy clouds deepening in the dusk, tugged her coat tighter against the colder wind coming off the nearby lake, but said nothing as flakes floated around her and melted on her nose.

Twelve miles on a cold, hard bench would be best done in the daylight, well-traveled road or not. "Then tomorrow we'll drive the dray out to the farm for a family meeting."

"Ja, *tack så mycket.*"

Swedish. Always Swedish with this family. If he never heard that language again it wouldn't be long enough. Rose died and all they did was chatter. Chatter about this and chatter about that. And not one word intelligible. Burton scowled. "No more Swedish, please. Speak English."

"I—yes, thank you so much." Maila translated her words then ducked around him to drop the rest of her belongings in the back of the sled. She yanked her travel skirt up, clambered into the seat, and stared straight ahead, blinking rapidly.

Burton grimaced at his brisk behavior. Maila hadn't caused the loss of his wife and mother. She had to be reeling from the loss of several of her cousins as well. It wasn't her fault the influenza epidemic wiped out so many people, including three men needed to help run the homestead, all in the last few months. Death had visited more people in their extended family than any other in the area. Maila's own sister and two children still needed nursing back to health, as did several people in town. The Swedish people lowered their voices and chattered and chattered and chattered. Did they think he couldn't tell who'd been the subject when a conversation stopped?

Sixteen years owning the general store. The first year alone was rough before Rose agreed to marry him. Her sweet way with others brought in business. Without Rose, how would he manage with people who refused to speak English? He couldn't risk losing customers to bigger city shopping or competitors. Maybe selling the store and moving on would be best.

He heaved a sigh. Still not Maila's fault. "I'm sorry for your loss, too." Burton settled beside her. "Your sister will be grateful you can look in on her and the children. Her husband is extremely worried."

She lifted her chin and turned away. "I'm glad I can be of use."

"Several more folks came down with the flu." Burton's words slowed and rang with reverence. "Seth, Johan, and Olaf passed in the last two days."

Maila swung her head to look at him and choked out one word: "All?"

His affirmation a bare movement of his jaw, Burton couldn't meet her gaze. Not when he'd leveled her with such loss within moments of her arrival. Not when the very people she arrived to help care for had dropped like wheat during the threshing season. Her sister's family, all that were left of those she'd come to aid.

"Each not far apart." He reached under the seat and brought out a heavy quilted lap rug. His muscles still ached from shoveling hard, cold ground when the sun warmed the land as a Chinook blew through. Just enough warmth to loosen the soil, with the farm's ox team and plow first. The rows of fresh graves seared into Burton's brain.

"How could no one tell me?"

"You were already coming. The family thought it best to allow you a peaceful journey rather than send another wire." As he covered them the best he could for the short jaunt through the streets from the station to the general store, he added, "There wasn't anything you could have done from the train."

Burton flicked the reins, though his forearms screamed at the smallest motion and his shoulders shouted back. Piling snow scattered off the horses' rumps as they pulled the dray against the strengthening onslaught. A sleigh normally used for hauling dry goods and farm equipment over heavy Minnesota drifts had hauled five coffins in the last weeks, his wife's the first, at Christmas. "We need some sleep. Tomorrow's a long day with the ride over to Foxhome." Would he ever celebrate Christmas with joy again? Probably not. How would he get through Easter? Rose's favorite holiday would have a new organist pumping the pedals.

∞

Tears dripped sideways off Maila's chin, salt mingling with sweet-tasting snow that blew in her face. She couldn't wipe them away fast enough before the next came sliding back toward her ears. Four cousins and Burton's mother. Compassion clung to each name as he'd said them like fog over the creek, blanketing the ground.

From the train. Did they all blame her? Did they think she could have saved them if she'd been here practicing her nursing instead of working so far away? What kind of miracle maker did they expect? This influenza epidemic didn't have a cure. Not one doctor had a clue how to stop its spread. She certainly wasn't God.

She'd hoped to help her family with emergency leave. To bring her skills home for a short time.

Maila hadn't caught the flu in Saint Paul. Perhaps she wasn't meant to because the good Lord had other plans. The high fever, respiratory distress, and then fluid-filled lungs moved fast. A person lived or died in less than two days. Why these strong men and women in their prime? Why did God let this disease dash her family to bits like hail blasting across their crops? But Burton had recovered, though he appeared a bit thin for his six-foot-three height. Was it from the flu bout or from grief?

Guiding the horses to the curb on Lincoln Avenue, Burton slid off the hard bench, taking the blanket with him. "I'll help you get your things inside, then after I've bedded the horses down I can bring up whatever you need." He shook piling snow out of the rug, rolled it, and tucked the bundle back in its nook.

"I'll be fine." Maila peered at the flat stone on the general store before hopping off the front seat into the street. Utilitarian flat-front buildings marched up and down Fergus Falls's main street. Smaller, simpler architecture contrasted with the more established elegance she enjoyed in the bigger city. The comparison fit Maila and her older cousin, Rose, too well. Maila dared a look in Burton's direction. Such a young, handsome man to lose the one he loved. Who wouldn't love a woman rich in heart, talent, and beauty? Maila had always wanted to be like the regal Rose when she grew up.

Resigned to her reality as plain and simple, Maila reached over the side of the sleigh. All her luggage had jumbled into the far corner nearest Burton.

"Yoo-hoo! Are you open, Mr. Rutherford?" A woman waved as she hurried toward the store. Not a small woman, she wore a man's woolen coat with a thick shawl tied around her head and shoulders against the strengthening gusts. "I need a bit of honey, please."

Burton ushered her in the dry goods store with half of Maila's belongings hanging on one arm. "Of course, Mrs. Anderson, come out of the storm." An electric lamp flared inside, spilling the golden promise of warmth out the window.

Left to wander in on her own as the sleet picked up speed and intensity, Maila collected the last two satchels. Didn't he keep normal business hours? She huffed over to the closed door. At least he could have—

Burton swung the door ajar, bell jangling with the motion and then writhing on its rope in the snowstorm. He spoke discreetly, close to her ear, warming her skin. "I'm sorry, Maila. Mrs. Anderson's husband already passed and now her little son has taken ill." His hands brushed hers as he relieved Maila of the bundles. "I'll just be a moment."

Maila scuffed through the doorway, eyes down. Burton took care of someone else in the face of his own exhaustion while she groused. She deserved to be left out in the howling cold for her selfishness. Her face flamed. She couldn't squeak out a word if she had to.

Burton set the bags on the floor near the back stair. He rounded the sales counter at the farthest end and plucked a jar of honey off the shelf. "What else can I get you?"

To Maila, the store looked more like the row houses she'd visited in a mill town during nursing training. Her professional focus became in-home patient care because of the experience. She loved caring for people one-on-one outside of the hospital setting. Here, glass displays lined both sides of the narrow aisle from front to rear. They seemed to run on forever, deep into the building. Shadows swallowed up the high shelves. She squinted to see the products in the lamplight while Burton served his unusually late customer. The store didn't look as well stocked as she remembered.

"Some are saying the coughs are quieting with a little peppermint. Do you have any that's broken? Some you can't sell maybe?"

"Mrs. Anderson, I have just the piece for you." Burton opened the glass jar holding straight sticks of red and white peppermint penny candies. He cracked the longest piece into thirds. "This appears to have broken." He dropped all three pieces into a tiny paper sack. "Keep a little piece handy for him to suck on like a lozenge."

"But you—"

"Want your son to get well?"

She smiled. "It's most appreciated, Mr. Rutherford. We'll be able to pay you soon."

"I'm sure you will. Now go home and see to your family without another worry."

"Thank you."

"We'll be praying for you and yours, Mrs. Anderson."

Her face registered sadness. "We'll miss your pretty wife, Mr. Rutherford. I've never heard another so talented on the organ, either. God keep you."

Maila stopped her at the door. "If your son gets to coughing too hard, you might try cupping to help him clear his lungs." She held her hands up to demonstrate. "Pat his back with some strength." She clapped her cupped hand against her opposite flat palm. Air popped between them. "Be sure you cover his entire upper back while he lies across your lap. I've seen this procedure relieve chest congestion and help several people."

"Thank you. I'll do that." Mrs. Anderson smiled at both Maila and Burton. In a flash of skirts, she scooted out the door and across the darkened street.

Burton took a deep breath. Then he motioned for Maila to come to the back. "Can you find your way upstairs? Second door on the right. I need to see to the horses."

"I can wait. Don't you need a moment to mark her account?"

"No, I'm not planning on remembering that order."

"Oh."

He put the lid back on the glass candy jar. "Sometimes other people need their pennies more than I do. She's wearing her husband's coat because she doesn't have one. He's no longer going to be able to provide."

No wonder Rose had fallen in love with Burton. He cared about the people he served, not just the money they spent on his dry goods. Maila was surprised at her next thought. *Would Benjamin have done the same?*

Chapter 2

T he hugs—no one gave just one—kept coming as her remaining family poured out of the small homestead cabin. Letters cheered her up, but to be with them now filled an emptiness she hadn't wanted to acknowledge. Mama opened her arms and Maila fell into them, inhaling the aroma of rye bread. Oh, how she'd missed Mama's baking.

"*Och*, but it's good you're home. You'll stay now, ja?" Mama held Maila's cheeks with both hands and smiled into her daughter's eyes.

Conscious of Burton nearby, Maila chose to answer her mother's Swedish with muffled English through squished cheeks and puckered fish lips. "Mama, I have a job."

"You're needed here." Mama patted Maila's face before releasing her. "You can work at the new hospital when everyone is well, if Burton can manage the store. They need nurses."

Needed. Everything hinged on being needed, not wanted. She could work at the Kirkbride, Fergus Falls State Hospital. Overcrowded conditions treating the mentally ill, though honorable and needed, wasn't the kind of nursing she wanted to do. "In Saint Paul, I travel a home care route. I prefer rehabilitating patients from injuries and illnesses." Work inside the sterile walls of a facility? It'd be especially tough since it wasn't completed. Construction went on in one wing while treating patients in the other. Who knew how long it would take? "Mama, I enjoy my work. I don't think I'm ready to move back yet. But I'm here to help now."

"You'll stay now."

"I—" *No, not my first day home.* "Let's enjoy being together today, Mama." Biting back further defense, Maila put an arm around her mother's waist and walked with her toward the small house. "How are Randa and her little ones? I should look in on them."

"The fevers have broken, but they ache all over."

"Any sign of pneumonia?"

Her mother's nose reddened. Tears glossed her eyes. "I couldn't bear to lose one of those precious children or their mama."

But you could do without me for nine years. Maila gritted her teeth then blew lightly between them, releasing pent-up pressure. "Mama, I'll do my best, but prayers are more important. I'm a nurse, not God."

"Ja. I know." She led Maila to the cramped bedroom. "But *Gud* has brought you home to *hjälpa*."

After examining her sister, niece, and nephew, Maila left them sipping on chicken broth Mama brought in on a tray. "*Krya på dig*," Maila said before closing the bedroom door. She laid her hand against the white wood and leaned into it, eyes closed. "God, please do help them get well soon."

"He will," Burton's low baritone responded.

Maila popped her eyes open and turned. This sense of faith from the man who'd lost two loved ones? She tipped her head back, looking into his compassionate face. "I hope so."

He scrunched his brows and scrutinized Maila's eyes closely. "They're not blue!"

"What?"

"Your eyes. They're. . .hazel?"

She giggled. "Yes? This is a surprise?"

He didn't stop staring. "They're. . .lovely."

"Um," Maila dropped her chin to her chest. "Thank you." When had she last received a genuine compliment like that? Benjamin complimented her hair. Such thick brown hair. He'd asked her to take it down once to see the full length. But no one had ever used the word *lovely* about any part of Maila Holmes. Rooted like trees, her legs wouldn't move. So why did it feel like squirrels raced up her spine?

"What's this, you two blocking up the hall?" Mama said in Swedish as she pushed between them, hands full of bowls and spoons. She stopped, looked up into Burton's face, and then swiveled to peruse Maila's.

A flush crept over Maila under her mother's inspection. "Nothing, Mama." She switched to English. "Burton came to see if we needed anything."

Her mother's eyes squinted and she slanted her head ever so slightly. She took one longer look between the two before saying, "Ja, come eat now."

Maila skirted Burton on her way to the table. She could feel his gaze following her movements. That little squirrel wreaked havoc in her rib cage.

❧

The entire family of cousins, aunts, and uncles from the area, minus the three flu victims, gathered for the noon meal around the long plank table, with shoulders and elbows bumping. Down so many, yet twelve souls remained to banter at mealtimes on special occasions. Burton would miss this if he sold the store.

"I think they're on the road to recovery," Maila informed everyone. "Randa and Inga have some color returning and little James's coughing is not nearly as deep as I expected. I believe they're already past the danger."

Randa's husband, George, spoke with a pained expression. "I won't lose my wife? My children?" Thick emotion clogged his words.

Maila placed a hand on his wrist in the tight space. "No. I don't think so. I'm not seeing any signs of pneumonia." She looked into his eyes. "They're getting Mama's chicken soup down. With rest and fluids, all should be well."

"Thank you, Maila. I've expected. . . I—" George closed his eyes and wiped a hand over them.

Mama Holmes bowed her head and thankfully said the prayer in words Burton understood. "We've lost enough. *Nej*, not one more, dear Lord. You've asked so many of mine family already." The family followed her lead for both a prayer of mercy and a blessing over their chicken soup and fresh bread.

"Mama Holmes." Burton picked up his spoon. "I can leave Maila here to care for them. She has her things in the sleigh."

Mama Holmes brightened at his words. "Ja, this is best." Her head bobbed.

George looked up from his bowl. "Will you be able to stay long, Maila?"

She swallowed the hot broth. "I took a month's leave."

"Nej, Maila. You will stay now. No more working so far away."

Spoons clinked on dishes like cymbals clashing amid the recent losses. No one would argue with Mama Holmes—except Maila.

Burton discreetly looked around the table. The only set of eyes not focused on a bowl, other than Mama Holmes and Maila, belonged to himself. He wanted to say something to ease the tension, but what?

Maila set her spoon down with a thunk. "I have a job and commitments, Mama."

Mama Holmes's eyes narrowed. "Family is commitment, and more important. We must care for one another now we have lost so many."

"I will do what I can until I must go back."

"I do not ask you to visit." Mama Holmes's voice rose. "I ask you to *komma hem*, Maila. *Du behövs!*"

What in the world did "du behövs" mean? Burton closed his eyes. English!

"I know I'm needed, Mama," Maila said quietly. "I'm willing to help in whatever way our family has need. But no one is ill enough to need a nurse."

Ah, needed. That's what those words meant. He shook his head as the argument escalated. The first day home and the two women were already at odds. But did this tinder and spark need to happen in the midst of heavy family grief? The coming month would be atrocious if mother and daughter locked antlers and couldn't manage to get along in the same house.

Burton held up a hand. "Ladies, please." But the two paid him no heed. The words flew in Swedish until he brought his hand down sharply on the table. The clatter of dishes caught everyone's attention.

"I believe we need to have that family meeting right now." Burton righted the saltshaker then straightened his fork and knife.

"You're forgetting my family is resting." George jumped in to support Burton while avoiding Mama Holmes's shocked stare. "We must all talk civilly."

Both ladies blanched.

Burton continued. "I've been thinking about our dilemma. We have a shortage of hands to do all the work both on the farm and in the store."

Several set down their silver, a few leaned back in their chairs, and Maila sent a grateful smile his way.

"What suggestions do you have?" Mama Holmes asked.

"I have stock still in boxes because I've been coming out to the farm the last week and"—he swallowed—"because we've buried family." The entire table crossed themselves. "I need help stocking the store and assisting customers. If someone worked in the store for me, I could help more on the farm with the heavy work of calving, preparing equipment for planting, and the like." *And a little time away from it would help me decide whether to sell or not.*

George tapped his fingers on the table as he listened. Then he offered, "We could send Randa when she's well. The children are good and can play quietly in the sitting room."

Burton wrinkled his brow. "Well, that could work." He turned to Maila and tried to warn her by widening his eyes. Would she catch his subtle hint? "How long will it take for Randa and the children to recover?"

Maila gave Burton a sideways look. "They're already getting better. They'll be weak for a bit. Nothing a bit more sleep and broth can't handle. Once Randa's feeling up to it, I think she'd do well to help here. She could rest when she wearies."

George rubbed his chin. "She must recover fully. I won't risk her health."

Burton let out the breath he'd been holding.

"What can we do then?" Mama Holmes joined the discussion. "We need every able body working, or the farm will fail. Papa has been gone only a year. We need good, strong men."

"If Randa and the children are recovering, what if Maila stayed at the store and Burton worked the farm?" Lars suggested. "It's the muscle we need in the fields."

Burton held back the grin and pasted a serious expression on his face. He needed to put the power of decision in the two women's laps. *Let them think they have to convince me.* "I'm not sure about that. Maila has been away at college and nursing. What does she know about running a store?"

"Excuse me?" Maila's indignant tone almost made Burton laugh. "You don't think I'm capable?"

Mama Holmes dove in to the conversation with a shaking finger. "My Maila can do anyt'ing she sets her mind to, ja? Ja!" She folded her arms. Something

Burton noticed she did when no one would sway her. "You chust be here to work, young man, and my girl will do her part. You take her back tonight and show what must be done."

He held both hands up in surrender. "If you all think it's the right thing to do. . ."

A chorus of agreement supported Mama Holmes's decision. Even Maila agreed as she raised one brown eyebrow in challenge.

If he hadn't intended the conversation to go this direction, the battle flaring in Maila's eyes might start a tremor in Burton's blood. But instead, triumph surged through his veins. The Civil War would not have a repeat in this household if he could circumvent the adversaries. Though judging from Maila's icy glare, he might have some explaining to do.

⌒∞⌒

On the stoop of the store, Maila whirled on Burton. The chilly drive, in more ways than waning light giving way to a frigid Minnesota evening, hadn't cooled the fire in her eyes. "What do you think I am—a complete dolt?"

"Maila, calm down and we can talk." Burton unlocked the door. "I thought—"

"You thought!" She fisted her hands on her hips. "You thought I couldn't do something as simple as stock shelves? You thought I couldn't add two plus two?"

"I thought you might like a little distance to make your own decisions," he shot back at her.

"I've been making my own decisions for years. I don't need you to—" A gasp on the sidewalk nearby caught her attention. Maila closed her eyes and pinched her lips into the finest line, forcing dimples to deepen at the edges of her mouth.

Two ladies quickly crossed to the other side of the street, casting disapproving glances back at Maila and Burton.

Burton held his tongue until the ladies passed out of hearing as he opened the shop door and pulled Maila inside. He closed the shade for privacy. "I thought it was very uncomfortable for you and everyone else this afternoon. I thought it might be better to have an intelligent, healthy woman help in the store rather than argue with her mother for the next month. And for your information, I couldn't take one more word out of either one of you."

Maila opened her mouth to speak. Closed it. Then her nose and cheeks turned red as tears formed in her beautiful hazel eyes. She left him standing in the narrow aisle without another word.

⌒∞⌒

Morning came all too early. Maila rinsed her face with cold water, dabbing at her puffy eyelids. She descended the back stairs, promising herself to at least try to ease the tension with Burton. She'd have to deal with her mother later in the week when she checked in on Randa's family. But one thing sank in from the discussion last night—she had to get through the month with some sort of decorum and courtesy.

"Burton?" She walked through the sitting room behind the sales area and looked around the small store then unlocked the front door and peered up and down the street. She wandered back down the aisle, puzzled. Then she picked up a paper that must have blown off the glass counter onto the wood floor.

Maila, gone to the farm. Please see the price list under the cash register to stock the shelves and assist customers. The ledger and customer cards are filed in the cabinet below it as well. I'm sure you'll figure it out. I'll be back before closing. Sincerely, Burton.

Oh dear. Maila scrunched her nose. Her mouth had run off with her senses again like a colt with no fence. The family wouldn't survive without each member pulling their weight, and she hadn't given Burton the chance to familiarize her with the store.

The bell jangled and a crisp breeze blew Maila's brown woolen skirt around her ankles. She whispered a quick prayer for help and turned to greet the customer.

"How may I help you?"

"Where's Mr. Rutherford?" the stout lady inquired.

"He's assisting at the farm for the next little bit. I'm Maila Holmes, his. . .uh. . . ." What was she now? Assistant? Clerk? She really didn't have a title.

"Oh, the young lady I heard about." She looked perplexed. "I'd heard Mr. Rutherford brought someone—in. Is your husband with you?"

Odd question, but if it helped the lady feel comfortable getting to know her, then Maila would oblige her with an answer. "No, ma'am. I'm not married." She smiled as she thought of Benjamin. "But I hope to be soon."

"Oh, you do, do you?"

The woman seemed quite out of sorts. Probably another family stricken by the epidemic. Maila smiled, hoping to ease her stress. "Yes, I'll be helping in the store for a few weeks before going back to Saint Paul."

"Ah, I see. Yes, well. . . ." She avoided Maila's eyes. "Here's my grocery list." The lady looked around at the shelves. "Could you fill it for me while I run a few other errands?"

"My pleasure." Maila's belly twinged. How would she get the chore done? Half the shelves were empty.

She could see the distrust and dilemma in the customer's eyes. "On second thought, I'm not sure." She reached out to reclaim her list.

"Ma'am, please don't worry. There's plenty of stock in back yet. If you'll give me a few extra minutes, I'll do my very best for you." At the woman's hesitant nod, Maila asked, "Do you have an account?"

"Yes, please put it on the Wright account."

"Thank you, Mrs. Wright. I'll do that."

Once Mrs. Wright left, Maila rolled her shoulders to relieve the tension. She knew where to find the billing ledgers. Now to see what on the list could be filled from the visible supplies before tackling the challenge of unmarked crates.

By the end of the day, not only had Maila filled several orders and filed the account cards, she'd sorted through and found several items to restock the displays. She'd also come to the conclusion that Burton could be right. Working here would help her family, minimize arguments with her mother, and keep Burton's business open. *I can do this.* She hummed the tune to "She'll Be Comin' Round the Mountain" as she faced peach cans from a stepstool.

"Haven't you been busy today?"

Maila startled at Burton's rich baritone, flipping cans out of the pouch she'd fashioned with her apron. They tumbled to the floor, rolling as fast as her blood pumped. She backed off the stepstool and took several deep breaths. Why did the sound of Burton's voice unsettle her so?

"You're really going to have to be more careful with the inventory. The dents can cause pinholes and ruin the product."

And irritate her, too! Maila clamped her teeth together. *I will not smart off. I will not smart off.* "Oh, really? Perhaps you'd like to let a body know when you've entered the building." *Fine. I will not smart off tomorrow.* "How did you sneak up on me, anyway?"

"I didn't sneak up on you. I came in the back so I wouldn't track snow and mud through the store." Burton wiggled stocking-covered toes at her. "I sweep the store each day, but there's no need for extra mess. When I come from the fields, I leave my shoes and coat in the mudroom."

Maila almost laughed at him standing in the middle of the shop with no shoes and a little toe peeping out of a small hole in his sock. "I see." She arched a brow and pointedly looked at his feet. "Then do you parade around in front of customers without shoes?"

"Of course not. I accidently left my indoor shoes behind the counter when I had to hurry and close up to get you from the train the other day. I forgot to move them with all the, shall we say, hubbub?"

"Oh." *Brilliant conversation, Maila. Spit it out. Tell him you're sorry.* "I'm—"

"You have a letter." Burton held out an envelope.

"A letter?" She took the letter and flipped it over to see the sender's address.

"Already?" Benjamin! Then she squealed and hugged it to her heart. The pretty stationery she'd picked up at Smith's Books would come in handy tonight.

Burton snagged his clean shoes and sat on the bench near the front door to put them on. "That must be some news."

"My friend must have received my message." Maila looked over at his cloudy face. What was bothering him? Then she doused her grin. Poor Burton. His wife must be weighing on his mind. "I'm sorry. You're not likely up for this kind of thing yet."

"I'm fine."

Maila set the mail down. "I know you're trying to help the family. I will work on being more courteous from now on." There. That was a pretty good olive branch.

"Maila, I only want all of us to work together the best we can under the circumstances."

"I know that now. I hope you'll be more comfortable with me from here on out." Burton stifled a yawn. "We'll be fine."

Maila closed up the cash register's storage cupboard. "We haven't figured out who should do what around here."

"Who should do what?"

The door jangled as Maila answered. "Housekeeping duties, dinner—"

Mrs. Anderson stood in the open doorway with a loaf of bread in her hands. "Maybe this will help you two." She walked the few feet to Burton and handed over her gift. "I made bread today. This loaf is fresh. I thought I could maybe take a little bit off my account with barter?"

Burton accepted the bread. "This will do very nicely, Mrs. Anderson. We were just discussing what to do about dinner with the long day we've both had."

She smiled, but her eyes darted between them. "I'm glad I could help. And thank you. My boy is recovering well."

Burton stood from the bench and held the door for her to leave. "Your bread is the best I've ever eaten. We'll enjoy it mightily." Once he closed the door behind Mrs. Anderson, he reversed the sign, officially ending the day's duties. The exhaustion showed in his slow movements. "How about I fix us a couple of eggs and a little of this bread for dinner?"

"How about we do that together?" Maila sent him a soft smile. "I can make delicious scrambled eggs."

"Sounds like we've struck a deal."

Chapter 3

Three weeks created a comfortable confidence. Maila knew where to find everything, and every item had an abundant supply. But business seemed to have dwindled the past two weeks. Some of the women placed an order and then didn't return to pick it up. Obviously, she didn't have Rose's way with people. Well, at least she could use the extra time to build up stock on the shelves before returning to Saint Paul. Burton would have to return to the store to regain his profitability. Although last night he talked of selling before he went under.

A woman stared into the shop as she walked past the window. Maila gave her a bright smile and wave, but the woman hustled past. Maila sighed. She wasn't a good shop clerk, no matter how hard she tried to be friendly. The customers just hadn't warmed up to her, even though she'd known some of them as a child. She needed to go back to what she was good at and back to the life she'd built. Away from this cold place where no one liked her.

The bells jarred Maila's nerves in the peaceful quiet of the empty shop as Mama burst inside.

Mama started the stream of questions before the shop door swung shut behind her. A few eggs left in the nearly empty basket wobbled when she plunked it on the counter. "I come in to sell my eggs and cream and find my daughter is the talk each place I go. What has gotten into you that you would shame your family so?"

Maila's elbow knocked over a tower of cans as she hurried from behind the counter. They cascaded over the edge, slamming onto the floor and rolling in all directions. Maila cringed at the clatter sounding like horse hooves kicking a stall door, but couldn't catch even one. Burton would have a word or two to say again if he knew. She really needed to stock something light and soft for a change or she'd be as responsible for the store's demise as the lack of customers lately.

"I don't know what you're talking about." Maila's brain raced to put the accusations together like pieces of a jigsaw puzzle.

"Mrs. Johnson told me that Mrs. Keller and Mrs. Berndt said they'd had to cross the road to avoid your lovers' spat." Mama's face turned a deep shade of scarlet. "A lovers' spat? You're supposed to be helping, not—och, what's the word?"

"Mama, we aren't—"

"Opp-or-tun-ist." She pronounced the new word she'd learned in English. "They say you're going to swoop in to dandy about with the poor widower's emotions and then leave."

Either she had lockjaw or the shock frazzled her mental facilities. She couldn't think of a thing to say in her defense. The pounding of her eardrums ricocheted pain into her temples. Was that why the women refused to shop at Burton's store? They thought she came from the city to take advantage of a man?

"Then Mrs. Anderson said the two of you acted like a married couple, coming in late together and talking housekeeping."

But Mrs. Anderson still shopped here? "Surely she didn't—"

"But the worst?" Mama shook her head and then sucked in a breath as if gaining courage. "Mrs. Wright said you even admitted it. She said she'd never step foot in here again."

"Admitted what? I've done nothing but work here. I told her so—" Maila tapped a finger against her lip. She'd had to send the delivery boy with the Wright order when the lady hadn't returned to pick it up.

"You must have done more than work. They're calling you a brazen hussy!" Mama's eyebrows drew together as they had all too often during Maila's childhood. "I know what that word means even in English, Maila. These things don't come out of the air."

"Well, this did," Maila groused. "I can't believe you'd listen to gossip." She picked the vegetable cans up off the floor and set them on the counter.

"Gossip?" Mama slapped her hands together. "It's only gossip when it's not true." She crossed her arms. "But I know, don't I? I have eyes in mine own head. Now it makes sense why he wants you here."

"*Lämna mig ifred*, Mama!" She stomped her foot. Her mother's shocked face cooled the heat in Maila. Had she just told her mother to leave her alone? This whole mess was a comedy of errors. But it certainly wasn't funny, especially if this caused Burton's financial bind! She gentled her voice. "You know I'd never behave that way. How could you think that of me?"

"I know that, child, but you have been gone such a long time. You're different now, ja? That big city has infected you with modern ideas. Taken modesty and good sense. Different."

"What's the ruckus?" Burton walked up the aisle from the rear rooms.

"You!" Mama pointed her finger. "It's not enough to bury a wife and not mourn her properly before taking up with another. No, you must destroy the family in the process? You hate us so much?"

Burton's eyes went wide. "Hate? I don't hate you."

Maila closed her eyes and said a silent prayer. *Mama must have cracked under the pressure of losing so many family members, trying to manage the farm's dairy sales, and keeping her household running.*

"Then how could you grieve me so much? First my niece I raise as mine own and now my daughter's good name?"

Maila moved between them. "Mama, how could you think such a thing of him? Burton's done nothing wrong."

"Mama Holmes, I loved my wife and I respect your daughter. What can I do to prove this to you? I'll do anything to prove I have only the best at heart for our family."

"Anyt'ing?" Mama's accent made the word sound like a chime tinkling in the breeze.

"Anything."

Maila gulped and a wave of desperation washed over her heart. Emily Holmes held people to their word. "Mama, why are you listening to gossip? That's just people with nothing better to do—"

"So you say, do you? But I know better. I saw the way you two acted in secret in mine own house!" She folded her arms.

"Secret!" Maila slapped her hands against her skirts. "We spoke in the hallway. That's all!"

Mama's eyes narrowed shrewdly. "Nej, you will not play me the fool. This has been going on since our pretty Rose was barely in her grave."

Burton turned gray. "Mama Holmes, nothing is going on."

She pinned him to the spot with her glare. "And what about all those letters Maila wrote about you?"

Maila's thoughts reeled. "My letters home?" She shook her head. "What in the world do they have to do—"

"You ask me in letters how is Burton. Then you admit you write to him. Nej, there is more to this than consolation."

Burton moved to stand between the women. "You're reading more into this than—"

"And in English!" Mama spat out as if English were foul. "You write in English so I must have someone read to me."

Nausea sloshed through Maila's stomach. Someone else read her mail? "Read to you? My letters are private."

"Ah, I see. So this is all a secret."

"I wrote in English because I had to practice for my classes. Honestly, Mama, this is—"

"Clearly this isn't getting us anywhere." Burton put a hand on Maila's shoulder.

She rolled her lips inward, trapping more angry words, and looked away from her mother.

"Mama Holmes, what do you need from me to stop the gossip? Let me do whatever I can."

Mama studied Burton's face for a moment. "This is what you two can do." She flicked her hands away from her body. "Make it go away."

Burton nodded. "I will. I promise."

What could he do? Maila studied his earnest face right along with her mother's stern expression. Every bit of Burton oozed honesty. Whatever he could do, this problem involved them both. "I will, too, then, whatever will help solve this problem."

"Then it's settled."

They both nodded.

"Mama, I can move to the Grand Hotel for my last week."

"That could get expensive, Maila," Burton protested. "I'll move out to the farm."

"And how will you do what you need for the store that way?" Maila asked.

Mama's arms folded tightly. "You will prove you have goot intentions toward my Maila and not ruin our name."

"Yes, somehow I will. I'll talk to the—"

"Nej, no somehow." She picked up Maila's hand and placed it in Burton's. Then she held them together.

Maila stared at her mother and tried to yank her hand back.

But Mama would have none of it and held on fast. "You will marry." One solid nod, as if she'd pronounced a law with a gavel.

"Marry?" both Burton and Maila said together.

Maila, positive she'd hit the highest note on the treble clef, couldn't close her mouth.

Mama's face turned to stone. "This is the way. You prove goot intentions." She turned to Maila. "You prove you're not opp-or—you're not a bad woman."

Burton broke in, "I believe we could solve this another way, Mama Holmes."

She turned to Burton. "You say the words, but when I tell you what to do—" She let go of their hands and then crossed her arms again. "So you do not mean the words you say."

"Mama! Burton is a man of integrity. He will do what he says. There's no call for—" The doorbells cackled a cacophony.

A cold breeze whisked through the store, stirring Maila's skirts as Mrs. Anderson walked in.

Burton looked from Mama to the startled customer and said, "Why, Mrs. Anderson, you're the first to hear our happy news."

Maila's eyes widened and a flush rushed into her cheeks. No! He wouldn't!

"We'll be getting married." He turned back to Maila and her mother. "Right, ladies?"

What could she say without making it worse? Maila bit her tongue. She could deal with this mess, but not with one of the gossips right there. It'd make the whole situation that much worse.

"I knew I saw a spark between you two. Yes, I surely did. I said so to the ladies at our church meeting." Mrs. Anderson crossed the planked floor with a hand extended. She shook Burton's. "Congratulations. Aren't you the lucky man? I'm sure Miss Maila will warm your heart and help ease the loss of your dear wife."

Maila's stomach twisted at the sudden stricken expression on Burton's face. He wasn't ready for another wife. The poor man hadn't been a widower for more than a few months.

Mrs. Anderson extended a hand to Maila as well. "When are the nuptials?"

Maila saw it now. Mrs. Anderson couldn't have meant to be malicious with her gossip. Even in her own loss, she seemed to believe in happy endings. "I, uh, we—" For a girl who couldn't stop arguing with her mother, Maila couldn't find the words yet again.

Mama supplied the answer. "Just as quickly as we can prepare for it. Ja, very soon. A good man like this must not be left to idle."

Mrs. Anderson smiled with kind understanding. "Yes, you're most certainly right, Mrs. Holmes."

No! No, no, no! Maila fought to find her voice.

Burton added, "Yes," looking at Maila. "It will be as soon as we can. But we'll keep it very small and private. It's best this way, out of respect for my dearly departed."

"Oh yes, indeedy. One must be appropriate with a loved one gone so short a time."

Burton's lips thinned as if it took every bit of willpower in his body. "Yes."

Maila had no intention of marrying without love. *Oh Benjamin, I must get back to you—and not as a married woman!* She'd find a way to quietly scoot out of town on the train. After all, she wasn't truly wanted here—she was just filling someone else's shoes. But. . .could Burton's store take it if he lost more customers? Would Mama ever forgive her for leaving without a good-bye? She sighed. No, she couldn't scurry away like a mouse fleeing into a field.

⧼∞⧽

The sun glared through the curtain corner, waking Maila. Groggy from the short night, she dug deeper into the quilts, but the ray of light burrowed behind her eyelids as if it were a mole in the vegetable patch. Why hadn't she fixed that curtain last night? She groaned and sat up. "Fine already. I'm up, Lord. Is this really what You want from me?"

Someone rapped on her door. "Maila, do you want breakfast before the ceremony?"

Burton. How normal. How very normal this would be, asking each other about the day-to-day moments of life.

He rapped again. "Are you up? We need to leave soon."

She clasped her hands together. "Yes, I'll be down in a few minutes."

"Did you want breakfast, then?"

She'd need something to give her strength. "Yes, I'll have some coffee and a biscuit. You go ahead and eat." She'd made drop biscuits the night before. That'd be a good way to settle her flip-floppy stomach.

Burton's footsteps faded down the hall and then clip-clopped down the stairs to where the sitting room and kitchen cojoined.

Maila slipped into her best dress, the one she wore for special occasions, then ran a brush through her long chestnut hair until it shimmered and crackled. She pinned it up, adding the small veil her mother had worn many years before. The only nice piece of jewelry she owned, the grape cluster necklace, added a splash of lavender and sparkle to the light pink gown's neckline.

"I'm sorry, Benjamin," she whispered into the mirror. Benjamin! He'd have no idea. The last letters they'd exchanged talked of a makeup dinner. How utterly inappropriate after. . . Maila swallowed and closed her eyes. Today she'd become the second Mrs. Burton Rutherford.

Maila gathered her stationery and tried to pen a letter. How did one say such things that had transpired in less than a few weeks? *Dear Benjamin, it grieves my heart. . .* She scratched through the line. She thought for a moment. *I must tell you. . .* She scratched through that line, too. *I wish it could have been different. . .* Maila struck two lines through that phrase. Now what? It had been easier to send for her things and write a letter of resignation to her boss than it was to write this letter to Benjamin.

She glanced at the newly arrived boxes. She would settle in no time—there wasn't much to unpack. But her heart would take a bit longer to get used to the new arrangements.

"Maila, are you coming? You're not going to have time for this coffee."

He'd made the coffee already? She sighed. This letter would take more thought and time than she had right now. The man she would call husband, until death do we part, must be first from here on out. "Yes, coming." She raised her voice so he could hear her through the door and downstairs.

With a deep breath, Maila opened the bedroom door to the narrow hall. The tiny upstairs apartment closed in on her. Would her life feel as hemmed in as it did right this moment?

Chapter 4

"Y ou look beautiful, Maila." Randa's eyes sparkled the compliment. "Where did you find that dress? Rosy pink is the perfect color on you!" She flounced the gauzy white veil passed first to herself and then to Maila. "It looks so pretty with Mama's veil, too. Just the right shade."

Maila fingered the edges of the veil that fell below her shoulders. "I've always loved her embroidery. I can't believe how fine a stitch Mama can make." Would she and Burton come to love each other? Or would it be a tightly woven prison as intricate as these golden threads? Maila blinked back the shimmer in her eyes. No sense in crying over spilled milk. That's what Mama always said. But the cow kicked over the whole pail this morning.

Randa walked over to the vanity in the church's dressing room. "What's this?" She picked up a small card on top of a thin triangular box. "It's addressed to you."

Opening the miniature envelope, Maila brushed away the mist from her eyes. Burton's familiar handwriting. So familiar now after a few weeks in his store pouring over customer accounts. Long, thin lines and loops that looked more artistic than utilitarian. Maybe he cared more than she'd given him credit for since Mama's edict.

For my bride, may your tears be few and only caused by joy. But should I cause them, may God grant them to evaporate quickly. Yours, Burton.

Maila lifted the slim cardboard lid and gasped at the most delicate handkerchief she'd ever seen. The elegant tiny satin ribbon matched the lavender grape clusters on her necklace. She couldn't tell where the lace insets were sewn in and the nearly transparent cotton began. The dainty thing would be perfect to hold as she said her vows. Maila tucked it carefully into the pages of Romans, the book she'd studied recently.

She'd carry her small Bible and the handkerchief. It'd taken only a short time to fashion a white silk cover for the holy book that helped her practice her faith. She prayed the Lord would help her become close to Burton. Maybe if they practiced acting like a married couple they'd build up their relationship to become a real married couple. She'd show the kind of love she'd always wanted for herself. She cast a glance toward heaven. "I'm sure that idea came from You, Lord. Thank You."

Randa smiled at her sister and handed over a nosegay of marsh marigolds. "I found a few of these and thought they'd be the perfect bouquet." She hugged Maila. "Are you ready?"

"Yes." Maila tucked the yellow flowers against the Bible. The handkerchief, Bible, and flowers—all little symbols of hope for the future. What would her husband see when she walked down the aisle? Maila glanced in the mirror. Pink dress, lavender necklace, yellow flowers, and a white veil. How appropriate. With the holiday only a few weeks away, she looked like an Easter egg. Maila rolled her eyes heavenward.

A moment later, Randa walked to the altar on the arm of Burton's nephew, Charles. Her two children, Inga and James, acted as the flower girl and ring bearer. Inga's little fingers clasped the basket of yellow flowers as if they'd gallop away like a herd of horses if she didn't hold them back. She stopped to touch the petals.

Her big brother called in a stage whisper for all to hear, "Inga! You're s'posed to be up here."

Inga tossed a grin to her grandmother and copied the stage whisper she'd learned from James. She cupped a small hand around her mouth. "*Mormor*, I gots pretty flowers in my basket." A burst of laughter came from the family gathered to witness the wedding.

"Ja, so pretty." Maila's mother grinned back as she leaned forward to motion with both hands. "Go on now, *flicka*."

James scooted back to the middle of the church and tugged his little sister forward by her elbow. More titters scattered through the sanctuary.

A wistful smile passed across Maila's lips at the antics. Would this be a story to tell her own grandchildren someday? At least these two were fully recovered and able to create such a ruckus. *Thank You, God, for answering my prayer.* She watched with a grateful heart as they moved up the short distance, to the adults near Burton. Then she lifted her gaze to him—and her breath caught at his handsome smile. His open admiration propelled Maila forward toward the hand he held out to her. An invitation into an unknown adventure.

"Will you take this woman. . ." Pastor Peterson began the ceremony.

Burton opened the door and turned to his new wife. The breeze picked up, swishing through her skirts until they rustled like the leaves in summer. None of this was her fault. He'd learn to love her. In the meantime, he'd be kind. "You are a lovely bride."

Maila's cheeks flushed to a becoming rosy shade.

He liked that about her, her true modesty. Maila stood out from other women because of her character. He'd been blessed a second time, and yet in such a very different way. Yes, he could learn to care for her. In time, they'd make a happy life together. "Every bride deserves traditions. Would you like me to carry you over the threshold?"

"I'm not sure. I—"

"There's no need to worry." He held out his strong arms. "I won't drop you." Then he winked. "I've built up some muscles working the farm lately." He looked over her shoulder and spotted the same two women who'd caught their spat weeks ago. "But it might be a good idea to smile and wave."

"What?" She followed the tip of his head. Then she whispered, "Pick me up, quickly!"

He chuckled as she jumped toward him full of trust that he'd catch her. He wrapped an arm about her. "Impeccable timing, those two. Don't you think?"

"Now, please." She laced her wrists behind his neck.

The panic in her voice tugged at his heart. He swung Maila up into his arms with pink fluff flouncing into his face. He waited for the second it took Maila to smooth the finery. And to solidify the scene for their gawkers, he turned so the ladies could see as he dropped a peck onto Maila's cheek. Her bemused expression made him laugh again. For all of Fergus Falls, Burton Rutherford would make a show of carrying the new Mrs. Rutherford over the threshold.

Burton strode through the doorway and kicked it shut behind him. "There you go, Mrs. Rutherford." He set her down carefully so as not to tear her gown on his buttons. Then he turned to lock the door again. The women stood as still as the otter statues dotted down Lincoln Avenue. He pointed at the closed sign and winked through the glass pane before drawing the shade. If that didn't help the word spread that he'd made an honest woman of Maila, nothing would.

"I suppose we should get out of these duds and get comfortable."

"Now?" Maila squeaked out. "It's barely four."

Burton felt the heat crawl up his collar as if poison ivy spread under his shirt. "No, I didn't mean that." He backed up into the counter. "I meant work clothes. I don't want to stay in my Sunday-go-to-meeting clothes. Do you?"

She shook her head. "No."

"How about we both go change and meet back down in the kitchen for some dinner?"

She gave him a searching look and then started toward the back stairs. She turned at the first step. "Wait, we haven't talked about room arrangements." She paused as if a little uncomfortable. Then she finished in a pinched tone, with her eyes lowered, "Now that we're married."

He stood straight as a tree, though that tree might be a quaking aspen, whose leaves shook at the slightest of breezes. He wasn't ready for this. To touch another woman so soon after losing the one he'd loved with every ounce of his being. And

Maila couldn't be any more prepared to give herself to him. He'd only been aware of her as an adult for a few short weeks. He remembered the day he'd held the jump rope for Maila outside the schoolhouse when Rose had been delayed with another of her students. Ten years Maila's senior, Burton realized he hadn't come to terms with her as a woman—or learned to desire his new wife.

He looked over at her with a new perspective. A woman of stunning character and a beautiful heart. Yes, perhaps he did have a pretty wife, after all.

Burton swallowed. "Maila, let's leave our arrangement be for now, shall we?" He tucked his hands into his pockets—as mothers told their children, to keep them from breaking expensive items in his store. A marriage, no, a wife was the most precious and priceless. How did he keep from breaking her in this marriage?

"You keep the guest room. Rose and I shared the other. I'll just stay there." She'd understand it was too soon after his wife's death. He glanced at her face. Was that hurt in her eyes? Why wasn't she relieved?

Maila studied Burton without giving him a hint of what she was thinking. She tossed a glance at Rose's picture above the alcove breakfast nook. Then she lifted her frothy pink skirt and climbed the stairs.

How had he offended her when he meant to ease the pressure on both of them? "Ah, Rose." Burton ran a hand through his dark hair and looked up at her portrait. "You always knew what to do with your people. Now what?"

❦

Burton's voice halted Maila at the top landing. She leaned on the railing and dipped down to see him addressing Rose. *Her people?* This was a really bad idea. Married to a man who loved his dead wife too much to let her go. So much so that he asked her two-dimensional paper likeness for advice.

Maila straightened and slipped down the short hall. She looked around the small room. Somehow this marriage had to have a chance. They had to work together and learn to love each other for a lifetime. Hopefully a happy one.

A tear dropped onto the small ruffle at Maila's décolletage. *Lord, what's my part in this whole thing? What am I supposed to do?* She sat at the vanity and let the tears roll.

As she dabbed the droplets off the papers, the unfinished letter to Benjamin caught her attention. If Burton had to learn to let go of Rose. . . Maila picked up the pen to end the letters coming from Benjamin. This would be the last one. Then she'd turn her attentions toward the man whose heart she still had to win from the cousin she also loved like a sister.

"Rose, if you can hear Burton, then I hope you can hear me. I promise to take good care of him." Although it felt a little dramatic, somehow the whispered vow gave Maila resolve. "But it's time for you to let him go for this marriage to work." If at all within her power, she would live at peace with Burton even if he never came to love her. Maybe if she first loved him, it would be easier for him to love her.

Dear Benjamin, I write with regret for any distress this letter may cause you. . . .

The ham steaks sizzled on the stove with cut potatoes beside them. Maila set out a jar of green beans Rose probably canned in the fall. The fluffy biscuits nearly done, she added the butter crock and a bottle of honey to the wedding supper. She didn't believe the way to a man's heart was through his stomach, but she would show Burton love through actions. Something tangible every day.

"It smells good in here." Burton leaned over the cast-iron frying pan. "I didn't mean for you to do all the cooking. And so fancy. I'm impressed."

Maila smiled. "Ham and potatoes aren't all that fancy. But I think we both need a good solid meal after all the excitement today." She handed him the spatula. "Want to help serve?"

"Delighted." He lifted the potatoes out of the pan and onto the platter while scooting to the side so Maila could pull the golden drop biscuits from the oven with a folded towel. "Would you mind if we talked a bit about getting to know each other?"

She stopped halfway to the corner alcove. He'd been thinking of ways to make this work, too. With a glance over her shoulder, she said, "I'd like that."

They settled in for the delicious meal. Burton folded his hands, elbows on the table, country style. Maila copied him, though she'd always folded her hands in her lap up till now. Small moments like this might build a huge foundation if they found a way to live in agreement. A tiny spark lit. She'd look for anything they had in common to put as many bricks in the foundation as possible. He'd have to meet her halfway, but look at the camaraderie in the kitchen already.

"Lord, for these Thy gifts, which we are about to receive, we thank Thee."

Was he done? She peeked through her lashes at his uncommonly short prayer and found Burton peeking back at her. "Thank You, also, for this good woman You have brought me. I will treat this gift with respect. Amen."

"Amen." Maila stared at him. "You think I'm a gift?"

"Of course you're a gift. I may not seem to be much of one to you, but you are to me."

"No, I mean, yes." She shook her head. "I didn't mean it that way. I—I don't know what I thought."

"Maila, I've performed marriages and preached sermons as a speaker in the Methodist church. I've read the Bible all my life. If I know anything, it's that God gives a woman to a man as a gift." He swished his cotton napkin through the air with a flourish. "We men don't always know what to do with a gift first off. Have you ever received a present and not known what to do with it?"

Maila cut her ham into bite-sized pieces. "Yes, that one." She put her utensils down and pointed at the amethyst glass pitcher on the table, "Beautiful, isn't it?"

"Quite." He examined the blue and white Swedish toll painting designs on the handblown purple glass. The scalloped top formed by a skilled artisan.

"I didn't know what to do with that."

Burton handed it to Maila. "It's pretty obvious, isn't it? It's an expensive water pitcher. What didn't you know?"

"How I'd survive with only that as my inheritance. What kind of an inheritance gift is a water pitcher and one matching tumbler?" Maila reached out and caressed the frosted belly of the piece. "But do you know what I learned, seeing that every day on my nightstand?"

"What?" He seemed to hang on her words. *God, please, let it be the case that we enjoy each other's conversations.*

"Where I came from." She picked up the pitcher, looked at it from several angles, and held it out until Burton slipped the glass under the spout. "I never forgot who I was or who my people were. I never forgot my family." She poured water into the tumbler. "I realized when my mother gave that to me and told me to go make my way in the world, she wanted me to remember home and tradition. You're part of my family and tradition now."

Burton drank deeply from the small glass. "I'm honored." He handed the glass to her. "I'm honored to have you share my home and join my family."

She smiled into his earnest eyes and sipped from the glass. Could they share so easily the rest of their lives?

"But I have one request."

"Anything." The memory of how this marriage came to be flashed into her mind. "Well, anything within my power."

"Today, as we married at your family church. . ." Burton took her hand. "A lot of the service was in Swedish. Then most everyone spoke in Swedish."

"Well, we are Swedish." A tremor started in her knees. Things didn't tend to go well when a person stated the obvious. At least not in her experience. Her mother's send-off when she was sixteen had started, "You know we have thirteen mouths to feed. . ."

"Maila. . ." He rubbed his thumb across the top of her hand.

A flutter started deep in her belly at his gentle touch. She watched his thumb like a clock pendulum, mesmerized. How could such a simple gesture flip her insides all around like that?

"I'm asking you not to speak Swedish around me and to please ask your family to speak English also."

"What?" The flutter dropped like a wagon of hay breaking a wheel. She yanked her hand out of his. "I just told you how important my heritage is and you respond by telling me not to speak Swedish? You were married to Rose for fifteen years and you never learned the language?"

"I didn't."

"I spoke Swedish until I turned eight. In our family, to preserve our history, that's how it worked." Images of childhood and traditions and then the schoolroom flashed through her mind. "My family all speaks Swedish. They're going to come here and visit and shop. It'd be impossible to never speak my mother tongue. You know how hard it has been for me to communicate with my mother as it is."

"Please listen." Burton captured her hand again as she fluttered it at him. "This isn't about your heritage or your family. I'm asking because I don't understand it. Rose used to translate for me. But even then it was irritating to rely on someone else." He released his hold. "I don't know what to do without her."

He looked so lost. Maila's heart went out to him even as a pang of jealousy stunned her. "Burton, she's gone. I'm so sorry." Taking time to get to know each other was a wonderful plan. "But you can't ask me not to—"

"Then I won't ask." His face set into stern lines. "I am done with not understanding."

"Then learn it. I'll help you."

"No. This is America. You'll need to speak only English here."

"But—"

"I said no. This is my home. I'm the captain of this ship, and I've chosen the course we're to follow."

Maila clamped her mouth tightly to hold back words she'd regret. Who went around ordering people not to speak their native tongue? Did he need her to be so different from Rose that she couldn't be herself—her Swedish self? Loving this man was going to be a lot harder than she thought. *Gud, hjälpa!* Or help him if she didn't walk away right now!

⟳

Burton shook his head at the empty kitchenette. An angry stream of Swedish trailed behind a departing Maila. He groaned. Women were even harder to understand than Swedish. "Maila, come back," he called at her retreating figure.

The words stopped. A moment of silence.

Then he flinched at the slam of the upstairs door. "Good job, Burton. You've just gotten the cold shoulder on your wedding night." He plunked his chin into a palm and leaned on the table. "She's certainly not you, Rose."

He told Maila he respected her heritage but didn't understand the language. Rose had understood any contention between them had been misunderstandings

79

caused by their language barrier. In her soft way, she'd learned to translate for him and to only speak English at home. She hadn't been offended by his request. So why was it such a problem that he wanted to start this marriage off without confusion?

He rubbed his neck. But then again, he hadn't ordered Rose not to speak Swedish altogether. Maila must think she married a boor. Pushing back from the table, he put away the food and set the dishes near the sink. Things would look better in the morning. But the image of Maila's stricken face played over and over in his head. He'd have to apologize for his heavy-handedness and try again to explain himself.

∽∞∾

"Let me know when you want dinner." Maila worked briskly at the sink.

"Please stop for a moment." Burton touched her elbow.

She inched away. "I'm not sure what else you could want."

He leaned against the counter and folded his arms. "Maila, I'm trying to apologize."

She finally paused, folded the towel over the wooden dowel, and turned to face him. "Go on."

"I thought if we started off speaking the same language all the time, we could avoid a few of the, uh, challenges Rose and I weathered."

Maila looked at the beautiful woman watching them from above the mantel. The warming stove reflected off the corner, and the room closed in on her. "There's your first mistake."

"How can that be a mistake?" Burton's confusion played across his handsome features. "I just want to start us off on the right foot. Don't you want to avoid unnecessary arguments?"

"Certainly. But this marriage is not the same as your last. I am not the same." She held out a hand toward the photograph. "There cannot be three of us in this— whatever this is." She closed her eyes. "I really want to make this work, Burton."

He stepped close and lifted her chin. "I do, too, Maila. Really I do." He leaned in and touched her forehead with his lips. "Please forgive me for the way I spoke to you last night." Then as quickly as he'd dropped the kiss, Burton crossed to the mantel. "I think it's a difficult situation we find ourselves in. Me, only months a widower, and you, married to your cousin's husband."

He took the sepia photo off the wall. "This can hang in my room. Maybe it'll feel less like we're trying to re-create something I lost"—he lowered his voice— "and more like we're trying to become the couple we are now."

"Do you mean we're going to work on making this a real marriage? Not just something that pacifies my mother and the town gossips?" The portrait still had a hold over her husband, but at least Rose wouldn't watch over them as they ate anymore. Her constant presence at the dinner table kept a reserve between them.

"In time, Maila. In time."

She bobbed her head. "Yes." At least he'd apologized. She could, too. "Burton?"

He waited.

"I shouldn't have stormed off like that last night. I'll work on calming my temper."

He grinned at her. "You certainly made me think."

Maila took a good look at him. "Did you sleep last night? You're looking a bit tired today."

He laughed. "Not really." He looked down at his shoes and then back at Maila. "I was a little concerned you wouldn't be here when I woke up."

"It crossed my mind." She stared at the back door. "But it was cold out." Then with a sideways glance under her lashes, the grin spread across her face.

He let out a guffaw. "Then I hope it stays downright frigid so you'll stay right where you belong."

Belong. Oh, that word soaked into her being like melted butter on biscuits. "I'm not going anywhere."

Tucking the portrait with its domed glass under one arm, Burton drew Maila in for a one-armed hug with the other. "I'm glad. In case you couldn't tell, I really need a wife."

"Oh goodness, I can tell." She looked around at the jumbled state of the kitchenette-sitting room and said with an impish wink, "But we'll get this place whipped into shape in no time."

Burton took the picture upstairs. A few minutes later he descended. "Shall we say six for dinner?"

"Six it will be." Maila wrung out the dishrag and dropped it over the edge of the washing bowl she used to conserve water. Time to put her plan into action. She met him at the bottom landing. "Burton, I'd like us to do something each morning."

"Take turns with breakfast?"

"No." She giggled at his logic as she placed fingertips on his freshly shaven cheek with a featherlight touch. "I'd like us to practice being a married couple till we figure it out. When you go to the farm or out for the day, would you please say 'I love you' and give me a good-bye kiss?" She rose on tiptoe.

"I, uh, a kiss?"

"And a hello kiss when you come home." She placed her hands on his shoulders. This concept seemed to be a little too far on the advanced side for Burton to digest.

"A kiss?"

"That's what I said." If she had to hold this position much longer her feet would start to cramp. "If we practice acting like we love each other, then maybe one day we will."

"Practice kissing?"

"Oh Burton, pish posh. Yes, practice. We have to learn to love each other, don't we?" She dropped back to flat feet. "Isn't that what married people do? Am I so distasteful?"

"No, uh. . ." Burton waggled his head. "I mean, yes."

"Oh." Maila's eyes widened and she backed up into the tabletop. "Never mind, then. I'm sure that was just a silly idea."

Burton reached out, circled her waist with his arms, and drew her to him. "I mean, yes." He lowered his head as he spoke. "But just a kiss right now. To practice." Then he gave Maila a sweet kiss that shot sparks to her toes.

Maila stammered, "I— I—" She cleared her throat and tried again. Her voice stayed on the husky side. "I think that's a good plan."

He kept looking at her as if stunned himself. "Well?"

"Well what?"

"This was your idea. Aren't you going to say it?"

She fought back the fear that he might not say it back. That it was phony. That the pretense wouldn't work. "I love you, Burton."

"I love you, Maila."

Chapter 5

Each morning, Burton kissed Maila good-bye. Each evening, he kissed her hello. At the end of the first week, the awkward start became a distant memory as the habit cemented. Maila looked forward to Burton's arrival for dinner—and to receiving her kiss, albeit a reserved one. A kiss that led to comfortable conversation about the farm, the store, and family.

"So James left the door open when he fed the chickens. Evidently a barn kitten found himself a cozy nap spot and woke up surrounded by a bunch of sleeping chicks in the henhouse." Burton's eyes lit up as he shared. "The mother cat and the harried hen got themselves into a frenzy squawking and yowling at each other."

"What happened?" Maila put her fingertips across her lips, fearing the grizzly ending for at least one of the animals. She spoke from behind her hand. "Did the poor little chickens get away safely? No, wait. Did the cats get pecked to death?"

Burton vibrated with laughter as he tried to finish the story. "I've never seen anything like it. The two mamas were squaring off for the defense," he snorted. "You never saw a hen or a cat puff up so big!" He laughed so hard Maila couldn't help but join the contagious humor. "When the hen hopped off to the side, the little kitty up and scurried away. All the fuzzy chicks ran after him cheeping to beat the band!"

"No!"

"It's true. Both the cat and the hen were so busy trying to round up their own young they completely forgot the other."

Maila clapped her hands. "Now that's a tall tale! I fear no one will believe you."

"Ah, but I have a witness." He held up his forefinger.

"You do?"

"Yes, my good woman." He pointed to the door as if someone stood there. "The mule saw it all happen." He kept a straight face, though his eyes glimmered with mischief. "Pretty stubborn old guy. He won't budge from his opinion no matter how you bribe him."

Maila doubled over in laughter at his imagery. "That can't be true."

"I'm telling you, ask the mule."

No wonder the church leadership had asked him to replace the retiring pastor. Burton could spin a tale and keep his listeners on tenterhooks, all while teaching an excellent lesson. Would she be expected to be a proper preacher's wife? The thought sobered her mirth.

Maila wanted to celebrate the appointment with him. Anyone who knew Burton knew the pulpit fit him like a hen in her nest. He farmed because the family needed him, not because he wanted to be a farmer. Burton's regular support as a substitute minister had finally earned him the permanent position. His flock would be well tended, and he could think about selling the store.

But what did this mean to her and her attendance at Augustana Lutheran Church? Didn't pastors' wives have go to the same church as their husbands—like Rose had? Rose played the organ. Rose taught Bible study. Rose had the biggest funeral the town ever saw, according to Burton, because she was so well loved.

Maila's shoulders drooped. She wasn't the beautiful, revered Rose. People still offered their condolences to Burton, although they quickly followed up with uncomfortable congratulations on his marriage. But Maila could see from the look in their eyes that she wasn't good enough to fill Rose's shoes.

She bit the inside of her lip. "When do you add pulpit duties to your schedule?"

"Next week." He beamed. "Holy Week takes a lot of planning. This will be Pastor Gilcrest's last one, so I'll shadow him in the evenings."

"I know you're busy helping with planting, and I know it's almost Easter." She folded her hands. "But I don't know how you'll do it all."

He looked confused. "You know I've wanted this for a long time. I told you that."

"But is now the right time?"

"I'm thirty-five. If not now, when will this opportunity come again?" He shook his head. "Did you know the pastor delayed his retirement when Rose passed? All to give me time."

She didn't know if he expected her to agree or disagree. "But that's the point. You still don't have time."

"Maila, I'll manage for the short stretch. A little less sleep won't kill me while the family works through getting a farmhand."

How did he not see this was a "we" situation and not an "I"? He'd already accepted the position without consulting her. Without discussing their needs as newlyweds. Was she a wife and partner? No. This roommate situation was getting out of control. She had to do something to change the situation before it became insurmountable.

"I just want you to know how much I enjoy dinner with you each night." Feeble. *No, Burton, don't realize your dream because I want to eat dinner with you.* She picked up the dish towel and wiped imaginary crumbs off her fingers. *Stupid. Stupid, stupid, stupid.*

"Is that your worry? Maila, we're not going to lose our dinnertime." He reached over and stilled her hands like a doting brother. "You'll see."

"All right." She stood to clear the table of their dishes. What else could she say? He'd already made up his mind. And clearly, his was the only mind that mattered. "But when are you going to write and rehearse sermons?"

He took her answer as agreement. "At night, after we go to our rooms. You can hear them on Sunday mornings, unless I'm too noisy when I practice them." He winked.

The Lutheran church she'd grown up in and the Methodist church Burton attended weren't far apart. But attending two services a week seemed difficult at best. "I thought I'd keep going to my church."

Oh, she did not like conflict. Why couldn't she avoid it even when she tried?

"Rose—" He cleared his throat.

The dishes rattled in her hands. Maila kept her back to Burton and closed her eyes.

"I'm sorry, Maila." He stood and turned her around by the shoulders. "I need you to support me as my wife. I've explained to the church board that we married to stop the appearance of evil. That nothing improper happened between us." He sent her a tentative smile. "They believed me and blessed our union. They said a pastor needs a helpmeet."

At least he figured out she existed, if only to support his dreams. What about hers? Maila clenched her teeth. Did he have to tell a whole bunch of strangers they'd married for appearances? Her face burned.

"Did you tell them we still haven't done anything improper?" She emphasized the last word as it scalded her tongue.

"No, Maila—"

"That we aren't living as a husband and wife because you don't love me? You only want one woman"—Maila's throat thickened her words to a husky whisper—"and she's dead. Or did you leave that part out?"

Her memory of Rose clouded. She was no longer the person Maila wanted to emulate. The cousin she'd loved became a ghostly adversary. Jealousy? Plain and simple. Jealousy of a woman whom she'd loved and admired. Jealousy of a woman who no longer breathed. The pain hit hard. Maila sucked air into her lungs.

Burton dropped his hold as his face stiffened. "A pastor's wife does not attend a different church. We may sleep separately, but it's not an option to worship separately. Beyond my calling, we have to find a way to handle the practical matters in our lives."

Practical? The breath whooshed out of her. The pain turned to anger. Like remembering the name of the woman standing right in front of him? Oh no. Maila stared at the buttons on Burton's vest. *Lord, I cannot do this on my own. He doesn't see me. He sees an employee existing to do his bidding. No, Lord, I can't do this.*

She refocused on the issue and ticked off the arguments in her head. Yes, he was right for the pulpit. No denying that. Burton was as good a man as she'd ever known. One so loyal it surpassed death itself. Her own vows said till death do us part. But would he ever part with Rose? A man needed time to grieve. But Burton's grief seemed too powerful a force.

Yes, they should worship together as a couple. She understood both the logic and his new station. But could she embrace a church she really knew nothing about in order to be a supportive wife?

Tears prickled Maila's eyelids. What happened? A month ago she'd anticipated a proposal from Benjamin, a future in nursing, and a completely different direction toward a loving marriage with children.

The rest of Burton's statement popped through her heart like canning lids sealing. Did he plan to keep separate rooms permanently? Surely he meant to become man and wife physically one day as they continued to grow closer. Eventually this would have to become a real marriage, or there'd be no children.

Maila raised her eyes to meet Burton's. "Do you want children?" Life would be so empty without the fullness of intimacy and family.

Burton's mouth opened, closed, opened again. And closed. His jaw pulsated as if he fought to keep his mouth shut. He turned and walked away.

No children, then. Maila dropped into her chair and buried her face in her hands. If they divorced. . . Could they be roommates for the rest of their lives while Burton mourned? Should they keep fighting for a marriage that didn't have a prayer? *Please, Lord, I've made a huge mistake. Either help me get this right or help me get out of this marriage.*

⌒∞⌒

Burton left quietly, before breakfast. No practiced kiss or treasured words. What had she expected? A few weeks of pretense did not a loving marriage make. Maila pushed away her plate. The food tasted like tree bark anyway. She tucked the bread back in the bread box.

Maybe a jaunt over to the hospital would be smart today. If she submitted an application, they'd likely appreciate an employee willing to work those hours when other nurses wanted to be with their families. Burton would have his dream and she would cope with some semblance of hers. But they wouldn't have to see each other. They'd simply be the roommates Burton expected. Maila missed the warmth of his lips. Not just this morning's kiss. She missed all the kisses that might have been.

Trudging to unlock the front door, Maila squared her shoulders. She could see a shadow cast by the bright morning sun against the drawn shade. A customer already waited outside. The last thing she needed first thing this morning, store finances or not. Well, no need to air their troubles for more gossip. She plastered a bright smile on her face. No one had to know how empty she felt.

She tugged the cord to retract the shade for the day's business. The gentleman stood with his back to her. At the sound of the banging bells when Maila opened the door, her customer turned around.

"Benjamin!" Her smile flashed from polite to deep and genuine. "How wonderful to see you!"

He grinned at her surprised greeting. "I couldn't stay away. I've been waiting a long time to have that talk with you."

"Did you get my letter?"

"Every one of them." He took off his hat and used it to point inside. "May I?"

She swept backward, let him enter, and stopped short as she noticed the passersby. No, no, no, no! Did those ladies ever walk anywhere else?

She closed the door on the gawking Mrs. Keller and Mrs. Berndt. It didn't help that Mrs. Berndt's husband handled the mail. The lady had likely seen the letters exchanged between Maila and Benjamin. Had they heard everything? Maila shivered. What did it matter? It was innocent enough. . .wasn't it?

"Are you all right, Maila?"

She turned back to Benjamin, a little tickle in her heart at the sight of him after so long. "Yes, fine." *I hope.* She shook off the impending gossip. Listening to what others thought of her had started this spiraling disaster in the first place. There'd be no more of that! From this moment on, she'd make her own decisions, based on what she knew to be right. Not on the pressure from any outside source. If only she'd done that in the beginning. Sadness washed over her even as curiosity propelled an invitation. "Come, have a cup of coffee." Why was he here?

Benjamin followed Maila through the store and into the sitting area of the kitchen. "I know you've been helping out, but can you leave the store?"

"Yes, trust me, I'd hear those bells regardless. I think they've created permanent tinnitus."

"Is that possible?"

"No." She giggled. "They give me a headache." She wrinkled her nose in the direction of the door. "I'd love to take them out to the cows they belong on. But I believe they'd drive the poor bovines crazy." She grinned. "But those noisemakers might find their way into the nearest pond."

Benjamin tipped his head back in a laugh. "I've missed you mightily, Maila." He dug in his coat pocket and pulled out a closed fist, turned upward. "I brought you something." He opened his hand.

Maila gasped. There lay the pretty grape cluster earbobs she had worked so hard to afford. "Oh Benjamin! You don't know how much they mean to me." The celebration of graduating nursing school. Her new job as a nurse. The very pair she'd stared at in the jewelry case walking home after work each night. She raised her eyes from his hand and saw the love shining in his eyes.

Her heart crumbled. She knew his love wasn't to be for a woman who'd already taken her vows. But she also knew the last letter couldn't have reached him, or he wouldn't be here, now, with such a lighthearted countenance.

Maila set down the coffeepot and cups. Then before speaking, she wiped her hands down the white apron she wore each day in the store. "Benjamin, I need to ask you if my last letter—"

"That's why I came, dear Maila." He scooted back his chair and, in a quick motion, stood and then dropped to his knee. "I wanted to ask you, Miss Maila Holmes," he said as he held out his hand again, "if you'd marry me?" His palm held more than her earbobs.

Maila gaped. "Oh!" He'd managed to drop a ring right in between them. "Benjamin, I—"

∞

"That's Mrs. Rutherford to you, sir," Burton announced from the back door in awe-inspiring authority. "Kindly refrain from stealing my wife." He took deep, controlled breaths.

If Mrs. Berndt hadn't run into him at the post office, Burton wouldn't have known this fox had entered his den. If it were her, she said, she'd hightail it over to the general store before his wife ran away with another man.

His stomach had plunged. He fingered the envelope in his pocket. He hadn't known, right up until the moment Mrs. Berndt handed him the evidence, that Maila meant so much to him. God had given him a second chance to have children. A second chance to love a unique woman. His chest heaved at the exertion to get home before the cunning fox outsmarted him and left ruin behind. Now he fought to control the desperate need for air and for his breathing to return to normal.

"Stealing your what?" Benjamin leaped to his feet. "Maila? What is he talking about?"

She stepped forward to touch his arm, but he backed away. "Benjamin, I'm so sorry. It happened so fast."

He looked utterly betrayed.

Maila let her arm drop.

He swiveled his head between Burton and Maila. "Then, it's true." He jammed his hand into his pocket. "Sir, you have my deepest apology. I would not stoop so low—had I only known."

Burton nodded an acceptance, though his jaw could be granite.

"Good-bye, Maila." Benjamin left so quickly dust spun off his shoes.

The triumph tasted sweet. Burton reached for his wife, but Maila's eyes filled with panic.

She lifted her skirts and rushed out of the room, following the wife thief. "Wait!" she yelled. "Benjamin, wait!"

Burton let her go and hung his head. He'd failed to claim his bride when he had the chance. He'd failed Maila, not the other way around. Maybe he'd been the bride thief all along, stealing another man's blessing right out from under his nose.

He took the letter Mrs. Berndt gave him out of his pocket. After dropping it on the table, he walked upstairs to his room. The fox had won because Burton had left the coop wide open.

Chapter 6

Was it in poor taste to ask for her jewelry back under the circumstances? She heard the cowbells bellow his exit. It didn't matter whether it was poor taste or not—she'd worked too long for those earbobs. They represented all of her achievements after Mama sent her off into the world. All her efforts to become someone of value. If she hurried, she could catch him before he boarded the train back to Saint Paul.

But as she shut the door behind her, Maila saw Benjamin drive away in a carriage. It would've been so romantic to be whisked away because he loved her. Now what? She looked over her shoulder at the storefront. Did that jewelry still represent what she wanted? Or did Burton's impassioned pronouncement mean they had a chance?

Maila crossed her arms against the brisk breeze and watched the empty corner where Benjamin had been. Go or stay? She stood at a crossroad, searching her heart. *Which is the good way, God? Is this You giving me a way out? Or did You set me on a new path I couldn't see on my own?*

She took a step forward as if testing a rickety old bridge.

"My, but your guest left in quite the hurry." Mrs. Keller meandered up the sidewalk behind Maila. "Is everything all right?"

Pinching the insides of her elbows, Maila pivoted. "Yes, thank you for asking." The woman wasn't getting the satisfaction of one more maligning morsel.

"Well, good then. We wouldn't want any more ills to befall your family." Mrs. Keller scrutinized Maila's face like a tomcat watching a seed-seeking sparrow. "I'd like a bag of sugar for my baking."

And that's the excuse. This little sparrow is flying away. "Mrs. Keller, you go right on home and start that baking. Unfortunately, we're closed this afternoon. But I'll have that sugar delivered as quickly as possible so you won't be held up. Shall I put it on your account?" Maila wanted to hoot at the woman's stunned expression, but she kept up an impassive facade with a will of iron.

"Well, I suppose that will have to do."

"Yes, we do aim for good customer service." The delivery boy down the street would get an extra nickel just so Mrs. Keller didn't have a chance to snoop one iota further. "What time do you require your delivery?"

"Any time before two will be fine."

"You shall have it." With that, Maila gave a perfunctory tip of her head and went back to the store.

She slowly twisted the knob, not willing to hear the bells jangle and bang against the door anymore. She reached around and captured the rope, stopping the swing. Once inside, she untied the infernal noisemakers and set them behind the counter. Burton would have to find some other way to announce customers' arrivals.

The sunlight streamed in, basting the floor like a turkey. Maila stopped herself short of yanking down the shade, and gently lowered it. She'd work extra hard to make up for the closure, if he wanted her to stay. But Burton and she had some talking to do. Right now!

⌒∞⌒

"Burton?"

He lifted his head from prayer. Maila? His heart sped up, sending thunderous rumblings through his blood like a summer storm.

"Are you in there?" She tapped on the door. "We need to talk right this minute."

The floor squeaked as he pushed himself off his knees.

"Burton? I'm serious. Right this minute."

A quick smoothing of his hair, and Burton opened the door to see his lovely wife planted in the hall, hands on hips, eyes more green than he'd noticed before.

Burton raised his eyebrows. "Why did you come back?" He blinked, trying to believe she hadn't run to Benjamin.

"Why what?" she sputtered. "Who do you think you are?" She flung the same unopened letter at him that he'd left on the table.

He jerked away from the spinning envelope. "Hey! Hold on." And then he saw it. He had a spitting wildcat for a wife. One with a mind of her own and a heart that just might belong with him. A grin spread across his face. They had one interesting future ahead of them. "You came back." He made a mental note to pay attention, if given the chance. Would her eyes turn more green when angry?

"I almost didn't, you know." She tapped a foot and pointed down the stairway. "And I almost walked right out that door down there when I found out you'd stopped my letter. How dare you! I wrote to Benjamin to tell him we'd married. Then through no fault of his own"—she waggled a finger at him—"and in good faith, mind you, that poor man came to honor me. You—" She sucked in a lungful of air.

As she started to speak, Burton grabbed the chance to get a word in. "You did?"

"I did what?"

"Wrote and told him you were married."

"Of course I did." She cocked her head and squinted. "Are you listening to me?"

"I'm listening, Maila. But hold on." He raised his hand. "I didn't stop your

91

letter. Mrs. Berndt gave it to me this morning at the post office. It was missing proper postage. I was going to go back to send it when I collected some change from the house."

"She did?"

"She did."

"You were?"

"I was."

"Then that would explain Mrs. Keller just happening to be here when—"

"Mrs. Keller was here?"

"Outside, yes. She ordered sugar."

"Sugar." Burton rubbed a hand across the back of his neck. "I don't understand."

"Oh, for Pete's sake, Burton. She wanted more gossip. The sugar was a ruse."

"Of course." He nodded matter-of-factly. Women were definitely harder to comprehend than Swedish. But it looked like he might have his very own translator.

"Ooh, those two women! They've caused all of this. If they hadn't—"

"Hadn't what, Maila?" Burton spoke so softly Maila had to lean in to hear him. He leaned across the threshold and tipped her chin up so she looked him in the eyes.

Silence. An electric silence held them in a visual embrace.

Burton leaned in and touched her lips with his. A whisper of a kiss. When he lifted his head away, Maila's eyes were peacefully closed and a light smile tickled across her lips.

Yes, there was hope. His prayer, the one he'd started on the run from the post office to the store. The one he'd desperately begged God to fulfill as he raced to protect the woman he'd nearly driven away. The one he continued on his knees as she ran after another man. That prayer was answered. He could see it all over his wife's face.

"Maila, I love you."

Her lashes fluttered open. "You do?"

"I do."

"And I do want children."

Tears welled up in her eyes but didn't fall. "You do?"

"I do." He circled his arms around her waist. "And I want them with you."

Maila's eyes traced his face as she looped her arms around his neck. But then she caught sight of something behind him and locked on to it. She stiffened in his embrace.

Burton swiveled to see what had such a hold over her attention. Rose.

In less time than it takes a cow to kick over a milk pail, Maila broke out of his arms.

"I can't compete with her." She pressed back into the hall wall as if it kept her from falling. "I'll never be as beautiful, talented, or beloved by the town. I'll never be able to be as wonderful to you as she was."

Burton moved out of his room and into the hall. He took her face in his hands, threading his fingers into her hair. "Maila, you are so lovely. You're beautiful in such a different way to me."

She tried to pry his hands away, but he wouldn't let go. He held her fast, but tenderly. "No. I'll never measure up to who she was."

"I don't want you to be like her. You know I loved Rose. She was sweet and kind and very, very stable."

"I loved her, too." Maila lowered her eyes.

"She was a reflection of me. She reflected back the man she saw. I loved what she saw in me." His thumbs gently caressed Maila's temples. "I believed that man didn't need to change. She thought he was the perfect husband."

"I'm sure you were. . ." Maila's voice hitched. ". . .to Rose."

"We had a very good marriage I'll always feel blessed to have experienced." He bent down to force Maila to look at him. "But when I see myself through your eyes, I'm challenged to be a better man and a better husband."

"I'm sorry." Her lips trembled.

"For what? You've shown me life is about growing as a person and into a marriage. Marriage isn't a woman reflecting a man." Burton tucked his chin and bent his knees, trying to catch her attention. "Marriage is about both people, not one. I've been given a second chance to have a family and a loving wife. A second chance to be a better man. Don't take that away from me."

"You really love me? The *me* me?"

"I really do. You. Because you're so smart and accomplished. Because you challenge me. Maila, you're funny, fascinating, and full of surprises. I love who you are. Please don't be someone else." He released her cheeks and began pulling pins from her hair. "I also love this amazing mane of yours."

Maila's eyes glowed. Not the glow from a mirror, reflecting him in a still pool. But the glow from a deep well of love he wanted to dip into and taste. She tilted her head to let him reach the rest of the pins holding up the thick chignon. "Then if I want to go back to nursing, you wouldn't stand in my way?"

"Never. I'm proud of you. The world needs the ministrations of your hands." He looked at her as he smoothed shiny chestnut waves down her shoulder. "And so do I."

Maila blushed. In a husky voice, she asked, "Do you want to practice kissing me?"

"More than you can even imagine." He dropped the pins into his shirt pocket. "Would you give me just a minute?"

"A minute?" The confusion rolled across her face.

"Just a second and I'll show you." Burton held her gaze with his as he backed into the room. He held up an index finger, signaling her to wait, and closed the door.

"Rose, I will always love and remember you." He picked up the frame and looked at the beauty that once was his. "Always. But it's time for me to love and live until we meet again." He opened the wardrobe, moved aside his suit coats, and gently faced the oval glassed portrait toward the back of the cabinet. Maybe one day he and Maila would be comfortable adding her picture to a family wall. One day.

"Lord, into Your hands I commend Rose. Thank You for the blessing she's been in my life. May we meet again in paradise." He closed the wooden door. "Now please turn my heart to the gift of this new wife and the life You've given us together. Bless me with the ability to show Maila every day that I love her."

He opened the door and invited Maila in by sweeping her up in his arms. "My bride deserves tradition. But even more, she deserves a husband who promises to love and cherish her."

Maila leaned her cheek against his shoulder. "I promise to love you, too." She peeked up at him. "And to practice kissing my husband every chance I get."

Burton laughed. "We might get pretty good at this marriage thing." He kicked the door shut behind him as he dipped his head to taste the sweetness of her kiss.

Chapter 7

One Year Later

The pains came hard and fast, with mother guiding daughter as the next generation emerged. The infant's squall whooshed through the parsonage like the month of March—a little lion entering and then quieting into a sleeping lamb.

After sixteen hours, Maila finally held her beautiful son. She tickled the tufts of freshly washed dark hair sprinkling the newborn's tiny head. "Och, you're beautiful," she whispered and then kissed the tiniest ear she'd ever seen.

"Mama, he's so precious." Maila held her newborn son tight to her chest. "I could never send him away." She caught her mother's hand as she tucked in the fresh sheets. "Why, Mama? Why did you do it?" If Maila could understand, then maybe she'd be able to put the sense of being unwanted to rest even as the swell of maternal protection sang in her heart.

"Do what, mine *lilla* flicka?"

The shocked expression on her mother's face surprised Maila. "Mama, you gave me this pitcher." She gestured at the amethyst water pitcher on the nightstand. "You told me it was my inheritance, that you had too many mouths to feed, and I must make my way in the world. And then you sent me away from you."

"You are so wrong. How could you think it so?"

Maila looked down at the peaceful babe, his eyelids fluttering in sleep. She pressed on. She had to find a way to forgive her mother. "How could I not feel abandoned? You sent me away, but you kept everyone else." Never would she allow that to happen to her child. Never!

Mama threw a hand across her heart. "Nej, lilla flicka. Nej!" She crossed herself then, before continuing, "That Gud would strike me down before I would send you so." Tears brimmed and spilled over her mother's round cheeks, finding rivulets in the crinkles baked into her skin by farming in the sun.

"Then help me understand why you threw me into the wild."

"Oh, that all of mine children were so smart. That I could give them the same chance I wanted for you." She picked up the purple tumbler, filled it with clean water from the ornate pitcher, and handed it to Maila. "Drink, you need to make milk."

Maila drank, if only to fill her mouth with something other than accusations.

Sweet water that would help her body nourish this child of her prayers.

Mama took the cup and set it back on the stand. "Maila, I gave you this inheritance to sell. I never expect you keep it. But to hjälpa you pay for the school you wanted."

"School?"

"I know it's very valuable. My mama bring it from the Old Country." She fingered the toll painting, tracing the little white flowers above the blue floral and curlicue design. "It was all I had. I want you become this nurse you talk so much about." She sighed and splayed a hand toward the handblown glassware. "But here it is."

"You didn't tell me." The tears coursed down her face now, too. "Mama, how could I know?"

"I had no more words." Mama bowed her head. "It was too hard to let you go. I watched you walk down the road. When you disappeared, I stayed at mine door. I wait. Maybe she comes back, I said. Maybe she changes her mind, I said." A tiny tremor shook her shoulders. "But not mine Maila. Not mine lilla flicka who is smart as she is so stubborn. Such a girl can be something more than a farmwife like her mama, ja? I'd have been an artist, if I could."

Maila gasped. Her mother wanted to be more than a farmwife? The beautiful decorations in their home were handmade. But Maila had taken those for granted. They'd just always been there. Mama had sent her daughter away in order to give her the chance she didn't have? "Mama, you were willing to give up the last thing you had from your mother? Why?"

Mama looked squarely into Maila's eyes. "There is no thing more important than your Gud-given dreams. Ja?" Her eyes radiated a sacrificial wisdom. "It could not be in my life, but I could do this for you." She raised both hands in dismay. "Who would think a girl would carry such a thing all over? You always do things the hard way, daughter. Always." She stroked the baby's cheek and then laid her palm against Maila's cheek. "I give it to you and think." She tapped her temple. "You know inheritance is to hjälpa you. But you don't think to sell?"

Maila smiled through misty eyes as if seeing the sunshine on the other side of a waterfall. Her mother hadn't thrown her away. She'd been trying to support her dream but didn't have the words to say it. "Oh Mama." She raised an arm to invite a hug while balancing her newborn against her shoulder. "It helped me so much. It helped me remember the people I love and to value my heritage. No, I never thought to sell it."

"Oh well, maybe I was wrong on the smart part." Mama lifted an eyebrow and delivered the line with a deadpan shrug. Then her lips twitched.

A laugh started deep in Maila's soul, rolling out of her like bells peeling in the belfry. "Yes," she chortled. "Evidently. Luckily, Dr. Baker thinks I am."

"I'm proud of you, daughter. You did it. You are a nurse." She hugged Maila. "And now a mama, too. I think you will soon understand wanting to give your son all you have, ja?"

"Ja, Mama." Maila curled her arms around the little boy. "What do you suppose he will be?"

"Smart like his mama and a good man like his papa. Anything else is for Gud to show when the time comes."

Burton pushed the door a smidgeon farther open. "Is it safe for a father to see his wife and son?"

"Ja, ja. Komma *hit*." The new grandmother waved him over. The bed creaked as she stood. "Now, you two, when do we baptize this mite at the church?"

Maila held out her hand for Burton. "We'll be sending you an invitation to the christening over at our church soon."

"But it is our tradition—"

"I realize now that I'm a follower of Christ, regardless of the building I'm in." Maila tugged her husband down beside her. "I choose to be in agreement with Burton and to raise our children living out our faith."

"Mama Holmes, I promise that as for me and my house, we will serve the Lord." Burton leaned toward Maila for a kiss. Then he touched the tip of his son's nose. "You're a dream come true, little man."

Epilogue

Christmas 1949

The Christmas tree blazed all evening with giant blue bulbs while Maila and Burton hosted their annual family decorating party. Their two sons and daughter came each Christmas Eve with spouses and children.

Maila returned from the big kitchen and put the candy canes in the crystal dish. The steaming cocoa, buttered toast, and marshmallows waited for the family to gather.

The last silver tinsel floated from petite fingers as William lifted his youngest daughter to finish the decorations.

William balanced his daughter's feet on his thighs, took one hand at a time until she stood tall and trusting like an acrobat. "Flip."

Rosa Lee grabbed tight, giggled as she jumped, and rolled in a ball until she unfolded safely on the rug with crinolines flouncing down around her.

All the family cheered and clapped at her gymnastics.

"Can I have cocoa with marshmallows?" Rosa Lee yanked on her daddy's pants leg. "Grammy says it's tradition. She said it all started during the Great Suppression!"

William laughed. "Depression, honey. It was a time when money was tight, sugar was hard to find, and we all gathered over toast and cocoa for our big feast. Grammy had just enough sugar to make cocoa for us for our Christmas present because her patient paid her in sugar that day when she did a house call." He swung her up in his arms. "Your grammy was a really good nurse. And you know what? We liked that treat so much we decided to keep on having it every year."

"Komma hit! I have it ready," Maila called, soaking in the home full of people and love. Burton waited in the living room, looking at the family wall. At Rose.

Maila slipped her hand into Burton's and laid her cheek against his shoulder. He wasn't as steady as he once had been, but then, she sighed to herself, they'd had quite a life.

"Maila, it's been fifty years since she went to be with the Lord." His voice sounded a little muffled. "Fifty years today."

She patted his chest. "I know, love. I know."

"I still miss her." Burton tilted his head to touch Maila's. "But I wouldn't trade the life we've had together, either."

Maila smiled. "We'll celebrate with her one day soon."

Burton turned and took his wife in his arms. "But we have our fifty years to celebrate first." His glasses slipped down his nose. "Mrs. Rutherford, would you do me the honor of renewing our vows for our anniversary?"

Maila slid his glasses back up into place and touched her nose to his. "What? You don't remember them?"

He laughed. "I thought you might like to hear them again, but this time because I mean every word from the bottom of my heart."

"Mr. Rutherford." Maila placed her hands on his cheeks. "I've known you meant every word every day of our lives. You've lived them for me." She pulled his face to hers. "But I don't think that was a proper proposal if you want me to say yes to it. A man is supposed to be down on one knee."

"Woman, if I got down there I couldn't get up again." He took her hands and laced them around his neck. "But I promise to keep loving you till the day I die."

"Just don't make that anytime too soon." And she flounced away, as only a grandmother can, leaving a glint of a grin in her wake.

William captured his mother by the waist before she reached the dining room. Walking her back to the Christmas tree, he called his father over as well. "We need a picture for that anniversary announcement."

With the tree on one side and their portraits on either side of the mantel clock, William snapped the photo with his Kodak. "There, we have then and now."

"Burton, do you remember little James tugging Inga up the aisle on our wedding day?" Maila's eyes crinkled into fans of humor.

"I only had eyes for my bride." He placed a tender kiss on her temple.

Maila patted Burton's cheek as she accepted his affection. "Oh Rosa Lee, you remind me of your Grand-Auntie Inga."

"Grammy? Who's that pretty lady by Grandpa's picture?" Rosa Lee asked as she pointed to an ornate, antique portrait in sepia tones. "I see Mommy, Auntie Mary, and that's even me." She grinned in the way only a seven-year-old could at seeing her own photo on the family wall. "But I don't know that lady."

Maila looked at the beauty softly smiling from behind the oval glass. She'd graced the family wall for nearly fifty years. She belonged there. They all did. Because they held a place in memories and hearts and family stories.

"That's Rose, my lilla flicka. Och, such an accomplished musician, she was." Maila gestured for the little girl to come sit by her on the sofa. "Bring your cocoa here and let me tell you about my cousin, the prettiest girl I've ever seen. I wanted to be like her, but God made me to be just who I am. . . ."

Angela Breidenbach is a descendent of Swedish, Scotch/Irish/English roots who loves genealogy and writing fictionalized versions of family stories. Yes, her grandparents really did marry because of town gossip! As the captivating host of *Grace Under Pressure Radio* on iTunes, Angela teaches how to become a woman of confidence, courage, and candor. Angela is the Christian Author Network's president, a bestselling author of Christian romances, a professional book judge, and she's half of the comedy duo, Muse and Writer, though her fe-lion, Muse, gets all the fan mail. Find her online at www.AngelaBreidenbach.com or in iTunes.

Mule Dazed

by Lisa Carter

Chapter 1

Montana Territory, 1885

S tep away from the mule and get your hands in the air."
The little feller stiffened. But keeping his back to Brax, he continued to unknot the lead that tethered the dun-coated mule to the railing outside the general store.

"You've caused the owners and me a pack of trouble this afternoon by setting the mules loose from the corral."

Ignoring Brax, the small guy's girlish fingers wrestled with the knot.

Brax—Sheriff Braxton Cashel—clenched his jaw. "I told you once. I don't aim to say it again. . ." He jacked the hammer with his thumb.

At the metallic *crack* of the gun cocking, the little feller froze.

"Hands where I can see them and turn around. Slowly."

The delicate hands convulsed around the loosed reins. "You sure you want me to raise my hands?"

High-pitched for a guy's voice. This varmint was about to get on Brax's last nerve. New to sheriffing, he'd never actually had to shoot anyone in peaceful Hitching Post, Montana. Yet.

But he might make an exception with this lightweight. The wiry figure in the too-large coat and ragged jeans tucked into black boots probably didn't weigh a hundred pounds soaking wet. Brax could take this dude down with one hand tied behind his back. "As sheriff, I'm ordering you to let go of the mule. Now."

Underneath the wide-brimmed straw hat, Little Feller squared his shoulders. "Whatever you say, Sheriff. Just remember this was your idea."

Brax started forward but too late. Little Feller slapped the reins against the mule's hindquarters.

Kicking free, the favored contender for this year's Mule Days Grand Champion careened down Main Street. Lining the boardwalk, women in their best bonnets screamed as the mule set off a chain reaction among the other mollys and jacks, wrenching free of their owners. Children cheered. Shopkeepers dashed out of storefronts. Men struggled to hold their prize mules in check. To no avail.

Dust billowed as the mules stampeded out of town. As the dust dissipated, all eyes swerved toward Brax. Waiting to see what he'd do. Expecting him to screw up again?

103

His eyes hardened as the shoulders under the little feller's bulky jacket bunched. In laughter.

Nobody disrespected the law in his town and got away with it. He—Braxton Caldwell Cashel—was the law. And it was high time people understood that.

Brax's finger tightened on the trigger. He'd been made to look a fool in front of the townspeople again. And by this whippersnapper no bigger than a tadpole. "I ought to plug you one just for practice."

Little Feller stopped laughing.

"If you don't turn around with your hands up this instant, you're going to have a sudden need for the doc. Maybe the undertaker, too."

With exquisite care, Little Feller pivoted, hands in the air.

Chocolate-brown eyes glared at Brax. Then widened. Petal pink lips parted into a gasp.

With equal shock, Brax's mouth fell open. "Crazy Hair, is that you?"

∽

Why did he always call her that? Hattie wasn't the same ten-year-old little girl with the wild, frizzy curls who constantly got into trouble. Trouble then fourteen-year-old Braxton Cashel had to rescue her from at the schoolhouse not far from her family's Wyoming ranch.

But now an ominous silence reigned the length of Main, broken by the distant thundering of fifty hooves headed for Canada. She closed her eyes. It couldn't possibly be him. Hoping—praying—the startlingly handsome young sheriff was a mirage of her fevered imagination. Hattie's eyes flew open.

He wasn't. She sighed. The square, lantern jaw. Those piercing sky-blue eyes rimmed in a darker indigo. The same tall, broad-shouldered boy she remembered.

Only no longer a boy. More broad shouldered. And more handsome, if possible. The former, somewhat lanky, boy who'd filled out in all the right muscular places. Her stomach did a curious flutter-flip.

Brax pointed the pistol at the ground. "Harriet from the Bronco B?"

The only one, besides her long-dead pa, who ever called her Harriet.

"Is it really you, Crazy Hair?"

She hated that childhood nickname. Her nose for trouble might not have changed, but in the decade since she'd last laid eyes on the handsomest boy in the West, the corkscrew curls—bane of her existence—had been tamed. Hattie tossed her head and allowed the hat to fall to the ground. Free of the confines of the hat, her golden hair spilled around her shoulders.

The indigo perimeter of his eyes deepened and merged with the black of the iris. "Harriet?"

"It's the girl who's ruined the festivities." Hostile murmurs crescendoed.

"What's the sheriff gonna do now?"

Brax's mouth snapped shut. Raising his firearm, his grip tightened on the Colt .45. He widened his stance. "Harriet Brimfield. You're under arrest."

"For what?" She started to cross her arms, but the black hole of the gun barrel beaded on her forehead. She let her arms drop to her side.

He jutted his jaw. "For disturbing the peace. For causing a riot and endangering lives. For. . .for anything else I can think of to tack on to the charges I'm filing against you."

"But I'm only trying to do the right thing for these pitiful animals."

His eyebrow rose like a question mark. "What're you talking about, Harriet?"

She waved her hands. "I'm talking about saving those mules from inhumane treatment."

He took a step closer. She stopped waving her hands. Braxton Cashel wouldn't shoot her, would he? Hattie cut her eyes at the angry Hitching Post citizens forming a horseshoe. Maybe, on second thought, he would.

She didn't know this grown-up version of the boy she'd followed around in one adventure after the other in the old days. After his ma died and he left town, she'd lost track of him. But one didn't grow up with five overprotective brothers and become a shrinking violet. Not her anyway.

"I'm talking about what *that* man said." Hattie motioned to the cowboy at the edge of the crowd. "He said the grand champion would be put permanently out to pasture. Lassoed, roped, and retired with a noose around his neck."

Laughter erupted. Brax's chest heaved under the brown vest with the shiny silver badge, setting off a ripple of muscular motion in his tan homespun shirt.

Hattie stamped her foot. "Mules are wonderful animals. Intelligent, patient. Hardworking."

"They're also stubborn, think they know better, and maddening. Mule-headed, hence the name. Like you, Harriet."

She balled her fists.

"You got it wrong, Harriet." Brax relaxed his stance and flicked a glance at the cowboy. "Jimbo here was just waxing poetic about one of our beloved Mule Days courtship rituals."

Other cowboys who'd taken off after the rioting mules returned. Pulling the reins short, their horses stopped, sending a cloud of grit over the crowd. "Couldn't catch 'em. We'll have to round 'em up tomorrow, Sheriff."

"Storm's a-comin' anyways." An older man, carrying a black bag, nudged his chin toward the darkening sky over the distant mountain horizon. "I can feel the chill in my bones."

And sure enough, Hattie shivered. Not because she was standing toe-to-toe with Braxton Cashel, either. Well, maybe. A little. But mainly because the west wind sweeping off the mountain range had kicked up a notch.

One man shook his fist. "Anything happens to my mules in the storm. . ."

A lovely lady in blue jabbed her parasol. "She's cost us our chance to find a beau at Mule Days." The mob tightened ranks.

Hattie backpedaled, hands in the air, till her spine pressed against the hitching post. All of a sudden she wished she hadn't been so quick to leave the safety of the Bronco B. Faced with her brothers' ultimatum that Hattie choose a groom or they'd pick one for her, she'd hightailed it out of the Wyoming Territory faster than you could say "Robinson Crusoe."

"She's a horse thief," someone from the back of the crowd shouted. "We hang horse thieves in the Montana Territory."

Hattie clamped her hands on her hips. "I did not steal any horses. If anything, I'm a mule thief."

The crowd pressed closer. "Somebody grab a rope."

Brax's lips did that thinning thing when he bit back words. Which he often did when they were together, Hattie also remembered.

"Harriet," he barked. "When will you learn to keep that mouth of yours shut?" Brax angled. "Nobody's hanging anybody. Not on my watch. We'll organize a rescue operation in the morning." His gaze panned to the snow clouds billowing on the horizon. "Provided we're not snowed in."

"What about Mule Days, Brax?"

Brax Cashel smiled at the redhead with the heart-shaped face.

He had a right nice smile, Hattie acknowledged. Those even, white teeth reflected well in his deeply tanned face. Not that he'd ever smiled around her. Not when they were little. Certainly not today. Around Hattie, his face only scowled.

The redhead gestured toward the bevy of ladies huddling in their shawls. "After a long winter, we've been looking forward to this for months."

Jimbo angled his Stetson on his head. "Especially the dancing. Judge Mitchell rode into town this afternoon. Ready for the marrying to commence."

Brax smiled at the redhead again. "Don't you fret your pretty head, Clarissy."

And something roiled in Hattie's gut. Must've been the beef jerky she'd eaten on the trail.

Brax held up his hand. "Fact is, nobody's getting married with a late-spring blizzard on the way. You folks need to clear the streets and take cover." He motioned toward the stately two-story hotel. "Everyone needs to find a warm place till the storm passes. And despite this recent crime wave"—the look he shot Hattie was not as sweet as the one he'd bestowed on Clarissy—"I'm not letting anyone ruin Mule Days."

Muttering, the crowd dispersed, heading for buckboards to outrun the storm to nearby farms or toward a hot meal at the hotel dining room.

Hattie took a deep breath of the evergreen-scented air and dusted off her hands on the ragged trousers she'd appropriated from one of her brothers. She retrieved the valise she'd hidden under the wooden planks of the sidewalk. "Glad we got that settled."

The gun cocked again. "Nothing's settled yet." Brax narrowed his eyes. " 'Cept you're going to be riding out the storm in a jail cell. 'Cause, Harriet Brimfield, I repeat, you're under arrest."

Chapter 2

A mule—the perfect result of the superior strength and stamina of a male donkey coupled with the intelligence and calm demeanor of a female horse.
FOR THE LOVE OF A MULE

B raxton brandished the gun toward the sheriff's office. "You're going nowhere but jail, Crazy Hair."

His former childhood friend winced. Got to be twenty, Brax reckoned, if she was a day. She fingered one of the corkscrew curls hanging over her shoulder. He scowled. Okay—maybe her hair didn't look so crazy now she was grown. A pretty shade of yellow. He motioned with the gun. "You'll be cooling your backside in lockup tonight."

Pesky tagalong, Harriet Brimfield had been nothing but trouble. Involving him much against his will in one harebrained—make that hair-brained—escapade after the other. Till he relocated to Hitching Post, Montana Territory, after his ma's death to live with his bachelor uncle, the former sheriff. A quiet life—just as he liked it—without Harriet Margaret Brimfield in it.

Head held high, she flounced past the ornate Farm and Ranch Commercial Bank, the pride of Hitching Post.

Brax aimed to show her the gravity of her actions. Misunderstanding or not. You couldn't go around messing with people's property. "Of all the towns in all the territories, you had to pick mine? Why are you always such a burr under my saddle, Harriet?"

Lips tight and shoulders stiff, she stomped past the feed store.

"If any harm comes to those mules. . . What were you thinking?" He snorted. "That, if I remember correctly, was always your problem, Harriet. You don't think. Not before you leap straight into disaster, dragging innocent bystanders into your chaos."

Harriet whirled. "Why don't you just save the taxpayers of Hitching Post the cost of a trial, Sheriff Cashel?" Her finger jabbed the badge into his chest. "Shoot me now and save the rope."

Brax stepped back a pace. Before he remembered who he was. The sheriff of Hitching Post. And who this little minx was. The bane of his existence. He glared. "Don't tempt me."

She glared back. Funny, he'd never noticed how deep brown Harriet's eyes were before. In the old days, she always smiled at him. Her eyes lit with new mischief.

Asserting his duly elected authority, Brax straightened to his full six-foot height. He towered over Harriet. Who wasn't much bigger than she'd been ten years ago. "I wouldn't think of depriving the fine citizens of Hitching Post the chance to see you pay for your crimes. I'll be telegraphing those wild brothers of yours in the morning. You owe a lot of people a lot of money for those missing mules."

For the first time, uncertainty coated her features. "Must we get the boys involved?" She moistened her lips with her tongue. "M–maybe we can work out a deal. I can work to pay off the cost."

Brax's gaze lingered on her mouth. "Not much a girl like you could do to work off that amount of debt."

He flushed and hustled her off the boardwalk away from the town's only saloon. "Nothing not illegal or immoral leastways." Brax nudged her shoulder with the barrel of his gun. Crossing over Main, they dodged buggies hurrying home in the face of the coming storm.

Reaching the jailhouse, he threw the door open with a flourish. "Why can't you ever do ladylike, Harriet?"

A stricken look crossed her face.

Brax tossed his Stetson on the desk. He holstered his gun and seized a brass key off the wall. "No surprise at your advanced age you're still not married." He wiggled the key in the keyhole till it turned. "But nobody's that stupid. Or that big a glutton for punishment." The hinges groaned as he swung the door wide.

Harriet slitted her eyes. "And what's your excuse? Too many sweethearts to choose from?" She lobbed the valise inside the cell. It bounced against the stone wall and fell with a clatter onto the floor. "Your problem is you think too much about everything."

Brax took hold of her arm. "Your problem is you don't think enough."

She looked at his fingers curled around her sleeve. And her gaze flitted to his face. Brax's heartbeat sped up. He dropped his hand.

Harriet scanned the cell. "You're really going to lock me in there?" Her mouth went mulish.

Brax hardened his heart. "Yes, Harriet. I am." He pushed her—albeit gently—inside. He shut the door with a *clang*.

She peered at him through the bars. Her mouth trembled. Not so cocky now. Not so all-fired sure of herself for once. She looked scared, and all of ten years old. Some of his indignation seeped away.

"Brax. . ." She wrapped her arms around herself. "Please. . .I won't ever do that again. I promise. I don't like it in here."

He poked the fire iron inside the potbellied stove. "You're not supposed to like it in there. That's the point, Harriet."

Brax shoved a few logs into the fire. "I'm going to the hotel for supper. And I suggest while I'm gone if you've got any girl clothes, you change. Judge's more likely to be lenient on a woman." Brax refastened the key to his belt and grabbed his hat. "If you can even do girly."

Her eyes flamed. "Aren't you afraid I'll escape while you're gone, Sheriff Cashel? S'pose I got a lock pick in my suitcase?"

"I'd enjoy dragging you kicking and screaming back to town." Brax shrugged into his jacket. "And with the mood of this town since you've spoiled their fun, I wouldn't advise escaping. You're safer in here."

Sounding not unlike Mayor Bledsoe's prize bull, Harriet hollered. She undid the clasp on the valise and snatched something out of its depths. "I hate you, Braxton Cashel."

Brax groped behind him for the doorknob. He also suddenly recollected she possessed the best throwing arm of anyone—male or female—at their school.

Should've searched her luggage before. But Harriet addled his brain. Made it hard for him to think straight. He'd rather tangle with a desperado than mix it up with Harriet. He'd pulled her off boy bullies double her size on the school yard more times than he liked to recall. Dragged her off because the bullies screamed for help.

Harriet let the object fly, hurtling with deadly accuracy across the space between them. Brax fumbled for the door. Flung it open. Stumbled over the threshold. Slammed the protective wooden panel behind him.

Something—the weapon of Harriet's wrath—thudded against the other side. Brax—the object of Harriet's wrath—blew out a breath. That was close. Too close. Best let Harriet cool off.

He adjusted the brim of his hat as snowflakes stung his eyes. Brax stuffed his hands into his pockets. Hunching his shoulders against the wind whipping the flakes, he set off toward the hotel. Brax planned to get stew from the dining room. And maybe, if she was over her little snit when he got back, give Harriet some food, too. Maybe.

'Cause he didn't fancy a plateful of food hitting him in the face or marring the cell he'd scrubbed this morning. And people believed sheriffing was glamorous? Not with the likes of Harriet Brimfield in his holding pen.

❧

Hattie fumbled with the buttons on her calico shirtwaist. She fought the urge to cry. Smoothing her skirt, she straightened the folds of the dark blue serge over the petticoat underneath. She propped her foot on one of the two benches and laced her black boots. As long as she didn't think about the small space. . . Or how the walls were closing in on her. . .

She bit her lip. *A fine mess you've gotten yourself into now, Hattie Brimfield.* But when her brothers got here, they'd soon sort out the charges. And hog-tie her all the way home to Wyoming, where a certain railroad suitor awaited. She grimaced. How was she going to get out of this mess?

A real woman would employ her feminine wiles on the sheriff. Sweet-talk the key off him. And then run till she crossed the Canadian border. Hattie adjusted her shirt cuff. Brax would never be taken in by her version of feminine wiles. Not that Hattie hadn't tried to attract his attention.

The best ten-year-old way Hattie knew leastways. Even then, girls flocked around Braxton Cashel like flowers to the sun. Not that he seemed to care one way or the other. Owing to some fatal flaw in the female gender, his apparent indifference only made the girls yearn for him even more. And his eyes? Her knees wobbled. She swallowed. Was it her imagination or were the walls shrinking?

Hattie squeezed her eyes shut. She'd been thinking about Braxton Cashel's eyes. Prettier than most women's. Longer lashes, for sure. Not that there was anything remotely girly about the ruggedly handsome sheriff. Then or now.

She put a hand to her throat. Her heart pounded. Upon reflection, his eyes might not be a safer topic. Because with all her up-close experience with the male species—five brothers and a ranch full of cowhands—she'd never met anyone like Braxton Cashel. She'd practically racked her brain to devise ways to force him to spend time with her after school.

Her gaze drifted through the bars and out the lone window facing Main. A hurricane of snow. Night had fallen. *Where was Brax?* For all she knew, he'd abandoned her. Leaving her to starve. Her frozen corpse discovered after the good citizens of Lynching Post, Montana Territory, remembered to dig her out.

Okay—that was a stretch. Brax had stoked the fire before he left. It was toasty in the stone-mortared jail. Stone. . . Hattie fought the hysteria building. Trapped like that day Brax pulled her out of a cave-in. Her mind flitted for something safer to dwell upon before she lost control.

Hattie focused on the battered wooden desk piled high with paperwork. At the Most Wanted posters mounted on the wall. To hear Brax tell it, her face ought to be right up there with the most brazen of outlaws.

In the flickering light, Hattie studied the pit-marked complexion of the leader of a gang of bank robbers. Double Dog Derring. Killed three men and a sheriff's deputy. His beady, paper eyes chilled Hattie to the bone. A meaner, uglier man, she'd never seen.

Where was Brax? The darkness outside the window deepened. The timbered eaves groaned at the gale-force winds. The entire building shuddered. Hattie's gaze darted to the ceiling, expecting the beams to collapse.

Unable to breathe, she sank into the corner of the cell where the two benches butted ends. Was the oxygen thinning? She'd suffocate. He'd promised he'd come back. Why wasn't he here?

She huddled on the bench. Her knees drawn to her chin, she tucked her boots under the hemline of her skirt. Arms wrapped around her legs, her head fell forward. *Oh God. Help me. Please. . .*

Chapter 3

This much-maligned beast of burden is the mainstay of the settlement of the West.
FOR THE LOVE OF A MULE

B rax stumbled across the threshold. He wrestled the door into its frame, fighting the forces of the storm until finally he heaved it shut.

Panting, he leaned his forehead against the splintered wood. Now to face a hurricane of a different sort. Brax pivoted and sucked in a breath at her motionless form on the bench in the cell. An inexplicable fear almost swallowed Brax whole. "Harriet!"

No sound. No movement. His boot sent the hairbrush—weapon of her wrath—scurrying. He dropped the pack slung across his shoulder. At the cell in two strides, he jerked the key ring from his belt. "Hattie!"

Her head snapped up to his short-lived relief. Short-lived because her brown eyes weren't so merry. She'd been crying. The little tomboy who never cried. Her eyes flicked to his face. "I thought you'd l–left me here."

And belatedly, Brax recalled the morning before his mother died. How little Harriet Brimfield enticed him to come see the cave she'd found. With an undiscovered treasure of dinosaur bones. Luring him as she'd known it would, with those big words from his books. One minute Hattie dashed ahead into the tunnel. The next? A portion of the ceiling collapsed, separating them. Trapping her on the inside in the dark.

Frantically digging Harriet out, he'd experienced a panic only equaled when his mother took her last wheezing breath later that same day. Probably why he'd forgotten the cave-in. He shouldn't have locked Harriet in the cell. If he'd remembered. . . Well, he didn't know what else he'd have done with a female prisoner, but not that.

Brax fiddled with the key. "I'm sorry, Harriet. Took me longer than I thought." He jiggled the key. Nothing happened. He should've gotten the blacksmith to fix this.

He didn't like the glazed look on Harriet's face. Catching, the lock clicked open. "There." He wrested out the key and tossed it with a *clank* onto the desk so he'd remember to get it repaired as soon as the storm finished wreaking havoc.

Brax swung wide the door and stepped inside. Like a blazing meteor, Harriet skedaddled off the bench toward freedom. Breath hitching, he instinctively grabbed for the iron bars of the door and yanked it shut. At the metallic clatter, Brax went rigid with disbelief, realizing what he'd done.

Harriet throttled the bars. "Of all the stupid things you've ever accused me of, this takes the cake."

Brax agreed with her, although he'd never give Harriet the satisfaction of knowing so. She made him crazy. So off his stride. Still, the anger was a far better thing than her white-faced fear.

Harriet whipped around. "Now you've gone and trapped both of us in this hole."

Brax gazed at the set of keys perched out of reach on his desk. Best-case scenario, someone would come looking for him. He'd be the laughingstock sheriff all over again. The sheriff who locked himself in a jail cell with his mule-rustling female prisoner. During a blizzard.

He gripped the bars. Stuck in the slammer with the likes of Harriet Brimfield. *Lord*—he sighed—*I thought we were friends.*

Never taking his eyes off the she-cat known as Crazy Hair, he retreated until the back of his knees hit the bench. "Might as well sit down, Harriet. It's going to be a long night." He dug a biscuit out of his jacket pocket.

Her lips pursed, Harriet condescended to take it from him. His conscience smote him, and he wondered how long it'd been since she ate. Since she chose to eat, Brax defended himself. The Brimfields weren't exactly hurting for money.

The fiery orange of the coals glowed from the open stove. At least they'd be warm. Brax surveyed the neatly folded pile of garments Harriet had used to disguise her identity. Harriet scooted to the conjoined angle of the two benches, her spine pressed against the wall.

"Are you okay? I should've remembered how you wouldn't like being closed up."

Her mouth quivered. "I'm fine with you here." A spot of pink tinged the fair skin above her lace collar.

Brax took in the blue calico dress. She'd scooped the hair on both sides of her smooth oval complexion out of her face. He'd wondered if Harriet could do girl. Question answered. She could.

Her mane captured in a garnet-studded clip, she tucked a stray tendril behind her ear. His eyes followed the movement of her hand. And with the greatest of effort, he managed to tear his gaze away from the locks of her hair. Pulse racing, Brax reminded himself Harriet was a felon.

Brax flopped onto the bench to stare at the ceiling. He'd never figured out why she'd chosen him to be her hero. The penniless son of the town seamstress. The one the other children taunted for never having a pa. Taunts that launched Harriet, fists flying, to his defense.

"Sheriffing long, Brax?"

He grunted and closed his eyes. "Go to sleep."

"Your uncle was good to you, wasn't he, Brax?"

Brax's eyes shot open.

"I prayed he would be after you left so sudden-like when your ma died."

Harriet—Crazy Hair—Brimfield had prayed for him? Brax didn't often think of those painful days after they lowered his mother's body into the ground. Probably why he'd chosen to bury the memories of pesky Harriet right there beside his mother in the grave, too.

A tough, fierce little thing, Harriet was also kind. He'd sat forlorn on the church steps until Harriet Brimfield plopped herself beside him. He'd forgotten how she'd been practically his last sight of the one-horse town where he'd spent the first fourteen years of his life. From the stagecoach window, he'd watched as Harriet waved good-bye from the middle of the deserted, dusty street.

Brax cleared his throat. "Uncle Wilbur was great. Former sheriff of Hitching Post. He taught me everything I needed to know about being an officer of the law." He crossed his arms over his chest. "And a man."

"I'm so glad."

Another good thing about Harriet? You always knew where you stood with her. Happy or sad. Mad or glad. Wore her heart on her sleeve. Her every thought on her face.

He fidgeted on the hard bench. "What about you? What other havoc have you wrought in the decade since our paths blessedly parted?"

She laughed. The sound rang high and clear and true. Brax smiled. He'd also forgotten about Harriet's inordinate—and sometimes wildly unfortunate—sense of humor.

"I'm sure I don't know what you're talking about."

"Like when you rescued that mule from the miner's pack train. Must've been when this fondness for nature's stick-in-the-mud started. Like calling to like."

She eased down, turning on her side, and faced the top of his head. "How about those kittens we rescued from the mean farmer when he threw the sack of them into the crick?"

Brax hooked his thumbs through the loops of his jeans. "When you forced me to dive in to the watering hole to drag them out and I near 'bout caught pneumonia."

"How could an itty-bitty girl like me force a strapping big boy like you to do anything he didn't want to do? You wanted to save those kittens as much as me. You just needed me to prod you in the right direction."

Brax caught a whiff of flowers. He scrubbed a hand over his face. "So you've managed to avoid trouble until this latest misadventure?"

Harriet propped her elbow and rested her chin in her hand. "After Pa died, the boys sent me East to finishing school until I ditched the city and headed for home again."

"Finishing school?" Brax chortled. "Obviously a job that only half baked."

She slapped the top of his head.

"Hey!" He rubbed his scalp. "Can we stop the chatter and get some shut-eye before dawn?"

⁓∞⁓

Hattie pushed back her shoulders. "What's the real reason an eligible bachelor like yourself isn't married?"

"I'm a bachelor sheriff like my uncle. The job and matrimony are a disaster waiting to happen. Although. . ."

"Although what?"

"Every winter I think about how nice it'd be to have supper waiting. . ."

Hattie sat up. "*I* can cook."

Brax ignored her like he always did. "And a sweet, quiet woman. A real womanly woman. Pretty as a Montana meadow in spring."

Her heart sank to her boots. She was definitely not the stuff of Brax's dreams. Nobody'd ever called her pretty. Much less sweet. And quiet? Hattie was about as quiet as a Kootenai war cry.

Brax was right. She was destined to forever live out her days an old maid. Rustling ill-treated mules and kittens till she dropped in her tracks. A dried-up old spinster. Unloved. Unwanted.

If only Braxton wasn't always so guarded with her. "You need to loosen up a notch, Brax."

"And you, Harriet, need to tighten up at least a couple of notches." Brax released a breath. "Oh, and one more thing, Harriet?"

"Yes, Braxton dearest?" She said that just to hear him gnash his teeth.

When he stopped growling, he added, "I think if we can regather the mules I can convince the owners to drop the charges, and we can send you on your way. The sooner the better. To wherever you were going."

Hattie wasn't ready to vacate Hitching Post or Sheriff Braxton Cashel any sooner than necessary. Because she wasn't sure until she ran into Brax's cocked gun she'd actually been heading anywhere.

Chapter 4

*The big secret to a mule that never kicks is to handle it firmly
but gently from the time it is born, or from the time you acquire the mule.*
FOR THE LOVE OF A MULE

Braxton opened his eyes as a shaft of sunlight poured through the jailhouse window. A sliver of blue sky. The storm had blown itself out. Bones aching, he slid his back up the wall. He stretched, and his hand brushed against something soft. *Harriet Brimfield's* soft golden hair. Brax snatched his hand away.

On her side with her hands tucked under her chin, Harriet resembled a sleeping angel. An illusion until she awoke and opened that big mouth of hers. But he resolved to enjoy the peace and quiet while it lasted.

Brax feathered a springy coil of hair off her cheek. Unable to fight the urge, he wound the silken strand around his finger. Her brown eyes fluttered open. Her gaze landed on the curl entwined around his finger. Outside, the wooden planks on the boardwalk creaked.

"It's morning." Brax cleared the hoarseness from his voice. But for the life of him, he couldn't seem to let go of her hair.

She smiled at him. A sweet smile. "A good morning." Faint lines crinkled out at the corners of her eyes just as he remembered.

Brax's heart constricted. His breath hitched. Brax moved closer. Her eyes widened.

His hand slid to cradle the nape of her neck, further entangling his fingers in her hair. And his mouth took on a mind of its own, edging nearer. He nudged her chin with the tip of his finger. Her lips parted. He held his breath. And—

The hammers of a half-dozen guns cocked.

Brax froze.

"Step away from our baby sister, mister, and get your slimy hands in the air."

꩜

He scrambled away from Hattie so fast, she placed a hand on his arm to prevent Braxton from crashing into the wall.

She gaped at the five men—guns extended through the bars of the cell. "Not you guys."

"You know these outlaws?" Brax's mouth thinned. "That figures."

Those wonderful lips had been about to kiss her before her knuckleheaded

117

brothers interrupted. "What," she hissed, "are you doing here, Gen?"

Brax's nose wrinkled. "Gen? What kind of name is that for a man?"

Her oldest brother growled.

She stepped between Gen's gun and Brax's chest. "He doesn't appreciate being teased about his name. It's Genesis and these are my other brothers. Exodus, Leviticus, Numbers, and Deuteronomy." The boys—never much for book learning—left the schoolhouse long before Brax's time.

Brax laughed. "You're kidding me."

Deut, the closest to Hattie's age, shrugged. "Pa was a chaplain in the war before he came west. A man of the Word."

Lev squinted. "Is that your little friend Braxton Cashel in that thar cell with you, sis?"

Ex peered through the bars and scrunched his face. "The same Brax Hattie was plumb nutty about? Why, she cried her eyes out for a month after you left town."

Brax's eyes darted to her, and he frowned. The heat rose up Hattie's neck.

Num, always more trigger-happy than the others, narrowed his eyes. "Won't be laughing when we put a hole in this snake for dishonoring Baby Sister."

Brax's eyes enlarged. "I never—"

"I'm not a baby." She stamped her foot. "How did you find me?"

"Hattie, you're 'bout as subtle moving across the land as a mule in a room of fine china." Gen, the thinkingest brother, released the hammer on his gun. "When you ran away from the nice railroad man we picked out for you to marry, sis, you knew we'd come after you. Pleased to make your acquaintance, Cashel." The other boys relaxed their stance and murmured their howdys.

Brax tapped the badge on his vest. "I'm the sheriff here in Hitching Post, and—"

"Woo-whee!" Lev tucked the barrel of his pistol under his armpit and folded his arms. "Little Braxton Cashel made sheriff. Congratulations."

Brax's brow furrowed. "Thanks. But your sister let loose a herd of mules—"

"Figures"—Ex pursed his lips—"it had something to do with mules if Hattie's involved."

Num twirled his pistol around his finger. "We came across the mules after the storm on our way into town. Left 'em at the corral. Folks appeared mighty happy. A festival going on?"

Brax's shoulders relaxed a tad. "People round Hitching Post love their mules. Mule Days is a good excuse to get together every spring after a long winter to do some courting. The judge and circuit rider come every year to perform the weddings. It's how we got the name, Hitching Post. It's where folks in the territory come to get hitched."

Ex straightened. "Say, with Hattie getting married—"

"I'm not marrying that railroad toad." Hattie crossed her arms.

Lev gestured toward Ex. "I'm not ready to return to your cooking, either."

Deut waggled his shaggy head. "Maybe one of us should tie the knot and bring another cook home to the Bronco B."

"Glad you boys came along when you did. Looks like things are going to work out for everyone." Brax's tone was crisp. "I'm sure with their property recovered, the owners will drop the charges against Harriet."

Lev snickered. "Harriet?"

"I think it's sweet." Deut smiled. "That's what Pa used to call Ma."

God, please. Hattie dropped her head. *Take me now.*

Brax motioned toward the key ring on the desk. "If you'd be so kind as to unlock the door?" He reddened. "There was a most unfortunate incident. . . . A silly accident really. . ."

Gen's bushy eyebrows arched. "Only unfortunate thing I see from this side of the bars is you spent the night with my baby sister. Nothing silly about ruining her reputation."

Brax reared. "It wasn't like that. I'm the sheriff. She's my prisoner."

Num glared. "Saying it that way, when she was at your mercy and all, don't make me feel any better, Cashel. Fact is, it makes me more riled." He pointed the barrel at Brax.

Brax froze.

Ex cut his eyes around to his brothers. "You fellas thinking what I'm thinking?"

Lev poked out his lips. "Snare two birds with one string."

Num's eyes glinted. "One ring. You want me to go find the judge, Genesis?"

"Harriet. . ." Brax gritted his teeth.

"Way I see it, Cashel." Gen rubbed a hand over his whiskers. "You've got one of two choices."

Deut, the most romantic of the boys, grinned. "I think it's right nice. Seeing as how they were childhood sweethearts."

"We were not—" Brax whipped around, panic in his eyes. "Harriet, tell them nothing happened last night."

For the life of her, Hattie's tongue seemed stuck to the roof of her mouth.

"You can either stretch out your left hand, Sheriff Cashel"—Gen and the brothers cocked their pistols, outgunning Brax five to one—"or we'll stretch your neck for you."

⌒≫⌒

"This isn't legal," Brax sputtered between clenched lips.

Judge Mitchell, hastily aroused from bed at gunpoint, paused in reading the wedding vows.

Num Brimfield pressed the round barrel hole against the judge's temple.

Judge Mitchell took a breath. "Repeat after me, I, Braxton Caldwell Cashel, take thee, Harriet Margaret Brimfield, to be my wedded wife."

Lev extracted a not-so-clean hanky from his pocket. "This is so beautiful. Ma and Pa would be so—"

"A marriage made under duress or threats of violence"—Brax flexed and unflexed his fists—"is not legal nor binding in any court of law."

Ex jabbed the rifle at Brax's chest. "Stop stalling."

"Say something, Harriet." Brax shook the bars. "Do something."

But head down, her cheeks two rosy spots of color, Harriet averted her eyes.

Gen propped his hand on his hip. "Cashel, you got 'bout two seconds before I let Ex draw blood."

Desperation swirled. "I, Braxton Caldwell Cashel. . ." He repeated the rest of the vow. Why didn't Harriet explain?

"Harriet's turn," cooed Deut.

Brax rattled the bars. "This isn't right, Harriet."

Married to Harriet Brimfield of all women? This couldn't be happening. *God, I could use a little help here. Maybe a bolt of lightning or a plague of locusts?*

Judge Mitchell's voice droned on. "You say, I, Harriet Margaret Brimfield, take thee. . ."

She bit her lip and swallowed. "I, Harriet Margaret Brimfield—"

"Don't, Harriet, no. . ." Brax pleaded.

A single tear tracked down her cheek. "I'm sorry," she whispered.

Before Brax could stop himself, his hand went to her face and caught the lone tear. Where it lingered on his fingertip and glistened like a dewdrop. Brax's eyes locked with hers. Something stirred inside him.

The judge cleared his throat. "Miss Brimfield, let's get this over with."

Harriet started again, her voice stronger this time. His heart did a funny lurch. His chest squeezed, making it hard to breathe. Like he'd been kicked by a mule.

And stammering promises to love, honor, and cherish, five minutes later Brax found himself roped, tied, and lassoed into marriage. With Harriet Brimfield.

Judge Mitchell heaved a breath. "I present to you Mr. and Mrs. Braxton Cashel. You may kiss your bride."

How had this happened?

The Brimfields holstered their weapons and slapped each other on the back. "We got ourselves a new brother, yes sirree."

"Go ahead." Deut grinned. "Kiss 'er, Brax. What ya waitin' on?"

Tough as a cougar, chip on her shoulder, Harriet dared and yet beckoned Brax with her eyes. Little Harriet Brimfield—Cashel temporarily—all grown up. Knees knocking, Brax moved closer. She tilted her head. He inhaled. She did smell like flowers.

Brax tightened his mouth into a straight line against the unexpected rush of feeling. He brushed his lips across hers. Came back for more. She cupped his stubble-covered jaw. His skin tingled from the touch of her hand. "Hattie. . ." His voice sounded husky.

She leaned into him. "Brax. . ." And on tiptoe, she kissed one corner of his mouth.

His lips curved. And parted. But she let go of him and stepped back. Smiling as if imminently satisfied about something.

Though not as surprised as he, he'd wager. Because strangely, Brax already missed the warmth of her hand. And the sweetness of her lips on his.

Chapter 5

The key to handling mules is to call your mule's bluff.
Once you do that, you have won.
FOR THE LOVE OF A MULE

Glaring at her brothers perched astride their mounts—Winchesters butted against their shoulders—Brax gathered Hattie into his arms. "Soon as the judge quits cowering in Helena, this farce of a marriage is over."

His muscles moved as he shifted her weight. "As soon as I get my gun back," Brax yelled, "you're going to regret you crossed the sheriff of Hitching Post, Montana Territory."

Brax kicked open the door to the farmhouse on the outskirts of town he'd inherited from his late uncle. Hattie stole a glance at his shuttered face. And wished she hadn't.

White-lipped with anger, Brax strode across the threshold. Her brothers had insisted on "escorting" the newlyweds to their new home to make sure Braxton did right by their baby sister. They also tossed a coin to see who'd walk down the aisle to secure a cook for the Bronco B. Deut won the honor—or lost, depending on your point of view.

Brax back-kicked the door. It slammed into the frame and vibrated the house. He dumped Hattie onto her feet. Collapsing into a ladder-back chair at the table, he dropped his head into his hands.

She took her first good look around her new home. One main room used for cooking, dining, and living. A pantry. Another door ajar at the back. A bedroom? Her cheeks pinked. "Maybe it won't be so bad married to me as you think."

Brax gave her a baleful glance. "That why you didn't say something? 'Cause married to me is better than the railroad man?"

Hattie busied herself in the kitchen, opening cabinet doors searching for a skillet. "You could've let them knock you out. You couldn't have married me if you were unconscious."

Brax huffed. "Or shot dead."

She seized a skillet. "They wouldn't have shot you. They were just funnin' with you."

"Didn't look like they were joking. Figured even married to you was better than swinging from a rope or gut shot."

Hattie banged the skillet onto the range.

122

Brax loosened his collar. "Feels like the noose still ended up around my neck, though."

Hattie pinched her lips. Saying those vows to Braxton, Hattie felt a rightness like nothing she'd experienced. Not since Brax rode out of her life all those years ago. She'd always had this fondness for him. But nobody liked to be forced to do something they didn't want to do.

The judge hightailed it out of town soon as the boys let go of him. At best, Hattie figured she had a week to change Brax's mind before the judge returned, probably with a marshal.

Hattie liked being Mrs. Braxton Cashel. And she was determined to do everything in her power to convince Brax that he liked it, too. Starting with breakfast. She got busy. Brax eyed the plate of fried ham and sourdough biscuits swimming in redeye gravy with trepidation.

"Go ahead. It's the best I could do. You don't have many supplies in your pantry."

He picked up a fork and stabbed the ham. "Eat my meals at the hotel."

She crossed her arms over her apron. "Now you have a wife, you won't need to eat there anymore."

He squinted at the ham as if it might rise on its hoof and attack. "How do I know you aren't trying to poison me?"

She rolled her eyes. "Suit yourself. Starve if you've a mule-headed mind to."

Brax sawed off a corner of the biscuit. "It ain't me who's the mule-headed one." He stabbed the chunk of bread with his fork.

Hattie did a slow circle, her skirts swirling. "This is a right nice place with those oak trees and view of the hills. Just needs a few feminine touches."

"From *you*?"

"Curtains." She gestured. "A few rag rugs on the floor."

"Knock yourself out, Harriet. But you won't be here that long." Brax stuffed the fork into his mouth.

She held her breath.

Brax chewed. A funny look crisscrossed his face. He chewed some more.

She clasped her hands under her chin. "How is it?"

Brax swallowed. "Not bad considering you're the one who made it."

Hattie deflated.

"Reckon it'll do." He shoved another forkful into his mouth.

Hattie's heart pitter-patted. High praise coming from the pay-for-every-word Braxton Cashel. Round one for her culinary charms.

Later, a southerly breeze heated up the temperature. "Escorting" them back to town, her brothers returned Brax's gun—on a trial basis only. The boys proceeded to win the hearts of Hitching Post by promising to shovel the remaining snow from the streets. And the town fathers voted to restart the festival come the morrow.

A rotating brother also vowed to remain at Brax's elbow as he went about patrol. But once their horses were stabled, Brax bolted down the block—with his current shadow Lev—as if the hounds of hell were on his booted heels. Hattie climbed down from the buckboard. How could she convince Braxton to love her if all he wanted to do was run away from her?

Hattie looped Sugarfoot's reins around the fence rail. The same eleven-year-old molly mule once upon a time Brax helped rescue from a cruel silver miner. She patted the mule's neck. And pondering how to yet win the war for Brax's affections, Hattie ran smack into Clarissy outside the mercantile.

"Couldn't get him to marry you without your barbarian posse of brothers, Miss Brimfield?"

Small-town grapevines being what they were, news of their shotgun nuptials had already leaked.

Hattie lifted her chin. "It's Mrs. Cashel."

Clarissy arched her delicate brow. "Not for long. I bet by the end of Mule Days, he'd have married me without putting him at the end of a gun. Maybe once the judge gets back, he still will."

Hattie curled her hands into fists. And released them. It wouldn't do for the sheriff's wife to punch this carrot-top in the nose and instigate a public brawl. Not very ladylike, either. She mustered her dignity and marched toward the feed store to buy a sack of grain for her palomino molly. Wrestling the sack out the door, Hattie stopped and took a breath.

"Need help there, little lady?" Jimbo, the cowboy, leaned against a post, legs extended and boots crossed at the ankle.

Hattie shaded her eyes with her hand. "If it wouldn't be any trouble. . ."

Jimbo grinned. "Way I heard it, you ain't been nothing but trouble for our poor old sheriff."

Hattie dropped her eyes.

"But I reckon you done me a favor. And one good turn deserves another." Jimbo hefted the feed sack and threw it onto his shoulder. "I've had my eye on Clarissy for ages."

"I guess there's no accounting for taste." Hattie bit the inside of her cheek. "Sorry. I didn't mean that against you."

Jimbo removed the sack from his shoulder. It landed with a dull *thud* into the wagon. "No offense taken. Clarissy, to be sure, is an acquired taste."

"I'll take your word for it."

Jimbo reclined against the side of the wagon. "Clarissy's fooled herself into thinking the good sheriff is more her sort. But now you've taken Brax off the market, I aim to win her heart by the end of the week."

Hattie's spirits rose. "You mean that?"

Jimbo resettled his hat on his head. "Perhaps we can help each other. Deal?"

Hattie stuck out her hand. "Deal." Jimbo clasped her hand in both of his. They smiled at each other in perfect understanding. Until Brax shoved Jimbo, sending him sprawling over the watering trough into the street.

"Get your stinking hands off my wife."

She took hold of his arm. "Brax."

He shook her off and jabbed his finger at Jimbo, who was grinning like a fool in the dirt. "And keep 'em off her."

"Brax, it wasn't what it looked like. Jimbo—"

"It never is with you, is it, Harriet?" Brax's mouth thinned. "You women are all alike." And he stalked down the street toward the livery.

Hattie put a hand to her throat. "What does he mean?"

Jimbo plucked his dripping hat out of the water. "Last little filly who strolled into town made a real effort to catch Sheriff Cashel's eye. And succeeded by all accounts."

Hattie's breath caught. What had she done? Had she forced Brax to marry her when he was in love with someone else?

"Besotted and blindsided while she and her oily partner cleaned out the church treasury. Got to Helena before the marshal there caught them and returned the money. Love has left a bad taste in Sheriff Cashel's mouth. Reckon Brax feels he's got a lot to prove. His uncle left tall boots to fill."

And Hattie, thanks to her overzealous brothers, had ensured Brax's continuing humiliation in front of the whole town. He'd never trust Hattie, much less learn to love her.

"Don't despair." Jimbo slapped the waterlogged Stetson against his thigh. "From the good sheriff's reaction, all may not be as lost as you think. It's Mule Days. And Mule Days in Hitching Post means love is in the air."

Hattie prayed Jimbo was right.

Chapter 6

Rather than pit your strength against the tremendous strength of a mule,
you must either outthink him or outmaneuver him.
FOR THE LOVE OF A MULE

Brax was still right befuddled as to what came over him three days ago. A sworn officer of the law, he kept his emotions under tight control. Utilizing violence only when the situation demanded action. And if any situation warranted violence, Jimbo's big paws touching Harriet qualified. Good thing Brax had telegraphed the judge it was safe to return. Two more days. Four days tops.

Then Brax would be forever free of Harriet Brimfield—he grunted—Cashel. The thought of finally getting rid of her, though, didn't bring as much pleasure as he'd expected. With Mule Days under way, the town settled into its pre-Harriet rhythm. Even if he, sad to say, hadn't. Hunched over his desk at the jail, his stomach rumbled.

He'd give Harriet her due. She knew her way around a kitchen. No wonder her brothers were so big. Nobody starved on Harriet's watch. It was getting to be a pleasure striding through the farmhouse door, anticipating a home-cooked meal. A man could get used to—

Brax scowled. He didn't aim to get used to nothing. He'd spent his nights sleeping in the same lofted bedroom he'd used when his uncle was alive. The boys hunkered down in the barn. And Brax wanted the whole lot of them gone.

She either pestered him to death with questions about his likes and dislikes or talked a blue streak about some book she wanted to write—a definitive guide to mules. Brax wanted his peaceful life back. And Harriet on her way to Wyoming. Before it was too late. Too late for what? The door banged open and he jolted.

Harriet bustled into the jail. Her arms sagged with the weight of a picnic hamper. Tendrils of pretty yellow hair curled around her face. Which lit at the sight of him. Like every evening when he came home. A man could get used to—

Brax's heart jerked, beating wildly. His fingers twitched, recalling the softness of her not-so-crazy hair the morning after the snowstorm. If anything, the hair— neatly coiled at the nape of her neck while she cooked—drove Brax crazy.

He hurried around the desk and took the hamper from her. She shifted toward the door without a word. "Wait." Absurdly panicked, he caught her hand. "Smells like fried chicken."

She stared at his hand. A pulse thrummed in the delicate hollow above her throat. "It's not for you. Unless you place the highest bid."

Brax scowled. "What?"

He'd hardly seen her in the last twenty-four hours. She was either in the barn training that blasted mule of hers. Or shaving whiskers off her brothers in a vain attempt to increase their matrimonial prospects. Lunch was usually their time, though.

Brax shook his head to clear his vision. Since when did he and Harriet have a "their" time? He wasn't getting much sleep. Not with thinking about Harriet.

"It's for the basket auction on the steps of the hotel."

Somehow Harriet Brimfield—Cashel—had become the darling of Hitching Post. The church women welcomed her with open arms while he sat stiff-necked beside her on the pew. A natural contralto, Harriet threw herself into the hymn-singing with the same gusto she tackled everything else.

"Bringing in the sheaves, we shall come rejoicing, bringing in the sheaves"—his eyeball, Brax vowed. It'd take more than a crook of her finger and biscuits to win him over. He knew Harriet better than anyone. Mischief, not Margaret, was her true middle name.

Yet whenever within arm's reach, Harriet had this curious, deleterious effect on his high-minded resolves. She moved toward the door. He held on to her hand, pulling her back in place.

Tilting her head, Harriet looked at him with those big eyes of hers, resembling a brown-eyed prairie sunflower. "We'll be late."

He twined his fingers through hers, loving the feel of her skin. "What else is in the basket?"

She shrugged. "Deviled eggs. Potato salad. Pie."

"What kind of pie?"

Harriet smiled. "Huckleberry."

Brax's insides quivered. "I love huckleberry pie."

She squeezed his hand and slid from his grasp. "I remember." Harriet slipped out the door.

Hoisting the basket and grabbing his hat, he followed her to the crowded steps of the hotel. Brax deposited the hamper amid the dozens of other delicacy-laden containers prepared by the fair hands of Hitching Post. He retreated across the street and leaned against the jail wall. Hitching Post citizens had already staked their spots up and down Main. Brax cast a practiced eye over the assembly. Mule Days provided a great economic boost for the town. And the chance to court the ladies. Bringing ranchers, miners, and farmers out of the woodwork.

But it also sometimes brought the disreputable element who frequented the Silver Dross Saloon. And with the telegram he'd received from the Virginia City

Mining Cooperative, Brax couldn't afford to be distracted by Crazy Hair. He grimaced.

At this rate, the only one going crazy was him. Or perhaps the whole world had gone crazy. Like Genesis winning the pie-eating contest this morning. Brax suspected an inside job. The oldest Brimfield brother had spent an inordinate amount of time in the hotel kitchen. With the help of Sugarfoot, Deut easily won the log-loading contest. And the attention of the shopkeeper's daughter.

Brax's gaze shifted to a pair of men he didn't recognize in front of the bank. Their hat brims shielded their eyes. Scruffy ruffians, they'd bear keeping a close watch on.

The bidding proceeded smoothly. Brax relaxed, arms crossed over his chest, one boot propped on the wall. Lev bought the doctor's sister's basket for the exorbitant amount of nineteen dollars. Looked like another Brimfield brother was destined for the matrimonial executioner's block.

His glee was short-lived when Harriet's wicker basket came up next. And Jimbo started the bidding on the high side of ridiculous. Brax's boot dropped. What ailed that cowboy? What part of "she's *my* wife" didn't that cow patty understand?

"I have ten dollars bid," the auctioneer rattled. "Who'll give me ten dollah fifty?"

Jimbo raised his hand.

The auctioneer pointed. "Thank ye, young feller, I see that hand."

Brax sucked in a breath. His eyes cut to Harriet.

"I have ten dollah fifty bid. Who'll make it eleven dollahs even?"

Brax pushed off the wall and planted his boots even with his hips.

"Ten dollah fifty going once..."

Harriet's lunch belonged to Brax by rights.

"Ten dollah fifty going twice..."

Something primal tore inside his chest. "One hundred and thirty dollars," Brax shouted.

The din of the crowd died away. All eyes swiveled to him. Except for Harriet. She never took her eyes off the auctioneer. Brax's heart threatened to burst out of his chest. If Jimbo raised his bid again...? Brax reckoned he could sell his horse.

"Sold!" The auctioneer pounded the table. "Sold to Sheriff Cashel for one hundred and thirty dollars." The double-jowled man grinned. "'Bout the going rate of a mule. Come get it, Sheriff. Belongs to you."

Brax crossed the street in three strides. Yes, she did. And he wasn't going to let anybody—including Harriet Brimfield Cashel—forget it.

⁓◌⁓

Clarissy's eyes almost bugged out at Jimbo's opening bid on Hattie's basket. But when only silence from Brax greeted Jimbo's bold move, Hattie started to sweat.

She turned to stone as the auctioneer accepted Jimbo's offer. Her own husband wouldn't buy her basket. Then at the last moment, she closed her eyes in relief when Brax's strong voice rang out. Okay—his belligerent, somebody's-going-to-pay voice. But it showed he cared—if only a little.

One hundred and thirty dollars. Not so little, Hattie's conscience chided. That was a lot of money to someone like Brax. That was a lot of money to a Brimfield, too. Brax—Hattie's heart thrilled at the thought—did care. Or—Hattie's spirit plummeted—his pride wouldn't allow another man to eat his wife's lunch in front of God and the whole town.

Now under the oak tree in the meadow, palpable waves of outrage radiated off Brax. And he chomped on the chicken leg like it was his last meal. Maybe on second thought, it was hers. Biting her lip, Hattie fretted at the lace collar at her throat. Skirts bunched around her legs, she rested her chin on her knees. And gazed over the wildflowers between Brax's cabin and the forested mountain range.

"Why aren't you talking?"

She kept her face averted. "I thought my talking annoyed you."

"Harriet."

She squeezed her eyes shut. Why did everything with Brax go wrong?

"Look at me, Harriet." A muscle ticked in his jaw. He threw the chicken bone as far over the pasture as he could. Cawing, a flock of crows rose from a tree.

Only Brax possessed the power to fulfill the longings of her heart. Like a bolt of lightning, the touch of his hand at the jailhouse earlier sizzled her brain. Sometimes she'd caught his gaze upon her over the last few days when he believed she wasn't looking. How she wanted him to say the words she yearned to hear. How she desperately longed for him to take her into his arms and pledge his heart to hers forever.

"What am I going to do with you, Harriet?"

Not the words she wanted from him.

Hattie choked back a sob. "I'm sorry." Cheeks burning, she pillowed her face in the pink calico. How much clearer did a man have to be? Brax didn't want her. He didn't love her. Braxton Cashel would never love her.

Chapter 7

Anything a horse can do, a mule can do better.
For the Love of a Mule

W hy must everything you do, Harriet, involve the outrageous?"
Harriet's chin dropped, distracting him from his anger. Her hair fell forward and shadowed her face. That hair. . .

Brax took a breath and blew it out slowly between his lips. Never having had a father, Brax worked extra hard to maintain his respectability. Which Harriet seemed determined to destroy. "I have a reputation to uphold as sheriff."

He'd no idea what possessed him to make such an absurd bid for chicken, potato salad, and deviled eggs. The pie he planned to eat as soon as he and Harriet finished this little talk in the meadow.

"I'll pay you back every penny. I'm sorry," Harriet whispered.

Brax didn't like not being able to see her face. And he didn't like Harriet's unnatural quiet. Far as he could tell, every thought in her head usually came out of her mouth. And another thing he didn't get—the more preposterous the exploit, the more Hitching Post loved Harriet Brimfield and her brothers.

What Brax *did* like was the puffy-sleeved pink calico on Harriet. She looked as pretty as the wild roses growing along the fence rails. And combined with the silky yellow of her—he gnashed his teeth. Stop. With. The. Hair.

"Two days, Harriet. Two days before the judge returns, and we get this marriage thing settled. All I'm asking is a little forethought before you decide to do something ridiculous. A little decorum as long as you're the temporary wife of the sheriff. Don't worry about repaying me. Truth is, the price of a mule is well spent if I can get back my peaceful life."

Her eyes flashed. "Whatever you want, Brax." She swept the hair out of her face and secured it with a pearl-studded clip.

Brax's eyes locked on to a curl dangling at her earlobe. "What I wanted was a real pa. I wanted to be good enough." Easing closer to Harriet, he rested against the rough bark of the tree. "What I got was a mother who made a mistake during the war she paid for the rest of her short life. One I've been paying for ever since." He raked his hand over his head. Where had that come from? He'd never said that out loud to anyone, not even Uncle Wilbur.

She jutted her chin. "Braxton Caldwell Cashel has always been good enough. I wish you'd see yourself the way I do. And understand how the whole town respects you."

Brax fidgeted. "Respect has to be earned. Don't know I've done such a good job of sheriffing."

"One mistake, Brax." She held up her finger. "You're new to this sheriffing business. You learn and you move on. This isn't New York City. The biggest part of sheriffing Hitching Post is your personal relationships in the community. At which you excel. The rest?" Harriet fluttered her hand. "I pray you'll never be called upon to exercise those types of skills. But if you do? You'll do as well as you do everything else."

Brax stared at her. She believed in him that much? Nobody ever—

"Least you didn't kill your mother like I did." Harriet folded her hands in her lap.

Brax frowned. "You didn't kill your mother."

"She birthed five brawny boys just fine and then died birthing one scrawny, brawling girl."

"That's not what happened, Harriet." Brax laced his fingers through hers. "Our mothers were friends. I was real little myself, but I remember one afternoon the teacup perched on her stomach rattled. The baby—you—were kicking like a mule, she said."

Harriet swallowed. "I guess I'm still kicking life like a mule."

"When I was older, I asked my mother what happened to yours. Ma said your mother was sick before she got in the family way. Some female—" How did he get into these conversations with Harriet? "Some female trouble killed her not long after you were born."

Brax draped his arm around Harriet's shoulders. "It's not your fault. Didn't you ever talk to your pa and brothers about it?"

"Every time I mentioned Mother, their eyes got wet. They brushed me off. So I stopped asking."

Brax hugged her closer. "I bet they were embarrassed because of their tears, not because of anything you'd done." The flowery fragrance she wore sped up his heart.

She tucked her head into the curve of his neck. "I tried my hardest to be one of the boys so Pa wouldn't remember I'm the girl who killed his wife."

He brushed his lips against her hair. "They love you to pieces, Harriet. I always wanted big brothers like yours. And you don't need to prove anything to anyone." Her alluring scent filled his nostrils. Violets? Brax's mouth went dry.

She wrapped her arms around his torso. "Trouble is, no one ever said it was okay to be a girl. Gunslingers or Indians, I can stand shoulder-to-shoulder with the best and hold my own. That's me, Harriet Margaret Brimfield."

No, she was Harriet Margaret Brimfield Cashel. Brax's heart thumped. Why did that sound like sweet music to his ears? "I like the way God made you, Harriet."

She raised her head. "You do?"

What in the blue blazes had gotten into him? Harriet's recklessness must be contagious.

"I do." Brax let go of her. "I've got to get to work."

Harriet was dangerous to his sanity. Good thing he'd see the last of her soon.

"But first?" He reached for the plate on the quilt. "I'm going to eat my pie."

∞

Hattie scanned the crowd in the hotel ballroom.

Couples dosey-doed. The auctioneer—now square dance caller—put the Mule Days sweethearts through their paces. The fiddlers sawed relentlessly. It was toe-tapping, boot-stomping fun. But where was Brax?

Hattie swayed to the rhythm of the music. She waved at Num cutting a fine figure on the dance floor with the spinster schoolteacher. Her brothers had taken Hitching Post by storm, a storm of love. Ex won the mule jumping event with Sugarfoot. He was courting Mayor Bledsoe's niece. And looked like Clarissy had come to her senses, too. Leastways from the way Jimbo twirled the redhead around the dance floor.

And since this afternoon under the oak tree? Life was once again full of possibilities. The possibility of a future with Brax. If Brax was glad God made Hattie the way she was, who was she to argue with Sheriff Cashel? Or with God? Her heart felt as light as dandelion fuzz blowing in a spring breeze.

Brax had told her in secret—the Virginia City Silver Co-op was sending an armed coach with silver bars for safekeeping to the Hitching Post bank until the federal marshals arrived and arranged a permanent transfer to Helena. He'd be busy, so Brax warned Hattie not to expect to see him anytime soon as he coordinated a secure transition of the silver ingots. But she hoped—wildly hoped—he'd manage to sneak away for one teensy dance with his shotgun bride.

After five more lively songs, Hattie gave Brax up as lost. Disappointed, Hattie reminded herself Brax had made no promises. Such a shame, though. She'd taken special pains with her lavender dress tonight. The boys declared lavender Hattie's best color.

Humming, she descended the curving staircase to the grand foyer as the strains of a waltz began. The front door opened and closed below.

"Mrs. Cashel?"

She halted mid-step.

Brax stood at the bottom of the stairs, clean shaven for once and his dark mane hatless. His broad shoulders in his best suit coat tapered to his hard-muscled waist. The badge glittered in the sparkling diamond light of the chandelier.

His gaze landed on the silver comb adorned with violets with which she'd scooped the ringlets of her hair. "Would you dance with me?"

Brax held out his hand.

Her heart beating faster than the three-four time of the waltz, Hattie took his hand. Brax's scrutiny never wavered as he drew her to level ground. One hand around her waist, he led Hattie in the box step.

But conflicting emotions rippled across his face. Doubt. And a fierce vulnerability. Yet his gaze traveled to her mouth. And lingered. His chest rose and fell.

Was Brax having as hard a time breathing as she? The heat from his hand scorched her skin. Brax stopped dancing. The music continued to flow around them. His eyes went opaque, a smoky blue.

"You are so—" He bit his lip and dropped his arms. Only to reach both hands behind Hattie's head. Unleashing the comb, he let her hair cascade to her shoulders. His face transformed.

"Brax. . ."

With a soft groan, he plunged his hands underneath her hair. His fingers entwined in her locks. Cradling the nape of her neck, Brax drew her head upward. She strained forward, and his mouth found hers. Tentative at first. Both of them trembling and scared to death. His gentle urgency curled Hattie's toes.

A small sigh of contentment escaped her lips—the one breath he allowed before he breathed Hattie in again. Her knees went weak as the pressure of his lips grew stronger, and she responded, deepening the kiss. It was the happiest Hattie had ever been in her whole life.

Her fingers feathered the damp, close-cropped tendrils of the hair above his ear. "I love you," she whispered.

Brax thrust her from him. "We shouldn't—" His gaze hopscotched around the deserted vestibule. "I shouldn't. . ." He stuffed his hands into his trouser pockets.

Hattie reached for him, but he dodged and yanked open the door. "Wait."

"I've got work to do." Brax bolted into the darkness. He closed the door behind him with a decided *bang*.

Hattie readjusted the comb in her hair. He loved her. She knew he did. Now he needed to stop running scared and admit it to himself. She'd change his mind. She'd always been able to talk Braxton Cashel into any adventure. Even the ultimate adventure of matrimony.

Chapter 8

Mules think for themselves, and that is not always a good thing.
FOR THE LOVE OF A MULE

During the judging for Grand Champion Mule, Sugarfoot's palomino coat shone. The molly's ears perked as the committee festooned the winner's garland around her stout neck. Hattie understood now she'd loved Brax as long as she'd known him. Something within him, even as children, sparking something inside her. A fondness that blossomed into something far more.

She wanted to stay in Hitching Post and be his wife. Fill the cabin with crazy-haired, mischief-making little girls and earnest, sweet-tempered young boys. Her children and Brax's. And, of course, write that book.

Love swelled in her heart at God's goodness in bringing her and Brax together after so many years. She was sure as shootin' Brax loved her, too. He had to, didn't he? They were meant to be together. Forever.

Hattie smiled and looped Sugarfoot's reins over the railing outside the jail. She might not be the meadow flower Brax imagined he wanted. But they were perfect for each other in every way that mattered. She skipped up the boardwalk steps, but stopped at the sound of male voices drifting through the open window.

"Are you sure you want to do this, Sheriff?"

Sounded official. Maybe she ought to wait until Brax was finished before she busted inside. Practice that restraint Brax preached.

"I'm sure, Judge."

Judge Mitchell? She hadn't realized the judge had returned to town. So soon? With the Mule Days parade in full swing, Hattie strained forward to hear.

"Paper. . .ready to sign."

What paper?

Brax blew out a breath. "Good."

Hattie pictured the love of her life seated behind the big walnut desk. His strong hands steepled. The dark hair on his forearms where he'd pushed up the sleeves of his undershirt. The brown pin-striped overshirt rolled to his elbows. She let out a sigh. Oh, how she loved, loved, loved Braxton Cashel.

Brax cleared his throat. "I didn't mean those words I said to her."

She tensed. Hattie's heartbeat accelerated.

"Not one of those vows I made was from my heart."

Hattie bit back a moan and laid her hand over her mouth.

134

"I've got to make things right, Judge."

Oh God. No... Hattie staggered back. Brax didn't love her. Not the way she loved him. He'd told her he intended to annul their marriage as soon as the judge returned.

Why hadn't she believed him? Why had she ever thought she could change his mind? He told her flat-out he wanted a real woman. A sweet, pretty woman. So not Harriet Brimfield.

She was stupid. Stupid to think a fine, upstanding man—a sheriff no less—would want someone as prone to disaster as she. All she'd ever done was embarrass Brax. His whole life, she'd caused him nothing but trouble. What man in his right mind would hitch himself permanently to a rescue project like her?

Brax... Her heart ached for the silly, beautiful dreams of a future that wouldn't be theirs. He didn't love her. And he never would.

Hattie's eyes burned with unshed tears. Her vision blurred as the proud citizens of Hitching Post marched by on their ribbon-winning mules. She had to get out of here. She wouldn't bring further disgrace to Brax. He deserved the best.

And with hindsight wrought through painful realization, Hattie understood someone like her would never be best for him. Brax was a good man. No need to punish him for feeling like he did. For not feeling as she did for him.

Untying Sugarfoot, Hattie led the molly toward the stagecoach office. She couldn't stay here, and she didn't want to go home. Too many memories of Brax in both places. Maybe her mother's sister would take her in. Hattie fingered the grand prize money she and Sugarfoot had won. She'd buy a ticket East. Go to the cabin and repack her valise.

And what about her shotgun marriage? Hattie's resolve quavered. She couldn't stomach facing the pity in his eyes. Somehow, without involving Brax, she'd have to find the judge and sign that hateful paper as soon as possible. The paper transforming the radiant Harriet Brimfield Cashel into unloved and unwanted Harriet Margaret Brimfield.

∽∾∾

When the judge left, Braxton came out from behind the desk. Was that Sugarfoot he heard braying before? Striding over to the unlatched window, he twitched aside the curtain.

The silly ruffled curtain Harriet insisted on sewing to "cheer up" the jailhouse. Brax rolled his tongue in his cheek. So not the point of a jailhouse, he'd told her. But so very Harriet.

He surveyed the street, congested with parade revelers. No sign of Harriet. Which was good. Good because he needed to rectify a few things. He'd made his wishes clear to the judge, who promised to make the necessary arrangements.

Dancing with Harriet last night. . . Brax recognized a hard truth about himself. So he'd run. And spent an endless night on the bench in his empty cell. Pondering the right thing to do. Trying to come to terms with how he felt. And his inescapable conclusion? A shotgun wedding in a jail cell under duress was no way to start a marriage. Harriet deserved better. Brax allowed the curtain to fall into place. So much better than being a sheriff's wife. And yet. . .

He massaged his neck, trying to unknot the kinks. He'd glimpsed snatches of a happiness he'd never believed could be his this week. But despite the childish hold—pull—she'd always possessed on his heart, Brax had to love Hattie enough to do what was best.

Best for them both. The federal marshals would arrive this afternoon. And with the responsibility of the silver off his shoulders, he and Harriet would talk. She'd be furious. Hurt and. . . His chest tightened.

He wished things between them were different, but he wouldn't have traded one moment of this week for all the silver in the Montana Territory. *God, help me be the sheriff Hitching Post deserves. Help me to be a man of integrity, worthy of respect. Help Harriet*—Brax squeezed his eyes shut—*to understand.*

Brax heaved a breath and ambled toward the door. Wondering what Harriet was up to, his lips quirked. Up to no good, knowing her.

∞

The CLOSED sign on the glass-fronted bank door snagged Brax's attention first. And the drawn blinds. Unless Christmas Day or Sunday, the Farm and Ranch Commercial Bank stayed open, rain or shine. Why—? Some instinct propelled Brax forward. Foreboding pinched his gut.

A dire dread confirmed when he sighted the shifty-eyed no-accounts he'd spotted earlier in the week. Loitering on the marbled granite steps of the bank without any possible bank business to attend to if, indeed, the bank was closed this Friday noon. A cadre of horses were tied and at the ready. The men examined the crowd in a professional manner Brax recognized as belonging only to lawmen. Or criminals.

Brax dodged the partygoers filling the street. At the forefront of his mind? How to stop the felons from robbing the bank and avoid unnecessary bloodshed. Because getting the drop on them without causing pandemonium meant the difference between life and death for the citizens he'd sworn to protect.

Crossing the dusty street, various scenarios flitted through his mind. And faced with the unthinkable, an unshakable calm took control. His focus narrowed. His head filled with a strange silence as his mission crystallized.

Emerging from the bank, Double Dog Derring pressed his six-shooter against the carotid artery of the Farm and Ranch bank manager. Three men scooted out

136

behind them. Their saddlebags bulged with ill-gotten gain. The two men on the street untied the horses and mounted. Heavily armed, their eyes never stopped calculating the danger.

The outlaw ringleader, his face plastered all over the West, had probably laid low until the most opportune moment to strike. When the citizens had been distracted with the Mule Days celebration. With the marshals in transition. When Brax and the manager were off their guard.

Brax assessed his chances. Outgunned; the silver wasn't worth the life of one of his people. Let the felons think they'd succeeded. Derring wouldn't kill the manager unless Brax forced his hand.

One conk on the head to prevent the manager from raising the alert and the desperados would be gone. Lulled into believing they'd gotten clean away, Brax would track them down. There wasn't a man or beast alive, Brax couldn't track. Uncle Wilbur had said so.

And Brax wasn't without recourse. Despite their greed and ruthlessness, Brax had a lot more on his side. Surprise. Speed. And God.

Brax fell back into the shadow of the mercantile. Steadying his mind, his hand hovered over his gun belt. He took slow, even breaths. Flexing his fingers, Brax craned his neck around the corner. The saddlebags were almost loaded.

If only the villains could clear the town limits without someone sounding the alarm. . . . Then what Brax most dreaded—a woman screamed.

Coming into the sunlight, Brax drew his weapon in one smooth motion. Derring tightened his stranglehold around the manager's neck. The others yanked rifles free of the scabbards strapped to their horses.

Brax waved his arm. "Get off the street! Take cover!"

Mayhem resulted as women grabbed their children, and men ducked into the storefronts. One child stood frozen in the middle of the street. Brax darted forward to put himself between the child and Derring.

"Look out, Sheriff!" someone yelled. "Ten o'clock! Balcony!"

Numbers? Brax spotted the metallic gleam of a shotgun high above his head on the second story of the hotel.

Shoving the child behind the safety of a buckboard, Brax jerked to the right. But in that split second, his gun arm swung up too late. A muzzle flashed with a deafening explosion of sound. White-hot lead whizzed past, inches from his face, splintering an adjacent post.

The outlaw clutched his shirt and fell face forward over the balcony onto the street. Numbers emerged from underneath the awning outside the feed store. His gun smoked. Genesis and Leviticus erupted from out of nowhere. They seized the bridles of the skittish horses and dragged the first two ruffians off their saddles.

Kicking like a mule, the manager dived for the bushes beside the steps. Derring jerked his man off one of the horses and vaulted into the saddle. The outlaw thrust his spurs into the horse.

"Halt, Derring! I'm ordering you to surrender." Brax had only time to pop off one shot. Derring reared, clutching his leg, but didn't stop as he disappeared out of sight heading for the hills.

Brax pivoted as another felon grabbed his shoulder. Landing an uppercut to his jaw, Brax followed with a fist into the man's belly, sending the outlaw reeling. Deut and Exodus subdued the remaining members of the Derring gang.

Though it played slow as molasses in Brax's head, as the smoke from the gunfire dissipated and the dust cleared, not five minutes had passed since the shooting started. His heart hammered. Numbers had saved his life.

"Woo-whee!" Numbers stowed his gun. "That was the most fun I've had in ages."

"If you hadn't spotted the gunman, Numbers. . ." Brax gulped. "I'd be as dead as him."

Numbers butted the toe of his boot at the fellow who'd taken the nosedive. The man groaned. "He ain't dead. He'll live to hang."

Brax passed Genesis a pair of handcuffs. "I don't know what to say, boys, but thank you." He holstered his gun and helped Exodus hog-tie another prisoner.

Leviticus shoulder-slapped Brax. "Well done, Brother Braxton." Lev elbowed Deut. "Reckon if he can handle the likes of these ne'er-do-wells, we can trust him with Sissy's heart."

Brother? Brax looked up as two federal marshals rode into town. Their gold badges shone in the early afternoon light. He motioned them over. "You're just in time to keep these lowlifes from cluttering my jail cell."

One of the marshals, an old friend of Uncle Wilbur's, laughed. "Looks like you got everything well in hand."

"Except the capture of Double Dog." Brax thrust out his jaw. "I plugged him. He's bleeding. Easy to track. I'll have him in custody by sundown."

Tall in his saddle, the lawman studied the streets and the citizens venturing once more into the daylight. "We'll wait and take the silver plus your prisoners off your hands then. Mighty fine town you've got here, Sheriff Cashel."

Yes. It was.

The marshal inspected the Brimfield brothers. "Mighty fine deputies you've got, too."

Deputies? The boys grinned at Brax.

Brax arched a brow. He reckoned they were at that. He'd quietly deputize them. Braxton Cashel liked things legal. Tied with a knotted bow.

Speaking of knots and legality, Brax was half-surprised Harriet hadn't rode in with guns a-blazing during the robbery. He wondered again, now that he had time to catch his breath, where she'd gotten to. And an inexplicable, nagging fear stabbed Brax. He started at a run for his horse stabled in the livery.

"Brax!" one of his new brothers called out. "What's your hurry? Derring can't go far."

"Derring took the road." Brax grimaced, mentally calculating the remaining number of cartridges in his gun. "The road that goes past the cabin."

Chapter 9

Mules must be handled just right. . . . There is simply no forcing
a mule to do anything he doesn't want to do.
FOR THE LOVE OF A MULE

Charging out of the underbrush, the outlaw bushwhacked Hattie halfway to town. Toppling from the saddle, she landed hard on the rocky ground. The man walloped Sugarfoot's haunches and sent the poor mule, hooves thundering, out of Hattie's reach. Flat on her back, she peered at the looming, pockmarked villain. Blood flowed in a steady stream down his pant leg. Pockmarked. . .

Gasping, she tried to scuttle free. He yanked her by the scruff of her hair and hauled Hattie to her feet. She cried out and fought to loosen his grip on her locks. "You're going to be my ticket out of this territory."

"Double Dog Derring, I wouldn't help you if you held the only cup of water in the Sahara."

He shook her like a rag doll. "Glad to see my fame precedes me. You keep quiet or I double dog daresay you'll regret crossing me."

She kicked his shin. Cursing, he backhanded Hattie. She reeled. Her mouth opened in a silent scream. Darkness clouded her eyes.

⤙∞⤚

Braxton had never known such gut-twisting terror as when he found Sugarfoot on the side of the road, riderless and reins dragging. Genesis retrieved the molly mule and pointed to Harriet's valise strapped to the saddle. Angry murmurs arose from the Brimfield posse.

Tightening his hands on the reins, Brax dug in his heels. "Come on. We've got to find her." A quiet desperation he might already be too late sucked the oxygen from his lungs.

Rounding a bend, he spotted Derring towering over Harriet's crumpled form in the road. Derring jumped into the saddle. Brax spurred his appaloosa as Derring fled. Drawing alongside Harriet's too-still body, Brax leaped off his horse and fell to his knees, uncaring whether Derring got away or not. "Harriet?"

Leviticus reined in his horse and dropped to the ground beside Brax. Jimbo, also newly deputized, and the rest of the boys slapped leather and galloped after Derring.

Scooping her into his arms, Brax cradled Harriet against his chest.

"Baby Sis?" Lev's voice broke.

"Harriet," Brax hollered. "Answer me." Why didn't she wake up?

Brax buried his face into her neck. And felt the pulse of her heart. "Hattie, sweetheart. Wake up." His lips grazed hers. "Please, honey. Don't leave me this way."

She stirred. "Brax. . ." She coughed and her body jackknifed.

Lev scrambled for the canteen tied to his bay. "Give her some water."

Brax grabbed the canteen and held the container to Harriet's lips. "Take it easy. Not too fast."

After a few sips, her eyes fluttered open. "Brax. . ." She heaved a deep sigh. "You must get so tired of rescuing me."

Something sad—something Brax didn't understand—dulled her eyes. His fingers toyed with the ends of her hair, and he searched her face. "Are you okay?"

With a ragged breath, Harriet struggled to sit upright. "I'm okay."

Brax and Lev helped Harriet regain her footing. The choking horror Brax experienced when he sighted Harriet lifeless on the ground sapped the last bit of energy from him. Relief washed through him like a flash flood in a canyon. He sagged against his saddle.

Harriet peered beyond Lev's horse. "Where's Sugarfoot?"

Lev raked a leaf from her hair. "Gen's got her. She's fine."

A cloud of dust arose. Jimbo and the rest of the boys rode up with Derring, arms bound, in tow. Ex vaulted off his horse. "You okay, hon? You 'bout had us and your husband worried sick."

Brax's breathing slowly resumed something resembling normal. Her husband. Yes. He was.

"I'm fine." Harriet flipped her hair over her shoulder. "I see you caught the scoundrel."

Numbers held the rope binding the outlaw. "Jimbo's lasso wrangled Derring."

Deut dismounted and touched his finger to Harriet's cheek. "What happened to your face?"

"Nothing." She veered away. "Hush now, Deut."

Brax angled. The fist-size whelp bruising her face socked Brax in the gut. Raw fury engorged him. He lunged for the outlaw. "You hit her!"

He tackled Derring to the ground and started slinging punches. "I'm. . . gonna. . .kill. . ."

"Genesis," Harriet cried. "Exodus."

Rough hands pulled Brax off Derring, who cowered in the dirt.

"He hit her." Brax struggled against their firm grip. "I'm going to—"

Numbers patted his shoulder. "Easy there, brother. Our law-abiding sheriff has finally lost control."

Lev removed the prisoner from harm's way. "Understandable, Brother Brax. But better to let justice have its way with this one."

Forcing back the killing rage, Brax mounted his appaloosa and reached to give Harriet a hand up.

Avoiding his eyes, she edged away. "I'll ride Sugarfoot to town."

Letting Jimbo, the boys, and their prisoner surge ahead, Brax maintained a plodding pace beside Sugarfoot on the trail. "Harriet—"

"Please don't say anything, Brax." She studied the watch fob pinned to her bodice. Curlicues of yellow hair shimmered like wheat in a summer breeze.

Brax opened his mouth and closed it. Something was wrong. An awkward distance gaped between them, and he didn't know why. Or what he could do to fix it.

Until they passed the circuit rider coming out of the church. And the judge coming from his chambers with the soon-to-be-annulled marriage decree in hand. A stagecoach driver heaved boxes onto the top of the carriage. The brothers rode Derring toward the waiting marshals.

Brax swung his leg and stepped down. "I'll get this sorted out, and then—"

"Don't bother." Harriet slid to the ground. She fumbled to free her valise from Sugarfoot's saddle. "Sir!" she called across the street and raised her hand. The stagecoach driver paused.

Brax's stomach knotted. "Harriet, you know our shotgun wedding wasn't legal."

The judge inched forward, pen in hand. "I need your signature, and then you'll be Miss Brimfield again before the reverend—"

"Here." Harriet snatched the pen from Judge Mitchell. She slammed the page against Brax's chest. He staggered a step.

She scrawled her signature. "Driver!" Harriet thrust the pen at Brax. "My bag, if you please, Driver."

"Yes'm." The driver snagged the valise and tossed it to his buddy who rode shotgun.

Brax frowned. "Harriet, what're you doing?"

"Trying not to make this any harder than it needs to be."

"Harriet, I don't think you—"

"I believe I owe you the price of a mule." She gathered Sugarfoot's reins and thrust them at him. "Grand Champion of Hitching Post, Montana Territory, 1885. A mature mule, but still probably worth more than the hundred and thirty I owe you."

Clutching the reins, annulment paper, and pen, Brax stared at her. "Harriet, you don't owe me." Why wouldn't she look at him?

"All aboard!" yelled the driver.

She wrenched away.

"Harriet!" Brax passed the pen and paper to the judge. The circuit rider lifted his finger to get Brax's attention. Brax handed him Sugarfoot's reins. "Just a minute, Reverend."

Brax strode after Harriet. "Where do you think you're going?"

"Last call for Helena!" the driver yelled.

Harriet kept her back to him. "I'm sorry, Brax. So sorry for everything. Silly, wasn't it? To ever think you and me. . . I'll never trouble you again."

Brax inhaled sharply. And dodging his outstretched hand, she slipped inside the stagecoach.

Pounding the side of the carriage, the assistant leaped aboard. The driver slapped the reins, and the horses took off at a trot.

Like a fool, Brax stood rooted in the middle of the street as the dust swirled in the wake of the wheels. *What just happened here?* Paralyzed, he watched the coach and Harriet disappear from sight. As suddenly exiting his life as she'd entered it.

This wasn't supposed to happen. Not like this. This wasn't what he'd planned. His heart sank to his boots. He'd lost her for good. Why hadn't he told her what he felt?

No more bossy Harriet. Brax could eat his meals at the hotel. No more Harriet hanging curtains in his jailhouse. Emptiness consumed him at the thought of the ruffled blue curtain.

Brax had his life back. All the peace and quiet he could stand. He drummed his fist against his thigh. Only now his cabin would be too quiet. Harriet Brimfield had ruined him for quiet. She'd turned his whole world upside down.

Without her, he was the same lonely boy who desperately longed to jump out of that other stagecoach in Wyoming. Taking him—so he'd believed—forever away from the crazy-haired little girl whose wide-eyed devotion had given him glimpses of a hope Brax only now understood could be his. She'd said she loved him. You didn't stop loving a person between last night and today. His heart ached. Did you?

He'd never—Brax straightaway realized—never stopped looking for the love she'd given him as a child. Not until he'd found that kind of love once more—with her—when she tried to rescue a mule in Hitching Post.

Brax wheeled. Some kind soul had already led his appaloosa away. The judge and the reverend stood, shoulders hunched in pity, beside Sugarfoot. Brax gritted his teeth.

For the love of a mule. . . He wouldn't give her up this easily. Not without a fight. He was far more mule-headed than Harriet could ever be.

Chapter 10

The way to a woman's heart may sometimes be through a mule.
FOR THE LOVE OF A MULE—A DEFINITIVE GUIDE
by HARRIET BRIMFIELD CASHEL

S tep out of the coach, Harriet."

At the sudden standstill, Hattie leaned out the stagecoach window. Her eyes widened at the sight of long-legged Braxton astride her molly mule, the Grand Champion garland still strung around Sugarfoot's neck.

Hattie jutted her jaw. "I don't have to do what you say. We're not married anymore, remember?"

Braxton bared his teeth and dismounted. "I'm still the sheriff of Hitching Post, and you're under arrest."

Hattie's eyes narrowed. "For what?"

"For disturbing the peace."

Hattie thrust open the door and stuck one booted foot onto the step. "What peace did I disturb?"

Brax pursed his lips. "Mine." He took hold of her arm.

She wrenched free and planted her hands on her hips. "I'm not going anywhere with you."

"Oh yes, Harriet. You are."

Seizing her about the waist, he slung her onto Sugarfoot. With a whoosh of air, she landed on her stomach across the saddle. Hattie squawked. The mule snorted and danced sideways. Hattie grappled to hang on. Brax swung into the saddle behind her.

"Always got to do things the hard way." He grabbed the reins. "Don't make me handcuff you, Harriet."

She raised her head. "You'd enjoy that, wouldn't you, Sheriff?" Hattie glared at him as Sugarfoot set off at a trot, rattling her teeth. "Y–you j–just tr–try i–t–t–t."

Her bones jolted with every step. Brax, with a firm grip, prevented her from sliding off. And so it went all the way to town—Hattie protesting a blue streak, Braxton ignoring her like he always did. She kicked her heels. Sugarfoot bucked.

Brax only just kept his seat and hold on Hattie. "For the love of a mule, if you don't stop that, Harriet, I'm going to get Genesis to tan your hide. Something, I suspect, is long overdue."

She growled as they clip-clopped through Main. Parading past the gawking stares of the Hitching Post citizens crowding the boardwalk.

Pulling the reins, Brax brought Sugarfoot to a halt. He swung his leg over and dismounted. He looped the reins on the hitching post in front of the jail. *"Bringing in the sheaves,"* he sang and tugged Hattie off the saddle to the ground. *"Bringing in the sheaves. . ."*

Hattie snarled. "You're making a spectacle out of us."

Braxton gave her a lopsided smile. "Sure am." He hustled her inside the jail and prodded Hattie toward the empty cell. *"We shall come rejoicin'—"*

"Stop singing and smiling at me like that."

Brax placed his finger at the corner of his mouth. "Why don't you make me?"

Gnashing her teeth, she sashayed into the cell. To her surprise, he marched in right behind her. Hattie whirled, her skirts swishing. "What're you doing?"

"Something I should've done first chance I got."

Brax wrested the key ring off his gun belt and tossed it out of the cell where it landed with a clatter against the far wall.

Her eyes enlarged. "Wait. . ."

Brax yanked the door shut with a decisive *clang* as the lock clicked in place.

She put a hand to her throat. "What did you just do, Braxton Cashel?"

"Can't run the risk of you getting away from me this time." Brax got down on one knee. "At least not until the reverend arrives."

The outer door opened, as if on cue. Her brothers, the reverend, and half the town flooded into the small jail.

"Harriet Margaret Brimfield." Brax kissed her hand. "Would you do me the honor of becoming my wife?"

If Brax hadn't kept a strong grip on her hand, with her knees knocking together so hard, Hattie reckoned she might've keeled over. "You want to marry me? But the judge? The annulment?"

"A legal marriage license this time. The reverend's here to do a proper wedding before God and Hitching Post."

"But I didn't think you wanted someone like me, Brax," she whispered.

"I want you—sweet Harriet, pretty as a mountain meadow—to marry me, the sheriff of Hitching Post." Braxton gazed at her. "Me, who has so little to offer in return."

She corralled his face between her hands. "You have everything to offer I've ever wanted. Yourself."

Brax cocked his head. "Is that a yes? Say it, Harriet. For the love of a mule and the sake of my heart." His lips quirked. "Will you be my cell mate for life?"

He moved closer until their foreheads touched, and he was within kissing distance. "Please, Hattie. . ." His breath fluttered the tendrils of her hair. "Marry me. I love you."

She felt the furious pounding of his heart against her hand through the muslin of his shirt.

"Why yes, Sheriff Cashel." Hattie brushed her lips across the upturned corner of his mouth. "Since you asked so nicely, I believe I will."

⁘

But theirs wasn't the next marriage ceremony performed. They were at the end of a long line of couples waiting to tie the knot.

Genesis and the widow woman hotel cook. Exodus and the mayor's niece. Leviticus and the doctor's sister. Numbers and the spinster schoolteacher. Deuteronomy and the shopkeeper's daughter. And not to be outdone, Clarissy and Jimbo—a.k.a. James Beauregard, owner of the largest cattle spread this side of the Rockies.

Braxton presented Hattie with two requests—to marry under the blue Montana sky in the wildflower meadow behind his house. And that she wear the "pretty purple dress."

There before God and the good folks who loved them the best, Harriet Margaret Brimfield became—at last!—Harriet Margaret Brimfield Cashel for real.

Instead of kissing his bride, however, Brax placed both hands around her waist and lifted Hattie onto Sugarfoot. She held on to the saddle horn as Brax swung up behind her. Wrapping both arms around her, he gripped the horn and Hattie angled. Only to give Brax a mouthful of hair.

She fingercombed her hair out of his face. "Sorry."

He buried his nose in her locks. "I love your hair." Brax clicked his teeth against his tongue and set Sugarfoot in motion toward the cabin.

She leaned back, not sure she'd heard him right. "You do?"

At the porch steps, Brax swung down. He reached again for her. "I definitely do. Almost as much as I love this, Hattie Cashel."

How she loved the sound of her name on his lips. She slid between his hands and nestled in the lovely embrace of his arms. And his mouth claimed hers. Full of love and promise.

Love for a lifetime.

Lisa Carter and her family make their home in North Carolina. In addition to *Mule Dazed*, she is the author of seven romantic suspense novels and a contemporary Coast Guard romantic series. When she isn't writing, Lisa enjoys traveling to romantic locales, teaching writing workshops, and researching her next exotic adventure. She has strong opinions on barbecue and ACC basketball. She loves to hear from readers, and you can connect with Lisa at www.lisacarterauthor.com.

The Sweetwater Bride

by Mary Connealy

Chapter 1

Montana
July 1897

Despite the worry about drought rabbiting around in his head, Tanner Harden's chest expanded as he rode around his property. He hadn't explored it all yet, and he *would* find water.

Nothing could stop him from making a home in this beautiful place.

Yes, it was in one of the meanest stretches of mountain the world had to offer—not that Tanner knew much about the world beyond his home—but it was hard to imagine anything more rugged than this. And he loved it. It was his.

But it wasn't just *mean*. What he and his family knew that nobody else did, was that between all these stretches of jagged rock and treacherous trails, the crumbling cliffs and the soaring peaks, were pockets of sweeping green meadows, lush, belly deep. Tall grass that'd fatten a cow and make a man prosper.

Pa had helped him scout this land, and then he'd left him to run it. . .unless Tanner needed help. He couldn't help but smile when he thought of how much his folks had done to help already.

Silas and Belle Harden were the best parents a family of nine kids ever had. They'd been generous to him when he struck out on his own. They'd said he'd worked for it and deserved it. And he'd worked mighty hard all his growing-up years—that was the plain truth.

They'd helped set his big sisters up when they married, too, so this seemed fair. But still, he knew he was starting out much easier than a lot of men.

This stretch was up where the eagles soared. It was between his folks' property and near his sisters Emma and Sarah and Betsy. And on past them was Lindsay. He closed a gap that might one day, if all his brothers did as he did and claimed stretches along the spine of the Rockies, connect Harden land all the way to Helena, Montana.

He'd bought his land, and Pa had cut some good young stock out of his herd. Then his family had come up here and helped him build a tight little cabin.

Just two days ago, he'd hugged his ma and shook his pa's hand, and they'd left him alone. . .at home. His chest expanded some more. His own home. His own land. And yes, he was worried because it was a dry summer, and he was out today scouting for springs. A couple that he'd thought he could depend on had dried up.

But he'd find water. It was all part of building something in a wild, unsettled land.

He smiled as wide as his face would allow.

A scream ripped through the thin air and wiped the smile away.

Gunfire followed. A rifle. One shot.

Another scream so sharp it seemed to rip into his bones.

That was a woman's scream. There were no women up here. But when a man's common sense told him one thing and his ears told him something else, a man was apt to believe his ears.

Tanner turned his horse trying to find the source.

The peaks and tumbled boulders, many taller than a man, echoed with gunfire, bouncing and surrounding him until he couldn't tell what direction it came from, but he had a notion and he was a man to trust his instincts.

Except his instincts told him the sound came from a pile of rocks that he saw no way to cross, a pile that seemed to lead straight to a wall of solid rock that reached overhead fifty feet. His black stallion, a descendant of Tom Linscott's prize thoroughbreds, might well break a leg crossing the rock—and this young giant was to be the foundation of a herd of horses Tanner planned to raise. He hated taking it onto the rock-strewn path, and if it got any more treacherous, he would leave the horse behind rather than risk its safety.

But the black moved forward with surprising speed, picking his way between scattered rocks. Tanner, who considered himself a mighty savvy tracker, finally realized this was a barely visible trail. Each step was taken carefully, and he was glad to trust his horse.

Another shot rang out. No scream this time. His horse responded to tension in Tanner's grip on the reins and picked up speed. They walked forward, approaching the sheer rock wall. He had no idea what he was supposed to do when he got there.

And then, only a dozen feet before he had to stop or run his stallion's nose into granite, the trail twisted right—Tanner wouldn't have seen it, but his horse did—then it turned left, and he looked straight into the heart of the mountain. A crack in stone that was only a bit wider than his shoulders. Yet the black kept going without pause.

His horse twisted through pure stone, open overhead. And then he saw green.

A thrill of discovery urged him onward. He entered a mountain valley that perched on top of the world.

Before he could study the valley, he heard a voice again, shouting this time, not screaming. And now inside this vast expanse of open ground, he could tell exactly where it came from. The ground was easy to ride now and he urged his horse to a trot.

The land rose gently then crested. He reached the top. Grass spread wide in front of him, a vast land, a thousand acres or more. The expanse was dotted with maybe a hundred longhorn cattle. At the far end of the meadow a small house stood, nearly swallowed up by a beautiful stand of majestic Douglas fir trees. Two smaller buildings were spread out beyond the house, also right against the woods that seemed to climb the edges of the mountain that created a bowl to conceal this beautiful land.

And in front of one of those buildings stood a woman.

A woman who looked nearly as wild as this hidden land. She wore leather, and her shining red hair was long and wild as if it had never seen scissors or a comb. She had a shotgun in one hand that she wielded ably. It was an old one that reminded him of a Sharps his ma kept hanging over the door, though it wasn't her preferred weapon.

He'd been in this area many times hunting a place to settle, and he'd never seen hide nor hair of a woman, nor a cattle herd, and he'd had no idea this rich valley existed.

She faced the woods near her house, gun in one hand, the other arm full of. . . Tanner wasn't sure what. It looked like a bundle of something brown.

Wary of that gun she held, he stopped at the top of the crest. "Howdy, miss."

The woman spun around, leveled her rifle, then froze. She stared at him as if he were a ghost. Something beyond her understanding. Her eyes got round, her tanned skin went pale as milk.

"Don't shoot, miss. I just came to see if you were all right." He braced to dive off his horse. He had no idea what she was thinking, nor what she'd do.

She dropped the rifle and the brown thing, which flapped its wings and went running. . .but not far. She covered her face with both hands, including her eyes, and some sound he didn't quite recognize came from her, a song maybe? No, not a song. No reason for a body to start singin' right now.

She was acting mighty crazy, which was bad. On the good side, she was disarmed.

"Are you all right? Was that you I heard yellin' and shootin'?"

She didn't move. Not sure what came next, Tanner pressed his heels to his horse's side and they descended the gentle slope.

He rode right up to her and she drew her hands down to uncover her eyes and stare. Her hands lowered farther until she clutched them together on her chest, maybe in prayer.

Her throat worked as if it'd gone bone dry beneath the collar of her strange leather outfit. He wasn't sure quite how to describe it. Leather, and very clearly made by hand. It wasn't an Indian dress, and she definitely wasn't a native woman with her bright red curls that hung nearly to her knees.

Then she said, "Wh–who?" her voice was like a rusty gear. He'd heard her scream then later shout. She'd sounded nothing like this.

"Name's Tanner Harden." He tugged the brim of his Stetson. "I'm getting down now. I mean you no harm."

He moved smooth and slow, no sudden moves. Her rifle was within grabbing distance, and he didn't want a nervous woman like this to decide she was in danger.

He ground-hitched his stallion and came face-to-face with her. She had eyes a shade of blue the Montana sky would envy. She licked her lips.

"Are you all right, miss?" He paused over the word, wishing she'd supply a name. Nothing, just staring. "I heard you scream and there was gunfire. Were you in danger?"

The woman glanced away at the bird she'd dropped. Tanner realized it was a grouse. Tanner had hunted them many times. But he'd never seen one that scratched and pecked at the ground ten feet from a man. They were always wild, flapping and running away. This one seemed to be her pet.

He looked back at her and saw her looking past the bird, past her house. Tanner looked at what must be a chicken coop, except a flock of grouse were inside a fence made of woven saplings.

Right near the pen lay a full-grown wolverine.

Dead.

Tanner had only seen a couple of them in his life. They were night creatures. Vicious killers who fought shy of people. He'd seen the damage they could do to a pen full of chickens. The time he'd seen their handiwork, a wolverine had killed the whole flock and only eaten a few.

That was what made her scream and shoot. He couldn't say he blamed her.

Finally a strange scratchy noise drew his eyes back to the woman. Who asked, "Where did y–you come from?"

The way she said it made Tanner doubt she'd ever had a visitor before. As suddenly as he thought it, he decided it might well be true. After all, the entrance to this place was about as hidden as could be.

She was probably about one thousand times more surprised to see him than she'd been to see that wolverine.

Tanner really didn't know where to start.

"I'm your new neighbor?"

Those beautiful blue eyes widened until he could see right into a mind full of pure terror. "You are moving in here? Into my valley?" She glanced at her rifle.

"No!" He'd started out all wrong. But maybe there was no right. "I'm going to live outside your valley. I've built a cabin and brought in my herd. I didn't know anyone lived near." He tried a friendly, neighborly smile. "I reckon we'll get to know each other well."

She just watched, her brow furrowed.

"Do you need any help? Did the critter hurt more of your animals?"

The woman opened her mouth, closed it, then as if forcing the words out, she said, "He was getting to my chicken house."

Tanner glanced at the tame grouse. "This is your. . .chicken?"

The girl smiled. "I know it's not a chicken, but I raised them. I gathered up hatchlings and brought them home and gentled them. I've got a nice little flock, and they provide eggs and—" Suddenly her eyes were filled with tears. She took a swipe at them and fell silent.

He decided he needed to ask simpler questions. "What's your name?"

There was a long moment of hesitation, as if she had to think the answer over. "Debba McClain."

"Debba. It's nice to meet you. I welcome company up here."

"No one should get in here. And I never go out."

"Never?"

"Why would I? I have everything I need."

Why indeed? Tanner could think of a lot of reasons. "You never go to the general store?"

She shook her head. "I went as a child. But I have nothing to buy."

Tanner had four big sisters and a ma. Women always needed to buy something. Why, they took the long ride to Divide at least twice a year. And of course once a year they made the cattle drive to Helena.

"Do you live here alone?"

Nodding, she said, "Since my pa and mama died."

"How long ago was that?"

"I don't keep track of such things. I think it's been four or five winters."

"You've lived here alone, completely alone, for four or five winters? And you've never gone out? Never seen anyone or gone to town?"

Those tears were back. She shrugged, the smallest motion possible. Her voice dropped nearly to a whisper. "I don't know where a town is."

Something odd and painful snapped in Tanner. Such sympathy for her swept through him he could hardly breathe.

He had to take her out of here. Take her to his mother. Ma would know what to do. She was something when it came to raising up girls. Boys, too, for that matter, but Tanner loved all his feisty big sisters, and Debba could use some kindness and attention from Belle Harden.

Of course, here she stood with a tame grouse and handmade clothes and a wolverine pestering her that had died for its trouble.

Add to that, she said she'd been here alone for maybe five years and she still had bullets left. This was a woman who knew how to take care of herself. Ma would love her.

"Can we talk?"

"We *are* talking."

At her confused look, he smiled. "I mean sit down and talk for a while, get to know each other."

Her nodding was as tiny a motion as her shrug. Tanner realized she was out of practice making gestures, the little clues people used to communicate. Maybe she yelled at wild animals all the time, but more likely, she spent more time in silence than any human alive.

"I don't have time."

Tanner fought back a smile. "You have an appointment somewhere?"

"Nope, I will skin that skunk bear before the smell sticks to the fur. And get my hen locked up before something else gets her."

Tanner had heard a wolverine called a skunk bear before, but mostly he had little experience with the critters. "I'll help you."

"Have you skinned a skunk bear before?"

He had to admit he had not.

"We must be mindful of the scent glands—the fur is unusable if they are punctured, and I shot it very carefully to avoid that."

She was a good enough shot she avoided glands inside a wolverine? Tanner was so full of admiration he felt a little dizzy.

"I'll catch the grouse for you, then, while you get on with the skinnin'."

She picked up the grouse and held it out to him. He wondered if she was realizing right now, having caught the bird herself, that he was not of much use.

He carried the placid grouse to the chicken yard while she headed for the wolverine.

As he looked at the pen, Tanner, who'd been trained by his pa in the way of building, realized it had been built without a single nail. It was a log structure, but the logs were saplings so it wasn't a heavy coop. And the fence was made by twisting and braiding branches no thicker than his thumb.

It stirred something in him to see the skill that went with this fence.

What's more, there were sections he could tell were new. His first notion was that her father had built this before he died. And maybe he had, but she'd learned enough to carry on.

Having spent all of two minutes returning the grouse to her little fenced yard, he went to watch Debba skin her catch.

Her knife must be razor sharp, and each motion was swift and sure. She might be shy of visitors, but there was no denying how skilled she was with that knife.

"You are really good at that."

"Thank you." She looked up from her work and smiled as she hadn't before. A full smile with true happiness lighting up her eyes.

It was a smile so pretty, Tanner followed her without looking left or right until just before he stepped inside. Then he did notice what he should have seen right from the first.

A stream, a good-sized one, flowing full and fast right along the far south edge of the valley.

Plentiful sweet water.

In a dry year.

When springs he'd counted on to water his cattle had gone dry.

She was already acting mighty friendly. He hoped that continued after he asked her to let him water his herd.

Chapter 2

D ebba's fingers itched to touch the man.

Tanner. Tanner Harden. The sound of his name was like music. Another person. The shock of it was almost too much to bear. He was tall and slim, with dark brown hair and eyes a startling color. Brown and green and golden all at once. She'd never seen the like. He had the sleeves of a blue shirt turned up to his elbows, and she saw the corded muscles in his forearms.

He wore thick brown leather chaps and brown jeans with rivets here and there. The clothes looked like some she remembered Pa wearing long ago.

She forced her attention back to her work, and he crouched beside her and watched in a way that made her clumsy.

It was almost impossible to speak, but it was even more impossible to remain silent.

"Where did you come from?"

"In through that keyhole pass on the northeast corner of the valley."

She nodded. She knew that pass well, but she'd never gone through it—not since Pa had died. He'd warned strongly against it. Talked of the dangers. Talked about how Mama had died. That had happened so long ago. Debba only had mixed-up memories of Mama.

"Are you alone, too?" The notion twisted through her that they might be the only two people in the world.

"I live in my own home a few miles away. Downhill from here. This is about the top of the world."

She was silent. She didn't know much about the world and if it had a top, bottom, or sides.

He added, "But I have a big family, and they live on a ways. I'd like to take you to meet my ma."

Her heart started pounding. He had a mama? The longing was wild. But she didn't dare leave her mountain meadow. Her pa's dying words, the last words he'd spoken, were too strong. And she'd heard no other words for all these years, which gave what Pa had said more and more weight.

"I—I can't go."

Tanner rested a hand on her shoulder, and she quit her skinning and turned to him. He looked at her, really looked hard, like he was memorizing her eyes or something. Then he said, "Well, all right. Maybe I'll bring them to meet you sometime."

That would probably be safe. She nodded, scared to tell him how much she'd like that. Wondering if Pa's warnings about the outside world included letting them in.

"You've lived alone here for years?" Tanner asked.

She nodded and got back to work, glad for something to do so she could force herself not to stare at this man.

"Don't you get lonely?"

"I'm used to it." She got so lonely she talked to her animals and the walls and sometimes she imagined her parents were at meals with her. She'd asked herself often enough if that made her a lunatic.

"Your meadow is nice. The house and coop and barn are well built." Tanner looked around. "Did you do it, or did you have family when you first came here?"

"I lived here with my mama and pa, but Mama died so long ago I can barely remember her. The house and barn were built when Mama was alive, but I was too young to help. Pa wanted a bigger chicken coop when I was older, and I helped with that. And I learned to build chairs and such with his help. And it's good that I learned because I've had to go on alone."

"I've never seen anyone skin a pelt this fast." Tanner's voice was quiet, like he really meant it. She looked and he was watching her hands whip along, doing the job.

"Th–thank you." She had a vague memory of proper manners.

"Did you build the chicken coop fence?"

"Yes." She stood and took the hide to the coop fence to hang it up.

"I've never seen anything like it before."

Debba felt her cheeks heat up. He'd embarrassed her. It was overpraise. Such a strange feeling. She didn't want to pursue his flattery. "A skunk bear, what did you call it?"

"Wolverine is the word I've learned."

She scowled a bit. "I prefer wolves to skunk bears. For that matter I prefer bears to skunk bears. Wolverine is a good name."

"I agree."

"A couple of years ago a wolverine killed every chicken I had. That greedy varmint ripped a board out of my coop and crawled in and killed them all. He didn't eat them either, just killed for sport. And this one was up to the same thing."

"So catching and taming grouse was something you did on your own?"

"Yep, they lay a decent-sized egg, so I trailed a grouse hen and found her nest, when it was still full of eggs. I waited for them to hatch and grow just a bit so they weren't too fragile, then I caught them, about eight chicks, and brought them home and raised them up. They are as tame as my chickens were."

"It's a good-sized flock."

Debba finished with the hide. "They've hatched out new babies every spring.

They give me plenty of eggs as good as any chicken."

"Do you want me to bury the carcass or cut it up and feed it to the grouse?"

"Bury it. They'll probably peck at it until they find the scent glands, then it'll smell too strong to interest my flock, and then I'll need to bury the reeking thing."

"Do you have a shovel?"

"I'll get it for you. It's in the barn."

Tanner walked along with her to fetch it. Honestly, as fascinated as she was to have company, the way he tagged after her made him seem almost as lonely as she was.

When that chore was done, Tanner said, "Can we walk around the meadow? You've got a stream running, and I'd like to see where it goes. Maybe I can find where it leaves this canyon and use the water."

She shrugged again. It was so easy not to talk, to make silent gestures. She had talked easily while she'd worked—to the grouse and her horse and herself. Maybe the chore had distracted her from fretting over how exactly a woman talked to a man.

They strolled together toward the far end of the pasture. She checked her cattle as they passed, looking for any sign of sickness or injury.

"Debba, what would you think of me bringing my ma or my sisters here to visit?"

The fear and excitement clashed until she couldn't speak. Whether that was because she had nothing to say, or too much, she wasn't sure.

He touched her elbow, and through the doeskin arms of her tunic his touch seemed warm.

When he tugged, she stopped walking and turned. He faced her, looking worried. "Does the idea bother you? I think you'd like Ma, but I don't want to do anything that will bother you."

"I—I think I would l–like to meet your mama."

"And you won't come with me?"

She shook her head frantically. "I can't."

"What makes you say that? Are you worried for your animals? I reckon another wolverine could come."

"No, or um. . .yes, the skunk bear could come, but no, that's not why I won't leave."

"Can you tell me why not then?"

"My papa said I mustn't ever leave this meadow."

Tanner frowned and studied her for far too long. "Why did he say that to you?"

"He always said it. Long before he died, but on his deathbed he made me swear I'd never go through that keyhole pass."

"But he was condemning you to a life of terrible loneliness. Why would he do that?"

"Because"—she wove her fingers together and stared at them—"the world outside this meadow killed my mama. And he said it would kill me, too, if I went out there. It's a dreadful, dangerous place."

Tanner opened his mouth and closed it about five times. Finally he said, "I live out there and it's not all that dangerous, Debba. I can't figure what your pa could be talking about. How did your ma die?"

She wavered, then, from her fear to confusion. "I'm not sure. I don't remember. She died when I was young, eight years old, I think."

"Was it sickness or an accident?"

Debba looked through him into the past. "I don't remember an accident. We'd been out, one of the few times we went to town. Pa liked keeping to ourselves. She wasn't hurt while we were there because I remember riding home together. Pa wasn't happy we'd gone. He always fussed, but Ma was in high spirits, teasing and laughing about how nice it was to get out and see others. Then one morning a few days later, I woke up and she'd taken to her bed. After she died, he rarely talked of her except to tell me it was dangerous outside of this canyon."

"So she must have caught something, a sickness, while she was outside. I can see how your pa would blame the trip. And he probably didn't plan on dying until you were full grown."

Nodding, slowly Tanner reached out and took both her shoulders. "But he can't have wanted you to spend the rest of your life, maybe forty or fifty years, completely alone. He just can't have wanted that. It sounds awful, cruel. Was your pa a cruel man?"

"No." She shuddered at the feel of his hands. It was deep inside so she didn't think he could tell, but to be touched!

She had no idea how wonderful it would feel. She lost all control of herself and threw her arms around him and hung on.

Tanner gasped and his hands came off her shoulders. She shouldn't have done this. She had to let go and step back. But just another second. Just one more second of contact.

Then Tanner's arms came around her and held her tight and close. It was like hearing him speak. It filled a desperately empty place inside her.

Until now she hadn't seen it, but it had been cruel of her father to make her swear to live this completely lonely life.

Was her pa a cruel man? She'd never thought of him as such.

Tanner released her, and she was going to let go of him in just one more moment.

His hands settled firmly on her shoulders, as they had when this started, and he eased her back far enough their eyes met.

Chapter 3

Come out with me. Come and meet my ma." Tanner now felt an almost overwhelming need to take her away from this canyon.

It was so strong he was determined to throw her over his shoulder and kidnap her out of here if he had to.

He hoped it didn't come to that. "We'll feed your grouse and hope that's the only wolverine that comes by for the year." He tried to sort out all she needed to do before she left. What chores did he see to before riding to his folks' place?

"Your cattle will be fine for a few days while I introduce you to my ma and my sisters, their husbands, and my little brothers—who are near grown-up men these days."

"You have a huge family."

Tanner smiled. "My sisters all have little ones, so it's even bigger than it sounds."

A bellow sounded from behind him and he whirled around to face the biggest longhorn bull he'd ever seen. Standing not twenty feet away, its head down, pawing the dirt. It was the color of midnight, with a spread of black-tipped horns that had to be more than eight feet. He lowered those massive sharp horns and kicked dirt onto his belly with his front legs. Tanner reached back to grab Debba and run.

"Shadow, you sweetie." She'd run all right. Right around him and right up to a bull that looked like a killer.

"Debba!" He drew his gun, knowing a single bullet would never kill this thing, not in time.

She didn't even notice his warning or his gun because she was busy hugging the monster. She wrapped her arms around his neck. Arms that had just been around him. The bellowing stopped, the pawing stopped. She pressed her cheek against his massive forehead and crooned. Then, with a pat on his massive black nose, she stood up and took one of his horns and led the critter right up to Tanner.

Well, he'd seen a lot of things in his life. Seen his skinny squirt of a ma throw a thousand-pound bull. Seen every one of his big sisters rope and brand a spring crop of jumping, running calves. Seen a neighbor, Mandy Linscott, shoot a running wolf from five hundred yards out. So Tanner didn't underestimate women, ever.

But this moment, right now. He looked old Shadow in the eye and saw his own death. That bull was as good as speaking to him, telling him no outsiders were welcome.

"Scratch him between his horns. He loves that."

Tanner could swear the bull's eyes narrowed, daring him to do it, daring him not to. Tanner figured either way, unless Debba could save him, he was bull fodder.

And, since there was no way to save himself, what the heck? He reached out and scratched the old beast. The bull lowered his head and tilted it as if he had an itchy spot Tanner wasn't reaching.

"C–can. . .uh. . .do you pet all your longhorns?" His ma had once told him that a longhorn was little more than a wolf that was good to eat. They were mean and wild and not to be fooled with, and especially not to be approached unless they were tied up or you were on horseback. And even the ones that'd been gentled for milking could turn on you and be deadly. It was one of the reasons the Harden family had switched away from longhorns. It'd taken years and there'd been plenty of mixed breeding, but these days the Circle H brand was slapped onto Angus or Hereford or a cross between the two.

"Well, of course. What's the use of them if I can't play with them?"

Tanner didn't mention food. He didn't think Debba would like that, and he was sure ol' Shadow wouldn't.

He stood there scratching a one-ton monster that had been gentled into a house cat. He sure hoped Shadow didn't take exception when the scratching stopped.

What would Ma and Pa make of this moment? One thing was for sure, Debba needed to get out of here. This life was nothing Tanner considered good or normal, and he was a man who prided himself on letting people live as they pleased.

He decided he'd make an exception to that outlook in this case.

Dear God, let me figure out a way to get this woman to come along with me. And let me live long enough to do it.

And then he had a thought, which, considering the praying he'd been doing, he took to be inspired straight from God. "I have some supplies in my saddlebags." He'd been planning to scout all day and maybe even be out overnight and sleep by a campfire. And cook by one, too. He wondered how long it'd been since there'd been any cornmeal, flour, or sugar in this place. He had a small pouch that had cookies in it—his ma had left them when she headed home. Maybe he could entice her with food. Give her a couple of bites of sweets then lure her out with a trail of cookie crumbs.

If the bull didn't kill him, that's just what he'd do.

A movement on past Shadow drew his gaze, and he had to admit it wasn't easy to take his eyes off the big beast. A whole herd of longhorns was wandering toward them. Based on their horn spread and the moss growing on them, some might be ten or twenty years old. Calves frolicked among them. Several horses came along, two of them ancient draught horses. Belgians, maybe. He'd seen a couple of them in his life. At least three mustangs and some that looked like a cross between the two. He counted ten horses, three of them colts. All as tame as dogs.

He wondered if she ever rode. Then again, why would she? That would suggest she had somewhere to go.

"Debba, the sun is high in the sky. It's time for a noon meal."

She stood, done with her hugging at last, and turned to him. "I have food in the house. Come and eat with me." Her voice rose with every word as if the idea was too exciting to bear.

Shadow bunted her in the back and knocked her right into him. She clasped his shoulders to keep from falling. His arms went around her waist.

Maybe the bull was annoyed the scratching had stopped, but Tanner decided to believe the old boy was matchmaking.

His eyes went to that stream. He planned to find a way to work with Debba because he needed her water. But to drive his black and red cattle in here with this strange valley full of gentle giants was hard to quite imagine.

Tanner slid one arm around her waist and turned her. Not making any sudden moves. He glanced back to see he led a parade. "Is Shadow going to follow us all the way to the house?"

Debba glanced back and patted the black head. "If he wants to."

Tanner decided if she wasn't afraid, neither was he. But he kept up a steady pace, not letting go of her, for fear she'd go back to her pets. Or that her pets would keep parading. So if Tanner and Debba stopped, the parade would walk right over the top of them.

They never got to the stream because having that bull on his heels made him head straight for Debba's cabin.

He let go of Debba and detoured to his horse. He puffed out a sigh of relief when the bull followed her. He didn't think that made him a coward; the bull was really fond of her.

Because his feisty stallion most likely wasn't a good fit for the friendly animal kingdom here, he took the black into the tight log barn near the house, stripped the leather off him, gave him a bait of oats, and left him in a stall.

The barn had several stalls, all empty, and the split log floor was clean enough that if he dropped one of his ma's sugar cookies on it, he'd pick it up and eat it without a second thought.

He peeked out the door and saw that the cattle had started grazing and were wandering off. With a sigh of relief he tossed his saddlebags, full of food he hoped to use on Debba, and hurried to the house before he had to shake hands with one of the Belgians.

Ɔ∞Ɔ

He was back!

She'd almost refused to let him care for his horse she was so afraid he'd vanish as mysteriously as he'd appeared. After years of having no one around, the few minutes he'd spent in the barn left her with loneliness flowing over her like the winter wind.

Tanner stepped inside, smiled, and swung the door shut. Those golden brown eyes flashed so friendly it was hard to look away. She was building up the fire to make him eggs and the rooted vegetables she always ate. Ma had called them potatoes, but Pa had said they weren't exactly that.

He set something on the table with a thump and started pulling things out, spreading them around. The fire needed to heat a bit so, fascinated, she went to his side.

"What do you have here?"

"Have one of my ma's sugar cookies."

Debba remembered sugar. Oh, she had honey, she'd found a hive she could rob. But sugar, it lay over the cookie in white drifts. She reached for it so eagerly she should have been embarrassed.

Tanner got another packet out and a small tin pan. "I'll make coffee."

"Coffee?"

"It's a drink. You boil the coffee"—he held up some black crumbs—"in hot water and have a drink to go with the cookies. It warms a man on a cool mountain morning or a bitter cold winter day."

"I've never had such a thing." She thought she'd heard of it but not for a long time. Her pa hadn't kept it in the house. How could he when he rarely went to town? They went without anything he couldn't raise himself or find in the forest.

Without asking for help or permission, Tanner made quick work of putting his pan into the fireplace, with the water and what looked like black dirt mixed together.

She looked at the cookie, practically crying out to her with its prettiness, round and thin and the sugar so appealing.

"My ma made those.

"Your ma." The words did something to her heart. A mother. What a wonderful thing.

"Ma is the best cook in the world." Tanner came and guided her into her chair, touching her again. Then he picked up a chair—from where she'd shoved it against the wall about four years ago—and dragged it to the table. He picked up a cookie and said, "I have a pack of them. We can eat one while we wait for the coffee and then have more."

He took a bite and then watched her take one. Her eyes went wide and she chewed slowly, like she wanted to live a lifetime in each bite.

She took her second bite and was chewing when he added, "And then we can talk about how fast you can get packed up and ready to come with me."

Chapter 4

That'd gone bad.

Tanner ducked when she threw her head back. She almost smashed him in the face with the back of her head.

A muffled scold kept up a steady rumble as he rode his black stallion out of the canyon. He didn't like gagging her, this was not a kidnapping, after all. It'd be a kidnapping if he wanted to get money for her. Taking her to meet Ma didn't count as kidnapping. Exactly.

It struck him that he'd never had call to hog-tie a woman before, and it wasn't something that suited him. And the gag would come off as soon as they were past shouting distance of her pet longhorn. He wouldn't put it past her to be able to summon that soft-hearted monster to come to her rescue.

"I swear I'll bring you back. But right now I have to go, and I can't stand the thought of leaving you behind. I don't know why you have to fight with me this way. Now settle down and I'll untie your hands and feet and take the gag out." She tried to head butt him again.

"Fine, Debba. Stay tied up. It's a long ride to my folks'. A long old day's ride, and we didn't get started until after noon. But we're going the whole way. And my stallion is strong enough to carry double and still set a good pace."

It was a good thing she was a little mite of a woman.

They threaded their way out of the canyon, and his horse picked its way through the jagged rocks, finding the nearly invisible trail like he had before. They finally reached open ground, and Tanner urged his horse into a long-legged gallop. It'd be long after dark when they got home, but he wouldn't sleep. It was wrong to keep a woman out alone with a man through the night. Even if the night was edging toward morning, he'd go until he got home.

He had to do that because he was an honorable man. . .for a kidnapper.

He rode a long way down the mountain before he took off her gag.

She yelled for a while. He probably oughta listen to her, but he had a fair idea what she was saying, and he was busy watching a tricky stretch of the trail. By the time he was on safer ground she'd calmed down.

He said, "We've been riding for over an hour. I'm sure as certain that if you jumped off my horse right now and headed home you'd never find your way back. Do you agree?"

She finally shut up.

The silence was nice so he figured if she didn't answer him, he'd just enjoy the quiet.

Finally, long after he'd given up, she said, "It's so big."

Since they'd come a long way down what had to be one of the biggest mountains in the Rockies, he figured that's what she meant. "Yep."

There wasn't a lot of fight in her, so he untied her wrists from the pommel and handed her his canteen. She didn't try to brain him; instead she took a good long drink and passed it back.

Maybe they were becoming friends. If she kept this up he might just give her another cookie.

He started telling yarns. About how his ma had married three times to three worthless men, then she'd married a fourth time to his pa.

He told all about his four big sisters and his four little brothers. Then he told about buying land not that far from her and building a cabin up near hers without knowing she was there and how many cows he had and plans for the future.

He found himself to be a talkin' fool, but she either wasn't speaking to him or she was so interested in the scenery that she was struck dumb, which amounted to. . .she wasn't speaking to him. And when he lapsed into silence, his kidnapping crime wore on him, so he kept telling tales.

When he thought his horse was about all in, he found a bubbling spring and pulled the black to a halt.

He swung off the stallion and lifted Debba down. She seemed unsteady, so he hung on to her while he tied his horse to a scrub bush.

He helped her kneel by the spring and drink.

"Sit here for a while and I'll fetch you something to eat." He eased her onto a flat-topped boulder that was about knee high and fished around in his saddlebags for the last of his cookies, figuring to sweeten her up.

"Debba." He sat next to her on the huge rock. "I am sorry about dragging you out of that canyon. I hope you know I will never hurt you."

Hoping she understood that he was sincere, he studied her as she ate her cookie. She finished it in several quick bites. No denying it, the woman liked sugar.

When the cookie was gone, crumbs clung to the corner of her lips, and he smiled and reached up to brush them away. As he touched her, something tugged deep in his gut. His fingers stopped then swept slowly along her bottom lip. Unable to resist, he leaned down and replaced his fingers with his lips.

A gasp stopped him. He drew back, shocked at what he'd done. Then she reached both hands for him, rested them on his cheeks and pulled him back.

He shouldn't kiss her. He knew it. He was innocent of women, but nothing compared to how defenseless she was.

Pulling back, he looked at those bottomless blue eyes full of loneliness and wonder. All he could feel was a powerful sense of confused longing.

"We mustn't do this." He kissed her again in direct contradiction to his statement. But he ended it and pulled her to her feet.

"We've lingered long enough."

The afternoon worked its way into evening. Tanner had to give his horse one more break, but this time he behaved himself, though he didn't want to, not one speck.

The break was short, and he pressed on as hard as the black would allow.

Finally, the sun fully set and Debba's head lolled back to rest on his shoulder. He leaned forward to see those pretty blue eyes closed in sleep. At last he was able to hold her as close as he wanted.

∞

Debba woke up being shaken around, no idea what was going on or where she was. The stars were blazing and the night was cool. A thudding sound brought her more fully awake.

"Ma, Pa, it's Tanner."

Tanner Harden, that kidnapping skunk bear. The thief of kisses.

He'd acted so friendly, and then it was over and she felt certain it was something she'd done. She knew nothing about men, and somehow she'd given him a disgust for her.

It made her fear this dangerous outside world and long for her home until the pain nearly cut her in half.

She had gotten tired of trying to fight him, especially since she had no luck, but she clenched a fist to take one more good shot at him just as the door swung open. A man stood there holding a lantern.

"Is she hurt?" The lantern man's eyes locked with hers. She blinked against the bright light.

"Nope, just tired. I'll tell you all about it after I put my horse up."

"Get in here. I'll see to your horse, you look all in." The man reached.

Debba thought he was going to grab her. She drew in a breath to scream.

The arm went past her and dragged Tanner inside. Then the man went out with the lantern and for a second things were dark. Then a light flared and another lantern lit up. . .this one hanging on the wall.

"You said she's not hurt?" A woman spoke. In the dim light, and with her eyes still blurry with sleep, Debba couldn't see her face.

"Nope, but I found her alone, Ma, stranded. Her pa died and left her alone in a high valley. It's a long story."

"I wasn't stranded," Debba mostly croaked. Her throat was dry and her temper was worn thin. This was his ma. Tanner had talked about her more than anyone else. This is who he wanted her to meet.

Tanner set her down, and when he let her go she ached at the loss of his touch. Before she could decide what to do with her first moment of freedom in hours, the woman spoke again.

"You poor thing." Another lantern lit, this one from behind. Tanner must've lit it, and it cast light on the woman's face and finally Debba saw her.

"I'm Belle, Tanner's ma." The woman came and rested two callused hands on her cheeks. Debba looked into brownish, greenish, golden eyes, a perfect match for Tanner's, full of kindness and strength.

With absolutely no idea how to act, she stood there, aching. Another woman. The longing from being near was so overwhelming she was incapable of moving or speaking.

Then Belle pulled her into her arms and hugged her. The second person to touch her in just one day. These arms were different. The coddling. The strength of them, matched with a mothering concern. . . Debba felt like she was breaking apart inside. When tears came flooding there was no stopping them.

She wrapped her arms around Tanner's ma as tight as she could hold on and wept. Tears came from so deeply inside they might well be tears for her own mama. And tears for Pa who'd stayed to himself completely after Ma died. And tears for all the years she'd been alone. At first she'd been terrified, in fact she'd barely cried because fear was so much stronger of a reaction.

Tears that had turned to stone from all their years of being stored away.

And now they broke free from where they'd been waiting, until it was safe. Until now.

⌒◯◯⌒

Tanner hated tears about as much as Pa did.

Not quite, but close.

He was mighty tempted to go help Pa strip the leather off his stallion—which was a one-man job and probably already done. Not a good enough reason to stay here. And while he was out there he'd warn Pa not to come inside anytime soon.

He even backed up and fumbled behind him for the doorknob when Ma noticed and about burned him to death with her eyes.

She was hugging Debba, crooning to her, patting her on the back and reading Tanner's mind all at the same time.

Not much got past Ma.

So Tanner hunted around in his head and decided he could feed himself. It was closer to morning than night, and much as he was near asleep on his feet, it didn't look like he was going to find a bed anytime soon. Since he was mighty hungry and his folks probably weren't going to get back to bed and his little brothers would be rising soon—in fact he was surprised they hadn't gotten up already what with all the ruckus of sobbing—he figured he might as well cook.

So he headed for the kitchen and stoked the fire, put coffee on, then started heating up skillets for breakfast.

Ma might not want him to leave the house, but he didn't have to stand right there watching, did he?

Debba was bound to quit crying and be hungry, too, in a minute.

He found his mind straying to that kiss they'd shared. He was about to crack an egg right into the top of the cookstove with no skillet when his pa came in the back door.

Which reminded him of the crying.

Pa was a smart man. He'd probably heard the sobbing and come around back.

They were out of the line of sight of the woman and probably, considering Debba's caterwauling, out of earshot, too.

"So, where'd you find the woman, son?" Pa heard the crying, but for some reason he wasn't running for the hills, and that just wasn't like him. In fact, he looked amused. Almost like he considered this crying woman someone else's problem, maybe Tanner's.

Tanner explained, and Pa listened and asked questions. He'd helped scout that land Tanner claimed.

"That mountain grows up on the west side of your property. And I remember the jagged rocks all around the base of it. I can't believe you found a trail across 'em."

"Debba screamed and there was a gunshot. The black followed the sound, and he found the way in. Even while he walked on it I had to use my imagination to see it." He thought the crying from the front of the house was fading a little. He hoped Ma was pulling Debba out of the doldrums.

"And a keyhole pass into an inner canyon." Pa had a spark about him in wild land. The Hardens lived a long way out, and though the town of Divide had grown and the train had come through, theirs was still a solitary life and it suited the whole family.

Tanner proved that by moving even farther from town. But to think a meadow like that existed. . .

"Don't you wonder what's left in these mountains to be discovered? Are there more meadows like that, in the heart of a mountain? I wonder if the Indians knew about it. Or if maybe her family stepped on land that no human had ever touched." Pa made that sound like the finest thing that could happen to a man.

"And I've been in there. Maybe the fourth person to ever see it." Tanner loved the thought of it. "It's a beautiful place, Pa, hundreds of acres of lush grass, with a fast-movin' stream, and she's got longhorns in there that may be twenty years old." He told about Shadow while they cracked eggs and sliced bacon.

Pa laughed and looked befuddled at the same time. "I don't suppose she's thinking that a hundred head of longhorn oughta be culled. Wonder how she'd act if I told her she needs a cattle drive?"

"I've got a feeling that if she got wind of a cattle drive having the end result of turning a cow into beefsteak, she'd be fully opposed to it." Tanner poured the eggs into the skillet, hot now on their rectangular cookstove. A luxury Pa had brought home for Ma a few years back. The livin' was getting mighty easy on the Circle H these days.

"It don't matter what Debba thinks; no one's gonna drive those cows anywhere." Tanner pictured himself trying to ramrod that big friendly bull out that narrow pass and across that rugged trail, just the first stretch on the long route to Helena.

"Maybe they'd come along if you lured them with buckets of wheat." Not unlike Tanner's plan to lure Debba with sugar cookies. Considering she ended up hog-tied, he might as well stop all his planning right now. He showed no talent for it.

Murmuring came from the other room. He heard Debba's voice break and Ma's soothing response, but he couldn't make out the words.

Then he heard Ma say, "He gagged you?" in a voice that wasn't one lick soothing.

"I've got to see this place," Pa said, "and see a one-ton longhorn that acts as tame as a house cat."

"I half expected her to weave him a necklace of dandelions and then ride him around the meadow."

Pa laughed and shook his head.

Which didn't distract Tanner from wondering what exactly Ma was going to have to say about his tactics. He decided to hurry with his cooking since he'd long ago noticed that Ma really appreciated help around the house.

He got real busy breaking eggs.

Ma came into the kitchen, her arm around her newest chick.

Tanner said, "Breakfast will be ready in just a few minutes."

At the falsely hardy tone, Pa gave him a strange look, arched a brow at him, then flipped the slices of bacon.

Ma settled Debba at the table and got her a glass of milk. They had glasses made of real glass these days, though Ma rarely let the boys touch one. She'd learned that in a hard school.

But Debba rated a glass. Then Ma set a pitcher of milk on the table, came over to get plates, and while she was close to hand, slapped Tanner on the back of the head.

"Hey!" He didn't say more. He figured he deserved it.

"A gag, Tanner?"

He shrugged helplessly. "I thought about leaving her there, but she really didn't want me to leave, did you, Debba?"

He looked at the poor soggy little red-eyed filly. He wanted to pull her into his arms and help her get through her upset.

She shrugged then shook her head. She really needed a haircut.

"But she wouldn't come with me. Her pa has filled her head with a lot of nonsense about never leaving that canyon."

"Don't you say a bad word about my pa!" She was angry, but he could see she was exhausted. The long night and the crying jag had about done her in.

"But I couldn't stay, and I—I—well. . .I just couldn't stand to leave her. . .but she wouldn't come." Tanner shrugged to match Debba. "I just thought no one could talk to her better than you, Ma."

"You thought you knew best, so you did what you wanted without regard to her feelings, is that right?"

He reckoned that summed it up nicely. "Yep."

Ma closed her eyes as if the very sight of him caused her pain.

"I'll take you right back, Debba." There was no possible way on God's green earth that he was taking her back. "We'll head out as soon as we eat." Except he'd think of a reason to delay it. Maybe if she slept for a while she'd come to her senses.

"I'm sorry." And that was purely true. He really had hated manhandling her. "I did *not* want to do that to you, but I was at my wit's end." Tanner gave her a weak smile that could hardly have been more unnatural. "Did it help at all to talk to Ma?"

Debba gave him such a forlorn look he half expected to get slapped in the head again. He was tempted to slap himself.

He scraped the cooked eggs onto a platter. Pa was taking up the bacon. Ma saw to the plates and such, along with bread, butter, and jelly. Tanner noticed he got a tin cup. He was probably lucky she didn't dump hot coffee over his head.

Ma urged Debba to her feet and settled her in a chair between the table and wall, with Ma and Pa at the ends of the rectangular table with the red-and-white gingham tablecloth. Tanner sat right across from her so he could read every expression in her bright blue eyes.

The smell must have done the work all the noise wouldn't do, because about the time Tanner swallowed the last of his breakfast he heard a stampede that'd impress old Shadow.

The noise made Debba clutch her hands together at her throat, her eyes wide as she turned to face. . .the dangerous outside world? Had she been waiting for trouble like this?

"It's two of Tanner's little brothers," Ma said.

"Two, there are more?"

Tanner was sure he'd told her about there being five boys, but maybe he'd mentioned that after she'd fallen asleep. Or maybe she was nervous enough she couldn't make sense out of anything.

"Mark came riding in and asked if he could have some help digging a spreader dam. We sent him your two littlest brothers. Emma can feed them for a while."

That left Si and Cade to come storming down the stairs, like a pack of hungry wolves on the scent.

They skidded into the kitchen, shoving at each other to get to the food first. Then Si's gaze lit on Debba, and he stopped short. Cade plowed into him and they both about tumbled to the floor, but Si held his ground and finally Cade noticed. He turned and looked, too, looked hard. Tanner was surprised to feel his temper rise up.

And he really didn't like it when he noticed Debba looking back, although he thought that might be fear. The house was filling with people, and for a woman too long alone it might be overwhelming. Which made Tanner want to toss his brothers outside and lock them out for good—or at least until he took Debba home—which he didn't see how he could ever do.

His little brothers were destined to live permanently in the barn.

"Howdy." Si was the image of Pa. He was twenty-three, only a year younger than Tanner, who figured all five of the brothers looked like Pa, except he alone had Ma's eyes. The rest of them had blue eyes like Pa's.

Si had Tanner's full six feet of height. Cade two inches taller. They'd finally had to leave off calling him Shorty.

Luckily Jake and Will were at Emma's.

Ma spoke, and it was a good thing because Tanner didn't want these two to know who Debba was—which was rude and mighty stupid.

"Debba, these are two of my five sons. Si is the oldest save for Tanner, and Cade is my third born. The next two, Jake and Will, are away." Ma rested a hand on Debba's arm to draw her attention. "I have four daughters who are older, but they are all married and moved to their own ranches."

With a sweet smile, Debba looked at the two knot-heads who'd come in. "Hello, Si. Cade."

They both came straight for her. Of course the food was right in front of her on the table, so Tanner wasn't sure what exactly they were aiming for. Tanner grabbed his plate and made a quick move to sit beside Debba. He didn't think she'd like sitting next to two strange men. And his brothers were mighty strange.

"Debba, that's a pretty name. Is your name Debra?" Si asked. "My real name is Silas, but with it being Pa's name I get called Si."

With a nervous blinking of her eyes, Debba seemed to be searching around on the inside of her head. "I th–think my name is Debra."

"You don't know?" Cade asked, sitting square in front of her.

Si slapped him on the shoulder to make him scoot down and leave room for another chair.

"No one has called me that for a long time. Not since before my ma died." She rested one hand on her mouth then said, "We have a family Bible. I am sure my name is written in it, but I haven't opened it to those pages for years. I could find out for sure."

Si and Cade settled in and started loading their plates with food, and loading Debba with questions at the same time.

About the time Tanner was ready to tell them to both shut up and let Debba eat, Pa's hand landed hard on his shoulder and lifted him out of his chair. He had no good reason to refuse to mind his father, though he wanted to. He resisted fussing and let himself get dragged to his feet and pulled out of the kitchen into the front room. He did his best to make it look like he wanted to go. He hated to look like a child in trouble in front of Debba.

The minute they were out of the room, Pa asked, "What should we do, son?"

"Can't we keep her, Pa?" Tanner flinched when he heard a little kid coming out of his own mouth.

"She's not an orphaned pup who showed up at our back door."

"Honest, she sort of puts me in mind of one."

Pa nodded.

"All I can think of is, can we find someone to go home with her?"

"Like hired hands? You think she needs hired hands? Or a housekeeper? To tidy a house for one that she tends just fine for herself?"

"Don't start arguing with me, Pa. It's a waste of time. I know all the troubles, none of 'em bigger than what to do with a two-thousand-pound house cat with an eight-foot spread of horns. But she can't go back in there and live out her life alone. I wondered if she could live here with you and Ma. She needs parents."

"She's a grown woman, Tanner. I'd say she's twenty years old at least. She doesn't seem real sure. The normal way for an adult woman to add to her home is to"—Pa's eyes sparked with mischief—"take a husband and have some children."

Tanner spun around and leaned sideways to look in the kitchen, where both of his worthless brothers were talking to Debba, and she was turning back and forth between the two of them and smiling to beat all.

"Who's she gonna marry? She don't know no one."

There was such a long silence that Tanner finally tore his eyes away from Debba and his two flirting brothers.

He looked at Pa, who said, "How about if she marries you?"

Chapter 5

That's the dumbest thing I've ever heard, Pa." Tanner sounded horrified.

"Nor will I marry you." Debba rushed from the room, looking widly between the two of them. Then she found the door and raced out.

She heard the door open and shut behind her and thudding footsteps closing in on her. Tanner grabbed her around the waist and swung her up in his arms.

"I want to go home!" She wanted to start crying again, but she'd done so much of it she really couldn't stand the thought. Being angry held more appeal honestly.

"You took me so far from home I have no way to return. I couldn't find my canyon if I searched for a lifetime." She balled up her fist and considered swinging it, though she'd never struck anyone in her life. That gave her pause. She might have swung a fist or two at Tanner earlier, and kicked him. And tried to smash him in the face with her skull. But she'd never hit anyone in her life, except him.

This was obviously Tanner's fault.

"Listen, what Pa said, Debba, we don't know each other nearly at all. We can't think of getting married. I'm sorry you heard that and it upset you. But you can't go back and live out your life in that canyon all alone." He dropped her legs so they swung down, and he stood her firmly in front of him, his hands on her shoulders.

She noticed the sun had come up. Somehow she'd passed an entire day and night with Tanner. Kidnapping was very time-consuming.

The sights around her stopped her from punching Tanner. She probably wouldn't have done it anyway. The house she'd been in was beautiful. Large and tightly built with spindles lining a porch. There were two huge barns and a corral with grazing horses that connected them. Cattle, black and red cattle of all things, spread out beyond the buildings. No horns anywhere. There was a low-slung shed with one side open, and parked in there were a wagon, a buckboard, and a buggy. She only even knew what a buggy was because it was referenced in one of the books she had in her house. Books she'd read over and over until they were nearly memorized.

There was so much life here. It overwhelmed her to the point of silence; at the same time she wanted to ask a thousand questions. There was so much she wanted to know she couldn't collect her thoughts to begin. Which made her realize how exhausted she was. Her anger and embarrassment drained away. She was simply too tired to do anything more right now. Her shoulders slumped.

Tanner was holding her up anyway—in addition to arranging her life. Why bother doing anything herself?

Lifting her chin took all her energy, and she looked into those unusual golden eyes. She didn't know quite what to say, but he took over, as he'd been doing since they met.

"You need some rest. Let's go back inside. Ma will find you a place to sleep. We can talk more later."

"Tanner, what are we going to do?"

She said *we*. That was wrong. What was *she* going to do? Tanner had caused this problem, but it was her life. Her problem to solve. Pa had always told her an adult had to stand on her own.

Tanner touched her cheek, drawing her back from her worry.

"I think, Debba, that. . .you can't go home. Not for good. Not alone. So when you ask what we're going to do, you need to spend time admitting you can't live walled off from the rest of the world, not anymore. So decide what you're going to do instead of what you've always done. It's your only possible choice."

⸎

Tanner watched Debba walk back to the house. Ma reached out an arm to wrap around her shoulders.

Pa left them to the house and strode toward Tanner with a glint in his eyes. "Let's go for a walk, son." If that didn't make a man nervous, nothing did. Tanner figured Debba's upset was mostly Pa's fault for his crazy notion about marriage. But there was no sign of remorse on Pa's face. Which most likely meant Pa was of a different mind.

Si and Cade picked that moment to come riding in, and Pa waited for them. It was something in the way he stood but his brothers slowed way down, like a person might when they were facing their own doom.

"Howdy, Pa." Si swallowed hard. "Uh, is something wrong?"

"I want you boys to ride out to the line shack."

They exchanged a glance. Cade said, "But we want to get to know Debba better. She's the prettiest woman we've ever seen."

She was about the only woman they'd ever seen. Ma and Pa didn't go to town much, and when they did, they rarely took their children along. And even in these modern times, Divide, Montana was a small town, mainly full of western men. The few respectable women were all married.

The boys all went along on the yearly cattle drives to Helena so they caught a glimpse of a woman on those trips, but they didn't linger in town after the cattle sold.

"The line shack, now. Do a head count while you're there. See how the spring calf crop is faring, and see if there's any trouble with wolves."

The line shack was right near a trail that went up and over a mountain, leading to the most treacherous trail known to man. . .well. . .that is, the most treacherous known to Tanner. They drove the cattle that way to Helena.

"Can we go up to the high country while we're over there?" They both had a rifle in a boot on their saddle and a holster with a six-gun and extra bullets. A man didn't ride out without being ready for trouble in the West. Besides, the line shack was well stocked with ammunition and food—even a few changes of clothes.

"Don't be pestering critters that aren't pestering you. But yep, you can go up in the high country. Stay together. Use your heads. Don't come back until I come and get you."

Si shrugged then flashed Cade a smile. "I reckon Pa wants Debba to spend time with only Tanner. Two good lookin' men like us around and it might confuse the little woman."

Tanner clenched a fist, and Si and Cade whirled their horses and rode off laughing.

Then Pa turned to Tanner. "I've been meaning to build a bigger chicken coop. Help me chop down some trees."

With a shudder, because he knew what was coming, Tanner followed Pa and shouldered an axe. Pa's own personal solution to every child that gave him any trouble was to put the problem child on the business end of the heaviest tool he could find. If it wasn't the axe, Tanner would be pitching the straw out of the barn all day and night, or swinging a hammer on the longest stretch of fence west of the Missouri.

"I don't know why you're upset at me." Tanner flinched. He was pretty sure he'd just said something that would have sounded better coming out of a five-year-old.

Pa sighed. "Maybe it's the kidnapping."

"I don't see how I could have avoided that, Pa."

"Maybe it's the gag."

"I thought her yelling might set off her cattle. I didn't put it past them to fight me for her." She'd tried to bite him, too, but he didn't mention that. He figured that was fair, considering the kidnapping.

"Or maybe it's that when I suggested you marry her, you said something so rude you should be ashamed of yourself. I made a mistake to suggest marriage when she could overhear."

Which didn't mean Pa thought it was a mistake to suggest it, he'd just needed to pick a better place and time.

"But you were downright unkind. What you said really hurt her feelings." Pa glared at Tanner. "She might've started crying again."

And that was where Tanner had really messed up. Pa's dislike of tears was legendary.

They walked on in silence for a long time. Tanner noticed Pa didn't bring an axe, which didn't bode well for who was going to be doing most of the work.

Then Pa pointed at a stand of slender aspens, the closest stand to the house. "You get busy chopping. I'll talk."

It's was Pa's very own version of a slap on the back of the head.

Chapter 6

Ma came into the kitchen late that afternoon with her hand on Debba's back.

Tanner couldn't quite decide if she was just giving the poor confused girl support or was she shoving her into the room?

Probably, considering how Debba was and. . .how Ma was, it was shoving—as gently as possible of course.

Then Tanner forgot all about shoving because Ma had combed Debba's hair and cut off about two feet of it, but it still hung past her shoulder blades. Washed her up and given her a new dress that Tanner recognized as one of Ma's own. Debba was shorter than Ma, but Ma was quick with a needle and the dress fit just exactly right.

Tanner had to admit it, Debba cleaned up real good.

Then Ma sat her down at the table in the same place she'd sat before, between the table and the wall, and gave her a long hug before she stepped back.

While he was really glad he'd brought her to Ma, the hug gave him a little jab that he suspected might be jealousy. Tanner kind of wanted a hug, too.

And it wasn't just the hugging that made him jealous. Debba got a nap, too.

At the rate Pa worked him today, Tanner probably could have added a room onto her cabin and just kept Debba up there and stayed with her. Which was all kinds of improper, but still the idea occurred to him.

Instead Pa got a bigger chicken coop out of the deal, and Tanner got some sore muscles.

And he shouldn't have said marrying Debba was the dumbest thing he'd ever heard. He knew that before he'd caught up with her outside. Chopping down all those trees would sure enough help him remember not to do it again.

Tanner was busy putting plates on the table. Ma had always expected inside chores from her sons as well as her daughters. And since Tanner's big sisters worked hard outside every day, that'd been fair. He'd been nearly an adult man before he'd heard such a thing as men's work and women's work.

Pa dished up steaming chicken stew. Ma put a plate of biscuits on the table and a bowl of mashed potatoes.

"Put the milk pitcher out, Tanner, and get the pie."

It was apple pie. Tanner had been smelling it ever since he'd come in. Ma always bought a bushel or two of apples in Helena after the cattle drive in the fall.

They feasted on them, and when they began to wither, Ma diced what was left for pie and applesauce. There weren't many to put up, and the apples were hard to find and costly. She must really want Debba to like being here.

It lifted Tanner's spirits. Despite his ham-handed tactics hauling Debba here, Ma was on his side.

Tanner took the chair straight across from Debba. Pa sat on Tanner's right at the head of the table, and Ma on his left at the foot and closest to the stove, so she could refill the serving dishes.

"Let's ask the blessing." Pa did a nice job. His prayers were always sincere but brief. But today he mentioned Debba, and it felt right and good to pray for the lonely woman.

Figuring a hard talk was coming, Tanner dug into his food and so did everyone else. He couldn't figure out if they were just dreading what had to be said or if the food was better eaten warm. Maybe some of both.

Tanner had his pie half eaten when Ma said, "Debba, have you thought about what you want to do?"

Debba stopped chewing and fixed her eyes on her dessert like she thought it held the meaning of life. Silence hung thick in the room. Tanner regretted it. He didn't want her upset. Ma was trying to let her make her own decisions. None of her daughters had ever had much trouble taking charge of their own lives. Ma was a whole lot nicer than he'd been.

Finally Debba lifted her chin as if her head weighed fifty pounds. Her skin was pale as milk. She looked at Tanner until she'd chewed and swallowed her bite of pie. "You asked me if my pa was a cruel man."

Ma reached across the table and slapped him in the back of the head. He'd be building fence in the moonlight if Debba didn't mind her words.

"I have never considered him cruel, but compared to whom?" Debba bit her bottom lip, and her eyes lost focus. Tanner thought she was looking into the past.

"I think we might have gone to town a couple of times a year when I was really little. But once Ma died, we probably went to town three times in my memory."

"Were you born in that canyon?" Ma asked.

"No. We moved there before Ma died, though. Pa told me we found that canyon when I was four."

"Do you know where you came from? Do you have aunts and uncles who might take you in?"

"No one." Debba answered slowly, and Tanner wondered if she was even sure of that.

"My birth is recorded in our family Bible, and Ma's death is, too. If there is other family, I might find names in there, but I don't know them and I've never met them."

There was silence for a time, and then Tanner spoke up with a notion. Chopping wood had a way of clearing a man's thoughts. "Did you see Luther when we were in Divide last spring?"

Pa nodded. "He had to be eighty years old."

"He's not as old as we think," Ma said. "That long gray beard puts years on a man. Mandy Linscott told me Tom built a cabin for him on their land and told him he'd earned some easy years."

"And did Mandy tell you that Buff and Wise Sister were coming to stay, too?"

Frowning, Pa said, "I didn't hear that."

Ma shook her head.

"Well, I talked with Luther for a while and he said he don't like it. He's been put out to pasture. His knees ache and he has to sit for longer between jobs, but he hates the thought of a rocking chair gettin' him in his old age. And he said Buff and Wise Sister have always roamed. They like the high-up hills, but it's a hard life, and coming down to live near Luther is what's ahead of them. They don't like it, either."

"This is all interesting, Tanner, but—"

"I wonder," Tanner cut Ma off, which was always dangerous, "if Luther, Buff, and Wise Sister would consider living in Debba's canyon."

With a little gasp, Debba said, "You want to give someone else my home?"

"No, I mean they could live there with you."

Debba blinked her eyes, as if stunned by the idea. As if shocked to think her choices might include going home.

"The thing is, Debba, I think you do need to consider coming out of there. And I think..." Tanner hesitated to say this in front of Pa and Ma, but he doubted they were going to give him much choice. "I think there is something between us."

Debba was watching every breath and word.

"I'd like to get to know you better, since we haven't known each other long." Tanner had worked hard all day and been slapped twice. He thought he'd learned his lessons well. It wasn't wise to say one of his misgivings about her was that she was furiously mad. He liked her, but before he proposed, he oughta make sure she wasn't a lunatic. That'd get old fast in a wife.

"We can ask them. I think they might like the idea of living up there. They'll have the wilderness, but they might need some taking care of. I'm not sure if they're up to much hunting anymore. And there might be days when keeping enough wood chopped will be too big a job. We'll lay up a good supply, but I'm not sure if I can get in and out through that narrow pass when the snow gets deep.

I'll do everything to help I can, and I'll be in during the spring, summer, and fall."

He was surprised at the pang he got from thinking he might not see her for months. "If the idea suits you, you can go home. And since I live close, we can get to know each other and see if we'll suit."

"I—I don't know if I want three strangers in my canyon."

No one responded for a time. It was up to her.

She seemed incapable of deciding.

Finally Ma said, "Would you like to meet them? Talk with them? They are fine people, and you'd be much safer with them around. Of course, they may object to the idea."

Tanner doubted it. Linscotts' ranch was two hours out of town, and on an earlier visit, Tanner'd heard Buff claim he could smell people. Luther fussed that the whole Rockies had been hunted out. Wise Sister, a Shoshone woman, had gotten quiet. . .even for her. She rarely left the cabin, and she sure as certain didn't come into Divide.

Debba smiled her quiet smile. "I appreciate this. I'm worried about it, but all afternoon I've been thinking I had no choice. Now maybe I do. Thank you."

Tanner nodded in satisfaction. "Good. Tomorrow we'll go find them and see what they say."

"Do you mean we're going to see more people?" She looked terrified.

"We'll skirt around town," Ma said. "You'll see the Linscotts but few other people. We'll have to hit the trail early. On a fast horse it's a five-hour ride—and just as far back. We can make it in one day, but it'll be as long a day as one of our cattle drives."

With a sigh, Debba shrugged and said, "I'll meet them."

Tanner sighed with relief, and then, his dessert gone, he said, "Debba, as for getting to know you better, would you like to step outside and take a walk with me?"

He glanced left and right at his parents and asked, "Is that all right with you?"

It was more than all right, they practically shoved the two of them out the kitchen door.

They walked a few steps, and, feeling like the world's clumsiest oaf, Tanner took Debba's hand. She smiled and hung on. Not acting crazy at all.

"You know, it's a funny thing, my folks fought it every time one of my sisters got married."

"Fought it, you mean they didn't like their husbands?"

"Well, no they never have met a man they thought was good enough for one of the girls. There was always a fuss. And my brothers-in-law are fine men and all live close around. But they don't seem to have much concern about you."

The smile melted off her face, and Tanner felt his eyes go wide. He could almost feel Ma slapping the back of his head.

"No, I don't mean to be insulting. I'm just stupid around woman. I've never been around a woman."

"Well, I've never been around a man, either."

"Then you know what I mean? You don't know what to say or how to act when you're trying to get to know a man better. How could you? You've never gotten to know anyone at all."

The hurt look faded off her face, but it wasn't exactly a cheerful expression.

"What I'm talking about has nothing to do with you."

"It doesn't?"

"Of course it does." Tanner covered his eyes with his free hand and sort of hoped he stepped into an open well. "I mean my folks are just treating me real different than they treated my sisters."

Then he got a bright idea. "Or maybe you're just so nice that they don't have any worries." He squeezed Debba's hand. "That must be it."

She smiled again, and Tanner considered shutting his mouth and never opening it again so he wouldn't say anything that hurt her feelings.

And then he realized they'd come a fair distance from the house, way outside of Ma's range of vision. He pulled Debba to a stop, turned her, and kissed her.

No talking now.

Finally he felt brave enough to say just about anything and believed she'd like to hear it.

"Debba, I—" A rush of something moving fast in the dark spun him around. He couldn't see what it was, but something was coming fast and quiet.

He'd come out without a gun, no way to protect them.

"Run!" He grabbed Debba's hand and ran toward the house as whatever came at them gained, running twice as fast as he could. He wasn't going to make it. He veered to the side and sprinted toward the barn, much closer. Whatever it was, all motion and silence beyond thudding hooves. No shout for them to stop.

"What is it, Tanner? What's going on?"

"Someone's after us." He couldn't talk and run at the same time, so he just dug in deep, getting every ounce of speed he was capable of. Debba kept up and he was grateful; he'd hate to drag her, and if he pulled her off her feet, whoever was out there would be on them.

They got close enough to the house that Pa was within earshot. "Pa, come quick!"

The pounding hooves closed on them. *A horse*, he thought. There was something eerie about it, but he didn't know what. It had to be someone on horseback. He braced himself for the sound of gunfire and prepared to grab Debba and throw her to the ground, shield her with his own body. Then they reached the barn and he wrenched the door open, hauled Debba in, and slammed it shut.

The hooves kept pounding for long minutes. Finally the sound stopped. Dead silence. He had the fleeting thought that Debba had been right. The outside world was dangerous.

Tanner pressed all his weight against the barn door. There was a heavy latch on the outside of it, but that did them no good.

From the house, Pa shouted, "Tanner, what is it?"

"Pa, look out. Someone's out there chasing us. We barely made it to the barn."

The silence lasted too long. Had the riders run off when Pa came out? Had they turned their attention to Pa? Tanner's stomach twisted to think he'd put Pa in danger. Taking a walk with Debba had appealed to him so strongly that he hadn't armed himself. He hadn't shown a lick of caution.

Then Pa shouted in fear, and the door to the house slammed.

Whoever it was scared Pa.

"Debba, my pa isn't scared of nothin'."

Which really sent him to thinking. He edged along the barn wall, keeping hold of Debba's wrist. He reached a window with a tight shutter, but not so tight he couldn't see out into the yard.

Nothing showed in the small crack. Then a rectangle of light appeared. The house. Pa stood, rifle in hand. He saw Ma behind him. They both just stood there. Not acting scared at all now.

"Pa, what's going on?"

Just then, Tanner heard a loud moo.

"Uh. . .there is a huge longhorn bull in our yard. Black. And he's just standing there. He came toward me earlier, but now he's standing right outside the barn door, staring. Uh. . .he has friends."

Debba slipped away and got to the barn door and flung it open.

"Shadow!" She rushed outside.

Tanner stepped out, and there wasn't a tame-as-a-house cat, two-thousand-pound bull in the yard. No, that would be too simple.

There was a whole herd of longhorns. They'd all missed their mama. Who had wrapped her arms around Shadow's neck and was kissing him on the cheek.

The yard was full of cattle, the whole herd came. They were really dangerous animals, all acting like they'd taken part in a parade from their mountain canyon to the Hardens'.

If Debba ever let them take her pets on a cattle drive, it'd be mighty simple. She'd just ride to Helena and they'd all follow.

Tanner would probably follow, too.

He gave them a wide berth as he walked to the house. He'd told his folks about the canyon. But honestly, how could a person believe it until they saw it?

"Is she hugging a longhorn bull, Tanner?" Ma asked, sounding confused to a point that could only be described as reasonable.

"Yep."

"That bull could turn on her and stomp her into the ground," Pa said. "You can't trust longhorns."

"Look, there's one of her Belgian horses. She said he's as old as her memory. Her folks had them already when they moved into the canyon." Tanner kept watch. "Just be glad her grouse didn't join the parade."

"Grouse?" Ma asked.

"Yep, she caught them and tamed them for their eggs. Leastways, I suspect they're just for eggs. She talks to them like they are family, so I'm not sure if she's up to eating one of them. But she shot a wolverine, and I watched her skin it. As fast as anyone I've ever seen with a skinning knife."

Ma whispered, "I like this girl more every minute."

"What are we going to do with that herd of cattle?" Pa scratched his head with the hand not holding his rifle. The yard was still filling.

"Not much you can do. They like Debba. They tracked her all the way here."

"That's the truth," Ma said, sounding like she wanted to laugh.

"That's the biggest longhorn I've ever seen. I wonder how old it is?" Pa was a cattleman to his bones. "I saw the ridges on Shadow's horns and the length."

"He's twenty years old at least, I'm guessing." Some of Debba's mustangs were here now. They mingled with the longhorns like a reunion of old friends. Pa usually kept the horses and cattle separate because the horses had some instinct to start herding and the cows didn't like it.

"I had one born on my place when I first started out that lived to be twenty-seven years old." Ma took the rifle from Pa, who gave it up without a fight. "An old cow who had a baby every year."

Ma stepped inside to return the rifle to the hooks over the door.

"I'm gonna bet this one don't drive worth a hoot." Pa stared, and then finally he made a decision. "I think I'll ride out right now and get Si and Cade home."

Tanner had to agree with that decision. Reinforcements were definitely in order.

Chapter 7

It took some wrangling, but they finally came up with a plan to get the cattle to go home.

Debba felt like she was lying to her cattle, but they really were inconvenient milling around the Hardens' ranch yard. She started out riding for her canyon, along with Si and Cade and Tanner. Si and Cade carried the clothes that Debba had worn down the mountain the first day and rode two of Debba's mustangs.

They got ahead far enough they were out of sight of her herd, her best friends, so when they reached a stream, instead of crossing, Tanner and Debba turned into the water and rode fast—hopefully out of smelling range since they hadn't had to see Debba to follow her.

Si and Cade rode on up toward her place. Tanner had given them careful directions to the canyon. He was hoping the horses knew the way and would take the trail with good spirits. If not, they'd just go to Tanner's house and let the cattle congregate there for now.

Debba listened carefully, in case she needed to get herself home later.

Tanner rode on, and Debba followed him. They eventually got back to his parents' house, and then they all headed out for the Linscott place.

Belle had promised to avoid Divide because Debba wanted no part of a town. Belle seemed to agree, so that was a promise easily made.

Silas had a gate across the trail they were taking to Divide. He'd spent some time reinforcing it in case the longhorns figured out they'd been tricked and came hunting Debba. She hoped it held.

"I hope that gate holds." Silas sounded glum. Like he doubted it.

Since Debba doubted it, too, it gave her a friendly feeling toward Silas.

"We could go tomorrow." Debba was pretty sure her heart was going to pound out of her chest—due to fear—which would kill her. Meeting new people was a terrible idea. Inviting them to live with her even worse. Thanks to her cattle and horses, they'd already put the trip off two days.

"Do you think Si and Cade will remember to feed my grouse?"

"You reminded them fifteen times, Debba." Tanner sounded tired and it wasn't even noon yet. "And besides, they know ranch life. They'd've thought of it on their own."

Putting this trip off a day wouldn't be so bad. Tanner had taken a walk with her both nights since the cattle had come. Shadow kept them company. The bull seemed to blame Tanner for taking her away, as well he should. And now he was guarding Debba so close she was afraid he might end up in the house with them.

The Hardens were good builders, though. The cabin door was sturdy and withstood all attempts by Shadow to breech it.

"Nope, no sense delaying." Belle seemed to be in charge in this family.

Debba had been in charge in her canyon for years. She was certainly no such thing now. She found herself surrounded by people with much stronger wills than her own.

She sort of missed being in charge. Then she thought of Shadow and wondered who'd really been in charge at her place.

Belle had wanted to start out before daylight, hoping to make the trip in one day. But she was afraid to wait for fear the cattle would come back, so they left just before noon and pushed hard.

Silas and Tanner had saddled eight horses, and they'd cut time by switching saddles and pressing on. The horses needed to shed the weight of a rider in order to keep moving fast, but it appeared that, with the saddle switched and the rider gone, the horses could rest while they galloped flat out.

Debba couldn't quite believe that was true—sure, a saddle and a person weighed a fair amount, but, well, it seemed like the running would be tiring regardless of the weight. But the horses—and the Hardens—kept going, so she did, too.

It was late in the afternoon when Debba saw evidence that they were nearing someone's property. The trails were widened, and there were magnificent black cattle grazing in herds. They were much rounder than her longhorns. And no horns anywhere. She'd seen a few of the Hardens' cattle, red and black and black with white faces, but these were all shining black.

Shadow would fit in here well, except of course for the horns.

About the time the trail became hard packed, they veered away into a faint trail that led into the woods. Debba was relieved because she thought that wide trail probably led to more people than she wanted to see.

They rode deep into a densely crowded forest, and when Silas, who led the way, reined back his horse, Debba was awhile figuring out why.

They were only a few feet away when she finally saw a house. It was almost a door in the woods, then behind the wall of trees, she saw a real house.

The door swung open and a woman with white hair stepped out. Debba knew she was an Indian by her clothing and old stories she'd heard of native folks. She wore two long braids and a brownish dress with fringe and leather decorations. This had to be Wise Sister, and the look in her eyes made Debba wonder if that wasn't the perfect name.

Right behind her an older man stepped out. Probably her husband, Buff. He had long hair around a bald head, with a full beard, more white than gray. He wore brown pants and a light-colored cotton shirt buttoned up the front.

Both of them nodded without speaking.

Silas said, "Buff, Wise Sister, howdy. Is Luther around? We'd like to talk to the three of you."

Another man came out of the woods just then, dressed much like Buff.

"Howdy Silas, Belle." His eyes shifted from Tanner to Debba.

"This is Tanner."

"Knew it was your boy, but I wasn't sure which one."

"And Debba is a young woman who lives in the high-up hills, and I'd like to talk with you about her."

"Light and set." Luther must do all the talking for the three.

They dismounted and headed inside, and Debba wondered where Luther's house was.

Debba was shocked to see a huge painting on one wall that didn't seem to fit with the otherwise simple but pretty house. The house was small, but there were benches along the table and they almost fit. Debba ended up next to Tanner, and it was a tight squeeze. They sat across from Belle and Silas. Wise Sister stood at the stove, leaning back, arms crossed, and when Silas offered her his chair she waved a hand and Silas didn't push it.

Belle said, "Debba lives in a canyon so high up we didn't even know it existed, and Tanner lives close. We'd never seen the keyhole pass that leads into it. She's lived there alone since her father died several years ago. Tanner found her and brought her to our place. She loves her canyon and wants to go back, but not alone. I've heard you speak of not liking to be so near people, and I wondered if. . ." She looked from one to the other, studying all three of them. "If you'd consider living up there."

She stopped talking.

Debba wondered if they'd even speak enough to say no.

"I'll help you get a cabin built, two cabins like you've got here," Silas added.

"Buff," Wise Sister surprised Debba by having a voice, "I am going."

Buff nodded. "Yep, we'll go."

Luther said, "Me, too. No decent fur to trap. No hunting. People everywhere."

Debba hadn't seen a single person, but she could feel them. She knew just how he felt. Of course, maybe she'd like them if she met them, but they all seemed so dangerous. And yet she felt no danger in inviting these three into her canyon. They looked like about the most dependable people in the world. And they wouldn't fill her ears with talk.

"Give us an hour to pack." Luther rose from the table.

"Hour?" Buff gave Luther a confused look. "I can go now."

"So can I, but I'd better ride over and tell Mandy we're leaving."

"She won't be surprised." Wise Sister stopped leaning and grabbed a pack and started loading it. Then she stopped and frowned at the huge painting. "We can come and visit that."

"Tell Mandy bye for me." Buff started filling his own pack. "We'll come for the picture."

"Shouldn't we tell them about the cattle?" Tanner asked.

"What's there to tell?" Debba couldn't imagine.

"No matter. Whatever you tell, I am going." Wise Sister didn't even pause in her packing. Neither did Buff.

"I'll pack your food." Belle headed for the cupboards and the icebox.

"I'll saddle the horses. Tanner, help me." Pa left and Tanner, too.

Debba hated to see him go. She'd have followed if Belle wasn't still in the house.

Buff seemed to be finished because he slung a pack over his shoulder, grabbed a rifle, and followed the men.

Once there were only the three of them, Belle started talking and working at the same time. Debba was the last up from the table and did her best to help.

There were details about what Debba's life was like. Wise Sister stopped packing and looked over her shoulder during the part about Shadow.

Then Belle talked about how fast Debba could skin a wolverine, and Wise Sister's black eyes flashed and she gave her chin one hard nod of approval.

"I will teach you to sew a dress in a different way. There are many things I could teach you. There are things you can teach me, too."

Which was about the nicest thing a wise old woman could have said. Debba decided she liked Wise Sister very much.

Suddenly going home wasn't quite so upsetting.

She decided it was time for her to talk. "My Pa always taught me that the world outside my canyon was dangerous."

"It is." Wise Sister dropped a pack by the front door and began filling another.

Belle was nearly done with the kitchen cupboards. She was leaving most things behind, and Debba had no idea how she was choosing.

"There is danger inside the canyon, too. And danger in being completely alone. You have been lucky to never fall and break a leg. With no help you might lie there until you died. There are bad men outside the canyon, but being alone can make you forget the joy of love and friendship."

This from a woman who was packing as fast as she could to leave a cabin that seemed very remote.

"We will talk of those dangers, and you can consider if a trip outside once in a while would suit you. Yes, there is danger to be faced, but you are strong enough to do it."

"You think I'm strong?"

Wise Sister quit packing. Belle, too. They both looked at her as if she surprised them.

Finally Belle said, "Debba, to have lived alone, cared for yourself in every way, all these years, is an act of strength. You may be the strongest woman, no, strongest *person*, I have ever known."

And all Debba could see was that she was scared.

Belle and Wise Sister went back to work. Debba noticed Wise Sister take rolled-up tubes of paper from a shelf and pack them with great care. She was taking only the minimum things. Debba wondered what those tubes of paper were.

Luther was wrong about it taking an hour. They were on the trail in forty-five minutes, and Wise Sister had been tapping her moccasined toe for fifteen minutes before Luther was ready to go.

She muttered about men who talk too much.

Chapter 8

Ma had been fretting about being gone overnight, but as Tanner had expected, they got home. It was full dark, but they slept in their own beds.

The next morning they all set out. Si and Cade were most likely at Debba's canyon already. If not they'd find the herd on the way there and lead them home.

The long days in the saddle were wearing on Tanner, mostly because he hadn't had a chance to take a walk with Debba or hardly even talk to her. They'd set a blistering pace yesterday, and today was little better. The land they were riding into was so rugged they made far slower time, and Pa had five pack horses with all the tools he needed to build a house. But slow didn't mean Tanner could ride side by side with Debba and talk to her.

Everyone was too busy making sure they didn't tumble off the steep, rocky trail.

As they neared that wall of rocks, Tanner didn't have to worry for one minute about finding his way in. They were following the footsteps, out and back, of a herd of cattle. That hidden trail wasn't so hidden now. A herd of cattle couldn't walk through a trail and not leave plenty of evidence that they'd come this way.

Tanner couldn't wait to see how Si and Cade had handled those critters.

"I hope my grouse are all right." Debba hadn't done much talking. Most likely she was weary to the bone.

They rounded the curve to that keyhole pass, and Pa said with wonder in his voice, "I never suspected this was here."

They went straight on in, and Tanner smiled to see that his brothers had already chopped down a stack of trees. They were good men.

Debba visited her grouse and satisfied herself as to their survival.

Luther and Buff did some hiking around with Pa to hunt for a place to build cabins. Si and Cade went along.

Wise Sister looked around, almost glowing at the beautiful meadow surrounded by high walls. She didn't seem like a woman who wanted to be walled in, but apparently it satisfied her to wall the rest of the world out.

In a few minutes, Buff came back and said to his wife, "Come see if this suits."

Wise Sister followed him into the woods.

"I thought they would be living right next door to me." Debba wove her fingers together, almost as if she were praying.

"Did you want them to?"

With a weak smile, she shrugged and said, "I like that they are here with me."

She gave Tanner a wide-eyed stare that he was sure meant she wanted him here, too. But he might be wrong. And it was too soon to propose.

She went on, "But I was wondering if we'd get to bothering each other. I like that we have a bit of space between us."

Pa came out and showed them where the first cabin went so they could get on with building. Then he left to explore some more.

"How deep does the snow get in winter?" Ma and Tanner, along with Debba, who followed orders with a sweet spirit, began dragging logs to the building site by hooking a chain to each log then to their saddles and hauling them along.

As they worked, Ma and Debba talked quietly. Tanner wanted to hear every word Debba said, but there was no time now, just like he hadn't had time to talk to her since they'd ridden out to fetch Buff and Luther.

The ring of an axe echoed out of the woods. Tanner's brothers were back at work.

The cattle and horses had spread to the far end of the canyon, some of them over the rise so they couldn't be seen. A few had watched the newcomers with placid curiosity for a time, but now they went back to crunching grass.

Tanner couldn't wait for Wise Sister to meet Shadow.

They'd gotten to the canyon with plenty of sunlight left. They burned it all and worked well into the dark. All the logs they needed were cut, and the first few feet of the walls of Buff's cabin were started before they quit for the night.

Ma and Wise Sister showed Debba a few cooking tricks. Tanner knew they used ingredients Debba hadn't worked with for years, like flour and sugar and coffee.

They next day went on at the same relentless pace, and the next. Finally on the fourth day, Si and Cade rode away. They needed to check the Harden place.

As he watched them go, Tanner decided he should do the same thing. He hadn't been to his place for nearly a week.

He asked Pa, who agreed he needed to check his cattle. Tanner rode for the pass out of the canyon, and as he neared it, he had a flashing memory of hauling Debba out of here against her will.

Somehow he felt like he was doing the same thing, only this time, with himself.

He slowed his black down, then down again. He drew closer and it echoed in his head, the way she'd protested. He pulled the stallion to a halt.

He couldn't make himself go. He turned his horse back and looked at the pristine beauty of this hidden meadow. A rise concealed Debba's cabin. Her cattle and horses weren't in sight. The new buildings were tucked back in the woods.

He thought of the dangerous longhorns as gentle as kittens. The wild grouse tamed into barnyard chickens. If he gave her half a chance, he wondered if Debba could make a lion lie down with a lamb.

It was as if he were the only man on earth and he was abandoning Eden. Even Adam was too smart to walk out on his own. God had to kick him out. The thought brought a smile to his face and helped clear up every confused thought in his head. He rode right back the way he'd come.

As he neared the top of the rise, Debba came running, her red hair loose and tangling in the wind. She saw him and stumbled to her knees. She was crying.

Swinging down, Tanner ran to her. "What's wrong? Are you hurt?" He caught her shoulders and lifted her to her feet.

She flung her arms around him and hung on like clinging vine. He held her just as tight.

Finally he was able to speak through his panic. "Did something happen?"

"Yes, something happened."

Tanner thought of Ma and Pa. Had there been an accident? Had—

"You left me." The grief in her words, the raining tears. They said to him exactly what he wanted to say to her.

But before he got to talking, he lowered his head and kissed her.

The moment stretched. The clouds overhead rolled by. A soaring eagle screamed on the wind. Babbling water and lowing cows, aspen leaves quaked and danced.

He was here, with her. The perfect woman in the perfect place.

At last he broke the kiss and looked at her, those deep-blue eyes that carried secrets and fears and loneliness, and a lifetime of hard-won knowledge of how to live in this harsh land.

The swollen lips that she so generously shared with him.

"Debba, I love you."

The fear faded. Her loneliness turned to hope.

"I love you, too, Tanner. That's why when your pa said you left—"

"I was leaving to go check my cattle. My land is low on water, and I might need to do some scouting. But only a bit today. I intended to only be gone an hour or two. I didn't think you'd even know."

Debba shook her head frantically. "The sun dimmed and the birds quit singing. The trees wept and the wind turned cold. I knew you'd gone out of my life."

He smiled and felt his heart fill—and he'd thought it was full before.

"I couldn't go. Not even for an hour. We've been together ever since we met. And Debba. . ." he kissed her again, long and hard. "I don't ever want to be away from you. Marry me. We can live here, or we can give the canyon to Wise Sister, Buff, and Luther and live at my place and come in here to care for your critters."

"Drive your cattle in here with mine and let them drink from my sweet-water creek. And I'll ride with you to scout for more, outside this place."

Nodding, Tanner said, "Thank you. Yes, I think I can go check my cattle now, if you'll ride along. I was thinking I couldn't leave this perfect place, but the truth is, I couldn't leave *you*. We'll live wherever you want, because my only wish in life is to find a way to make you the happiest woman who ever lived."

"Then marry me, soon. Because that would make me blissfully happy."

Tanner smiled and hugged her close. "We're going to have to hit the trail for a bunch more hours."

She pulled back just far enough to meet his gaze, her eyes wide and worried. "Why?"

"Because we need to find ourselves a parson."

Her furrowed forehead smoothed, and she smiled. "And say some vows before God."

"That's right. We need to get married, and I don't want to wait another day."

This time she kissed him first. They were a long time thinking of anything else.

Tanner said, "Let's go tell my ma and pa they've got another long ride ahead of them."

Debba laughed, and they walked arm in arm back to tell everyone the good news.

Epilogue

They didn't manage to get married that day, nor the next.

And when they did ride away, Tanner had no trouble leaving the canyon, not with Debba along. Pa built a fence across the keyhole pass that was so sturdy it just might keep Debba's cattle in.

They didn't get married that day, either, because, before Ma set to cooking, she sent Si and Cade and Pa in different directions. Tanner, too. His job was to get Red Dawson to come and perform a ceremony.

The rest of them were gathering family.

They had about the biggest wedding any of them had ever seen. Especially when Tom and Mandy Linscott showed up. Red brought his wife, Cassie. Wade and Abby Sawyer came over, too. All of them brought their young'uns and a bunch of food.

All Tanner's brothers and sisters and his sisters' husbands rode in. They all brought a passel of children.

Red smiled as he held his prayer book and had them speak their marriage vows.

Ma managed to get a side of beef roasting while the family gathered, and they had a feast, though Debba was horrified that they'd cooked a cow.

Tanner would talk to her about that later.

Then they all split up to head home before Shadow arrived demanding to be a bridesmaid.

Mary Connealy writes romantic comedy with cowboys. She is a Carol Award winner, and a Rita, Christy, and Inspirational Reader's Choice finalist. She is the bestselling author of the Wild at Heart series, Trouble in Texas series, Kincaid Bride series, Lassoed in Texas trilogy, Montana Marriages trilogy, Sophie's Daughters trilogy, and many other books. Mary is married to a Nebraska cattleman and has four grown daughters and a little bevy of spectacular grandchildren. Find Mary online at www.maryconnealy.com.

A Highbrow Hoodwink

by Rebecca Jepson

Chapter 1

Aspen, Colorado
February 1883

Katie Dupont tried to focus on serving the hotel's hungry guests, but she was distracted by the man seated in the far corner. The flickering light cast by the fire barely reached him. In the smoky darkness, he was little more than a shadow. He kept hidden under the brim of his gray bowler hat and blended seamlessly with the miners and entrepreneurs that filled the room.

Still, she was sure she had seen him before. . .and equally sure she had not. What was worse, she feared her shameful past had just returned to plague her.

Her shoulders sagged as she cleared away empty bread plates and stew bowls, then piled them onto a tray. A strand of curly brown hair slipped from her coiled braid and stuck to her damp forehead. She pushed it back, lifted the tray, and walked toward the kitchen.

Once there, she raised her voice above the din. "The men want more whiskey."

Meg, the red-haired cook, jerked her chin toward the worktable. "It's over there. The jug's full, so mind you don't slosh."

The words were sharp, but Katie took no offense. *It's a wonder she even speaks to me.* The thought caused her brow to furrow. *Isn't twenty-one too young for this much regret?*

She forced the depressing thought away and carefully picked up the jug. The guests had an unquenchable thirst tonight, but she didn't mind. It gave her a chance to learn more about the man in the corner. She wove through the crowded room as swiftly as her full jug would allow, and approached his table.

He didn't look up while she poured. She kept hoping he would, even for a moment. Then he spoke, and she nearly jumped.

"I need to talk to you."

Gentlemen of his class did not speak to serving girls. Yet his voice was quiet, as if he didn't want the other guests to hear him. *Whoever he is, he knows better than to draw attention to us.* She knew he was waiting for an answer, but she stole a quick glance at him. She saw that his eyes were dark blue and his features even, except for a slight upward curve at the end of his nose. He gave no indication of recognizing her, and scarcely met her eyes before he turned back to his drink.

She wished she could linger, scrutinize him further, try to get him to talk some more. But she had a supper to serve.

"I finish my shift in an hour," she said.

He nodded, and she returned to work.

∽∾∾

Supper lasted longer than usual, and Katie stayed late. By the time the guests were finally sated, her arms ached from carrying heavy kettles and sturdy platters. She hurried from the kitchen to the silent dining room to wipe the tables, her last chore of the night.

The stranger stood by the hearth, still waiting for her.

A sudden prickle of dread entered her chest, and she began cleaning one of the tables with unsteady hands.

"Might I convince you to sit a moment?"

She paused mid-wipe. Turned and sank into the nearest chair.

The stranger crossed the room and stopped a few feet from her. She noticed his relaxed stance, the lack of tension in his shoulders. *He's confident, used to getting his own way.* She twisted the dishrag until it was nearly a knot. *Why, why does he seem so familiar?*

He met her gaze. "I fear I must be direct, Miss Dupont."

Her hands stilled on the dishrag. "How do you know my name?"

And then he spoke the words that chilled her to her very core.

"Because your child is my brother's son."

The room tilted, the fire in the hearth blurred to a vaporous haze.

She knew now why he seemed so familiar.

She remembered serving a man quite like him almost two years ago. He always sat at the same table beside this very hearth. The sight of him never failed to bring her a tingle of excitement. No man had ever affected her that way. She recalled the thrill she felt when he noticed her at last. And then he offered to give her a ride home in his buggy one night. . .

How I wish I had known what a kiss could lead to.

She willed herself to return to the present. To focus on the man before her— who inexplicably quickened her pulse. *But why is he here?*

"I don't usually act as my family's carrier pigeon," he said with a grin that caused a dimple to appear in one cheek. "But someone had to handle this. . .situation."

Situation? What situation? Then it struck her. *Georgie.* Her dread increased tenfold. "How did you find me?" she asked in a shaking voice.

"My brother's coachman. He said Jackson had built a hunting lodge near here, and often dined at the hotel." His eyes narrowed. "We did not know about the lodge. Nor about his. . ." He snapped his mouth shut.

But she knew what he was too refined to say. *Affair. Dalliance.* It had only been one night, but it was enough. She was damaged. Tarnished. A fallen woman.

She had known little about intimate matters before meeting Jackson Baxter.

200

No one had told her how a girl became compromised. By the time she figured it out, it was too late.

The consequences were dire. The stigma rested on her son like a heavy cape, the disgrace of being born out of wedlock. Better he had died, according to some. She remembered hearing a doctor say as much to one of the chambermaids, after the woman's infant was stillborn. *But my child is very much alive.* And she would fight to protect him.

She drew herself up. "Why are you here, Mr. Baxter?"

"Henry." A trace of bitterness tinged his tone. "I'm preserving the illustrious Baxter name, though whether I'm worthy of it myself is subject to debate."

I don't care a whit about your illustrious name, only about my son. The brave thought remained trapped in her mind, words she didn't have the courage to speak. Despite Henry Baxter's devil-may-care exterior, rumpled cravat, and two days' growth of stubble, there was no masking his educated speech and the keen intelligence in his eyes. *But I cannot let myself be intimidated.*

She lifted her chin. "I should be getting home, sir. Mr. McLaughlin locks the doors himself on occasion, and he must not see me loitering with a gentleman guest."

He gave her an even stare. "And I would rather be squandering my family's money at some garish gambling house. Unfortunately, here we are."

She waited.

"Miss Dupont, I am prepared to offer you a great deal of money to part with your child."

A dreadful silence filled the room.

She didn't even have the strength to gasp. If the chair had not supported her, she might have failed to stay upright. She had expected many things, perhaps a cabin in northern Montana Territory, where she and Georgie could disappear and never be heard from again. *But this?*

"Why?"

He laughed without humor. "Because my brother has somehow managed to trump my hand yet again." He paused, and his expression grew sheepish. "Terrible thing to say, now that he is dead."

An icy jab pierced her chest. She'd long ago given up hope of a life with Jackson Baxter, but she'd cared for him once—and now he was gone. She swallowed hard.

Henry cocked a brow. "You wish to know why I am here?"

She nodded.

"I have come to buy your silence. To purchase your child, and present him to the gilded echelons of Denver society as my son."

At his words, the icy chill spread clear to her limbs. "Why?" She held her breath.

"Simply put, your son has just inherited the lion's share of the Baxter fortune."

Chapter 2

Henry noticed that her wide-eyed stare and oversized apron gave her a childish look. *Don't they bother to attire their servers in clothing that fits?* Despite the disagreeableness of his errand and his longing to be elsewhere, he nearly smiled. *Perhaps they were unable to find anything that came in waif.*

She continued to stare up at him, blue eyes huge in her pale face. The sight almost made him wish he had not been so flippant with her. Then he remembered the illegitimate child she had conceived, and steeled himself. *She is far from innocent.*

She spoke in a small voice. "I don't understand. Jackson didn't want anything to do with Georgie. He never even met him."

Henry concealed the sudden emotion that welled within, masked his disgust for his brother behind a smooth shrug. "It is not inconceivable that a year of consumption brought the boy to Jackson's preoccupied mind."

At the mention of the disease, she grew even paler. Colorado natives were all too familiar with consumption. Sufferers of the illness amassed to the state, hoping the clean mountain air and steaming hot springs would soothe their damaged lungs.

He quickly changed the subject. "At any rate, my family's fortune belongs to your son now, and I intend to secure it."

She tilted her head. "Wouldn't your friends be suspicious if you suddenly appeared with a child they'd never heard of?"

"One would assume. But I've been living abroad since my mother shipped me off to study at Göttingen in Germany. The moment I was expelled, I became a wanderer. My whereabouts and activities were hardly known to my own family, much less Denver society. The lot of them will be informed I was married while overseas, and my wife died in childbirth. I find it best to keep my stories simple."

She toyed with her dishrag. "So, Georgie's mother is to be. . .taken out of your story?"

His voice was even. "Yes, but she will be well-compensated for it."

She studied him. "My son has inherited a fortune. I don't need compensation."

"He won't have access to the funds until he turns eighteen. Meanwhile, they remain untouchable." He grimaced. "I assure you, that clause is every bit as unwelcome to my family as it is to you. We will be forced, after paying you, to greatly reduce our expenditures and live off the revenue brought in by our banking house. That is, if I can persuade our clients that the child is mine, and so keep them from leaving us."

She shook her head. "I don't think they'll believe you."

"Oh, but I will be convincing. If there's one thing I've learned from gambling my way through Europe, it's how to be convincing."

A log fell in the hearth and sparks shot upward, then all was still.

"If you intend to separate a mother from her son, you will have to be."

Her soft words coiled around him, threatened his confidence. He weighed her with a look. Was it possible she couldn't be coerced? *But there's always an angle.* He glanced around at the room. The firelight cast a glow over the dark blue carpets and cherrywood tables. Though all was peaceful now, he remembered the place overflowing with a stampede of hungry, soot-smudged men. The hotel was new, of higher quality than most such wilderness establishments, but already the red leather chairs seemed covered with a film, the layered smoke and grime of mining territory. Careful to keep his expression casual, he pulled a chair from a nearby table and sat across from her.

"This job keeps you pretty busy, I imagine," he said.

She didn't respond.

"Your duties probably don't leave much time for caring for your son." He hesitated, then forged ahead. "Nor does your status as a serving girl offer him much of a life." Girls in her profession were seen as little better than prostitutes. Offering drinks to crowds of rowdy males hardly gave a girl a sterling reputation.

She flushed.

"You want your son to be happy, I presume?" he pressed.

Once again, he was taken aback by her soft words.

"Being separated from his mother won't make him happy."

He forced his irritation aside and hunkered down before her. Elbows on his knees, he met her gaze. "Do you really think the life you can offer here will benefit him?"

She didn't flinch from his gaze, but he saw the pulse in her throat. He had unnerved her. Good. But had he convinced her?

Firmness tightened her jaw. "I will not be separated from my son."

His eyes hardened, matched hers, and he sat back on his heels. "Tell me what you want from us."

"Nothing."

He'd spent years reading faces across countless card tables. She couldn't be bought. He stifled a curse and schooled his features. This wasn't over. He wouldn't allow his life to be ruined by a penniless ragamuffin and her deplorable offspring. But for now, he needed to confer with his mother. She might have more ideas, and at the moment, he did not.

He stood to his feet. "Very well, Miss Dupont. I'll not take any more of your time." He nodded curtly. "Good night."

Without a backward glance, he strode from the room.

❧

Henry mounted the steps under the domed turret of his family's Queen Anne home and flung the door open without knocking.

"P–pardon, sir," a fresh-faced footman in knee breeches stammered, "but shan't I announce you?"

Henry brushed past him. "No need."

He hurried to the staircase and hollered up it. "Mother!"

Seconds passed, then Margaret Eleanor Hatherly Baxter appeared, empress of Denver society and matriarch of one of its most prominent families. She stood motionless, her perfect brows arched, intense brown eyes giving him a cool look before she descended the stairs.

"Things did not go as I had hoped," he began, "but I did manage to travel from Union Station to Capitol Hill without bumping into anyone we kne—"

She pursed her lips and glanced at the footman, who, unbeknownst to Henry, had followed him and now stood in the hall awaiting her command.

Henry knew what she was warning him of. Not only was it vital to keep Georgie's true parentage a secret, it was bad manners to speak of private matters before a servant.

His mother turned to the footman. "My son and I will take tea in the drawing room, Philip."

If she was chagrined to hear of the ill success of her plan, she didn't show it. She had sent for Henry by letter when Jackson was sick, but by the time Henry docked in the New York harbor, it was too late. His brother was already gone. His mother, having been made aware of the contents of the will by the family lawyer, warned him by telegram to lie low for a while. She had a plan, she said. *A plan that would have worked, if only that stubborn girl had cooperated.*

Henry traveled from New York to Denver without drawing attention to himself. Once he arrived home, his mother told him the whole distasteful tale. *How loath she must have been to topple Jackson from his white steed.*

Now she led the way to the drawing room, brushed back the red velvet curtain, and gestured for him to sit across from her at the little center table. She waited until Philip brought in a silver tray and poured two steaming cups of fragrant tea.

"That will be all, Philip," she said.

The servant inclined his head and departed.

"The girl refused our offer?" she asked as soon as he was gone.

Henry nodded.

She picked up her teacup, fingers unsteady. "This threat has the power to ruin us all." She sipped her tea and lifted her gaze to his. "I hope you realize that, Henry."

He scowled. *Does she think I'm that stupid?* An illegitimate child in the family was a disgrace too terrible to speak of. Everybody knew that. Though Denver had begun crudely, it was becoming a veritable beacon of propriety, at least in his family's circles. Men of birth from the East, members of the Old Guard, had come to the city for its gold, silver, coal, and the railroads needed to transport them. If word of Georgie's origins leaked to them, his mother's proper Fortnightly Club existence would be no more. J. A. Baxter & Co., the investment bank started by his late father, would collapse, and its income would be lost. Cigar-smoking clients with their Waltham pocket watches and starched collars would never do business with the sons of Baxter again.

Ruined.

Henry told himself he didn't care. There had never been a need for him in his family's lofty world, not when Jackson managed things so well. And yet. . .

He was sorry for his brother's death, of course. He'd been stricken to learn that the childhood playmate he'd shared a nursery with was gone, just like that.

But he was the heir now. The Capitol Hill mansion was his. Baxter & Co. was his.

He leaned forward, folded his hands on the Russian lace tablecloth, his teacup still untouched. "What must I do?"

When his mother told him, he drank all of his tea in a single swallow and called for whiskey.

Chapter 3

Katie's arms ached from carrying Georgie through the alley. She chose each step, careful not to walk in the patches of yellow-gray slush. She knew it had been created by dishwater, flung onto the snow from the row of windows above.

"You're getting too big," she murmured.

Georgie twisted in her grasp and regarded her with serious blue eyes, then stuck his fingers in his mouth and resumed looking straight ahead. He was just ten months old, but he grew heavy during the weekly trek from the mountain shanty to Katie's west-side tenement. She was forced to leave him with a miner's wife six days a week. Her long hours at the hotel prevented her from fetching him until her day off. *If only someone who lived nearer would look after him. Then I could at least bring him home at night.*

But the miner's wife was the best a girl with her reputation could do. The woman also took in laundry. . .and the children of prostitutes.

Does Georgie even know I'm his mother?

The thought brought a sting to Katie's eyes. The time they'd spent together was limited, yes, but she'd tried to make it special. And she was saving every spare cent in hopes that someday she could take him away from here, to somewhere no one knew about her past. Where she could give her son a better future.

Katie ducked through the brick entryway and felt her way along the pitch-black corridor that led to the staircase. She clutched Georgie close and braved the rickety stairs.

"We're home," she announced as she stepped through the door.

The two women who shared her tenement glanced up from their places at the table. One acknowledged Katie's presence with a grin, the other a grunt. The room greeted her silently with its stained, uneven floorboards and cracked walls of the same shade as the slush she'd avoided earlier.

Despite the dreariness of her surroundings, Katie considered herself fortunate. She couldn't afford her own place and was glad when two chambermaids at the hotel said they needed a roommate. One of them, Sylvia, was a bold black-eyed girl who sometimes painted her face; the other, Helen, a world-weary killjoy whose husband had run off with a fancy-house girl. As long as Katie paid her third of the rent, they didn't mind about Georgie—unlike the respectable boardinghouse matron who evicted her the moment her pregnancy became noticeable.

"Your kid's bathwater is heating," Sylvia said. "I wanted to use it, but Helen wouldn't let me."

Katie saw the steam that rose from the cookstove, a reassuring sight. She had laboriously packed snow into the iron kettle this morning before dawn, shivering on the gigantic snowbank behind the building.

Georgie's bath was always a battle. By the time she brought him home, he was so tired he either wailed in protest or barely stayed awake.

Tonight, he did the former.

Sylvia raised her voice above his shrieks. "Didn't I hear some high-and-mighty gent at the hotel offer to take that kid off your hands?"

Katie gave her a startled look. She hadn't known anyone else had been working so late that night. "You heard us?"

Sylvia's gaze darted to her plate of boiled potatoes, but not before Katie saw the truth in her eyes. *She heard everything.* She glanced at Helen. *And she told Helen.*

Katie sighed. "I admit I have thought twice—a hundred times, actually—about his offer."

Georgie kicked his legs, and she tightened her grip on his slippery torso. Water sloshed from the washbasin and soaked her brown twill work dress.

Sylvia flipped her hair over her shoulder. "I would have handed that imp right over. Glorious freedom, I'd say."

Helen said nothing.

But later, after Georgie was tucked into bed and Sylvia had gone out with friends, Helen came over to the washbasin and helped Katie lift it. They carried it to the window together.

"Don't mind Sylvia," Helen said. "She's just young is all. You go right on being a good mother."

Her words stayed with Katie the rest of the night. She tossed and fretted as she tried to fall asleep. Her cot seemed hard as a wooden plank. Or rather, her father's cot. She'd folded it up and brought it with her when she'd come to Aspen in search of work after his death in a mine collapse. She knew there was no respectable employment for a girl at the camp, so she'd taken the small amount of money he kept stowed under the floorboard and used it for travel expenses. Before long, she'd landed the job at the Clarendon.

Hardly respectable, but at least it pays.

She forced her thoughts to happier times, before her father's death. Her mother left them when Katie was a small girl, but her father did his best to give her a pleasant upbringing. Better to think of those days than to dwell on the enormity of the decision she'd just made for her own child.

Her agonized mother's heart couldn't bear it, all that she'd denied Georgie. The best schools, travel to exotic places, the prestige of being a Baxter.

Helen's kind words drifted through her mind again. *A good mother.*

But at that moment, Katie didn't feel like one.

~∞~

The next morning, Georgie happily banged his spoon on his breakfast tray, his cherubic face covered in fried mush. Katie placed a kiss atop his silky head and knew she could never give him up. *Whether the decision was right or wrong, I couldn't make a different one.*

Peace settled over her. There would likely be times of doubt, but for now, she was certain. *God, let me never fail him.*

Her roommates were at work, and Katie basked in the quiet. She wiped Georgie's face and hands, laid a blanket on the floor, and set him down. He immediately craned his head toward the table, his attention fixed on the spoon. A disgruntled furrow creased his forehead. She laughed.

"What an impatient little scamp you are." She reached for the spoon and was just about to hand it to him, when there was a knock on the door. She rose to answer it, expecting to find the man from the tenement next to theirs, who sometimes came to borrow coal. But the visage that greeted her was a far cry from sagging trousers and a soot-blackened grin.

Henry Baxter stood before her, tailored, pressed, and scowling. His dark gaze flickered to the spoon she still held. He lifted a brow but said only, "A chambermaid at the hotel told me I might find you here." He paused, and added, "May I come in?"

She nodded and stepped aside, her mind in a whirl. *Why is he here?* Was he trying again to persuade her to give up Georgie? *Well, it won't work.*

She left the door open. It wouldn't do to further damage her already battered reputation. When she turned, she saw that he stood in the center of the room, bowler hat in his hands. She thought he'd be looking at the musty walls and scant furnishings around him, but his eyes were on Georgie. Though Henry wasn't much taller than average, he seemed formidable as he gazed down at her son. His expression revealed nothing.

She knew she should offer tea but hated to serve him from a rusty kettle and chipped cups. Nor did she want him to stay any longer than necessary.

He faced her abruptly. "I'll not waste your time, Miss Dupont, but get straight to the point." He rolled the brim of his hat in his palm until it nearly bent in half. "I have come to do whatever it takes to gain your cooperation on the matter we spoke of."

She felt a tingle, like a bitter wind swept through the window.

He continued. "You were disinclined to part ways with your son, as I recall. Let me assure you, you may keep him."

The tingle did not lessen. *Why am I not reassured?* "I mean to."

His eyes narrowed. "Do you have any idea what it would do to my family if it was discovered that all our money had been bequeathed to an ill-begotten child?"

She clenched her apron in a tense fist. "Yes, sir, I do." *I'm quite familiar with the treatment of the fallen.*

He went on as if she hadn't spoken. "When I last saw you, you observed that Georgie's mother was to be removed from my story." He spoke through tight lips. "As it happens, Miss Dupont, my mother noticed it, too. She suggested I should revise that part."

For the first time, a tiny flame sputtered inside her, a blaze of hope. And turned to ashes with his next words.

"She told me to ask you to marry me."

Her thoughts scattered in a dozen directions. Time ticked by, and finally she realized he was speaking again.

"Mother had it all planned out, you know. How we would get married in some obscure town where no one has ever heard of us. We would be welcomed home with as much fanfare as a family in mourning is permitted to display. The press would be informed that the second son of Alexander Branson Baxter has come home to comfort his family, bringing with him the wife he married while overseas, along with their young son, George Alexander."

Only one thought crystallized in her mind. "Georgie's middle name is not Alexander."

"It will be."

Her retort didn't escape, but the hostility must have shown on her face.

"Don't you see that this is best for him?" he asked.

At the moment, all she could see was the brother of the man who had shattered her life, standing before her asking her to marry him. *But is it really fair to compare him to Jackson?*

He looked similar, it was true. They shared the same aristocratic features and dark hair, though in the light of day, she saw that Henry's was more brown than black. Wavy with a hint of auburn. They were alike in manner, too. Both men had a diplomatic charm that made them very convincing. But while Jackson's aplomb never failed, it seemed that Henry couldn't quite keep his true feelings to himself.

She remembered something he'd said about being unworthy of the Baxter name. *If the brother who claimed my virtue was the worthy one, what does that say about this one?*

But none of that mattered. Not if the farce wasn't believable. "I'm a miner's daughter, not a duchess. No one will believe I'm anything more."

"It's risky, I'll admit." He gave a regretful sigh. "A pity you don't have a foreign accent. People would just assume we'd met and married abroad, without our having to invent a story. Your unknown origins would be considered exotic and mysterious, rather than appalling and suspicious."

So much for charming. But she overlooked his bluntness and spoke softly. *"Mon nom complet est Katriane."*

He stared at her, for once speechless.

"My full name is Katriane," she translated in a perfect French accent. "My father, Pierre Gerard Dupont, began calling me Katie when we first immigrated to America. For seven years, I have worked very hard to sound truly American."

He recovered his ability to speak. "This should be easy for you then. Simply go back to being Katriane, and sound as French as you please."

"Of course, it would be nice not to have to be so careful."

"Well then." He cleared his throat. "Say you'll marry me, Katriane."

In such close quarters, she couldn't help noticing that he smelled like pine needles and cloves. *Only better.* She looked away.

Georgie whimpered and she hurried to kneel beside him, grateful for the distraction. She lifted him into her arms and gave him his long-awaited spoon. He clasped it as joyously as if she'd offered him the world.

And in that instant, she realized she could.

"Yes, Mr. Baxter," she said. "I will marry you."

Chapter 4

The bellboy plunked Katie's trunk near the narrow bed and crossed the room to light the kerosene lamp. Henry knew he should be glad this ramshackle hotel at least provided them with assistance. But as he looked at the lumpy quilt and peeling damask wallpaper, gratitude was not the sentiment he felt. *There isn't even a hearth or a washstand.*

He paid the bellboy and flung the door shut behind him. He glanced at Katie and forced a smile when he saw Georgie staring at him, motionless and wide-eyed in his mother's arms.

"The boy must be weary after such a long day." *And after all that howling he did in the coach.* Henry ran a tired hand through his hair.

Katie didn't quite meet his gaze. "Would you mind very much, keeping an eye on Georgie while I—while I . . ."

He waited.

She blushed. "Prepare for bed."

Undress, she means. He wanted to groan. Or sigh. Or kiss her.

He shook his head sharply, jarred by the last thought. The sensation reminded him of times when he'd stood up too quickly and grew faint.

He'd imagined all the difficulties of schooling Katie once they arrived in Denver. Of teaching her to act like a lady of refinement. Of the challenge it would be to present her to society as his proper, poised wife. But there was one thing he hadn't considered—this night.

I hope she doesn't expect me to behave like an eager bridegroom. Theirs was a union of necessity only, and he would make sure it stayed that way. Stray thoughts such as the one he'd just had must be firmly dealt with.

Katie stepped over to the bed, still avoiding his eyes, and removed the quilt, which she arranged on the floor. She lowered Georgie into its scratchy folds and disappeared behind the dressing screen.

Henry almost asked what he was supposed to do if the boy cried, but decided against it. He sat awkwardly on the bed, very aware of the creak of springs in the quiet room. He gazed down at Georgie and reviewed the events of their journey. *Anything to keep myself from listening for the rustle of clothes behind that screen.*

He'd hired a private coach to take them from Aspen to the depot in Leadville, and they traveled by train over summit passes. Toward evening, they'd stopped at a sooty little mining town, a backwoods place—ideal for getting married. Neither of them had been there before, so there was scant chance of being recognized. After finally finding a judge in town who would marry them, they arrived late at the only hotel in town. In the dark, they could barely see the false front, the sign that greeted them with the single word *Rooms*. The place had no name, as if the owner himself didn't want to claim it.

Henry fumed inwardly. Two dollars tossed to a half-deaf judge, a harried witness trying to soothe a wailing Georgie, and a bride who would never wear white.

The evidence of that last fact sat gurgling before him, drool on his chin. *He hardly looks like the dignified heir of a fortune.* The child busied himself playing with the handle on his mother's trunk, eyes alight with concentration. Then the handle got stuck in one position, and he frowned. He smacked it just once, his little brow stern.

Henry smiled. *Now he looks like Jackson.* At that moment, in fact, the only difference between the two appeared to be their hair. Georgie's was blond, while Jackson's had been dark. Though on second thought, Henry recalled Jackson's being white-blond when he was a child, just like Georgie's. *It's as if Katie wasn't present at all for the making of him.*

But she was very much present tonight.

Without really meaning to, Henry glanced at the screen. It was black on the edges, and dark tan in the middle—but not dark enough to hide the shadowy outline behind it.

He swallowed and averted his gaze.

When he'd first met Katie at the Clarendon, she'd resembled a street urchin, swimming in her gigantic apron. Her rounded nose and pointed chin had added to the childish impression. He would think of her like that.

She emerged and knelt beside Georgie to unbuckle her trunk. She opened it and dropped her clothes inside in a single, unfolded heap. With the motion, her curvy hips swayed beneath her cotton slip.

A street urchin, he reminded himself.

She straightened and peered at the bed, eyes as big and cowed as Georgie's had been earlier.

Henry had no intention of sleeping with her. *But she needn't act like she's facing the executioner's block.* "I'll take the floor," he said.

She bit her lip. "Please don't. I'm used to hard surfaces, while you're a sophisticated gentleman—"

"And you're my wife. A grand lady, didn't you know?" He saw that she flushed, and feared it might be with pleasure at his words. "You mustn't arouse suspicion. Any notion of behaving as a serving girl must be done away with. Do you understand?"

Her eyes flashed, but she nodded.

He softened his tone. "Anyway, the bed would be better for Georgie. He could use a good night's rest."

She smoothed a wayward curl and smiled apologetically. "I'm sorry he was so difficult today. He's not used to traveling."

He shrugged.

She turned and lifted Georgie into her arms. Henry tried not to notice the tender way she laid her son in bed and spread the quilt over him, or the grace in her movements. *It isn't hard to see why Jackson was so beguiled.*

The thought soured him, reminded him with stinging clarity that this woman was once a common, *quite* common, acquaintance of his brother.

He flopped his cape onto the floor and laid down on it.

The minutes went by, then hours. Sleep eluded him, and he knew by her restless tossing that she was awake, too. But he kept his back squarely to her.

Chapter 5

The Baxters' matched bays turned onto Grant Street with a *clip-clop* of perfectly shod hooves. Katie gazed out the window of the buggy at the row of Victorian houses with their multi-gabled roofs, her mouth open.

"This is where you live?" She couldn't keep the wonder from her voice.

"No," Henry replied, "this is where *we* live."

His words made her feel like a chastised toddler. She looked away, sure the flame would flare in her eyes. . .and sure he wouldn't care.

He'd hardly spoken to her during the entire journey, other than to try to teach her his fancy city ways. Worse, she thought she'd seen a hint of revulsion on his face the night before.

It doesn't matter, she told herself whenever the sting came. All that mattered was Georgie. *Please let this man accept my baby*. But she feared the request would be too difficult, even for the Almighty.

She cuddled Georgie close to her. He squirmed and reached toward the purple tassel hanging from the curtain, and she captured his plump hand in hers. Then she sat and rigidly waited for the grand entrance into her new world.

Henry's voice broke through the tension.

"Here we are."

The horses turned onto a circular brick driveway, and Katie beheld her new home for the first time. Of all the Capitol Hill houses they'd passed so far, it had the most gables, the most windows, the most balconies. It even had two porches, one of them round, with a dark green spindle on top.

The team followed the driveway around the side of the house to the back. The driver pulled on the reins, and the buggy rolled to a stop.

"This is the carriage house." Henry's voice was low, presumably so the driver wouldn't hear him. "We keep a chaise and a sled in here, in addition to the carriage we're presently in. It's called a landau."

She rolled her eyes toward the landau's roof and reached for her trunk.

Henry stopped her with a hand on her arm. "The coachman will bring the luggage in after he unharnesses the horses and turns them over to the groom." He kept his hand on hers, even pressed it a little until she met his gaze. "These are things you need to know, Miss Dupont."

She couldn't help herself. "Don't you mean 'my dear'?"

A troubled look flitted across his face, and he lowered his voice further. "You're right, of course. I won't make that mistake again. If I do, we're in danger."

The sun, partly concealed behind a towering cottonwood, seemed suddenly dim. *This is serious.* The future of her son, indeed, of an entire family, was at stake.

She looked up, hoped her expression would reassure him. "We'll be careful."

But as she mounted the stairs, the looming stone tower overhead, she was the one in need of assurance.

Henry barely lifted the knocker before the door was swung open by a butler, who, like the house, was tall and looming. For the first time since she'd met him, Henry broke into a genuine smile.

"Manfred!" he exclaimed.

The butler gave a short bow. His own smile flickered, almost as if against his wishes. "How very good to see you, sir." He spoke in a faint British accent. "I greatly regretted being away the last time you were at home."

Henry shook his head. "Don't concern yourself." He clasped the butler's shoulder to turn him toward Katie. "Manfred, please see that my wife is shown to her room and properly assisted with dressing for dinner. And fetch Miss Oliver for the child."

Katie tightened her hold on Georgie. Who was Miss Oliver?

She didn't have time to ask, for Manfred was already leading the way across the entrance hall to the staircase.

Lustrous images passed before her in a blur, a vague march of portraits and stained-glass windows above a carved banister. She scarcely knew what had happened before she found herself seated in a girlish room, looking into a cheval glass mirror flanked by two dainty sconces. Behind her stood a maid, who met her gaze in the mirror.

"I'll have you ready in a wink, ma'am." Without a pause, she swept Katie's hair up in deft hands.

Through Katie's haze, one thing was clear. Georgie was safely in her arms, held snugly in her lap.

Just as the last pin was tucked into her hair, there was a knock on the door. Another maid entered the room, clothed in a white blouse and finely made skirt of checkered wool. *A lady's maid.*

"Mrs. Baxter is ready for dinner, Bridget," she informed the first maid. "See that you show—ah—Mrs. Baxter the way to the dining room."

A smooth voice spoke from the hallway. "We will refer to my son's wife as Mrs. Henry when we are at home, Francine."

The maid's cheeks turned pink.

The lady of the house herself stepped through the door, and Katie hurried to her feet, awkwardly lugging Georgie with her.

Margaret Baxter looked her up and down over a straight nose; thin lips twisted in an expression Katie couldn't read. *Disdain?* She held Georgie closer, as if to shield him from the aloof eyes. Alas, Margaret's gaze shifted to him.

"Where can that Miss Oliver be?" she murmured. She glanced toward the maid who'd labored over Katie's hair. "Bridget, do take the child and find his nurse."

The maid dipped a curtsy and reached for Georgie.

Katie stretched as far from the reaching arms as possible. "I don't mind holding him. Really, I don't."

Her new mother-in-law's brows rose.

She didn't expect me to have an accent.

The surprise faded and a coldness took its place, a coldness not quite buried beneath Margaret's poise. "We leave the tending of our little ones to capable nurses here on Capitol Hill, my dear."

Katie stared at her for the length of several heartbeats. *This is best for Georgie,* she reminded herself. But with every heartbeat, she felt a mother's protest. It didn't help that her son had fallen asleep, downy head pillowed on her shoulder, body slumped in a way that was entirely trusting.

He didn't awaken as Bridget carried him from the room. Still, everything within Katie wanted to snatch him back and depart the house, never to return. Especially when she saw that Margaret looked after him, too, her face devoid of grandmotherly warmth.

At that moment, Henry appeared in the doorway, and his single dimple filled Katie's vision. If she hadn't known better, she would have thought his smile bordered on sympathetic.

"I see young George is off to the nursery," he said.

Unsolicited tears welled in her eyes. "*Oui*, but—"

"It's past time for dinner," Margaret broke in. She addressed Henry. "Your brother and Alice are here, awaiting your arrival in the drawing room."

"Ah, good old Thomas. Finally overcame his habit of tardiness, did he?"

Margaret ignored the question and turned to Francine. "Kindly inform Mister Thomas and his wife that dinner is served."

The maid left, and Margaret again addressed Henry. "You'll find that your brother has changed in your absence. He's no longer a child. Both he and Alice are aware of the. . .circumstances of your marriage." She gave Katie a pointed stare. "But the servants are not. Let's preserve their ignorance, shall we?"

Katie managed a dazed nod, and her mother-in-law swept through the door, her black mourning skirt trailing behind her.

Henry extended his elbow to Katie, and together they followed the velvet train through the hall and down the stairs.

Dinner was a strained affair, made worse by Margaret, who apparently had some delicate matters to discuss with her offspring.

Katie ate forkfuls of steaming duck and sipped vintage wine, all the while afraid she'd chosen the wrong fork.

Henry's brother Thomas sat across from her, his intense brown eyes—his mother's eyes—on Henry. *Almost as if he is weighing a stranger.* Thomas's pretty, blond wife, Alice, had smiled at Katie when they'd first entered the room. Just a small smile, but it seemed a veritable beacon of sunlight in this wainscoted cavern with its dark mahogany table and claw-footed chairs.

The footman set a dish of currant jelly on the table, and Margaret waited for him to leave the room before she spoke.

The jelly is supposed to accompany the duck. Katie realized she'd been the only one eating the savory meat. She chided herself for her blunder and hoped the others hadn't noticed. She forced her mind to what her mother-in-law was saying.

"You are aware, Thomas, that I sent for Henry when your brother was ill." She didn't wait for a response, nor did she seem to think it odd that she spoke of Henry as if he weren't there. "I decided it was time for him to come home and take up his family obligations, primarily concerning the bank."

Thomas tightened his grip on his wineglass. "Pardon my bluntness, but. . .do you really think that's wise?"

A droll look appeared on Henry's face. "You're referring to my inglorious record of being more an embarrassment than an asset, I presume?"

Thomas flushed, and his voice rose. "You deny it?"

"No."

There was silence.

Margaret broke it, nonplussed. "Nevertheless, Henry will take Jackson's place as senior partner at Baxter and Company, and head of this family."

"That will hardly be necessary, Mother." Thomas spoke icily. "I know enough about the bank to manage its operation."

She looked at him. "You are more than capable, son, but you're too young. We need Henry to be the one who makes deals over drinks." Her shoulders slumped just slightly. "Jackson had a way about him that made people trust him. Who knows?" She reached across and patted Henry's hand. "Perhaps Henry will as well."

But even an outsider could see she didn't have much faith in the notion.

Katie could barely swallow her bite of duck. It would seem she'd joined a family who not only rejected both her and her son but also had little respect for her husband.

Chapter 6

Through the open oak door, Henry could see his brother's knee bobbing. He could hear the tapping sound of the sleek Stylographic pen on the ledger. He'd been troubled by Thomas's behavior lately—the sending and receiving of mysterious telegrams, hasty departures, constant fidgeting. But he wouldn't ask. *Let him come to me for once.*

Henry's massive book-lined chamber was separated from all others, accessible only through his brother's office. He preferred it that way. During the months since he'd been home, he'd focused on learning his new trade. He'd poured over accounts, studied earnings books, checked and rechecked collateral. He was content to let Thomas deal with the clerks, bookkeepers, office boys, and runners even the clients. *At least, all but the most salient of clients.* As senior member, Henry was expected to meet with certain ones.

But he didn't dare do it without Thomas. Not until he learned more.

He heard a scraping noise and looked to see his brother standing in the doorway, one hand braced against the frame, the other holding a folded piece of paper. Henry recognized the insignia stamped on the creamy page, a winged lion.

Randall & Son.

A chill crawled up his back. The head of Randall & Son was a bitter enemy, a former business partner of Henry's father before a terrible disagreement caused them to separate. Their rivalry grew fiercer as the years went by, and Henry knew that Arthur Randall would love nothing more than to ruin his family.

Then why is my brother holding a message from him?

"I'm headed home," Thomas said.

Henry searched for a reason to object. *If I keep him here, he might tell me what this is all about.* "Couldn't you stay and help me with these joint transactions? I can't quite decipher the postings."

Thomas crossed his wiry arms over his chest. "Isn't that something the chief manager should know?"

Henry sighed. He'd tried to be patient, earn respect little by little. But a hostile glint still shone in his brother's eyes. "Yes. It is." He waited.

Thomas jerked his hand through his light brown hair. "I thought I explained it to you already." He gave Henry a sudden piercing look. "Yes, I did. You do know how to do it. Don't pretend otherwise."

Henry treaded with caution. He'd discovered a knack for business lurking inside him, and suspected his brother had seen it as well. *If he doesn't feel needed, we could lose him.* The company couldn't afford that. "Kindly remember that my business expertise consists of one uncompleted term at a university and two summers as an intern under Father's junior clerk."

There was a brief silence.

"I've been here for hours, Henry. My wife is waiting."

There's more to his urgency than Alice's eagerness. And Henry was sure it had something to do with that note from Randall & Son. But it was true Thomas had worked long. They'd both kept the newfangled electric lights on late tonight.

Henry shrugged. "Very well, go."

Thomas left, and Henry resigned himself to learning more about the note another day.

Their strained exchange put him in a foul mood that followed him home.

His mood did not improve when he entered the house and the footman told him that his mother was waiting for him in the drawing room. He groaned inwardly and surrendered his hat to the servant, then walked down the hall and drew aside the curtain. He proceeded into the gas-lit room—his mother considered electricity downright perilous—to find her pacing.

"What is it?" he asked.

She stopped in the middle of the immense Oriental rug and faced him with a grim countenance. "You're spending too much time at work."

"I thought you wanted me to take the reins of the business."

She turned sharply, moved to sit on the floral settee. With a sweep of her hand, she gestured for him to sit across from her. "Not if it means neglecting your wife."

"So you're fond of her now?" He nearly smiled.

She glared.

He let out an exasperated breath. "If you're worried about the servants being suspicious, you needn't be. They've no doubt thought I was merely preoccupied with my new profession."

"It's not only the servants. Do you realize that in a few short months we'll be out of mourning? We'll host the expected reception for her. We'll have guests. You and your bride must begin acting more affectionate now, or you'll never convince them."

He didn't reply.

"And what of the boy? You've hardly glanced at him in weeks."

Something built inside, a simmering he'd kept under the surface. But now it bubbled over. "Do you think this has been easy for me, Mother? Do you think it's easy knowing that the offspring I must claim as my own came from that. . .illicit union? Surely you've noticed the child is the very image of Jackson. Every time I look at him I remember his tainted origins." The edge in his voice grew. "And my wife, formerly my brother's mis—" In the widened white of his mother's eyes, he saw he'd gone too far. One didn't speak so bluntly in the presence of a lady.

He studied her more closely. *Or is it only that?*

She was gazing beyond him. He twisted and saw, framed in the entrance, Katie's stricken face.

She met his eyes for an instant, then whirled and hastened away.

For a time he stared after her, numb. Then a sharp sensation knifed through his chest, and he sank his head into his hands.

∽

Katie looked in awe at the many-paned windows, gilt-framed portraits, and golden lambrequins that led the way to a vaulted ceiling. The ballroom had been unused all spring and was shadowy, covered in a layer of dust. *Still, the men in the portraits should be smiling, being in such a grand place.*

So should the woman standing before her. Katie knew her mother-in-law enjoyed dancing, yet her mouth was drawn in a sour line.

"I've no notion whatever," she said, "of how to be the man."

Katie would have laughed if she hadn't been so tired of being blamed. *It isn't my fault her summer is spoiled.* There were no excursions to Twin Lakes Village or the summer resorts at Bear Creek for a family in mourning. *Teaching me to dance should be a welcome diversion for her.*

"Maybe I could be the man?" Katie suggested.

"Don't be absurd. You can't very well waltz with my son or dance a quadrille with our acquaintances if you can't follow a lead."

Katie swallowed. She hadn't considered that she might be dancing with Henry. It had been days since she'd overheard him talking to Margaret in the drawing room. She hadn't spoken to him since. It wasn't difficult to avoid him. He left the house before breakfast every morning, worked late, and though their rooms were adjacent, had yet to seek her out at night.

She couldn't imagine the intimacy of a waltz with someone who so disdained her. *Or who despises my child.* Her eyes stung, and she forced her thoughts to the matter at hand.

The fall and winter seasons would bring many social engagements, dinner parties, teas, and balls. If Katie was to fit in at these events, she must learn whatever Margaret had to teach her. *Even if she treats me like a soiled dishcloth—and even if I must dance without a man.*

At that moment, the door swung open, and a solidly built figure strode into the room. Katie felt herself stiffen when she recognized the confident gait of her husband.

"Dancing, are we?" he paused to ask. He continued forward and halted before them. "I believe I can help with that."

And then, without warning, he lifted his brows pointedly at his mother, who lost little time in departing the room. Katie longed to call out after her. *No! Don't go. I forgive you for being a tyrant.*

But she was already gone.

In the silence, Henry made no move toward her. He put his hands behind his head as though reclining in his favorite chair. He did that sometimes, she'd noticed.

"Hard at work, I see," he said. "Learning the social niceties."

She bit her lip and looked away. *I am not making trivial conversation with him.*

He hesitated, then spread his arms wide in an invitation to dance. "Shall we?"

She bore holes into him with her eyes. Then a lump formed in her throat and she dropped her gaze.

Mistress. That's what he'd almost called her. His brother's mistress. She hadn't been, not really. Jackson wasn't married, and their relationship hadn't been ongoing. She knew the latter was what Henry assumed. *But once was bad enough.*

That was then, she reminded herself. This was now, and she needed to learn a new skill. For her son's sake.

Before she could think better of it, she stepped forward and slipped her hands into his.

His clasp was warm. Masculine hairs darkened his wrist. *Jackson hadn't had those,* she remembered absently.

Her husband slid his arm around her waist and drew her nearer. She pulled back, spine rigid. His face was impassive as he led her through their first turn.

The sway of his steps lured her, relaxed her. She followed his lead, gradually began to move with him—most of the time. He turned in a direction she hadn't anticipated, and she lurched forward, her chest inadvertently brushing against his.

His face changed. A flicker of. . .something. . .flitted into his eyes.

He cleared his throat. "I suppose my mother has schooled you in a dizzying array of social rituals by now."

She didn't respond.

"The ceremony of the call, no doubt. The leaving of cards, the folding of corners to indicate the purpose of the visit, the proper length of time to return the call."

Why was he here, with his casual banter? *As though nothing has happened.* Well, something had. She couldn't forget the way he'd insulted her. Couldn't answer him. And yet she heard herself speaking.

"I've discovered that it's bad form to make introductions in the street. Or to arrive early to the opera, or wear the same gown to dinner as one wore to luncheon. My mind is forever racing, trying to keep track of it all."

He stopped. Dropped his hands to his sides, tired eyes telling of sleepless nights. "The other evening I was a rake. I should never have spoken that way about you."

She noticed he didn't disclaim what he'd said, only owned that he shouldn't have said it.

"Please say you'll forgive me. My behavior was unpardonable."

Her heart sank. Behavior, not feelings. *He still despises me.* He was merely begging pardon for saying so. But she nodded.

He smiled, just a little. The dimple appeared, then was gone.

The wall between them remained.

Chapter 7

Y ou look lovely this evening, Mrs. Henry."

Katie managed a smile. "It's nice to be out of black."

She tried to hold still while Bridget buttoned her bodice, but she longed to flee the stuffy room and go to Georgie, who was outdoors receiving his daily dose of autumnal air. Only he could quiet her nerves tonight.

The buttons were finally fastened, and Katie stood and smoothed her hands over the emerald-toned overskirt. This gown was special, made of satin by Worth, shipped from Paris. She'd donned it just once, allowed Georgie to carefully stroke the jet-beaded trim.

"How shall I arrange your hair tonight?" Bridget asked.

"However it would be expected, *non*?" Katie reseated herself before her rosewood dressing table, her bustle making the movement difficult.

In addition to her usual chores, Bridget had helped Katie dress for dinner through the summer. The necessary cutback in spending, brought on by the inaccessibility of Georgie's inheritance, had forced the Baxters to dismiss some of their staff.

Though surely no expense was spared when this gown was ordered.

A knock on the door interrupted Katie's musings.

Bridget rose to answer it, and when she opened the door a crack, Alice peered in.

Katie brightened. Over the eight months since her arrival in Denver, she and Alice had become friends. On one occasion, Alice had even confided in her, confessed her fears regarding her husband's recent secretive behavior.

Alice entered and crossed the room to sit on the chaise at the foot of the bed. "Thomas sent me to see if his mother needed help." Her dark eyes, a contrast to her fair hair, twinkled. "I shan't confess to him that I neglected his command."

Katie chuckled. "You're getting quite adept at sneaking past her."

Alice grinned. Then she toyed with the piece of lace draped over the arm of the chaise. "Actually, there's something I've wished to ask you."

Bridget secured the last tuck of Katie's hair with a jeweled pin. "Will that be all, Mrs. Henry?"

"Yes, thank you, Bridget."

After the maid left the room, Katie turned to Alice. "What is it?"

A blush covered her friend's perfectly oval face. "How did you—how did you know when you were expecting Georgie?"

Katie's own cheeks flushed. She gave a faltering reply, then asked, "Why? Are you. . .?"

"No, I was simply curious, for the future." Alice hesitated. "Was it—difficult? Telling Georgie's father?"

Katie thought a moment. "I suppose so, but I don't remember very well. I was in shock. I didn't expect to be with child."

In the silence that followed, Katie's flush deepened. *She thinks I was Jackson's mistress, just like Henry does.* Only Alice hadn't condemned her for it. "I didn't consider the possibility of a child, because there was only. . .the one time, you see. I was quite ignorant about such things."

Alice was quiet again, for a long while. "Does Henry know it only happened once?"

Katie shrugged and said nothing. But the answer must have shown in her eyes. "Why haven't you told him?"

Katie busied herself pulling on her long white gloves. "He never asked."

She didn't add that he'd avoided her since the day they were married, other than that one dance. Though it stung, Katie wasn't surprised. She couldn't forgive herself, why should he?

She peeked up to find Alice studying her.

"May I tell you a story?" Alice seemed to consider Katie's silence as an assent, for she began in a soft voice. "There once was a man named Peter, who saw a vision from God. In this vision, a giant sheet came down from heaven, filled with animals that Peter, a Jew, considered unclean. Three times, God repeated, 'Do not call anything impure that I have made clean.'"

She must think I've never heard a sermon before. "I know the story. A traveling minister came to my father's mining settlement and told us. He said God was telling Peter to include everyone in the Christian faith." She remembered another sermon, preached by a fiery evangelist at a camp meeting. After hearing the man's message, she'd knelt down under the starry sky, pregnant belly notwithstanding, and asked Jesus to forgive her sins. In that moment, she'd felt His love, His nearness and mercy.

But since then, doubts had arisen.

Alice nodded. "That's what ministers say, that the animals symbolized the Gentiles who wanted to become Christians, too. And they're right, of course. But sometimes I think there's something more. Three times, in the Gospel of John, Jesus asked, 'Peter, do you love me?' How grieved Peter must have been, to think his Lord had to ask him so many times. It must have brought back another 'three times' incident, a terrible one. When Jesus was on trial, Peter denied Him three times. The guilt, the shame he must have experienced over and over, as he relived those dreadful moments. He must have wished, more than anything, to go back and do things differently."

Katie knew the feeling.

Alice continued. "How wonderful it is, that as many times as Peter cursed and swore his denial, God later repeated, 'Do not call unclean what I have made pure.' It's almost like He was saying, 'I forgive you, Peter. I have made you clean.'"

The beautiful words filled Katie's spirit, poured over her like warm honey.

But as she finished preparing for the momentous evening to come, she only wished she could believe them.

⟡

Henry pulled aside the curtain to view the procession of carriages in the circular brick driveway. From the drawing room, he could just see through the front window to the teams of blooded horses and liveried footmen, illuminated by gas lampposts. Top hats bobbed and parasols swayed as the guests stepped down from their conveyances and approached the house.

He let the curtain fall back into place. "They're here," he said tersely.

Katie's almond-shaped eyes grew wide, and she snapped her fan shut.

His mother remained motionless on the sofa beside her. "Manfred will admit our guests, then show them upstairs to the dressing rooms before we formally receive them." She looked as unruffled as a pond on a windless day.

But Katie doesn't. The determination he'd begun to admire in spite of himself was nowhere in sight. Her slightly pointed chin, often lifted in assertion, now trembled. And who could blame her? Despite his family's period of sequestered mourning, they knew there'd been speculation.

Denver society had good reason to wonder. It was odd that an occasion of such importance—the marriage of a Baxter son—should have transpired with so little to-do. Of course, people assumed Henry had been out of the country at the time. But the event still deserved a formal announcement. The same held true for the birth of a Baxter heir. Yet Georgie's arrival hadn't received so much as a one-line sentence in the papers. *Granted, I'm just the second son. But still...*

Thankfully, church on Sundays had been their only outing during the spring and summer months. Even in that sacred place, he could see the women peering at Katie as though wondering, *who is this interloper?*

Gentlemen at the Denver club no doubt pondered the question as well. *Do they suspect there's a scandal attached to her?*

Well, he would remain mum. Grandly so, as his mother had taught him.

"Katriane," his mother said, "go stand at your husband's side and prepare to receive your guests."

Katie's face went white.

Henry offered her his arm. She rose and took it. He could hear the shallowness of her breaths, and pressed her hand with his. She clung to his arm like it was a lifeboat, and something within him softened.

He leaned down to whisper, "You look lovely." His mouth lingered near her ear longer than he'd intended. He straightened but could feel her touch through his sleeve.

He glanced at her gown. Ruffles, bows, and graceful train were expertly made in costly satin. Whatever their guests thought of Katie's manners tonight, they could not criticize her appearance. *And no man will be able to keep his eyes off her.*

Just then, the first guest arrived. An unaccompanied gentleman, whose round belly and thick mustache made him appear jolly. But he regarded Katie with hawklike intensity.

Henry bowed. His mother stood, as imperiously as if she were rising from a throne. He didn't know how she managed it. His legs were so tense he feared they might snap in two.

The man turned his beady eyes toward Katie, who lifted her chin.

"How pleased I am to meet you, monsieur," she said in her soft French accent.

The man brightened. "Ah, madame, you are French. I spent many glorious summers in Paris as a boy." He grinned.

Henry's limbs slowly began to loosen. He watched as Katie greeted their next guest with as much poise as she had their first.

Now the evening held promise.

Chapter 8

Henry knew he should be overjoyed. The reception for Katie couldn't have gone better. She'd behaved impeccably.

But Monday morning, as he looked through the office doorway at his brother, he felt weighted. Even from here, he could see the deep lines between Thomas's eyes. *Something is still troubling him.*

Henry snatched up the sheaf of papers on his desk and strode into his brother's office. Thomas glanced up, but offered no greeting.

"Will you review these statements?" Henry plunked the papers down without waiting for an answer. "I think we've been doling out credits too readily. This isn't enough financial history to ask from prospective clients."

He expected his brother to protest, to defend the risks he'd taken. But Thomas merely nodded, his gaze on the papers, his mind clearly elsewhere.

Henry propped himself against the desk. "What, no lectures today? No monologues about Randall & Son stealing all our business if we fail to act with 'due promptness'?"

Thomas's eyes sparked to life. "Arthur Randall is no laughing matter. He would destroy us if we'd let him."

Henry settled his hands behind his head. "Why don't you tell me what's bothering you?"

His brother's expression grew guarded. "I'm fine."

"Even if I believed that, I couldn't say the same of Alice. She seems drawn lately, like she's worried about something."

Thomas's gaze narrowed. "I would prefer it if you keep your observations about my wife to yourself."

"Tell me the truth, then."

Thomas let out a forceful breath. "Very well." He rose and went to the door, looked first one way then the other. In the area directly facing his office, the hallway opened up into an elegant sitting room, encircled by a railed balcony overlooking the lobby.

Thomas shut the door and returned to his desk. "About two months after you arrived home, I saw a stranger sitting in the back row at church, watching us. When he realized I'd noticed him, he looked elsewhere. But then I spotted him again, getting out of a carriage one night, just down the street from your house."

Henry's brow furrowed. "It could be a coincidence."

"I thought so, too." Thomas opened his drawer and pulled out a card with Randall & Son's insignia on it.

Finally, the mysterious note explained.

"Then I received this message from an old colleague," Thomas said. "A man who now works for Randall. He warned me that he'd heard a rumor about an investigation of our family—he has connections with some of Pinkerton's men. You know how they always know things."

Henry's heartbeat quickened. "What kind of investigation?" He paused. "Something to do with the bank?"

Thomas shook his head.

Katie. Henry gripped the edge of the desk. *If this involves her, we're finished.* "You think Randall's behind the investigation?"

Thomas's incessantly bobbing knee was answer enough. "I asked my friend to keep an eye out, and we've been exchanging telegrams ever since. I've even tracked the stranger myself, though it's done little good. He was no doubt aware I was following him, and never uttered a single useful word in my presence. My efforts kept me out late at night, took me out of town, for nothing."

"No wonder Alice is distraught."

Thomas sent him a warning look. "Don't say anything about this to her."

"You'd rather she think the worst?"

"No, but if I tell her, it might somehow get back to Mother. She's had enough troubles these last few years." His voice turned to a mutter. "As you'd know, if you'd been home."

It was true. Thomas was the one who'd comforted their mother, both through the loss of their father and Jackson's illness and death.

Henry determined to do a better job of caring for his family, starting with this newest threat.

⟨∞⟩

The fog was denser here, he noticed, as he and Thomas made their way through the Cherry Creek Bottoms district. Rows of brick buildings hemmed them in on either side. Worn clothes hung overhead on lines strung from the rooftops. Streetlamps shone bravely through sooty glass enclosures.

Henry and Thomas darted as furtively as possible across the alley and hid in a clump of evergreen bushes. They could just glimpse the stranger's billowing cloak up ahead in the December twilight. They watched him disappear into a small tavern.

Through the orange glow of the single window, Henry saw him approach the bar, then straddle a stool beside a man wearing a fine brown Mackintosh.

"Can you see anything?" Thomas whispered.

"Barely." From this distance, the Mackintosh-man didn't appear to be a miner.

Or anyone who might have known Katie in Aspen—a hotel lackey, silver baron, or smelter. But Henry had to be certain. If the man had somehow seen her there with Jackson. . .

"I need to get closer." He pushed the scratchy boughs aside and stood up.

Thomas yanked him back down. "Don't you dare. If he didn't know we were following him before, he's sure to know it if we go in there. It's only one room, with nowhere to hide."

Henry stared at him. "Are you telling me we trekked clear across this miserable neighborhood for nothing?"

"Essentially, yes."

Henry muttered to himself and shoved past the dense shrubbery. When he reached the alley, he glanced back and saw Thomas brushing stickers from his sleeves, and then—Thomas froze.

"Did you hear that?" He shifted his gaze toward a row of weathered barrels they'd passed earlier.

Henry looked, too, but saw nothing.

Thomas gestured for him to follow, and they crept together down the alley. By the time they arrived at the barrels, Henry's muscles were tight as bedsprings.

All was still.

Then someone sneezed.

"We hear you," Thomas said. "You can come out."

There was a commotion, and two sets of silk violets poked up behind the barrels. Black bonnets followed.

Henry gaped as Katie and Alice emerged.

His first impulse was to rail at them. *What are they thinking, out in this district unescorted?* But soon a very different emotion arose. He felt his lips twitch. *How bold they are, in their stealthy black clothes.*

Thomas didn't appear to share his amusement. "What are you doing here?" he demanded of Alice. "Do you have any idea how dangerous it is, a woman out alone like this?"

"Shhhh." Henry sent a cautioning look toward the tavern.

"I'm not alone," Alice said. "Katie is with me."

"And she has every right to follow you." Katie's eyes flashed. "Every reason to be suspicious."

Like a mother tigress, defending her young. Henry grinned.

Thomas turned to glare at Katie, and Henry hastened to her side. He gripped her shoulders and steered her away, to the other end of the alley. Once safe in the cloaking shadow of a building, he dropped his hands.

He looked at the other two, awash in the streetlamp's glow. What had started as a hostile encounter began to change in tone. At first Thomas's arms were folded rigidly over his chest, Alice wildly gesturing. But then his brother shook his head. Told his wife about the stranger. Her mouth formed an *O*, and tears welled in her eyes. Her shoulders began to tremble.

"I thought you were sneaking around with another woman," she sobbed. "That you didn't love me anymore."

Thomas shook his head again, his expression gentle, and drew her to him.

Henry averted his gaze and looked at Katie. Escaped curls wisped about her neck, bits of dried grass caught in the tresses. He wanted to pull the grass free, an excuse to see if her neck was as soft as it looked. She stood only inches from him but seemed miles away. A sudden ire burned inside him. *How careful she's being, making sure even our sleeves don't touch.*

He glanced at Thomas and Alice, and wished he hadn't. They were kissing, most passionately. It was difficult to ignore the desire that kindled in his chest at the sight. He envisioned being entwined in his own wife's arms.

Then he remembered another brother, one whose claim on Katie had preceded his.

Maintaining his distance was easier after that.

Chapter 9

On his way to the library, Henry approached the staircase and saw Georgie arduously descending, one stair at a time, his hand clasped in the hand of Bridget, the maid. Miss Oliver had been summoned to her ailing sister's bedside earlier that evening, and Katie was at the opera with Alice.

Henry noted the determined furrow in Georgie's brow. It would have been much simpler for the maid to carry him. *But he can do it himself—he's Jackson's child.* The grandeur of the sweeping staircase, the broad mahogany steps marching down either side of the Oriental carpet runner, made the boy seem the size of a doll.

Henry began climbing the stairs and was about to pass by the pair when, out of the corner of his eye, he saw Georgie wrench free from the maid's grasp and take a step on his own. He watched in horror as the stocking-clad foot missed the carpet, and Georgie slipped on the polished wood.

Henry and Bridgett lunged to try and catch him but couldn't reach him in time.

A sharp cry accompanied the thud at the bottom of the stairs, followed by wails loud enough to bring Henry's mother rushing into the entrance hall.

"What happened?" she asked, hand at her throat.

Henry didn't respond but brushed past the frozen Bridget and ran down the stairs. He knelt beside Georgie, his gaze roving quickly over the child's body. His racing pulse slowed when he saw that, other than a small bit of blood on one knee, he seemed relatively unharmed.

"Let's get you fixed up," Henry murmured. He scooped the sobbing boy into his arms and carried him upstairs to the bathroom.

With Georgie propped on one hip, Henry rummaged through the medicine cabinet and pulled out a bandage. He set Georgie on the marble floor, sat next to him, and reached for his wounded leg. When the boy cried out and tried to jerk away from him, he had to force himself to remain unyielding. He bandaged the knee as gently as possible, and, once he finished, Georgie crawled into his lap.

After a thorough soaking of Henry's serge coat, Georgie raised his tear-streaked cheeks and drew in a great, shuddering breath. Then he turned and held one finger out to Henry's mother, who had followed them and now stood framed in the doorway, face gray and eyes stricken.

"Ouch," he said.

She backed away from him but paused to give Henry a reproachful look. "The child has a splinter."

"I didn't give it to him," he snapped.

Her lips pursed. "Just be sure you tend to it."

Henry heard it in her voice, saw it in her eyes. She was terrified, had been petrified at the thought of something happening to Georgie.

So had he.

When did it happen, this change of heart? Had it occurred over time or in an instant—a terrible moment of watching a small boy plummet down a flight of stairs? All Henry knew was that he no longer regarded Georgie as a reminder of something abhorrent. The dimpled lad, with his angelic hair and stubborn chin, was a Baxter.

Accepting a baby born out of wedlock went against age-old prejudices for Henry. Doubtless it was even worse for his mother. She probably grieved anew every time she saw her beloved Jackson's eyes gazing up at her from that illegitimate face. *But it would seem she's finally succumbing to his charms, too.*

The sleigh stopped before Alice's driveway, and the coachman helped her alight. Katie leaned out and waved good-bye. Once the sleigh started again, she flopped against the velvet seat with a sigh.

The opera had been lovely. But she'd missed putting Georgie to bed tonight. Nearly a year had passed since her arrival in Denver, and she still hated leaving him in Miss Oliver's care. In a useless attempt to please Margaret, she'd faithfully attended teas, receptions, balls, and numerous literary luncheons and charities, hosted by Denver's exclusive Fortnightly Club.

Georgie always stayed home.

The horses trotted up Grant Street and turned into the Baxters' circular drive. When the sleigh came to a halt, Katie peered at the house—and peered again. *Why is the nursery light on?* But it wasn't the gaslight, it was much fainter. *A candle.* Perhaps one of the maids was merely checking on Georgie. *But he should have been sound asleep hours ago.*

Without waiting for the coachman's aid, Katie gathered her skirt in her palm and climbed to the ground as fast as her steel hoops would allow.

She entered the silent house and hurried up the stairs. The nursery door was slightly ajar, and she pushed through it and into the room.

All was peaceful.

In the candlelight, she saw that the ancient rocking horse stood guard in its corner. Noah's wooden animals were neatly placed in their ark. Best of all, Georgie lay slumbering in his bed, blond lashes against flushed cheeks, round bottom in the air.

Then Katie saw his bandaged hand.

A sharp breath escaped her mouth, and she rushed forward and knelt before him. With shaking fingers, she touched his silken curls, careful not to bump his wee injury.

A voice spoke from behind her.

"He fell down the stairs this evening after dinner."

Katie twisted about, hand on her heart.

In the rocking chair on the far side of the room, her mother-in-law sat clothed in a dressing gown, holding Georgie's one-eyed corduroy bear.

The sight was so incongruous, neither aloof nor imposing, that for a moment Katie only stared. But soon she recovered.

"And just where," she asked, "is my son's 'capable nurse' tonight?"

Margaret shrugged. "She was called away suddenly, to be with her sister. A frail woman." She paused. "The sister, not Miss Oliver."

Katie returned her gaze to her son's hand. It was impossible to still the quivering of her chin.

"You really have no cause for dismay." Margaret's voice seemed less cold than usual. "It's only a splinter."

Katie's quivering gradually stilled.

Margaret went on. "The child has precisely one scrape on his knee and one very small splinter, which has now been removed."

The words were like a healing balm. "Who took the splinter out?"

"Henry."

Tears formed in Katie's eyes. "And who tended his knee?"

"Henry."

Silence prevailed until Margaret broke it. "I wouldn't have thought the bandage necessary for a splinter, of course, but the child would accept nothing but a thorough dressing to soothe his chapped soul."

Katie sniffed, smiled through her tears.

"He's had a trying night, I'll admit. After Henry put him to bed, I passed by and saw he'd somehow thrown off his coverings. Once I'd properly secured them, he clung to me, and I was forced to stay with him."

Yet he's asleep, and here you still are. Katie turned and met Margaret's gaze. "Thank you."

Margaret shrugged again. Rose from her chair.

"Please," Katie said quickly, "tell Henry thank you, too."

After an almost imperceptible nod, Margaret walked across the room, ruffled mobcap askew over prim brown curls. She hesitated, her hand on the knob. "He's become quite gentle with him, you know."

No, Katie hadn't known.

"My son is changing, whether he realizes it or not."

Katie dared to venture a question. "Maybe he's not the only one?"

Margaret stiffened, angular shoulders taut. She didn't speak right away, and when she did, her coldness had returned. "Perhaps you think you alone have had to make adjustments, Katriane. But your husband is safely abed, while mine rests in the churchyard." She gestured toward Georgie. "And here lies your firstborn, sleeping serenely, while mine is lost to me."

Katie's usual instinct was to shrivel before her mother-in-law's stare. But tonight, she could detect the pain that lay beneath it. "I'm sorry," she whispered.

Margaret continued to stare at her in the flickering light, unmoved. Then slowly, she inclined her head.

An acceptance of sympathy.

It was a start.

Chapter 10

K atie was just about to lay Georgie into bed one night, when he squirmed assertively in her arms.

"What is it?" she asked.

"I think he sees someone," Miss Oliver said with a knowing smile. She placed another of his little garments in the dresser then pointed at the nursery doorway.

Henry stood there, partly concealed in a shadow.

Katie set Georgie down, and he toddled eagerly toward the door. She grinned at the sight. Her son had finally grown at ease with her husband.

But her delight vanished abruptly when Henry stepped into the light. Even from across the room, she could see the grimness of his countenance, the sober look in his eyes. *Something's wrong.*

He offered Georgie a small smile, then glanced at Katie and tilted his head toward the hallway. "May I have a word?"

Katie hastened to her son and swept him up. She carried him to Miss Oliver and deposited him in the woman's arms despite his protests, then went to Henry.

He stepped into the hall and waited for her to join him. After closing the door behind her, he opened his mouth to speak but shut it again when Bridget approached. She curtsied and proceeded past them, followed by a footman, then another maid.

Henry frowned. "It's a bit crowded out here." He turned and led Katie toward a thick, carved door at the end of the hallway.

It was a door she was familiar with—from the outside. Apprehension darted through her, along with a fluttery feeling she didn't recognize. *Why is he taking me to his bedroom?* But she trailed after him, down the hall, and through the carved door. *He wants to speak privately, is all.*

Darker colors prevailed here. Rich greens and browns, severely striped wallpaper, heavy drapes, walnut furnishings.

Henry strode to his bed and tossed his hat on the austere velvet spread, its simplicity contrasted by the massive Gothic-style headboard behind it.

He turned to face her. "Our snooping stranger—Simon, I discovered his name is—went to Aspen last week."

Her pulse raced. Henry had told her about the man, about his too-keen interest in the Baxters. He'd also told her of his concern that the investigation might involve her. It would appear his fears were warranted.

"I was surprised it took him so long," Henry said. "Throughout the winter, he holed up in his suite at the Windsor Hotel, only emerging to play cards in the gambling room downstairs. If he acquired any leads in December from the man at the Cherry Creek tavern, he either chose not to pursue them or was deterred by the cold weather."

"Did you follow him to Aspen?" Katie asked.

"Not personally. After our fruitless attempt at tracking him at Cherry Creek last winter, Thomas and I decided to hire a professional to do our investigating for us. We enlisted a man named Casey from the Pinkerton agency. He knows his business, and he's the one who followed Simon to Aspen."

"Maybe this Mr. Casey didn't learn anything important." Even as she said it, she knew the hope was futile. The look on Henry's face confirmed it.

"He told me that Simon met an old friend of yours," he said. "A chambermaid at the Clarendon Hotel, a girl named Sylvia."

Sylvia was Katie's former roommate. *And for a price, she'd talk.*

Tears gathered in Katie's eyes. She'd brought all this on Henry and his family. "I'm sorry," she whispered.

He shook his head but said nothing.

Her heart seemed to cave into her chest. *He's angry with me.* And she didn't fault him for it. *Still, we both knew this marriage was a risk.* That risk was becoming a reality, one that must be dealt with.

"Are we in danger?" she asked.

He hesitated. "Thomas and I will do all that is possible to protect the family."

An evasive answer. Things were bleak indeed.

He leaned against one of the tall walnut columns that stood like sentinels at the foot of the bed. "Simon asked your friend Sylvia about Georgie and Jackson, and I'm afraid she told him everything." He drummed his fingers against the column, his eyes fixed on some point beyond her.

Moments passed.

"He must have been something," he muttered finally.

"Pardon?"

His dark blue gaze moved to hers. "My brother, the way he captured your attention. Three-fourths of the men in Denver are fascinated by you, and you don't even seem to notice. Makes a man wonder what might have been done to merit such regard."

Katie swallowed. She'd often considered telling Henry about that night with Jackson. Yet now that the time was upon her, she wished she were anywhere else. "I am *mortifié*, discussing this with you."

"I can see that." But there was a tension in his posture that indicated he was still waiting for an answer.

She wanted to explain, tell him she'd been young. Stupid. That she'd committed a grave wrong, one she'd give anything to rectify. *Must I be without words at this precise moment?*

He laughed, a hollow sound. "But then, Jackson always did know how to get his own way."

She longed for the strength to tell him that her interest in his brother had been fleeting. Superficial. That he, Henry, was the one who truly drew her, with his single-dimpled grin and knack for making Georgie laugh. That she loved the scent of cloves and pine needles that clung to his woolen coat—a coat that barely buttoned across his strong chest.

Which now rose and fell in erratic motions.

Is he nervous? The thought somehow bolstered her courage. She reached out, tentatively, and touched his lapel. She thought she heard his breath catch in his throat but couldn't be sure.

His focus shifted to her fingers, which toyed lightly with the coarse fabric at the base of his neck. He lifted his gaze to hers and gave her an inscrutable look. Then he stepped away, beyond her reach. He wheeled around and walked out of his room.

Later, while tunneled in the softness of her pale yellow quilts, Katie cried into her pillow. His rejection had stung. The abruptness of his departure made her ache. But there was something worse that plagued her.

She couldn't rid herself of this clinging shadow. The past gripped her and wouldn't let go. The memory of that one night with Jackson haunted her, followed her like a faithful hound. *Will I never be free of this shame?*

Words came to her then, clear as day. They were sweet, spoken in Alice's soft voice. And yet, they were deeper. More assertive. A powerful command.

"Do not call unclean what I have made pure."

She sat up, wiped at her tears. *But I'm so sullied, God. How can anyone, even You, wipe away my disgrace?*

A part of her heart that had no voice asked Him to help her. Pleaded wordlessly with Him for mercy.

And then she felt it—peace. An unexplainable, spreading calm. A knowing that He'd heard her, that He really did forgive her. She was sinful, yes. Her wrongdoing had been real, certainly. But *He* was clean. He was pure. He alone had the authority to give her that same cleanness. . .and He had done so. Freely.

She buried her head in her pillow once again, but this time her tears were not of sorrow.

∞

The library, with its rows of gold-lettered volumes and masculine aura, was Henry's favorite room in the house. He cherished his after-dinner glass of port by the hearth, time to unwind after a long day. And he knew Thomas was waiting for him there.

But he didn't hurry to leave the table, where his mother and Alice were planning their Fortnightly Club's upcoming summer events. Katie had excused herself some time ago, no doubt wishing to avoid him.

He could leave, too, of course. But the moment he did, he would be alone—if only long enough to climb the stairs. And he would have to face it, how he'd botched things last night with Katie. Over and over it would plague his mind, the scene with her in his bedroom. He groaned inside. Why hadn't he reassured her, taken her in his arms, instead of turning away from her?

Regardless of the answer, he feared she'd be reluctant to let him close to her again.

He forced himself to rise from the table and bid the women good night. As he left the dining room and climbed the stairs, he did his utmost to think of. . .nothing.

When he arrived at the library, Thomas met him at the door, hands on hips.

"Do you realize how urgently I needed to see you?" he demanded.

"Pardon, Master." A faint smile twitched Henry's lips. He strode past his brother and claimed the armchair on the far side of the hearth.

Thomas hastened after him and sat in the chair opposite him. "Alice told me that Casey went to Aspen. She said our secret has been discovered."

"News travels swiftly, I see." Henry pulled a cigar out of his pocket and lit it.

Thomas frowned, gaze troubled. "Does our stranger know everything now?"

"I think so. His name is Simon, by the way. Casey couldn't tell if it's a given name or a surname."

"That's more than we've been able to find out so far."

It was true. Despite diligent attempts, Casey hadn't succeeded in getting much information on the wily stranger. He'd seemed to come from nowhere, knew everyone, but somehow no one knew *him*. He had no criminal history that the state of Colorado was aware of. No background of any kind, at least none that Casey could find.

Thomas flopped back against his chair in a despairing manner. "Only Arthur Randall could have dug up such a man."

Henry nodded and blew out a puff of smoke. "So. . .what are we left with?"

Thomas loosened his cravat. "Threaten or bribe, I'd say."

After much discussion, they settled on the latter. The venue would be a letter, with a convincing amount of money enclosed.

The next morning, Henry spent intense hours poring over the letter's contents.

He conferred with Thomas, and they labored together until they were satisfied.

But two weeks later, their money was returned to them, every cent. They tried again, this time with an even larger bribe. But again, it was returned.

And so they abandoned their efforts and waited. On edge, they waited.

Henry wondered—would Arthur Randall choose to trumpet his newfound knowledge, or would he merely blackmail and gloat?

He feared he knew the answer already.

Chapter 11

Henry was almost grateful when Georgie began to wail. It ended a silence fraught with strain.

Tonight was Miss Oliver's night off, and Georgie had been playing with his wooden animals, which he'd placed in a neat row on the drawing room windowsill above him. He'd been content with his toys for a time, and quietness prevailed despite the fact that the whole family was present. Then Georgie accidentally knocked a giraffe over and it toppled onto an elephant—and all the animals crashed to the floor. He erupted into tears.

"He must be tired," Katie said. She rose from her cushioned piano bench across the room.

Henry hastened to stop her with a raised hand. "I'll get him."

She sank back down, and he stood and went to the window. He stooped and lifted Georgie into his arms, hiding a smile at the way the boy's legs dangled limply in the air. *Aren't we despondent tonight?*

"There, there, lad." He patted Georgie's back and stole a glance at Katie. Her face was turned unswervingly from him, but he could see her reflection in the burnished rosewood piano before her. She looked lovely in a blue taffeta dress that cascaded from the bench to the floor. He considered going over and talking to her but knew they would be keenly observed. Though the others were busy reading or sewing, he could feel their knowing looks. *Noticing me noticing her.* The thought made him want to clout someone.

He hadn't slept well these past weeks. Whenever he tried to doze off, he remembered that night with Katie, and berated himself for it. He also envisioned pulling her back into his bedroom and kissing her, again and again.

Georgie's pathetic sniffs brought Henry back to the present. The boy settled his plump cheek against Henry's chest, his small body now relaxed. *If only a grown man could be so easily consoled.* Henry held the boy closer, rested his chin on the soft waves. *Ah, Georgie, life is so complex.*

He'd just determined to do whatever was needed to get Katie alone, at least attempt an apology, when he heard a commotion coming from the direction of the entrance hall. He could identify Philip's voice, raised in protest, and later, Manfred's. But neither the footman nor the butler's objections were very effective, judging by the swift footsteps that sounded in the hallway.

Every eye in the room went toward the drawn red curtain. In an instant, it was swept aside.

And then, just ahead of the two flustered servants, Simon the stranger strode into the room.

⁓

Katie watched as if in a slow-moving dream as Henry brushed past her, Georgie still in his arms. He didn't pause when he neared the stranger, but reached out, snagged the man's sleeve, and pulled him back across the Oriental rug toward the curtain.

"Come with me."

Something in her husband's voice told Katie who the man was. *The very person who could ruin us is standing in our drawing room.*

The chilling thought caused Katie to realize something else. It wasn't only Georgie she was afraid for. She looked around the room at each face in turn, and a clogging sensation filled her throat.

Thomas was perched on the edge of the settee, weight forward, as if prepared to lurch to his feet. His bold dark eyes and mannish form seemed incongruent with the flowery upholstery beneath him. Alice, seated across from Margaret at the center table, was motionless as a statue, her face wan under her blond halo. Even the matriarch herself, normally so composed, had an unusual alertness about her.

The obstruction in Katie's throat swelled when she looked at Henry. She knew he would do everything in his power to protect his family, to rid them of this threatening presence. A wash of tears made it difficult to see him, but she could envision him, wavy brown hair that hinted at auburn, aristocratically straight posture. A Baxter to the core.

At times they were overly gratified with themselves, yes. The Baxters were stiff, reserved. Plagued by many flaws. *Not Alice, of course, she has none.* But Katie had learned to care for them.

Especially Henry.

She knew her hopes for a real marriage were futile. He could never forget her past, much less return her affection. He'd proved that by his actions the other night. Still, she couldn't help herself.

A sharp movement drew her focus to the front of the room.

She watched as the stranger shrugged off Henry's hand and crossed the floor. He approached the piano, and for a terrible moment, she was sure he meant to speak to her. But he turned and faced Margaret instead. Before he could open his mouth, he was jostled by the footman, who pushed his way forward, cheeks pink and eyes earnest.

"I tried to stop him at the door, ma'am."

Margaret didn't respond but looked past him to Manfred, gaze pointed. The butler gripped the footman's shoulders and steered him from the room.

When they were gone, Margaret lifted her brows at the stranger, her most noticeable movement so far.

"My name is Simon," he told her.

At the distinctive inflection of his voice, Katie started. *He's English.*

His arms were slack at his sides, his manner unhurried. "I'm here on behalf of my employer. I fear I must speak candidly regarding a certain—"

Thomas sprang from his perch and joined Henry, who was standing near Simon. "My brother and I will hear you first, sir."

Henry's jaw was tight, his tone measured. "Yes, come to the library, where we may talk freely."

Simon ignored them both and continued. "My investigation brought me to Denver in the late spring of last year. I had to satisfy myself as to the origin of a certain member of your family, names being changeable, as they are."

Katie felt as though her chest were being squeezed between two heavy objects. She looked over at Henry. He returned her gaze, but other than the expected graveness, his expression was impassive. *He must hate me for what's about to happen.* Warm tears threatened to spill, and she had to will herself to concentrate on what Simon was saying.

"It didn't take long for my ruddy good detective skills to unearth the truth about. . ." He blew a thatch of fawn-colored hair from his eyes and gestured toward Georgie. "You know."

Oh, yes, we know.

"But of course I needed to be sure," he went on. "The winter proved to be the most disobliging I'd ever encountered, so I waited until spring to conduct my interviews, chiefly one in the mountains, in the frostbitten netherworld you call Aspen."

Katie's chest squeezed tighter. She braced herself for what was coming.

"Once my suspicions were confirmed, I notified my employer. I felt obligated to tell him of my findings, you see, out of regard for his best interests—"

He was cut off by a deep voice from the doorway. "But I didn't care."

They turned as one, every soul in the room.

The curtain had been pulled aside to admit a tall figure, an imposing man in a brown beret and high-buttoned gray suit. His eyes were fixed on one person, and one person only.

"I had to see you, Maggie," he said.

Katie swiveled around slowly, slowly on her bench, to behold the ashen face of her mother-in-law.

"Nicky," she breathed. She half rose from her chair, folds of her skirt clutched in a trembling fist.

Simon went to stand next to the imposing man, and faced the room. He looked so pleased, Katie wondered how she could have ever thought him threatening.

"Allow me," he said with an imperial sweep of his hand, "to introduce my employer, His Grace, Nicholas Morgan, Duke of Kentworth."

Chapter 12

The realization that their menacing stranger hadn't been hired by Arthur Randall at all, that he'd never intended to ruin anyone, caused a glorious, loosening sensation in Katie's chest. But she had little time to revel in it, for her attention was once again captured by her mother-in-law.

Katie hardly recognized her, this pale woman who groped with unsteady hands for her chair. *As if she wants to assure herself that it's actually there before she sits down.*

"I didn't mean to upset you," the duke said from the entrance.

Katie glanced over and saw that he hadn't moved. He was gazing at Margaret out of clear blue eyes, accented by distinguished silver brows.

"No, you haven't," she answered. "I just—I never—I thought—" She drew in a long breath. Squared her shoulders. "I never thought I'd see you again."

A soft smile turned his lips upward. Margaret blushed under his unwavering gaze.

She looks almost. . .girlish.

Alice cleared her throat, a dainty sound. "Perhaps Katie and I ought to see to Georgie. It's well past his bedtime." She gave her husband a telling look. "And I know how you and Henry enjoy your after-dinner cigar."

Her gentle suggestion that they offer the pair some privacy was roundly ignored by everyone but the duke, who seemed suddenly aware that he and Margaret weren't alone. His gaze broke from hers, and he removed his beret and glanced at Henry.

"May I come in?" he asked.

Henry hesitated, then stepped aside to clear the path to his mother.

The duke moved forward but stopped several feet short of her. "I heard some time ago, through a rumor I came to believe, that your husband had passed away." He twisted the supple woolen hat in his hands. "Please accept my sincere condolences."

She nodded.

The duke inhaled, pressed on. "As soon as I heard of his passing, I determined to find you. But I didn't know your married name, the surname of this man you'd chosen"—he tilted his head and gave her a self-depreciating grin—"over me."

Margaret seemed about to protest, but remained silent.

Perhaps she is remembering the presence of her sons. Katie was sure they wouldn't wish to hear that their mother had preferred another man to their father.

"I had never asked your fiancé's name, not once." The duke chuckled ruefully. "Hotheaded young fool that I was. I regretted it later, of course, this rashly cutting you out of my life. I didn't have the faintest notion of how to locate you, so I called on my friend, Commissioner Henderson at Scotland Yard, and asked for his best man, preferably one who had connections 'across the pond.'" He shot a look at Simon. "The commissioner gave me precisely that, and my new sleuth left for America. He docked at the New York harbor and began his search in New York City, as might be expected. Then he learned you'd moved, and followed your trail to Denver." His eyes fixed on Margaret. "When he wrote me regarding your eldest son's. . .indiscretion, and the subsequent marriage of your second son, I hardly heard him. All I cared about was that I'd finally found you. I boarded a ship that very day, hoping against hope I might have a second chance with you."

Margaret looked everywhere but at him. Her face, partly hidden beneath her fluttering fan, seemed almost despairing, and Katie wanted to come to her aid. Before she could, however, Alice stood and faced Thomas, her manner resolute.

"Thomas, I think we should be getting home."

He didn't protest this time, but followed her meekly from the room.

Henry shifted the now-sleeping Georgie in his arms and addressed the duke. "I must take my boy to bed." His expression turned warning. "But I shall be back very soon, in case my presence is needed."

Katie almost laughed. *As if his fully grown mother requires a guardian.* She rose from her bench to join him and was surprised when Margaret stopped her.

"Stay, Katriane."

Katie sat back down, eyes wide. She watched Henry leave, then focused her attention on her mother-in-law.

Margaret lowered her fan, still blushing but no longer hesitant. "You must understand, Nicky, when Cousin Sara invited me to join her family on their European holiday, I thought I'd be miserable. Leaving New York just before the social season seemed a dreadful idea." Her brown eyes grew warm, like melting molasses. "But that winter I spent with you was magical. You've no idea. Until then, I'd always done the proper thing. But in England, at your charming country estate, with so many young people my own age, I became another person, one who could skate across the ice with abandon. Toboggan down a steep slope without a care in the world." She shook her head slowly, met his gaze. "The trouble is, you were part of all that."

He seemed to understand her meaning, for he winced. "That was all I was to you? A moment of freedom?"

"I thought so, yes. But I soon realized I'd been mistaken. Only. . .I was already engaged to Alex." She shut and latched her fan, eyes fixed on the motion as though it required great concentration. "I never told you how earnestly my parents desired the match. They were thrilled about Alex. And Mother, whose health was poor, would have been devastated if her one and only child had remained across the ocean, never to return."

There was silence.

"Did you love him?"

Margaret looked not at him, but at Katie as she answered. "No. Not when I married him. I wed him out of family obligation." She held Katie's gaze. "Truth be told, though, I learned to care for him in time."

Katie ached inside. *I already do*, she cried silently. *But your son doesn't feel the same way.*

"And me?" The duke seemed to hold his breath. "Do I have any chance at all?"

Margaret turned her head and looked straight at him. "Yes," she said simply. "You, I always loved."

⁓

Henry basked in the September twilight. He sat in an armless wicker chair in the garden, surrounded by fragrant perennials and pungent herbs. He'd come outdoors to reorder his thoughts, to distance himself from his mother's whirlwind courtship. No party had been too costly, no ball too lavish, no newspaper proclamation too flamboyant for the duke and his bride-to-be. Henry needed a moment to recover from the bustle of it all.

After announcing their engagement, the duke and Henry's mother had made plans for a winter wedding. Henry recalled her shining eyes when she told him she'd decided to be married in England, during the same month she'd first met her Nicky. Henry was glad for them, of course, but his own romantic affairs were so hopeless he had to force down a groan whenever he saw them together.

The back door opened and shut, summoned Henry from his troubled thoughts. He turned to see the duke descend the steps and approach up the stone pathway.

"May I?" The duke gestured toward the chair across from Henry.

Henry nodded.

The duke sat down, and moments passed. Sparrows scratched the damp soil; a swan spread its wings in the small pond. Otherwise, all was still.

"I realized I never asked your permission for your mother's hand," the duke finally said.

Henry managed to look past the fact that this man was taking his mother away from him, and instead saw the trembling fingers, steepled against the noble Grecian nose. "Certainly, you may have it."

The duke's smile began slowly, then spread until crinkles appeared in the corners of his eyes. "I know it isn't easy. I regret the necessity of stealing your mother away so permanently."

Henry picked up a pebble and threw it into the pond. "Well, I suppose it can't be helped."

"Yes. It's rather too bad you can't join us. Katriane will be an adequate chaperone, no doubt, but surely you'll miss her and Georgie."

Henry froze.

The pond, the flower beds, the herb boxes became a haze of shapes.

"Pardon?" It didn't sound like his own voice asking the question.

"When they accompany us on our voyage next week. Of course it wouldn't do for an unmarried couple to travel alone, and your mother will need help if she's to be properly fitted for her trousseau in Paris."

"And just when," the frigid voice that wasn't his asked, "will my family be returning to me?"

A frown creased the duke's brow. "After the wedding. I thought you knew."

Henry's mind turned from frost to steel. "Oh, but I didn't."

The duke put his hand on Henry's shoulder. "Come with us," he urged.

"That's not possible. I have a bank to manage."

"Let Thomas—"

"Thomas is efficient, but not careful. He needs someone to temper his brash ambitions."

The duke hesitated. "It's only for a few months. Surely you can be away for such a short time."

Henry pulled his shoulder free from the warm hand and stood. "Take Alice with you." *She, at least, is certain to return to her husband.* "My wife and son are going nowhere." With a feeble smile intended to soften his words, he departed the garden.

He had a thing or two to say to Katie.

Chapter 13

Henry strode into the girlish room without knocking, dismissed the maid mid-brushstroke, and thrust the door shut behind her.

Despite the rage boiling inside, he almost stifled his tirade when he saw Katie, twisted in her chair to look at him, eyes startled and vulnerable amid her riot of curls.

Almost.

"Might I inform you," he seethed, "that Georgie is *my* child, and I will not allow you to whisk him off on a perilous voyage, with his third birthday not yet behind him." He glared at her. "And may I ask, whether you were ever planning to tell me about this little venture?"

Katie rose from her dressing table, chin trembling, and laid the porcelain mirror on her dresser alongside several delicate perfume bottles. She faced away from him, fumbled with her chemise, presumably securing the loose ribbons at her neck.

He clenched his jaw at the knowledge that she considered it necessary to be so modest in his presence. Not that it did much good. Her arms were bare and white, her shapely ankles exposed beneath her long slip. Such a vision mightily jeopardized his resolve, but he refused to be moved.

"Well?" he prompted once she'd finished.

She turned around, the evidence of tears on her cheeks. His resolve wavered.

"You'll pardon me for wanting to be of assistance to your mother." She wiped at her cheeks with the inside of her wrist. "And for not guessing you'd miss Georgie. Until this moment, I didn't know you thought of him as much more than an obligation."

"Don't do that."

She sniffed. "Do what?"

He hated himself for softening, for letting her tears affect him. "You know Georgie is my son in every way that matters—and I'm not about to lose him."

Her hands slipped up to cover her face and her slim shoulders began to shake. "No, I didn't know."

Muffled as her voice was, he'd heard her. He stood there for a moment, the sound of her weeping colliding against his ears like a crashing wave. He wanted to go to her, to hold her and console her. But he was sure she wouldn't yield to his embrace, that she'd keep herself apart from him.

He warred with himself for a few tense seconds, then surrendered with an expelled breath. He crossed the room, reached out, and awkwardly patted her arm. The pats soon turned into a soft grasp, a pulling her toward him. And by the same instinct that often prompted him to comfort Georgie, he drew Katie into his arms.

And by an instinct that was nothing like the one that prompted him to comfort Georgie, he lowered his head and kissed her, tentatively, just above her right brow. Then again near her ear, and in her loose hair, more than once.

She went rigid and jerked away from him.

Though he'd expected her reaction, it still cut like a blade. *Am I really so repellent to her?* The thought worsened his pain for an instant. But then he looked closer. In the rapid rise and fall of her chest, he saw something very unlike repulsion.

He summoned his willpower and stepped away from her. Watched as her hands formed fists at her sides. From her safe distance, she blew the hair out of her eyes, the puff forceful.

"You came storming in here," she fumed, "and berated me like a child."

He kept his voice even with effort. "I'd just had some disconcerting news."

Her eyes shot flames at him. "Don't pretend you care."

The boiling within him, formerly diminished to a low simmer, leaped back to life. "You decided, without consulting me, to take our child and sail across an unpredictable sea, and you say *I* don't care?"

"I assure you, I'm perfectly capable of watching over him for a few short months."

"My concern for Georgie's safety is nothing compared to my concern for. . .his desire to return at all." The moment he'd spoken the nonsensical words, he wished them back. But it was too late.

Her expression turned from obstinate to quizzical. "He's two years old. He won't know the difference between one side of the ocean and the other."

"He's not the one who's keen to get away from me. Nor the one breaking my heart."

She stared.

He longed to unsay it. There was no way she could mistake it now, his caring. He might as well follow through with the rest. *Yes, I'm in love with you. Please, please, don't go.*

But she'd loved his brother once, and he knew he couldn't bear hearing that she still did.

❧

Katie steeled herself against the guilt. She shouldn't have made plans without consulting him, of course. *But does he think I've enjoyed being treated like a used-up pair of shoes?*

She searched her mind for a civil response. *Help me, Father.* "It's been difficult," she said finally. "Knowing you haven't forgiven me for my—for Jackson."

There was a lengthy silence.

"I'm hardly qualified to throw the first stone," he said.

Had she only imagined his bitterness? "That night in your room, when you spoke of Jackson, I reached out to you, and—" She faltered under his steadfast gaze.

"I pulled away?" A ghost of a grin touched his lips. "If you must know, confounded helpless passion can take odd forms at times. I was afraid that my brother held a place in your heart, a place I might never possess."

A tingle began, somewhere in her middle, a sprouting of hope. But she maintained her wary distance.

"The truth is," he said, "I've wanted to make amends for some time." He reached to brush the back of his hair, a discomfited gesture. "In the beginning, I did condemn you, which I greatly regret. But then I stopped seeing a fallen woman and began to see the mother of my child, a faithful wife, a true Christian. By that night in my room, my feelings had changed completely. Only. . ." Again he seemed to have trouble looking at her. "I was jealous, pure and simple."

She gaped at him. All these months, she'd thought he'd rejected her, and he was merely jealous? "You had no reason to be."

He hesitated. Swallowed. "Then tell me you don't still care for him."

She hoped her eyes would assure him. "I never did, not really. It was a fleeting infatuation, gone long before the sun rose." Her cheeks burned, her gaze departed from his. It mortified her to discuss such a subject with him.

Apparently he didn't suffer the same embarrassment. He narrowed the space between them in two steps, tipped her chin up with one finger. "You've no need to blush in front of me. I'm your husband, you know."

At the moment, all she knew was that his finger now traced a path along her jaw and across her lips. And that the expanse of his chest, soft in its gray pullover, beckoned her, as did his scent of pine needles and cloves.

"I was—" She strained to formulate words. "The reality was, I was naive. I had accepted a ride home in his carriage, very stupidly. He asked if he could come inside for a cup of tea, and then. . ." Tears formed in her eyes. "It was one time, Henry, and it was over."

"Hush, you've told me now." He slid his hand up, tilted her chin upward once again. "Let's be done with it, shall we?"

She nodded but couldn't quite meet his gaze.

"I've been a wretched lout of a husband," he said. "But God is different than I am. He promises to forgive our sins, and our lawless deeds to 'remember no more.'" He broke into a charming smile. "Might we try to do the same?"

At his question, her heart overflowed with joy. *God, how gracious You are.* She was clothed in mercy from on high and never wanted to leave the heavenly warmth.

She was drawn back to earth by the husky sound of her husband's voice.

"I assume you know I want to kiss you?"

She nearly lost her breath, had trouble nodding.

He rubbed a hand across his barely whiskered jaw. A flush began in his neck and continued up to his hairline. "I also assume you know that—that I love you."

She knew how hard it was for him to say it. Men in his highbrow world didn't care to make such deeply personal confessions. So she wound her arms around his neck and gave him a cheeky grin.

"Tell me again," she said. Then she raised her face toward his, to welcome the words of love he whispered against her lips.

Rebecca Jepson is a homebody who loves a good book, a cup of freshly ground coffee, and all things autumn. She dreamed of being a writer since she was thirteen and has been creating stories ever since. She has traveled extensively, to places that inspire her stories. Her favorite destinations include Russia, New England, and the Alaskan wilderness. She lives in sunny Reno, Nevada, with her software engineer husband, Mike.

Not So Pretty Penny

by Amy Lillard

Thou art all fair, my love; there is no spot in thee.
Song of Solomon 4:7

Chapter 1

Kansas, 1867

P enelope Pinehurst marched down the wooden sidewalk ignoring the looks she received. She was accustomed to people staring at her, and frankly she didn't care. She had a mission today, and she was going to see it through.

Her heart thumped in her chest at the thought of what she was about to do. Still, regardless of her anxiety over the situation, she had prayed about it, and she knew this was her only answer.

She paused at the entrance to the sheriff's office and nervously smoothed her hands down the front of her dress. She really wished she had something better to wear for such a special occasion, but the war had been hard on them all. Still a day dress made from twice-turned-out flour sacks wasn't the best attire to meet one's destiny. And that's exactly what she was here to do.

She stiffened her shoulders, cleared her throat, and strengthened her resolve. This was her answer. The only answer she had. With more aplomb than she truly had, she trooped into the building.

The sheriff sat behind his desk, feet braced on top, hands behind his head, hat tilted to shade his eyes from the sun streaming through the windows. She didn't know if he was asleep or merely ignoring her. He didn't move as she halted in front of his desk.

"Ahem." She cleared her throat hoping to gain his attention. No such luck. "Ahem." Louder this time. But still he didn't move.

"Sheriff." She tried again. And still he didn't move. Looking around she found a large book sitting to the side of his desk. She had no idea what it was doing there. As far as she knew the sheriff couldn't read. Not one to cast stones, she was glad the book was there. It would serve her purpose nicely. She picked it up with both hands and released it, allowing it to land on the desk with a loud *thwack*.

"What—?" The sheriff was on his feet in an instant. It might've been hard for her to wake him, but he seemed to be very alert once she got him there.

He looked around as if he was somehow expecting to be ambushed, then caught sight of her and grimaced.

She didn't mind. She was used to such looks. She got them from everybody she encountered. He could look at her however he wanted. Just as long as he found her a husband.

"Sheriff Riley," she started, "I'm in need of a husband."

He eyed her warily as if he wasn't sure how to respond. Was he afraid that she had set her sights on him? Not likely. The sheriff wasn't marrying material, and a lawman running off and getting killed was the last thing she needed. Her brother and her father had gone off to war and never came back. She still prayed every night that they would return, and in her heart God assured her they would. She just had to keep on—to persevere. She had to have faith. And so she would. But more than faith, she needed a strong back to work the land, plant the seeds, and help bring in a crop. A strong back that she didn't have. And then there was the matter of her neighbor.

"A husband?" the sheriff asked.

She nodded, her straw hat moving slightly with the motion. Her hat pin was slightly on the worn side, not quite as strong as it used to be. But that wouldn't matter as soon as she got this crop in.

"I heard about this town where a woman could buy a husband if'n she had enough money. A husband from the gallows, see?"

The sheriff gave a soft nod. "Go on."

"I find myself in need of a husband," she said. "And I'd like to buy one of these men from the gallows to help me bring in a crop this year." She had done what she could last year on her own. And the year before. She'd barely had enough to eke out an existence, but everyone around her had fared about the same. The war had devastated their small town of Cooper, Kansas. But now she needed more than to scrape by. She needed a full crop. She needed to start living again. The war was over, and she didn't want her father and brother coming home to empty fields, no money coming in, no way to support themselves.

"Now, Miss Pinehurst," the sheriff started in that condescending tone she knew all too well. But she was prepared for it.

She tossed a small purse onto his desk. It jangled as it landed—the last of the money she'd saved. She only had enough for seeds and some supplies to get them through until the harvest. She didn't turn loose of the money lightly. "You'll find enough in there, Sheriff, to compensate the state for the release of the prisoner."

The sheriff rubbed his scruffy beard and eyed her dubiously. "Miss Penny," he started again, "why would you want to go and buy yourself a rascal for a husband?"

Penny shook her head. She didn't really want to buy a rascal for a husband, but considering the visit she got from her closest neighbor the night before, purchasing a husband was the one thing she had to do. Jackson Alexander might be the best-looking man in the county, and he might have the most money in the county, but she knew he only wanted her for her land. He had come in all "You're so beautiful," and a bunch of other bunk that she knew wasn't true. She hadn't reached the ripe old age of twenty-five not knowing what she really looked like. And not to know what the children called her behind her back. Not So Pretty Penny.

That she could handle. She had lived her whole life with her face. What she couldn't deal with was a lying man and empty fields.

"As I see it, Sheriff, a rascal husband might make for a very grateful man. Wouldn't you be mighty thankful if someone saved you from hanging?"

He only had to think about it a moment before he nodded. "But—"

Penny shook her head. "I just need to know how this works. Do I get my choice?"

"I reckon," the sheriff grumbled.

Penny suspected that he would rather not allow her this at all, but she wasn't going to call him out on it. She needed the sheriff as an ally not an enemy.

"You just go on down and give them a look-see and let me know if you see one you think might be a good. . .match," he finally finished.

Penelope gave a small nod, and with her heart pounding and shoulders back, she walked toward the iron-barred cells. She'd just reached the first one when the sheriff called, "You know they can turn you down, right?"

She did, but she was banking that the man she chose would be so grateful to be free that he wouldn't care what she looked like. Well, she could only hope.

The first cell held a man as old as Methuselah. He had scraggly white hair surrounding a big bald patch smack in the center. His beard was gray and tangled, and he leered at her, revealing several missing teeth. Aside from the fact that he was old enough to be her father, he didn't look strong enough to hold up a plow, much less guide it behind a horse.

A younger man sat next to him, a *much* younger man, and regardless of his sad eyes and soft-looking brown hair, she knew he was nearly half her age. What he was doing in jail was anybody's guess, but she knew he would have to stay there. She needed a man not a boy.

The second of the jail's two cells held a man who appeared so dirty and unkempt that Penny was unsure of his age. His long dark hair hung in his face. She couldn't tell if it was naturally that dark or an accumulation of months of grime and dirt.

Maybe this isn't such a good idea, she thought. It had seemed like a perfectly solid plan last night sitting at her dinner table, praying and sorting through her options. Coming to town and buying a husband from the gallows. She'd heard other women who had done it, and as far as she knew everything came out just fine. Though she really didn't know. She had faith. The Lord had given her this idea, and she was going to see it through. She turned from the last prisoner and walked back toward the sheriff. "Are there any more?"

"Sorry." The sheriff's lips twitched as if battling a grin. "That's all we got today.

You want to check back tomorrow and see if we have any new ones come in?"

He was making fun of her. But she had been made fun of her whole life, and frankly she didn't care. She needed a husband and she needed one now. Today. This could not wait any longer. The crops needed to get in the ground so they would have time to grow and mature before harvest. That meant marrying somebody, dragging him out to the farm, and setting to work.

She turned on her heel and looked back toward the jail cells and the scraggly band of criminals there. She just had to trust in the Lord. Hadn't He led her here? Hadn't He provided these men? Though she thought she might need a little more than faith if she took home the older man or even the younger man, really. That left her only one choice.

"You're sure there are no others?" A girl had to make certain.

"Nope."

"*What's he in for?*" jumped to the tip of her tongue, but she bit back the words. She wasn't sure she wanted to know. The only solution she had was getting married. She couldn't back out. Not now.

The dark-haired man stirred, as if he sensed her eyes upon him. He opened them and they looked as black as pitch. Black hair, black eyes. She had never seen anything like it. A small shudder ran through her.

"H–him," she stammered.

"Oh, Brannock over there?"

Penny gave a reassuring nod, though it was for her own benefit more than the sheriff's. "Yes. Him. The one with the dark hair."

The sheriff slipped around the desk and made his way to stand over next to the bars. "Well now, Brannock, it seems like it's your lucky day. This here lady wants to marry you. Ain't that something?"

Brannock didn't move from his slouched-over spot in the corner of one bench. He simply let his gaze rove over her as if taking in every detail of her appearance. He neither flinched nor sneered, but she didn't need a facial expression from him to know that she was homely.

Her hair was of no particular color at all. Sometimes it looked brown, sometimes it had a reddish tint to it. Sometimes it looked blond, but never did it look the same two days in a row. She had a nice curl to it she supposed, but that wasn't saying an awful lot when it was compared to a nose that was too big for the rest of her face and a mouth that was a little too wide. Her jaw was squared off, and she had a small indent in the middle of her chin. To top it all off, she had an unfortunate gap between her two front teeth. Even more unfortunate, she tended to be the tallest person in the room.

Once upon a time her father had told her she was striking and imposing, but those were just nice ways to say that she wasn't very pretty, and she tended to put men off because of her stature. She understood. It was just the way the world was. For some reason God had seen fit to make her this way, and though she wouldn't understand it in this life, she knew one day she would sit at His hand and could ask Him why He had given her this cross to bear.

"So whaddya say?" the sheriff asked. "I can't make you, but if you want to marry her that can be arranged."

"Today," Penny said, reaffirming her urgency. That was ridiculous really. Of course it was urgent. Why else would she pick a man about to hang for unknown crimes if she wasn't at least a bit on the desperate side?

The man stood slowly as if he had all day and then some. Penny supposed that he was in no hurry to die. Or maybe he was in no hurry to get married. He made his way to the bars never taking his eyes off her as he approached.

Even though invincible iron stood between the two of them, Penny took a quick step back.

He wrapped his hands around the bars and dragged his gaze from her, settling it on the sheriff. "And if I marry her I get out of here?"

"I reckon so," the sheriff said.

The man shook his head. "There's no reckon to it. I either get out or I don't." His voice was hard as flint.

"Yeah," the sheriff said. "You marry her, and you get out of here. But let me tell you something. You make a run for it, and I will hunt you down and hang you on the spot." For all his bumbling and laziness, Penny knew he meant what he said. A chill ran down her spine at the words.

The two men stood, their gazes locked in some sort of primitive showdown.

Finally the dark-haired man gave a quick nod of consent.

She was getting married! The thought should have filled her with joy beyond joy. Now she would have someone to help her farm the land, bring in a good crop, and keep her land in the family. When her father and her brother got back, they would be so very proud of everything that she had done.

But she couldn't rejoice just yet. There was something entirely too sinister about the man. Whether it was his brooding gaze or his dark hair she wasn't sure. Or maybe it was the slant of his mouth that said he had seen too much and he just didn't care anymore. Whatever it was, she didn't know. But this felt less like salvation and more like a deal with the devil.

⌒∽

George Washington Brannock had never given much thought to wedding days. Never even thought he would have one. But had he been asked, he would've never thought he'd be standing next to a woman while his hair felt so dirty he was certain it had bugs in it and his clothes hadn't been washed in weeks. No sir, this was not at all how he imagined his life going.

"You may kiss your bride," the minister finished, smiling jovially and looking from one to the other.

Though Wash had never thought much about weddings, he would have certainly been able to come up with a better place than the front office of the jail to hold such a service. But, alas, that was the predicament he found himself in.

Wash turned toward the woman at his side. She was tall. Nearly as tall as he was. She had a strong face, not quite attractive but striking all the same. It was the kind of face that a person didn't readily forget.

Every bride deserved a kiss on her wedding day, but he was in no condition to be kissing anyone, however much it was only a marriage of convenience. He was beyond filthy and was certain he had more crawlies than he did hairs on his head.

He stuck out his hand to shake then looked down at his grime-crusted fingernails and cracked skin.

He mumbled something that he hoped passed for an apology and retracted his hand.

The sheriff leered at them. "Well, now, ain't that special?"

Wash wasn't sure what was so special about it. Except that now he was out of jail and he could find the man who framed him and put him in jail in the first place. The sheriff's warning from earlier came back to mind. He would have to hang out there for a while longer and keep up pretenses. The gentleman in him knew that he owed the woman at his side a little something for releasing him. The least he could do was stay through the harvest as she wanted him to, then head out. He'd been waiting almost a year for his revenge. What was a couple more months?

∞

Penny pulled the wagon onto the dirt road that led to her farm, all too aware of the stranger she had just married. Almost home. What then?

She tried not to notice the sad and sorry state of the house. She had done the best she could, but keeping up with everything was more than she could handle. She was only one person. She had done okay for a while, but then everything had gotten the better of her. Now so much needed to be done that she wasn't even sure where to start.

She pulled the wagon to a stop and got out, not bothering to wait for him as he scrambled down the other side.

Red, the brown-and-black hound dog she kept for both security and companionship, strolled out of the barn to see who had come out to the house. Catching sight of her, he wagged his tail and nudged his head against her affectionately. She scratched behind one floppy ear then turned back to Wash, unsure of what to call him.

During the ceremonies she had learned that his given name was George Washington Brannock but that he preferred to be called Wash. Crazy name if she'd ever heard one, but who was she to say? Wash just seemed like such a tame label to put on a man who appeared as dangerous as the devil and twice as handsome.

Yes, she had watched him a bit as they were riding home. She'd glanced at him from under the cover of her lashes. Under all the grime and dirt were strong cheekbones and an even stronger jaw. His eyes were piercing, his hair midnight-black, and he carried himself with a regal bearing worthy of the prince of England. In short, he was dangerous. Dangerous to a homely girl like her. She could only hope that he would do his job, abide by her rules, and help her get the farm ready for her brother and father to return.

"I suppose you want to wash up," she said. How did one address the husband after the wedding? She had no idea. Aside from the fact that her mother died when she was just eight years old, and her father never remarried, she had no experience with men whatsoever. She didn't know what men did after a wedding. She didn't know what men did at all. "I can get you some warm water."

He gave a small nod, his expression masked. Even those dark eyes hid whatever was going on inside his head. He looked neither displeased nor pleased, neither happy nor unhappy, neither scared nor courageous. "That would be good. It's been a long time since I had a bath."

Heat rose into Penny's cheeks. Her face felt hot enough to fry eggs, but she continued on as if nothing out of the ordinary were happening. She gave him a quick nod. "If you give me a few minutes, I can heat some water and have you a right nice bath in no time at all."

She didn't have to ask him twice. "Thank you." A grin worked its way across his expression. Slightly crooked, a little mischievous, and a whole lot of handsome. When he smiled like that, Penny's knees got week, and she wanted to collapse into a heap at his feet rather than press on with her promise. Her heart gave a flip in her chest as she walked past him toward the door of her snug log house.

If he could make her react to him like that when he had done nothing but casually smile. . . She shook her head. What had she gotten herself into? A deal with the devil if she had ever had one.

Chapter 2

Penny stirred the beans and checked the corn bread baking in the oven. Everything was almost ready to put on the table. She didn't know what kind of food Wash had been accustomed to before his incarceration, but she was fairly certain anything she put in front of him would be much better than what he'd been eating at the hands of Sheriff Riley.

She had laid some clothes out for Wash to wear. He was about the same size as her brother. Maybe a bit taller, maybe a little leaner, but she was fairly certain that Harvey's clothes would suffice in a pinch. And after looking at the sorry state of Wash's only set of clothes, the situation could definitely be called "a pinch."

"I hope this is okay." Wash came out from behind the screen that Penny used to separate the hallway that led to the bedrooms from the kitchen and living room where she now stood.

He wore one of her brother's shirts with a tie at the neck. The sleeves were too short and the tan pants had a good two inches from the hem to the top of Wash's ratty black shoes. He'd used a length of rope to tie around the waist and cinch the pants up tighter, and she vowed to make him something better to wear. Surely she could let out a pair of Harvey's old pants in the length and take them up in the waist. Maybe she could find a halfway decent flour sack and make him a new shirt. Times were hard, yes, but that didn't mean he had to go around in someone else's clothing all the time. He was her husband, after all.

Husband! The word slammed into her like a runaway bull.

Dear Lord, please let me know I did the right thing. I brought a stranger into my home, but I didn't see any other way. Please keep us both safe, and get us through this trying time, she prayed. *In Jesus' name, amen.*

"Are you hungry?" she asked, not able to address the state of his clothing at all. Somehow that seemed too intimate for two people who'd just met, even if they were married.

Wash smiled, and if she thought his earlier grin was irresistible, this one was doubly so. She started to close her eyes and pray again but instead, just ran the words over in her head. *Dear Lord, please let this be the right decision.*

She set the table quickly then came around to one side of the bench and sat down. Wash sat down opposite her, his eyes feasting on the food before them. He reached for a piece of corn bread and had it halfway to his mouth before she admonished, "We need to pray first."

He looked sheepish as if he'd forgotten that was one of the rules of the outside. Who knew what he had experienced in jail? Or how regular his meals had come. Penny hadn't thought to ask him if he'd been in the war or if he'd served in either army. Times like that made a man pray when he could and not so much when the world thought he should.

He set the piece of corn bread down and clasped his hands in front of him, bowing his head without another word.

Penny blessed their meal somehow realizing that it'd been a long time since Washington Brannock had talked to the Lord.

The silence surrounding them as they ate fairly hummed with tension. The situation was strange, not the same situation a person found herself in every day. Married to a stranger, one day in jail and the next trying to save the family farm. Neither one of them had anything to talk about, yet both felt the need for conversation.

Penny knew that she wasn't much to look at, but she could sew, she could cook, and she could clean. So what if she wasn't the prettiest girl in Crawford County? She could hold her own with anybody when it came to cooking.

Wash wiped his mouth and patted his stomach. "I know this may not mean much, seein's how I've been in jail for a few months. But that was the best meal I've had in a long while, Miss Pinehurst." She didn't bother to correct him. She wasn't Miss Pinehurst anymore. She was actually Mrs. Brannock. Though neither one of them was fooling themselves about the state of their marriage.

"I'm glad you enjoyed it, Mr. Brannock." Who knew she would be calling her own husband "mister"?

He pushed back from the table and remarkably enough took his plate over to the washboard and set it down. Then he turned back to her, his expression unreadable. "Is there anything you'd like me to do tonight?"

Penny shook her head. "We can get started first thing in the morning with the plowing and the planting. If that's okay with you?" she asked.

"And what are the other. . .arrangements?" His expression never altered as he said the words. Yet Penny's face filled with red-hot heat. "I'm sure you'll agree that our marriage is not one of the traditional nature."

He nodded.

"For now, if you wouldn't mind sleeping in the barn."

She watched his expression for any flicker of emotion, but there was none. He simply gave a quick nod then spun on his heel and headed out the door.

Penny stood at the window and watched him stride across the yard to the barn. It was a disgraceful way to treat a guest, a man she'd just married, a fellow human being on the road to postwar recovery, but she couldn't ask him to stay in the house with her. There were three other beds besides hers, but somehow it seemed too intimate, too much like a real marriage to have him under the roof with her. As much as she daydreamed about faraway places and being beautiful, she knew better than to attach a fantasy to this situation. She wasn't plain, she was downright homely. And she knew it.

The next morning Penny woke with the sun and started breakfast. They wouldn't have much, just biscuits and coffee, but it was better than nothing. Wash was in for a hard day's work, and she vowed to make up for the lack of meat as soon as she could. Maybe once all the planting was complete she would see if a hen wasn't producing and they could have chicken for supper.

Smiling to herself, she set about her chores. Wash headed to the field and she was left alone for the morning. Aside from knowing that Wash was plowing, her morning was no different than it had been before she had gotten married.

She cleaned the breakfast dishes then headed outside to hoe the weeds from the garden plot. The small household garden had been her salvation in the past couple of years. It had provided her enough food to keep her going, but now she had a hungry man to feed. She would need twice the crop this year that she had the last. But with a husband in the fields, the two of them stood a better chance at success, at having a bit of money left over after everything had been paid.

The sun had risen to directly overhead when Penny stopped and wiped an arm across her brow. Spring in Kansas could be unpredictable, and the weather had turned hot today. But it wasn't the heat that caught her attention, but the rattle of a wagon. She looked up to see someone coming down the lane that led to her house. From this distance she couldn't tell who it was, but she stood there and waited until she could make out the driver.

"Lord, give me strength," she prayed.

She loved going to church in town. She loved the small church and all the people in the town, getting together and hearing God's Word. She loved the preacher and how he took the Word of God and made it understandable, how he brought it to all the good citizens of Cooper every Sunday. But his wife. . .

"Yoo-hoo!" The falsetto voice called as Margaret Benson waved enthusiastically from her perch in the wagon.

"Hello." Penny waved back.

"I just wanted to come out to see you today," Margaret said.

Penny gave her a small smile, one that she hoped wasn't too encouraging and yet wasn't too much of a scowl. If she had learned one thing since being in Pastor Benson's congregation, it was to limit her time with Margaret to as little as possible.

"What brings you out today?" Penny asked, saying a quick prayer that she didn't sound too inhospitable.

She had a lot of work to do. And she didn't know if Wash was coming back to the house for a meal. She supposed he would, that was what men did, wasn't it? They went out in the fields, plowed all morning, then came home and had a meal and went back out and plowed some more. But how was she to know? She had never been married before. That was what her father had done. She could only assume that Wash would do the same thing. Yet as it was right now, the sun was high in the sky, and she didn't have anything for him to eat.

"I hope you're not too busy." Margaret lifted up her skirts and made her way toward Penny.

"Of course not." She smoothed her hands over her dress, hoping she wasn't too dusty and grimy from being outside all morning. Margaret Benson looked as fresh as a spring rain, but the young woman always appeared that way. She had to have been at least ten years younger than her husband, but secretly Penny suspected it was more like twenty. Margaret was beautiful, and any man could see why she would catch a man's eye. Blond hair in perfect ringlets, blue eyes that sparkled like the sky after a rain. Her skin was smooth, and her teeth perfectly straight. Her chin a feminine point.

"I was just going in the house to get a drink," Penny said. "Would you like to join me?" She had to ask. Didn't she?

Margaret shook her head. "Oh no, I can't stay for long. I have to head out to the Tyrell place. Becky is supposed to have her baby soon, and I wanted to check on her beforehand."

Margaret smiled, that perfect, beautiful smile that made Penny feel as plain as dirt.

"But I did want to talk to you about something."

That was exactly what she was afraid of. "Would you like to go to the porch and sit a spell?"

Again, Margaret flashed her that beaming smile and nodded. "That would be lovely."

Penny led Margaret up the porch steps and over to the rocking chair and the bench she had placed there so long ago. It was a favorite place for her and her father to come out and sit. Sometimes her brother joined them as they watched the sunset. They whittled and drank lemonade, talked, and otherwise enjoyed each other's company. They would have those times again. She was sure of it. She just had to be patient and keep things going until her father and her brother returned.

"What's on your mind, Margaret?" Penny settled down onto the bench, allowing her guest to have the more comfortable rocking chair.

Margaret sat and fanned herself, rocking back and forth as she mulled over her words. "I just received some distressing news," she said. "I was in town and Sheriff Riley told me that you bought yourself a husband from the gallows. Please tell me this isn't true."

Her solemn words almost made Penny laugh. Almost. Except there wasn't anything particularly funny about the situation. Nothing funny about the desperation of others. She'd simply done what she had to do. "I'm not in the habit of lying, Margaret. That's true. I bought a husband yesterday."

Margaret drew back as if she had been faced with the serpent himself. Then she shook her head. "Oh Penny, Penny, Penny," she moaned. "Why would you do such a thing?"

"I need a husband," she replied matter-of-factly. Women like Margaret would never understand situations that faced women like Penny. It was a man's world, and the men were in short supply these days. Penny had to do what she had to do to keep the farm running. Not to mention Jackson's not-so-wonderful suggestion that she marry him. She might have, too, had he not started spouting off about her beauty. That's when she had known that Jackson Alexander was only after her father's land. He cared nothing for her. Nothing at all.

"The sheriff told me that he was arrested for murder."

Murder? Penny's heart gave a hard thump. To say that she hadn't instinctively known that would be a lie, but to hear Margaret say the words. . .

"Surely there's a better way." Margaret stood. "There are other ways, to be certain."

Penny shook her head. "But this was the only way available to me, so I took it."

"I don't understand."

Suddenly uncomfortable with the situation and the conversation, Penny pushed herself to her feet and fortified her resolve. She had made her decision. "I appreciate your concern, Margaret. But really, I'm fine. There's no need for you to worry about me."

"Of course I worry about you."

Penny herded Margaret toward the porch steps. The quicker she got the preacher's wife back into her wagon and on the road once more, the quicker she could forget this conversation ever happened. "There's no need, really."

"But you don't know this man," Margaret protested as she took the first step.

Penny plowed on. "I'm fine," she said.

"But—" Margaret continued, still reluctantly making her way down the stairs.

"I hate that you wasted your time coming out here." Penny made her voice as cordial as she could. She didn't have to—shouldn't have to—defend her decision to anybody. This was her farm, and she could do with it as she saw fit. If that meant going into town and buying herself a husband, then that was what she would do. Did.

She continued nudging Margaret toward her wagon. Once she got the woman back on the road, she would make them something to eat and have about the rest of her day.

As if sensing her plan, Margaret stopped and raised one hand. "Penny, I have to say that this idea of yours to buy a husband from the gallows is a terrible one."

Never mind that it was already done.

"I need help with the farm, Margaret," she patiently explained once again. "I know it might be hard for you to understand. But I need to keep this land in my family for when my father and my brother return."

"Surely there's another way." Margaret suddenly dug in her heels and refused to go any farther. They were standing closer to the house than to the yard and the wagon Margaret had been driving.

"If there is, I've had yet to find it."

Margaret looked as if she was about to say something else, but Penny shook her head and cut off her words. "Margaret, let's be honest here. I'm not exactly marriage material."

Margaret sputtered. "There's a lot more to marriage than beau—I mean, look—uh, pleasing attributes."

That might be true, but a pretty face went a long way when men knew they had their choice of the women. Even if men hadn't been in such a short supply, she still would be the last one to get married in these parts.

"Margaret, I appreciate your concern, but I'm quite aware of my lack of beauty."

Once again Margaret started to speak, but Penny knew that if this conversation was going to end before supper, she needed to be blunt. "I didn't get to be twenty-five years old and unmarried without a reason," she said. "If I was ever going to find a husband, this was the only way." Not often did she have to say those words aloud, and though she was used to them rattling around in her head, it hurt to hear them. No matter that they were true, no matter that she lived with this every day, they still hurt. So she was proud that her voice was steady and even as she spoke.

"But, Penny—"

Penny cut her off once again. "Thank you, for your concern, Margaret. But I think Becky Tyrell needs you more than I do right now."

Thankfully the preacher's wife got the hint and climbed into her wagon. "If you ever feel in danger. . ." she started.

Penny hid her smile. "I'll be sure to let you know."

Margaret's starch deflated as if the worry had seeped out of her rapidly.

She turned her buggy around and started back down the lane.

Penny watched her go, trying to pretend that words didn't cut. Even when they were her own.

❧

Wash stood at the side of the house, tin cup halfway between the fountain and his lips as he listened to the two women talk. He felt as if someone had taken a flying leap right into the middle of his chest. His breath hung suspended, not quite in his lungs, not quite out.

Is that how she saw herself? Not attractive, without beauty? No, he couldn't say that Penelope Pinehurst was beautiful. Not like the woman who had just left. But to hear her say the words aloud, to hear her speak them to another human being, cut him like a knife. Is that what they thought was important around here?

He remembered the square set of her shoulders as she marched into the jailhouse yesterday and demanded a husband. She hadn't known he was watching at the time. But a man didn't sit in jail without keeping at least one eye open at all times. He'd learned that the hard way.

But to think that she didn't deserve a husband because somehow God had left her out. . . He shook his head.

"Wash!" Penny came around the side of the house and was brought up short when she saw him standing there. She looked back to where she had come from then turned to him once again. "I didn't know you were here." Her voice became small. He could almost see the wheels in her head turning over, trying to decide if he had heard what she'd said about herself or not. Trying to decide whether or not she should say something to him about it. Evidently against won, and she kept her mouth shut.

"I'm hungry." Finally the water made it all the way to his lips and wet his parched throat. It had been a long time since he'd plowed a field, and he'd forgotten how dusty and dirty it could be.

"I–I'll make us something to eat." She lifted her skirts and started for the house.

He had a hard time concentrating on the meal. Or rather her continuous chatter during the meal. She talked about each field and what her father and brother had planted there in the years before the war. She rattled on about what the almanac said about planting this year and anything she had heard lately concerning President Johnson.

She hadn't been this nervous yesterday. Now he had to wonder: Was she upset because of what the woman had forced her to admit about herself or because she knew his supposed crime?

"And then I asked for the recipe—"

"I didn't kill him." His quiet words cut through hers.

"W–what?"

"I didn't kill him." He laid his fork to one side of his plate and leaned back. The bench around the table had no back to it so the motion was small, but he realized as he ate and she talked that he had hunched over his plate as if someone was about to take it from him. Old habits and all that.

She shifted uncomfortably in her seat. "Well, then. . ." she trailed off as if she didn't know what to say.

"I was framed. See—" He stopped. What did the details matter? He was still accused of murder, and the guilty man was still out there. There was no justice in this world, but he would extract his. "The true killer is still out there, and I aim to see him pay for his crime. I'll plant your crops. I'll even bring them in, but after that..."

"I see." She didn't appear surprised by his revelation. He could only muse that she had realized his plans from the beginning. Or maybe she thought that he viewed her as everyone else did, all these people who talked about her and to her as if she were somehow less of a person.

"It has nothing to do with you."

"Of course not." She swung her legs around and stood, making her way to the stove as if she had forgotten something there.

Suddenly, his plans seemed less important than the feelings of the woman who had saved him. Without her, he would be swinging from a rope, and yet the need for retribution burned in his gut.

Still he wanted to go to her, comfort her somehow, let her know that he was there. She was not alone.

Instead, he pushed back from the table and crammed his hat on his head. He mumbled something about work needing to be done and stalked out the door.

⌘

By supper time, her emotions were still raw, but she had managed to pull herself together. She should have known better than to have placed all her trust in one man. Never mind that he was an accused criminal.

They ate in silence, and afterward he headed for the barn without another word. Penny watched him go, sadness dragging at her. What had she expected? That he would somehow miraculously change into a real husband? The idea was more than ridiculous. But she had let her guard down for a brief moment and imagined what it would be like if George Washington Brannock were a real husband.

Chapter 3

She was being foolish she thought as she knocked on the barn door. Like he could hear her soft rap. She slid the door open and eased inside. "Wash?" She hadn't noticed where he had bedded down the night before.

"Up here." He started down the ladder from the hayloft. "Is everything okay?"

She gave a quick nod. "I like to read the Bible every night. I thought you might want to come in and, uh, join me."

"Read the Bible?"

She nodded even as Wash shook his head. "I haven't read the Bible in. . ." He stopped.

"If it's been that long, then perhaps it's time to get back into the Word."

His jaw clenched, and she could almost hear his teeth grind together. Then he gave a swift nod. "I'll be there in a few minutes."

Penny let herself out of the barn, the feeling that she had won a battle filling her with joy. But was it a battle? Or was it the simple fact that tonight she would have the company of another person for the first time in a long while?

She started water boiling for coffee and wished she had a little extra money to buy some sugar. But it was too much of a luxury at this time. But maybe next year, once this crop came in. If what the old-timers at the mercantile said was correct, then this would be a good year for wheat.

A knock sounded on the door, then Wash eased inside. He had cleaned up a bit, his hair gleaming from the water he'd used to brush it back from his face.

"Go ahead and have a seat. The coffee will be ready in a few minutes."

He settled down in one of the wooden rockers in front of the fireplace and waited as she got the coffee ready.

She handed him a cup then found her own seat. "I've been reading in the book of Romans."

Wash gave her a quick dip of his chin as she opened the book and started to read chapter twelve. She started at verse one and continued on until nineteen. "Beloved, avenge not yourselves, but rather give place unto wrath: for it is written, Vengeance is mine; I will repay, saith the Lord."

He cleared his throat then pushed to his feet. "Maybe this wasn't such a good idea."

She stood as well. "I meant no harm. I didn't realize. . ."

"Right." He stalked to the door and had it open before she caught up with him.

She laid a hand on his arm, stopping him. "Wash, I didn't do that on purpose. I've been reading Romans for the last two weeks."

"I understand." But he didn't look understanding. He looked angry. Or was that frustration? He shook free of her hold and made his way out the door.

∽∾∽

It wasn't a sign. It wasn't a sign, Wash told himself as he plodded back to the barn and climbed into the hayloft once again. And she wasn't getting to him. What did he care if she prayed before every meal and read the Bible at night?

Except that her Christian ways brought to mind better times. Times he didn't want to remember while he was awake. They haunted his dreams so often that allowing those thoughts in at other times was more than he could bear. Thoughts of the family he'd once had. But all of that was a long time ago. War, heartache, and smallpox had taken them from him at one time or another, leaving him alone in the world and asking God why? No matter how many times he asked, he never got an answer. Eventually he stopped asking, stopped going to church, stopped caring.

The last wasn't true. He did care. As badly as he didn't want to, he cared. With those thoughts still knocking around in his head, Wash settled down in the hay and let sleep wash over him.

∽∾∽

The next three weeks fell into a similar pattern: a strained breakfast, followed by a morning of separate chores. A strained dinner and an afternoon of chores. A strained supper and an offer to join her in reading the Bible. He turned her down then retired to the barn to sleep, only to get up the next day and start it all over again.

He had just come back to the house for the noon meal when he heard the rattle of a wagon coming down the lane. Wash turned back to the water fountain, using his bandanna to wipe the grime and grit from his face and the back of his neck. Whoever had ridden up was not there to see him.

"Mr. Alexander." Penny's voice carried to him from around the side of the house. Like the woman herself, the voice was strong, confident, and sure. "To what do I owe the pleasure?"

She said the words, but she didn't sound like it was a pleasure at all.

"I recently heard the most distressing news." The man's voice sounded pampered and soft. Or maybe that's what Wash wanted him to be.

Did he stay where he was? Did he see just who this visitor was? Was it any of his business?

Penny took the choice from him. "And what is that, Mr. Alexander?"

"That you married a common criminal."

"I don't know why that news would cause you any discomfort."

"Penny, I can't believe that you would marry another. Not after I just asked for your hand."

Everything made sense now.

Wash stepped around the side of the house. As expected, the man who visited was a dandy. Where he got the money for such clothes in these trying times, Wash could only suspect. The man was too slick, too smooth. Wash hated him on sight.

"What have we here?" Alexander looked from Wash to Penny, then back again.

Wash gave him a curt nod of greeting then loped up the porch steps to stand by his wife. For good measure, he slid one arm around her waist and tugged her a little closer.

She gasped but didn't resist his hold. "My husband," she said, her voice cracking on the last word.

Alexander stared at them. "I see," he finally said. His tone was neutral, his true thoughts undetermined.

Wash waited there by her side as Alexander apparently mulled over the situation and decided to cut his losses.

"I guess I misunderstood your feelings," he said. He gave them each a nod then turned his wagon and headed back down the lane.

Wash stood there, Penny at his side, and tried not to think about how warm she was and how sweet she smelled. She was his wife, but thoughts like that didn't have a place in their relationship. He took a step away from her. "I take it that's the man who wants your father's land?"

She nodded. "Thanks for your support."

He smiled at her. "That's what husbands are for."

The rest of the day fell into the same pattern as the ones before it. Wash went back to work in the field and Penny stayed near the house doing her chores. But by dinner it seemed something had changed. Penny was quiet, more withdrawn than she had been before, and Wash could only surmise that her neighbor's visit had caused this difference in her attitude.

"I think I'll go hunting tomorrow," he said. It would be good to have some fresh meat on the table. Salt pork could only take a man so far, and beans... Well, beans were good, but not every day.

"Is something wrong with your meal?" she asked. Her tone was level, but he could hear the thread of frustration underneath.

"No, it's fine. Good even, but wouldn't it be nice to have some rabbit? Make some stew?"

She sniffed. "Be even better if we had some vegetables to go with it."

"How about dumplings? Rabbit dumplings are good." His mouth watered just thinking about it. Suddenly his beans seemed less appetizing than they had before. Despite this, he shoveled in another bite. Hunting and plowing, those things took energy, and energy required food. Regardless of how tired he was of eating it.

"I suppose."

"I didn't mean to offend you. I was just trying to help."

She ducked her head and swallowed hard, but she nodded all the same. Then she picked up her plate and made her way toward the wash pan, her back turned toward him as she effectively ended the conversation.

The last thing Wash wanted to do was hurt her in any way. Maybe her attitude would change come tomorrow night when they had more than beans on their plates. But until then he was going to give his wife a wide berth, give her time to work through whatever was going through her mind and heart. He hadn't grown up with a mother and a sister not to know that sometimes women needed time to themselves.

He scraped the rest of the beans from his plate and guzzled down the last of his coffee then took his dishes to the wash bin and laid them next to hers. Without another word, he turned on his heel and headed out the door.

∞

He managed to avoid Penny for the rest of the evening. He kept to the barn, and she kept to the house. At least he thought she did. A light burned on the table, the same one that had been going while they were eating, though he hadn't seen her at all. He figured she was mending or something. He had been grateful when she let out her brother's clothes for him. At least his ankles didn't get cold in a strong wind these days. She was probably working on something else, but he wanted to tell her good night. Check on her one last time before he went to bed. Once more to make sure she was okay. Not that he would know what to do to help her, but he couldn't leave it like this.

He loped up the porch steps and gave a small knock on the door before he opened it. He peeked in but couldn't see her in any of the main rooms.

"Penny?" he called, but he heard no answering rustle, no sound of her voice. "Penny?" he said louder, but she was not there.

He had not known her to leave the house this time of night. He'd been out in the corral with the horses. So he would have known if she had left with one of them. She had to be close. He shook his head and made his way back outside.

He might not be able to tell her good night, but surely he would see her in the morning. And that might be just as good. He made his way across the yard and back into the barn. The couple of horses that had been boarded for the night nickered as he came in. He could hear their soft weight shift in their stalls, their breath even.

273

He knew there were more beds in the house, but it was better this way. All the more reason after his reaction to her that afternoon. Their relationship could never be more than it was now. As soon as this crop came in he was going to find the man who killed his sister then framed him for the crime. And after that. . . Well, he hadn't given much thought to after that. He would figure out what to do with the rest of his life later. But until then—

The sound came to him, soft and mewing, like a cat who had lost his mother. But he had seen only one cat out here, and that was an old yellow Tom. Which meant no kittens, unless he had found himself a girlfriend and Wash hadn't noticed.

The mewing sound came again. He listened intently, realizing that it came from one of the horse stalls. They weren't all full, just a couple. Maybe old Tom had found himself a girl and brought her home.

Just what they needed, a couple more mouths in need of vittles. At least cats were good at finding their own food.

The first horse stall had a mare in foal that he wanted to keep separate from the rest. The next held one of Penny's older geldings. The horse seemed to be dwindling fast, and Wash thought it better to bring the old horse in out of the night air. But the next horse stall down was empty. Or at least he thought it was. He pushed open the door, and there, huddled in the hay, was his wife.

"Penny?" He eased inside.

She jerked as if she'd only just then realized he'd found her. Then she pushed herself up straighter and used the backs of her hands to wipe her tears from her eyes. "Sorry, I didn't mean to intrude," she said. She pushed herself to her feet, still wiping away tears as she stood. Her caramel-colored hair had bits of straw entwined in the curls and somehow that made her look all the more desirable. No longer was she the formidable woman who stood beside him on the porch facing down her oily neighbor, nor was she the spitfire he watched march into the sheriff's office demanding a husband. Now she was just a soft, sweet-smelling woman whose heart had been trampled on. By the war? By a man? Who was to say?

"I'll just go now." She started to push past him, but he reached out a hand to stay her leave.

"What's wrong?" He said the words gently, in the same voice he used when talking to skittish beasts and small children.

"I— Nothing." She sniffed loudly as if somehow that would hide all the evidence of her tears.

"I don't believe that for a minute." Then something inside him shifted. He pulled her closer and closer still. She was stiff in his arms, holding herself away from him like a board bowed in the weather. But he wasn't about to let this go. A girl didn't come out to the barn and cry like the world had ended for no reason.

He cupped the back of her head with one hand and pushed it to his shoulder, offering what comfort he had.

She was warm and sweet in his arms. But he tried to concentrate on other things. Anything else but the feel of her in his arms. This marriage had no place for gentler feelings.

His plan had been to embrace her like he would his sister and show her compassion and understanding. But once he had her in his arms, his feelings were anything but brotherly. What made a woman as strong as Penelope Pinehurst dissolve into tears? He had to know.

"Why are you crying?" he asked again. He continued to hold her close, rubbing one hand down her back in a measure of comfort but knowing he was digging his grave deeper.

"It's all so much." She shook her head and pulled away from him.

Common sense took over, and Wash allowed her to step from his embrace.

"Every day I pray that my brother and my father will return, and every day nothing. Sometimes it just gets me down."

"What will you do if they don't return?" He hadn't wanted to ask the question, but it'd been two years since the end of the war. If they hadn't come back by now. . . They could be starving in Andersonville or buried in an unmarked grave in some field. Who knew? The war had been devastating, taking fathers, brothers, sons, and uncles. Before him stood the worst casualty of all: a woman who had lost near everything.

"I don't know." Tears welled in her eyes once again, and Wash immediately regretted asking. But as much as he wanted to comfort her again, he knew it was best to keep his distance. Something was happening between him and Penny, though he couldn't say exactly what "it" was. Love? Mutual need? Or maybe it was just what happened when two people found themselves married and alone. Whatever it was, nothing of it was acceptable. Just a couple more months and he would be gone. Wash would not leave a broken heart in his wake.

He reached out a hand and wiped the tears from her cheek. Her brown eyes widened, as fearful as a doe's, then she pressed her lips together. "I'm sorry to bother you." She started to push past him once again. This time he let her go.

Chapter 4

Penny hurried to the house as if the devil himself were on her heels. What had she been thinking? She shared this farm with a stranger, a handsome devilish stranger who had a heart as big as the sky. Just the thought of the comfort he offered brought a blush to her cheeks and a warmth to her heart.

Washington Brannock had something different, though she couldn't say what it was. Her experience with men had been limited at best, even more so when it came to men like Wash. She hadn't bothered to ask what he'd been in jail for. And when Margaret had told her that it was murder, her heart sank to her toes. Wash didn't look like a murderer, didn't act like a murderer. And though she was surprised that he had managed to stay this long, he seemed to have more integrity than she would suspect from a killer. But that didn't mean he was any less dangerous.

She pressed the heels of her hands to her eyes and continued up the porch steps. She needed to keep her distance from her farmhand husband. Because regardless of the title of *husband*, he was still a hired hand. She had bought his life from the gallows in order to have him plant crops for her. It was an uneven exchange, but one that worked in her favor as well. She needed those crops. She needed him to stay, but more than anything she needed not to fall in love with him.

She sat herself down in the rocking chair in front of the fireplace and stared into the dying embers. "Dear Lord in heaven, I have done what I thought best. What I thought You wanted me to do. And yet now I'm not so sure about that decision. Help me, Lord, help me understand if my decision was right. And help me, Lord, to know what to do each day, so that I walk with You in every aspect of my life. And, Lord, wherever Pa and my brother are tonight, please let them make it home safe. Take care of them and watch over them as You watch over me. And Wash," she added. "In Jesus' name, amen."

∽∾∾

Something had changed between them. Penny wasn't sure what it was, but it existed all the same. They seemed to be working more toward a common goal now. And whether the change came from her or him, she wasn't sure.

Two months into their marriage, and more than ever Penny felt the excitement of a brand-new start. Tiny green sprouts were pushing through the dry earth. It rained just enough to get them through, but she wasn't complaining. The garden was taking off nicely, and before long they would have fresh vegetables for the table. Wash had started hunting in the mornings, and though most of the fare was squirrels and rabbits, at least they had fresh meat. For that she would be eternally grateful.

The door flung open, and Wash stuck his head in, a grin on his face like she had never seen before.

Penny jumped sending flour in the air.

"What are you doing?" Wash asked.

Penny wiped the flour from her face and sputtered, "Making bread."

"Oh," he said, just his head still visible through the door frame. "Well, stop for a bit and come here. I've got something I want to show you."

"I'll be right there." Her tone was skeptical. What did he need to show her?

She grabbed a dish towel and wiped as much of the flour from her face and hands as she could before starting out the door. She stepped onto the porch, her gaze scanning the yard to see where Wash had gotten off to. She found him in an instant, a deer hanging by its feet from the skinning post in the yard.

"You killed that?" She knew her eyes were huge as she stared at the doe. She hated that the beautiful creature had to die for them, but venison!

She rushed down the steps to stand next to him. He was grinning even broader than before, apparently proud of himself.

"I've been watching her for a while now. Just waiting to get the right shot. Hunting's hard going if you're only out for a bit every day, but it's going to be good eating tonight."

"Yes, it is!" Penny launched herself at her husband, wrapping her arms around his neck.

She stood there for a moment feeling his heart beat so close to hers, then his arms came around her and pulled her closer still.

The hitch in his breath drew her gaze to his. His eyes were black as night, so deep and dark she couldn't fathom one emotion from them. All she could see was their intensity, and the heat she hadn't known existed.

"Wash?" She needed him to say something to let her know everything was okay. But instead of words, he lowered his head and pressed his lips to hers.

The realization hit her like never before. Was this what it felt like to be kissed? Girls like her weren't kissed very often, and this was her first. And what a kiss it was!

His lips were soft and sweet as they moved over hers. And she felt as if every good thing in the world was wrapped up in that one embrace. She felt herself falling and falling, until she wasn't sure if she would ever make it back up.

Then Wash pulled away, breaking their kiss and setting her an arm's length from him in one jarring motion.

"I'm sorry."

Penny couldn't say a word. She just stood there, the back of her hand pressed to her mouth, her eyes wide as she stared at her husband. He was sorry? It was the best kiss of her life, the *only* kiss of her life, and he was sorry?

She shook her head. Then she took two more steps backward, the joy of the venison lost in the confusion she now faced. Her husband had kissed her, but he was sorry.

"Penny?" He took a step toward her, his arm outstretched, his hand reaching, his eyes remorseful.

She shook her head then turned on her heel and ran for the house.

Penny shut the door behind her and leaned against it, like that would keep him out. Like he wanted in. He had kissed her and then rebuked her. In one swift moment, she had fallen in love with him, only to have her hopes shattered a second later.

She shook her head at her foolish ways.

Lord, whatever this is I feel for Wash, take it from me. I do not want to love him. I do not want to love a man whose kisses are sweet but whose heart isn't true.

And he couldn't have a true heart if he was sorry.

She pushed herself off the door and made her way back into the kitchen. Flour still dusted every available surface where she had been making the dough, but suddenly she didn't feel like baking bread anymore. Not that she had much choice.

She wiped her hands on her apron and started kneading the dough once more. This time praying that Wash would be so busy with his deer that he wouldn't come in until supper.

≈

He told himself not to go after her. As much as he wanted to follow behind her, explain, kiss her again, he had to let her go.

And he wanted to explain and maybe kiss her again. But his explanation and kissing did not go together. He should've never kissed her to begin with. She was his wife, but in name only. In another couple of months he would be heading out to get his revenge.

Nancy, his sister, had been his world. After their parents had died, after they lost everything at the beginning of the war, Nancy was his everything. He would have given her anything, and when she had asked to marry Ralston James, Wash had given his blessing despite his misgivings.

Ralston seemed a little too slick, a little too smart, a lot like Penny's neighbor. Not wanting to deny his sister, Wash kept his mouth shut about his reservations. That was his first mistake. His second came two days before the wedding. He had gone to Ralston's house to go over some last-minute plans. He'd expected to get Ralston alone, and what he got was Ralston and his sister. Except Nancy was no longer with them. Ralston had choked her, cut off her air until she could breathe no more. Then he managed to convince everyone in a fifty-mile radius that Wash had killed her instead.

Wash was flabbergasted that everyone believed Ralston, but money can buy almost anything, even innocence. Wash had none, and though Ralston was still trying to build his postwar, carpetbag fortune, he still had more than the Brannocks. James had gotten off scot-free, and Wash was left to hang.

Why he hadn't hung before now was anybody's guess. It seemed as if no one wanted to take the responsibility for putting the noose around his neck. Instead they traded him jail to jail until he ended up in Cooper. And that was where Penny had come in.

Penny. He had never met anyone like her, so strong and tough on the outside but soft and womanly on the inside. She was a product of the war, a product of survival, and the grandest creature God ever made. Heaven help him. He was starting to develop feelings for her. Feelings that had no place in a heart filled with revenge.

He didn't have time for love, didn't have time to be a proper husband to anyone, much less the kind of husband that Penelope Pinehurst deserved. He didn't know if her father or her brother would ever make it back from the war. For all he knew, they could have died in Andersonville years ago. But she prayed every night that they would return, just as she prayed every night for healthy crops, good rains, and a long growing season. Even the fact that she prayed. . . That was more than he could do.

He'd stopped praying a long time ago. Yet these days when she bowed her head, he bowed his without question and let her words wash through him and on up to heaven. Maybe some of her goodness would rub off on him and God would listen, if only through her.

But that kiss. . . He had apologized, should do so again, but he didn't think she could listen to it now. He gave one last look to the shut door of the house, then with a sigh he turned back to his kill. She might accept and offer her forgiveness if he came bearing a gift.

⁂

Supper was too cordial by far. Penny wouldn't look him in the face. She skimmed everywhere except his eyes. The tip of his ear, this side of his cheek. She seemed to have a special love of his collarbone. But she wouldn't meet his gaze.

"The bread's good," he said, complimenting her on the tenth thing since he'd sat down. He had complimented her hair, the table setting, the pickles she had canned, the jam, and a host of other things he couldn't even remember.

"Thank you." Her gaze centered on his upper lip. Then she turned beet-red and pulled it down to his collarbone once again.

He planned to say something after dinner, but he'd had about all of this he could take.

"Penny, about this afternoon. . ."

She jumped to her feet and headed toward the stove, snatching up the pot of coffee and returning to the table in a heartbeat. "Would you like some more?"

He held his cup up for her to fill it, even though he really didn't want any more coffee.

"Penny, I'm trying to apologize."

She whirled back around, her back to him as she set the coffee onto the stove top. But once her hands were free, she didn't face him.

"Penny?"

She shook her head then whirled back around. "Please don't tell me you're sorry. Please." Tears filled those amazing brown eyes once again.

Wash stood, intending to offer her comfort of one sort or another, but she held up her hands as if to keep him at a distance. "No," she said.

"Why can't I say I'm sorry?" All he wanted was her forgiveness. They had been married for two months, and she had come to mean more to him than just someone who lived in the house while he slept in the barn. As much as he didn't want to examine any of those feelings he held for her, her forgiveness still meant a great deal to him.

"Because," she cried, her eyes fluttering closed as if she was trying to gather thoughts too painful to look at. "Because that was the best kiss of my life, and I can't stand it if you're sorry for it."

"The best?"

Her eyes flew open. "I should have never told you that." She moved to flounce around him, but he grabbed her by one arm and pulled her back. Holding her at an arm's distance even as he chuckled.

"It's not every day a man gets told he's the best."

She harrumphed. "Don't be so smug. It was only the best because it's my only one. Ever."

He frowned. "You've never been kissed?"

"Well, I have now."

Wash shook his head again, trying to get ahold of the thoughts and what she was telling him. "When I kissed you, that was your first kiss ever?"

She reluctantly nodded.

"Are you joshing me?"

She shook her head again.

"Why? What about—" He didn't even say the man's name before Penny shook her head again. "I never kissed Jackson."

"No school days boyfriend?"

"Are you having trouble understanding me?"

It was his turn to shake his head. "What's wrong with the guys around here?"

Penny let out a bark of laughter. "Now you're joshing me."

"Why would I do that?" Why were they talking in circles?

"Look at me." Her voice was so matter-of-fact that he flinched. "I am not pretty. I did not have boyfriends. I do not have a boyfriend, and I have never been kissed."

"But you are pretty," he said, realizing even as he said them, the words didn't fit Penelope Pinehurst. *Pretty* was too vapid a word. She was striking. She was memorable. She was. . .strong.

"You don't have to lie to me."

Wash turned serious, realizing that she was telling the truth as she saw it. "You know what I see when I look at you?" he asked.

Her eyes darkened until they were no longer the tawny color of strong tea, but deep and rich like the chocolate he'd seen imported from Europe.

"I see a survivor. I see a woman who was left to fend for herself, who made do for years but kept everything going regardless of the enemies she faced. I see strength, resilience, and fortitude."

She took a deep breath, the air shuddering. "But not beauty." She said the words quietly; they were no more than a whisper between them.

"When you have all that," he said, "what is beauty?"

Chapter 5

Penny held her breath as he said the words. Could he really mean them? Never before had she met someone like Wash. Never before had she truly dreamed of getting married. Those dreams had died a swift death a long time ago. Once she realized that she wasn't like the other girls. She could cook and clean, and keep a house. She could take care of her own, and she had for the longest time. But now it seemed everything was different. Because of him. Because of Wash.

"Kiss me," she invited. She knew it was bold, but they were married, after all. And he had said the sweetest things to her that anyone had ever said in her entire life.

Wash let go of her arms and took a step back. Immediately she felt bereft, and though her heart cracked at the rejection, her logical side said that it wasn't the first time. Most likely it wouldn't be the last.

"I can't do that," he said with a shake of his head. "I can't lead you on that way. I can't make you think that I'm something I'm not. And I'm not husband material."

"Because you killed someone?" she whispered.

He shook his head. "Because I didn't kill anyone."

"I don't understand."

Wash took her hand into his, and Penny allowed him to lead her over to the rocking chairs next to the fireplace. Dinner was half eaten and still sitting on the table. Maybe they would get back to it, maybe they wouldn't.

They settled down side by side, Wash still holding her hand in his.

"My family was very wealthy, once upon a time. We lived over in Butler. We had quite a large farm there. A plantation I guess you could say, and everything seemed to be going really well until Kansas decided to enter the Union as a free state. Then the talk began to give up what we had and move to Missouri. That decision was taken from us by others, and before it was all said and done we had almost nothing. But we did the best we could, so we were still an upstanding family in the community. For the most part." His voice took on a far-off quality, as if he were in another place as he told her his tale. "Then my parents died. My father had a heart attack, and I think my mother died because she missed him so much. That left me and Nancy, my sister. And I vowed that I would take care of her always. She was a little younger than I was, so wonderful and full of life." He gently traced the outline of each knuckle on her hand. Penny didn't know what to say, she just listened. Somehow she knew she wasn't going to like the ending.

"Then Nancy met this man, Ralston James, and he swept her off her feet. I really didn't care for the man, but she was in love, and I agreed that they could get married. Because it meant so much to Nancy. Then two days before the wedding I went over to James's house, only to find—" His voice broke.

Penny waited as he gave a small cough and regained some of his earlier composure.

"He had killed her," he said.

Penny gasped and blinked back her tears as Wash continued.

"He thought we had money." He shrugged. "I don't know where he got such an idea, but when he found out that we were poor, he grew angry and strangled her. Then he framed me for the murder, and here I am." He let go of her hand to spread his wide.

Penny shook her head. "I don't know what to say."

Wash gave her a bitter smile. "There's nothing to say. He killed my sister then sent me to prison. You walked into my cell and offered me freedom. And I'll stay here and I'll bring in your crops, but come the fall I'm going to find Ralston James, and I'm going to kill that man."

"Wash, you can't do that. You can't go around seeking vengeance," she said. "Vengeance belongs to God."

Wash shook his head. "An eye for an eye, isn't that what the Bible says?"

"That's not what it means," Penny started. "I mean it is, but it doesn't mean that you get to take an eye for an eye. You're supposed to turn the other cheek."

Wash stood so fast he knocked the rocking chair over behind him. "I can't turn the other cheek. He killed the one thing I had left in this world, the one person I loved more than anything. And then he sent me to prison for it. My family lost everything in the span of just a few years. And he's not going to get away with it."

Penny stood, her insides trembling, even as she straightened her shoulders and looked him square in the eye. "Vengeance is not ours, Washington Brannock. I'll pray for you."

⁓∞⁓

As the next weeks turned into another month, Wash grew tired of Penny's constant Bible quotes. If it wasn't one about vengeance belonging to the Lord, it was one where Jesus said to turn the other cheek. She never missed a chance to tell him the verses, tell him that she was praying for him, or to stand in the middle of the yard and raise her hands to heaven and say a prayer that he would come to his senses. But there was no coming to the senses.

She would be the same way if she knew that something had happened to one of her beloved family members the way he did. It was really easy to say turn the other cheek when she wasn't the one having to turn it.

"Hello!" someone called from the road.

Wash looked up as a lone rider came down the lane. He shaded his eyes to get a better look-see, but he could see only that it was a man on the roan horse who rode near. "Hello," he called in return.

"I was looking for a place to water my horse," the man said.

Wash pointed to the water trough just this side of the corral. "You can get some water there, and I can get you a scoop of oats for your beast, if you want to sit and rest a spell."

"Much obliged," the rider said.

The stranger's voice rang familiar, but Wash thought perhaps it was merely a trick of his ears. He hadn't heard another man's voice in quite some time. He and Penny, despite their differences of opinion on the matter of vengeance, had been working very closely side by side to get everything in order. She made it known that she hated the fact that he was leaving soon, but she knew she couldn't make him stay.

The rider dismounted and led his horse to the trough. Like many in this postwar time, the man wore a gun on his hip and had a rifle in a scabbard on the side of his saddle.

"You just coming in from town?" Wash asked.

The man took off his hat and wiped his forehead with his sleeve then turned to face him.

Wash would have known those eyes anywhere. Green as meadow grass and evil to the core.

Ralston James!

Somehow Wash kept his wits about him. He might've recognized James, but the man did not recognize Wash. He supposed he'd changed a lot in the last few years. He had lost some weight. His hair was longer, and he knew that his face bore the pinch of bitterness.

His heart pounded hard in his chest. He looked to where his own rifle lay several yards away. He kept it out here in case coyotes or small game happened by. He had no idea the man he wanted to kill more than he wanted his next breath would be riding up. But he'd never get to his rifle before the man in front of him could raise the gun from his hip.

"Hello there!" Penny came out of the house wiping her hands on a towel as she surveyed the newcomer.

The man tipped his hat at Penny then flashed her that devilish smile Wash had seen him use too many times to count.

Watch out, Penny. The man's a snake.

"I just stopped in for some water and some oats. I won't be troubling you long. I appreciate your hospitality."

Penny gave a small nod then came down the stairs. "I'm Penny," she said. "Penny—"

"Pinehurst," Wash interjected. "Her name is Penny Pinehurst. And I'm her husband. . .George."

Penny frowned at him but seemed to realize something was up. The woman was nothing if not smart.

"That's right," she said.

The man reached out a hand. "Ralston James."

Wash looked from the hand to the man who extended it. The last thing he wanted to do was touch the hand that had killed his sister. Those hands, together, had choked the life out of his Nancy. How was he supposed to shake it in good faith?

Penny elbowed him in the ribs. "Don't go all day-dreamy on me now, George. Shake the man's hand."

It took all the strength he could muster and a small prayer for more before Wash could shake James's hand. Strange, but when their skin touched, he didn't burst into flames.

"It's a pleasure," James said. "Like I said, I can't stay long." He looked behind him nervously, and Wash wondered if perhaps someone was following behind.

"You can stay as long as you need." Penny beamed at him. Wash wanted to elbow her back in the ribs. The man could *not* stay as long as he wanted. Wash wanted nothing more than to shoot him on sight.

"Can I speak to my wife for a moment alone, please?" Wash didn't wait for James to respond. He grabbed Penny by the elbow and pulled her to the other side of the yard. "What are you saying?"

"I'm saying that he can stay as long as he needs to, because if he can't then he might realize something's up."

"I want to kill that man."

Penny plopped her hands on her hips and eyed him skeptically. "Oh yeah? Then why haven't you?"

"I—why, I—" Wash sputtered. Why hadn't he? He'd had the perfect opportunity. The man that he wanted to seek vengeance on had ridden up in the front yard, right there in shooting distance. He could've moved closer to his gun. He could've gone inside and gotten a different gun. He could've jumped James from behind. He could've done a number of things to bring Ralston James down. So why hadn't he?

"I'll tell you why," Penny said, "because vengeance is not the way. And you know it."

He looked to the woman in front of him and in that instant realized that his decision not to kill Ralston James had nothing to do with vengeance and everything to do with love. More specifically love for the woman he'd married.

"He cannot be allowed to get away with killing my sister."

Without waiting for her to respond, he stalked across the yard. James stood with his back to them, and Wash had only a split second to wonder if perhaps that was a gift from God, before he'd jumped on Ralston's back and wrestled him to the ground.

"Wash! What are you doing?"

Wash was breathing heavy. Ralston had managed to land a few punches of his own, but Wash had the element of surprise on his side. Now he sat astride the dandy, the man's face in the dust, as he pulled both arms behind his back. "Quit hollering at me, woman, and go get some rope!"

For once Penny did as he asked, running into the barn and returning a few moments later with a length of rope just long enough to hog-tie Ralston James. The man sputtered and fussed until Wash took a bandanna and tied it around the man's mouth to stifle his acid words.

"Now what?" Penny looked from him to Ralston.

"We're taking him to jail. Can you help me load him in the wagon?"

She smiled, obviously relieved. "Thank the Lord for answered prayers."

"Penny?" he prompted.

"Yes," she said with a smile. "I'll help you load him into the wagon."

The look on the sheriff's face was worth more than anything as Penny and Wash pulled into town. In fact everyone wanted to hear about how Ralston came to be hog-tied in the back of Penny's wagon. Wash told his story to the sheriff, who promptly locked Ralston up in the jail where only months before Wash himself had been incarcerated. Then Wash promised to come back and testify as soon as the judge came through town. And before Penny knew it, she and her husband were on their way back to her farm.

They were quiet on the trip. Penny couldn't speak for Wash, but she didn't know what to say. Somehow Wash had given up his need for vengeance and settled for justice instead. She wanted to tell him that she had prayed for some sort of peaceful resolution and that God had delivered Ralston to their yard so that it could come to be. God was good, and Wash needed to realize that.

He had turned the other cheek whether he realized it or not. But more than the circumstances surrounding Ralston James and his arrest, Penny had to figure out what to do with her gallows husband.

Penny climbed down from the wagon and went into the house. It was close to time for supper, and she needed to get them something together to eat. Wash took the wagon and unhitched the horses. But an air of expectancy hung around them both. What was to become of them now?

Wash would stay until the crops came in, which might be another month, and then he'd planned to head off after vengeance. But what were his plans now?

Penny's heart thumped hard in her chest. She was just being foolish. Why would his plans have anything to do with her? *You silly, silly girl. You just had to go and fall in love with a man like that. A man who could never love you in return. How could he? He is so handsome and so strong.*

Despite his sweet words to her from a few weeks ago, she doubted they held true today.

They sat down to dinner, still no words of importance spoken between them, just "please," "thank you," and a "here, this is for you," when she passed him the salt. But nothing of any substance, nothing of any importance.

She said grace over their meal, and they began to eat, each one busy with their own thoughts. Was he thinking about their marriage? Or was he thinking about his sister as he thought about Ralston James?

Penny was being ridiculous. He was more than likely thinking of his sister, needing time to come to terms with the justice served to her killer. And his thoughts would probably not hold much else until all of that was resolved.

Finished with her meal, she stood and took her plate over to the washstand. She supposed even homely girls could be foolish over boys. And she had been the biggest fool of all.

"Penny?" He spoke directly behind her, and Penny jumped, so lost in her thoughts that she hadn't realized he'd come close.

"Yes?"

"About the harvest..."

He couldn't leave! She needed him! And he had promised.

She turned on him then, punching one finger in his chest. "You can't go. You promised to stay until the harvest came in. And I can't allow you to leave without you helping me. I can't do it alone."

"Wait! I mean, why are you poking me? What's wrong with you?"

"Isn't that what you're looking to tell me? That you're leaving before the harvest? That's not acceptable. I need your help. My father and brother are coming back. I know they are. And I need to do everything I can to help feed them. Bring in the crops and keep this farm running until they return."

Even as she said the words she doubted that her father and brother would ever return to Kansas, but she couldn't let loose of that last shred of hope. And she needed Washington Brannock to help her regardless of his desire to be anywhere but with her.

"I'm not leaving. I mean, I can't—" His face turned a shade of red she had never seen before. "Penny, my time here with you has shown me something different.

I hadn't thought about getting married in a long, long time, much less getting married to someone who paid for me from the gallows. When you walked into the jail, I saw my chance at vengeance. But you wouldn't even allow me that." He chuckled, taking the sting from his words. "This is not anywhere I thought my life would be now. I expected to find Ralston James, shoot him dead for killing my sister, and then live my life on the run in Indian Territory, just trying to stay alive. Never had a farm, a wife, or crops ever come into it."

Penny's heart skipped a beat. "A wife?"

He gave a small nod. "Yes, a wife. I never thought I'd have one, and now I do. And I've got crops to bring in. What I want to know is after the crops are in, can I stay?"

"Can you—"

He nodded again. "Stay. Can I stay?"

"With me?" Surely she had heard him wrong. Why would he want to stay with her?

He took her hands in his and held them up close to his heart. Penny's mouth turned to ash as she waited for him to continue.

This time he laughed. "Well it won't be much fun here by myself."

"I don't understand."

"I'm saying, Penelope Pinehurst Brannock, can I stay and be your husband? See, I found myself falling in love with this woman. Some folks say she's not very pretty, but there's something about her that I love."

Penny's heart thumped back to life. "Oh really? Like what?"

"She's strong, for one. And she's a little bossy, but I can overlook that. But she gives me a different perspective on things. And that's one thing I really need in my life."

Penny grinned. "Yes." She could hardly believe this was happening to her, Not So Pretty Penny. "Yes, you can stay."

Wash pulled her close, holding her tight and kissing her like he had that day in the yard. Penny had never felt so loved.

He lifted his head and smiled, the sweetest smile she had ever seen. "There's just one thing," he said.

"And what's that?"

"I'm no longer set to hang, and you did buy me from the gallows."

"Does your story have a point?"

"I don't think the sheriff can give you a refund."

And that was just fine with her.

Blessed are the merciful: for they shall obtain mercy.
MATTHEW 5:7

Amy Lillard is a 2013 Carol Award–winning author who loves reading romance novels from contemporary to Amish. She was born and raised in Mississippi but now lives in Oklahoma with her husband and their teenage son.

All's Fair

by Gina Welborn

Dedication

For my sister Dawn for driving me there and back again, and for the Hogwarts stop along the way. I promote you to Chief Research Assistant. No pay, but it's cool to have a title.

Acknowledgments

Many thanks to the Cache Police Department; the Kansas State University Special Collections Department; the Wichita-Sedgwick County Historical Museum and Kansas Historical Society Museum in Topeka (I love museums!); the Kansas State Archives for the old map of Wathena and Doniphan County; and Cargill for donating five hundred pounds of bacon to Wichita's First Annual Bacon Feast. Amen.

*If you are going to set out an orchard of any kind, plow the ground deep-
very-deep and if the soil is not naturally rich, make it rich by the application
of manure; then cultivate the field intended for trees as you would
a field intended for a prize crop of potatoes.*
KANSAS FARMER, 1864

*Our field is large, our labors will be somewhat arduous, but with willing minds
we can overcome all apparent obstacles, and place our State on
an equality with the most favored fruit-growing regions.*
WILLIAM TANNER, president, Kansas State Horticultural Society, 1867

*I therefore, the prisoner of the Lord, beseech you that ye walk worthy of the
vocation wherewith ye are called, with all lowliness and meekness,
with longsuffering, forbearing one another in love.*
EPHESIANS 4:1–2

Prologue

What deep wounds ever closed without a scar?
GEORGE GORDON, LORD BYRON

Wathena, Kansas
July 4, 1900

oral Davies turned away from the tranquil Missouri River to look at the thousand or so people milling about the lawn and riverbank after a day of swimming and picnicking in the sweltering heat. Her heart beat frantically in her chest. The orchestra had started the last stanza of the national anthem before the mayor would read the Declaration of Independence. Everyone in Doniphan County had to be at the celebration, including every Kent and Davies keeping to separate sides of the pavilion and clearly on their best behavior since no altercations had broken out. Yet.

She could feel worry etching lines into her brow.

"Please, Coral, talk to me."

Her attention shifted to Hiram Kent standing a few feet from where she was near the edge of the ten-foot-long pier. Her traitorous heart fluttered. Tie askew, shirtsleeves rolled up, dark brown hair mussed—he looked adorable, charming, and stubborn as always. After five months of clandestine meetings, not one stolen kiss. If that didn't prove his honorable character, she didn't know what would.

Which was why she had to be the one to do the right thing.

She tapped her straw hat against her green-striped skirt and hardened her gaze. "I can't keep disobeying my parents by sneaking off to see you. You have to leave. Go," she ordered. "Jack said he'd beat you to high heaven if he saw us talking again."

His chin raised like it did when someone told him he couldn't do something. "I can handle Jack."

She didn't want to see what he looked like after he "handled" his cousin who had six years, twenty pounds of muscle, and at least eight inches in height on him.

"Then go before my brothers see you," she warned in a low voice.

"Earning a black eye from talking to a Davies will be worth it," he said. "Because you are worth it." He winked, and her resistance weakened.

He stepped closer, leaving a handbreadth's distance between them. While she

293

didn't retreat, she did grip her straw hat with both hands to keep from touching him.

"You know we can't be together," she whispered.

"No, I don't."

Even in the dimming sunlight, she could see unabashed adoration in those sultry dark eyes that had haunted her dreams and waking thoughts ever since the St. Valentine's Day Sock Hop. Ever since she agreed to "Fine, Hiram, one dance," despite him being a Kent and her a Davies. While Hiram was the most popular guy in Wathena High School, without a mean bone in his body, considering the hatred their families shared for each other, he wouldn't have asked her to dance if he hadn't wanted to.

If he hadn't liked her.

As she liked him.

He held out a torn sheet of paper. "Write to me. Please."

She didn't have to take it to see he'd written down the address for the University of Missouri boardinghouse where Jack also lived.

"If I write to you, everyone in town will know. Every. One."

"I don't care who knows." A muscle at his jaw flinched. "I love you, Coral, and I know you love me, too, or you wouldn't try to protect me."

Her hat slid from her grip to the pier. Something—joy, fear, shock—gripped her heart. She liked him, felt giddy when he was near, but love? How could either of them know about love? They were eighteen, barely out of high school.

Hiram brushed his knuckles across her cheek then tucked behind her ear a red curl that had loosened from her braid. Her pulse pounded in her ears. He was going to kiss her.

For anyone—everyone—to see.

She wanted him to. She didn't.

She did.

Just once. Just once, for memory's sake, and then she'd end it good and proper.

Argumentative voices rose over the orchestra, drawing her attention. Jack Kent and her brothers, Gil and Whit, shoved at one another as they ran down the pier while spewing what sounded to be invectives toward Hiram. Gil reached Hiram first. His fist connected with Hiram's mouth. Jack grabbed Gil's arm and kneed him in the groin. As the pair fought, Whit's hands encircled Hiram's neck, squeezing his throat, lifting him up off the pier.

"Stop!" Coral screamed.

Hiram clawed at Whit's hands. He coughed. "Let—go—"

Coral jumped on her brother Gil's back before he could punch Jack again. One arm around his neck, with her other hand, she yanked his hair, jerking his head backward. Gil howled.

"Get off me," he yelled.

"I will once Whit lets go of Hiram," she yelled back.

Whit dropped Hiram to the dock.

Hiram doubled over, hands on his throbbing throat, gulping for air. "That's my girl."

Coral slid of Gil's back. She breathed deep. "Let's relax and—"

"Relax?" Jack gripped Coral's arms. "I warned you to stop leading him on." In one fluid motion, he swung her into the river. The left side of her head smacked the cold water before she could even scream. A sharp pain burst in her ear.

As Coral struggled to right herself, someone jumped in the water beside her. She gained her footing and stood in the chest-high water, gasping air, hair plastered to the side of her face, a buzzing in her left ear. She wobbled. Pulse pounded. Head ached. She wiped the dank river water from her eyes. On the pier, Whit and Jack—first time ever a Davies and a Kent unified—held Hiram's arms behind his back.

Gil's torso rose out of the water. He grabbed Coral by the waist.

She pushed him back and almost lost her balance again. "Stop, Gil. I can manage on my own." She glared at Hiram. "I am not your girl," she seethed. Never again. She turned to Jack. "Didn't you swear to do no harm?"

His jaw set in a very tight line.

"I hate you, Jackson Kent," she ground out. "I will hate you forever."

He shrugged.

"Don't you ever come near me again, you hear?"

He gave her a smug grin despite his bloodied lip. "I can live with that."

Coral turned away in disgust. With a hand over her ringing left ear, she trudged out of the river. She didn't look over her shoulder to see who followed. As soon as she had the means, she was leaving Wathena to the Kents and the Davies and their stupid feud.

Chapter 1

There is no charm equal to tenderness of heart.
JANE AUSTEN

Saturday
September 3, 1904

I t seems, Miss Coral Davies, this is your lucky day."

Coral gasped as Inez returned to the counter with a paper-wrapped bouquet of thirty petite white roses—exactly what Judge Swayze had asked Coral to find on short notice and under seemingly impossible odds. She accepted the fragrant flowers from the only other girl from their graduating class who had yet to marry. The roses appeared even whiter against the sleeve of Coral's royal-blue walking suit and black Irish lace gloves.

"They're perfect," she said. "I can't believe no one wanted these for their parade float."

Inez chuckled. "Many did. I hid them Wednesday after you called."

"I owe you one."

"Oh, you don't have—"

"I insist." Coral paused until Inez gave an accepting nod.

As Inez filled out a receipt, Coral sniffed the bouquet. The sweet scent reminded her of Mrs. Swayze's elegant home. One rule of being a social secretary was to not put herself or employers in debt to anyone by accepting favors. In light of the decreasing lack of purchasable roses this week because of the upcoming parade, owing Inez a favor was the right thing. While she and Inez had never shared intimate secrets, they were friends. Someday when Inez had a great need, Coral would find a way to fulfill it—hopefully before Coral left Wathena next month for her future in Cleveland.

Coral laid the bouquet on the counter next to the alligator-skin briefcase her brother Whit had made for her twenty-third birthday last month. "I think if anyone is lucky, the town is, because the rain has stopped last night and there's not a cloud in sight. What would Wathena do without the Labor Day carnival?"

"Are you going?"

"I have work."

"You always have work," Inez chided.

"True"—Coral grinned mischievously—"but I have a feeling the next thirty days will afford me a much-needed holiday."

Inez leaned over the counter. Her gray eyes sparkled with curiosity. "Do tell."

Coral started to comment but was cut off by a bell jingling above either the front or side entrance to the corner shop. Probably another frantic Labor Day float designer desperate for extra flowers or ribbon for Monday's parade. Having grown used to being incapable of pinpointing the direction of the sound, she ignored who'd entered. She opened her briefcase and removed the fringed parasol—apple green and "an abomination" according to her father. Not that she carried it to defy him. The vivid color made her happy. And life was too short not to enjoy simple pleasures, as long as they were legal, moral, temperate, and the enjoying harmed no one.

She withdrew her wallet wedged underneath the ribbon-tied box of chocolates.

"How much. . ." Her words trailed off once she noticed how Inez's flushed cheeks beautified her plain features.

Whenever Coral blushed, the ruddiness in her cheeks and neck combined with the redness of her hair made her look splotchy and feverish. Although curious at who'd caused this reaction in Inez, she clicked open her wallet. Her job—and good manners—necessitated she mind her business.

She withdrew a dollar. "How much do I owe you?"

"It's, uhh. . ." Inez brushed at the front of her white apron. "Good afternoon, Dr. Kent."

Coral froze. So much for this being *her* lucky day.

He didn't speak for an excruciatingly long moment. "Afternoon, Miss Potter." Pause. "You the only one working today?"

She nodded. "Everyone else had carnival invites, including Ma. Pa says just 'cause they're married doesn't mean they can't still court. Can I help you find something?"

He grunted as if to say, *Since you're the only one working, I'll permit you to help me.* "Yellow ribbon?"

Inez motioned to the display on the other side of the counter. "Ribbon over five yards is twenty percent off this weekend." She smoothed her dark hair, drawn back in a simple bun. "All, uhh, hands must be busy at the orchard if they sent you."

"Something like that."

Heels clomped against the wood floor as the handsome yet surly man in his snakeskin boots and three-piece beige suit passed behind Coral, making her breathless and uneasy as Inez, although for a different reason. Out of the corner of her right eye, she could see him standing at the ribbon display. His face was bristled instead of clean shaven. His left hand clenched his Panama hat, his right rested on the yellow ribbon, yet he didn't pick it up. Jack Kent ought to be at the carnival. Or at the orchard overseeing the harvest. Or attending to a sick patient. Or—or—or anywhere else than where she was.

They had an understanding.

In the last four years and two months, he'd given her distance, and she'd reciprocated by giving him his, even though she'd felt his continued disdain. Not a word spoken.

No hateful glares, either.

Polite avoidance.

Until last Sunday after the worship service. For decades the Kent and Davies families attended churches on opposite sides of the street. The moment Jack had taken a step in her direction—his distraught attention solely on her—she'd dashed inside her parents' buggy. Not the most fitting behavior for a woman of twenty-three years. If he hadn't thrown her into the river, she wouldn't be deaf in her left ear and Hiram wouldn't have become the Kent family prodigal son who missed his father's funeral seventeen months ago.

Two lives damaged because of Dr. Jackson Kent.

Why didn't he just leave Potter's Flowers and come back after she was gone?

Inez walked around the counter and stopped (posed, actually) at Coral's left. Within Jack's line of sight, if he were looking Coral's direction, and from what she could tell, he was more fascinated with the ribbon roll he now held.

If he was not leaving, then she would.

While Inez's besotted gaze stayed on Jack, Coral withdrew a few more dollars. "How much do I owe you?" she said the same moment Inez blurted, "Dr. Kent, can I help you find something else?"

"I'll wait," Jack answered brusquely, "while you tend to. . .your other customers."

"He means me," Coral put in. She smiled because, by golly, she would not permit Storm Cloud Jack to dampen her joy. She laid the money next to the register.

Inez blushed again. "Oh yes, I. . .uhh. . ."

She hurried around the counter and punched numbers into the register, her gaze continually shifting to Jack. She pulled the lever. Bell rang, drawer opened.

"Here you go." Inez offered two quarters.

"Thank you." Coral took the change. She placed it and the receipt in her wallet.

Boots pounded against the floor. One step. Two. Approaching or walking away, she wasn't sure, nor was she going to wait and find out. She stowed her wallet, grabbed her briefcase, parasol, and the bouquet, and dashed outside into the summer sun, turning in the direction of the carnival, leaving Inez to flirt with Jack. He had a solid reputation in the community. Polite. Kind. Generous to a fault.

Some said he had a wonderful sense of humor. In many ways, he was much like Inez. And they attended the same church.

Coral sincerely wished them well. Even Jack Kent should be loved.

As she made her way down the sidewalk, she opened her parasol. Then she wedged the precious bouquet in the crook of her arm, holding it against her chest while she kept the parasol upright, clenching her briefcase in the other hand. She had a job to do and her own future to secure in Cleveland, home of The Arcade (a nine-story shopping mall!), Millionaire's Row, and a theater district like nothing she'd ever experienced.

Most of all, no feud.

Coral continued to smile as she walked past the businesses bedecked in red, white, and blue bunting. Buggies, horses, automobiles, and bicycles lined St. Joseph Street. Pedestrians like her bustled both ways, bumping her shoulders as they passed coming from or going to the carnival. If any offered apologies, she wouldn't have known. The traffic on the road and music from the carnival hindered her hearing.

She glanced at her wristwatch. Three sixteen.

In two and a half hours, Judge and Mrs. Swayze would return home from the carnival to find their dining room set for a romantic meal and a will-you-marry-me-again proposal. Per the judge's detailed plans. As long as the judge and Coral assuaged Mrs. Swayze's worries about who would care for the estate while the couple was gone (Coral would), then she would agree to leave tomorrow for a surprise second honeymoon to The King Edward Hotel in Toronto, Canada. Thirty roses and thirty days in Canada for the thirty years that Jane—God bless that woman—Swayze "has put up with me," or so the judge had said.

Someday she would have a love like the Swayzes had.

Someday she'd have a husband who made her laugh and who treated her like she was his greatest treasure, instead of one who only shared a house with her because they were married. Her parents argued more than talked. They seemed to make the most of their marriage for the sake of their children. Lately, they hadn't even done that.

Into her mind popped the faces of those at the orphanage. She'd adopt them all today if she could. Being unmarried, she couldn't adopt. Not even a partially deaf little girl who liked drawing ponies and had an imaginary friend named Fire.

No one deserved loneliness.

Her smile died, heart ached. Coral breathed deep.

She had to stop wallowing on what she didn't have. Stop wishing. Stop thinking about anything, save for doing her job.

Considering the extra work she'd put in this week after the judge stunned her with the news of how he wanted to surprise his wife, there was no way the Swayzes wouldn't be on the outbound train tomorrow morning. She'd stake her job on it. In all reality, she had. This was the last test for her to earn the precious reference she needed to secure a social secretary position elsewhere. Life in a city with electricity and streetcars.

And the opera!

An automobile honked somewhere along the street.

A man yelled for Carol. Or maybe he said Coral. She didn't have time to wait and look around to figure out where the sound had come from. She hurried past the ice-cream parlor and young Teddy Kent's glare. For once, the teenager and his friends didn't toss expletives in her direction.

The honking increased.

Coral reached the intersection. She grimaced.

A wooden board lay on the muddy street across a water-filled pothole.

"This could be a problem," she muttered under her breath.

She could backtrack and take a different—longer—route to the jeweler, and waste precious time, or she could cross the board. An easy task *if* she had good equilibrium. And she didn't. She had no balance, struggled to hear well in crowds, no longer danced with rhythm, and couldn't tell where sounds originated. Still, all in all, being deaf in one ear was more of an inconvenience than a handicap. Not that she would announce news of her deafness in the *Wathena Times* or *Weekly Republican*. The pitying glances she received from her family were enough. She didn't need everyone in town feeling sorry for her, too.

Someone again yelled for Carol.

The devil wagon honked three times in a row. Likely at the pedestrians crossing the street, darting around the wheeled and horse-drawn traffic.

Coral eyed the muddy road and footprint-covered board. She didn't have time to lose. She drew upon every ounce of optimism she had. If she walked on her tiptoes, she could keep the hem of her skirt from the mud.

"Coral, stop!"

She jerked her gaze upward. Halfway up the block ahead were Gil and his wife Ann, waving.

"Wait!" they both said in unison.

Coral released a sigh of relief and nodded. Instead of continuing on to her, they stopped to chat with a cluster of teeners that included their brother Richard, and Ann's nephew, Ronnie.

A hand touched her shoulder then drew back.

Coral turned around. Gasped. Standing this close, she could see the dark circles under Jack's blue eyes and could smell his leather and soap cologne. His forehead furrowed, wrinkling deep from more than two decades of working in the Kent family orchard. If Inez knew his true character, like Coral did, she may not find his exterior so appealing.

Jack tipped his hat and a lock of ash-blond hair fell across his forehead. "We need to talk."

⁕

Six days of fitful sleep. Of having no focus morning, noon, and night. Of promising God he'd make things right between him and Coral if God would orchestrate an opportunity.

Not once during the last six days had Jack seen Coral anywhere about town. Only when he decided to live with his guilt, here she was. In a flower shop he'd never stepped inside before today. Not but five feet from him. And what had he talked about? Yellow ribbon. If it weren't for him, she'd be married with a baby or two. It was time he apologized. God help him, he'd do it even if it meant losing every last bit of his pride.

That's what You want, isn't it, Lord?

The automobile horn blared again.

Jack glanced over his shoulder at a green Ford Model C, the driver's face obscured by the afternoon sun's glare on the windshield. Not recognizing the automobile as belonging to anyone he knew, he narrowed his focus on the pretty redhead. Coral stood before him, clenching her briefcase and looking like she was about to breathe fire. Considering the number of Kent and Davies kin milling about the street and at the nearby carnival, he wasn't about to risk a skirmish breaking out if things between them became heated.

He grabbed her elbow. "Let's go somewhere private."

Coral jerked free of his hold. "If you have anything to say to me, Jack Kent, you can say it here."

Dozens of pedestrians stopped walking and looked their way.

"Shh," he cautioned. "No need to draw attention by yelling."

"I'm not—"

"Coral?" came an out-of-breath voice. "Is it really you?"

Her blue-eyed glare shifted from Jack to his wayward cousin who wore a fancy high-collar black suit and a top hat—clothes more fitting for a bank president than a soon-to-be orchard manager. Coral offered no smile of delight. No jumping into her first love's arms, kissing him repeatedly and confessing the love she'd kept hidden these last four years. If anything, she looked put out. With Hiram.

The corner of Jack's mouth twitched. If she was wary of Hiram, then she was shrewder than he'd given her credit for.

Jack nodded toward the Model C parked on the opposite side of the street. "That yours?"

Hiram slapped Jack's shoulder. "Sure is, coz. She's a beaut, isn't she?"

Jack didn't respond. Or ask where Hiram had secured the funds to purchase the vehicle.

"Ahh, Coral darling." Hiram took a slow, predatory step toward her. His gaze moved from her face to the curves her blue suit accentuated. "You've become even more beautiful. Forgive me for being a fool and not returning home sooner."

Jack's brows rose at the word *home*.

Coral continued to regard Hiram as if he were a stranger offering candy.

Smart girl.

"What are you doing back in Wathena?" she asked.

Hiram cocked his head to the side. "You don't know?"

She shook her head.

"You, Coral Davies."

"Me?" she blurted in an unladylike manner.

As Hiram talked to Coral, Jack looked past her, up the sidewalk where her brother Gil was shoving people out of the way. His wife Ann pulled at his arm. Whatever she was saying, they were too far away to hear, yet gaining ground.

Jack slapped Hiram's shoulder. "We should go."

Hiram had eyes for no one but Coral. "I've spent the last four years agonizing over how things would be different if we would've eloped. I would have returned sooner, but I've been making plans."

Coral's mouth opened, but no words came out.

Jack felt his jaw drop as well. What yarn was his cousin spinning? During that last year at university and whenever he'd returned to visit Hiram, as soon as his cousin noticed a pretty girl, nothing Jack could say would distract him. Never once in the last four years had Hiram asked Jack about Coral.

"What kind of plans?" Jack put in.

"To elope," Hiram said to Coral as if she'd been the one to ask.

Panic widened Coral's eyes. "Elope? It's been years since—"

"Not to me. I've never stopped loving you." Hiram reached for her arm.

For a split second, Jack would have sworn her gaze shifted to him, a silent *help me*. Jack shoved Hiram to the side as Coral backed onto the wooden board. She wobbled. Jack lunged for her, but she lost her balance and fell backward into the street with an *oomph*. Mud splattered everywhere; her briefcase and parasol slide from her grip, yet she clung to the bouquet.

Hiram scowled at Jack. "Why did you—"

Gil swung Hiram around; his fist connected with Hiram's face. Someone shoved Jack from behind. He stumbled forward, tripped over Gil's boot, and twisted in time not to land on Coral. Instead he hit the ground next to her, mud seeping into his suit. Coral's other brothers, Dan and Richard, arrived and attacked Hiram. Then, out of the corner of Jack's eye, he saw Teddy grab a handful of mud.

"Don't," he yelled in unison with Coral.

A glob hit Gil in the back.

Gil scooped a handful. "Why, you little—!"

Ann screamed.

Jack shielded Coral as mud flew from all directions.

Chapter 2

He that demands mercy and shows none,
ruins the bridge over which he himself is to pass.
THOMAS ADAMS

The next morning

D o you even know why you hate each other?" The calm voice broke the
silence in the jail.

From where Jack sat on the cot in the corner of his cell, he looked from
Judge Swayze, dressed in his Sunday finest, to the Kents, then to Coral with her
bright red-orange hair a startling contrast to that of her kin. All six cells packed
with two or three people. While this wasn't the first time he'd been in jail after an
altercation with a Davies, it was the first time since his university days when he
used to run head-first into any battle unconcerned with the consequence. Years of
taming his temper and establishing his reputation as an upstanding citizen—as one
of the town's esteemed doctors—ruined in the blink of an eye.

In a mud puddle, to be more precise.

A steeple bell in the distance rang, calling worshippers to service.

Tin coffee mug in hand, Judge Swayze looked over the rims of his spectacles
as he walked down the corridor between the two rows of cells. "Well," he prodded,
"you've been given the night to think it over. Surely you've figured it out."

Murmurs and shrugs were the only response.

"In all my fifty-two years, I've never seen such a bunch of fools."

"Sir, the reason the feud began doesn't matter anymore." Coral's girlish voice
came from behind her brothers Gil and Dan.

Richard sulked in another cell with two cousins. Whit was the Davies brother
not involved in the mudslinging. Jack wasn't surprised. Since the incident at the
river four years ago, Whit had kept with his leatherworking business while also
helping Mr. Davies manage their orchard. If anyone had the ability to end this
feud, it was the oldest Davies son.

Coral pushed her brothers aside and made her way to the cell door, to where
Swayze now stood. Her dress was more brown than blue, likely as ruined as his
beige suit. Most of her lovely face was covered with dried mud, hair matted. Unlike
Jack, she'd slept through the night, he knew because he'd watched her. She'd lain on
her right side, using Dan's coat as a pillow. Never stirred at any sound, which made

him more assured of his diagnosis.

"I do think everyone has learned his lesson," Coral said with a cheerfulness Jack never had until he'd been awake at least an hour. "This won't happen again."

Hiram walked to the door of the cell he shared with Jack. "I agree, sir. We're all changed men."

A *humph* came from the district attorney, the Honorable Lew Peters, standing at the entrance to the jail cells.

Judge Swayze sipped his coffee. "You are ever the optimist, Miss Davies, and you. . ." He scowled at Hiram. "Considering you've been away from Wathena these last four years, you no more know those sharing this jail with you than they know you. Besides, a man's nature never changes, wouldn't you say, Dr. Kent?"

All eyes, including Coral's, turned on him.

Jack leaned forward, resting his elbows on his knees, gaze on the brick floor. He steepled his fingers. Last Sunday the judge had sat in the same service as Jack, and every Kent save for Hiram, and listened to the same sermon on how believers were the temple in which the Spirit of God abided. That could only happen if a man's sinful nature was removed. Crucified. Changed. Replaced with a new nature, one holy, blameless, and beyond reproach. It'd taken Jack almost seventeen months to finally understand God had forgiven all his sins—past, present, future—and made him a new man in Christ.

A sinner to a saint.

He looked at the judge. "God changes a man."

"Indeed." Swayze took a leisurely sip from his tin cup.

Jack would wager the man did it to hide a smile.

Coral's head tilted as she stared at him. He wanted to say she looked impressed with his answer, but he no more knew her than she knew him. Her faith may be no more real than his had been prior to his uncle's death.

Swayze cleared his throat.

Coral and Jack looked his way.

His gaze narrowed and shifted about, looking no more pleased than he had the moment he'd first questioned them all yesterday afternoon following their arrest. "Still, I'm neither convinced a lesson has been learned here nor hopeful this won't happen again. Disturbing the peace is a misdemeanor criminal offense. Anyone charged can face jail time up to ninety days plus fines."

"Ninety days," echoed about the room.

"Plus fines," muttered Jack.

"Your warning is duly noted." Hiram grinned. He shoved his hands in his trouser pockets with that devil-may-care attitude of his. "Since we've all agreed not to press charges against one another for assault and battery, you can let us go."

Jack shook his head. University hadn't changed his cousin one bit. Hiram still had that uncanny ability to keep criticism from getting under his skin.

Not a flaw, but not necessarily a virtue, either.

"Not so quickly, Mr. Kent," the DA put in. "I have the paperwork ready to file charges against you all for creating a public disturbance. Trust me, you will be found guilty. Your families—every last one—are waiting outside to hear what the judge decides. You're under his mercy at the moment."

As murmurs and grumbles grew, Jack stared at the dried mud on his hands. Ninety days of no house calls. Mary Zeizer's twins wouldn't wait that long to be delivered. He'd promised Mr. McKinney he'd be by the man's side when his wife passed. While misdemeanor conviction would be a black mark on them all, disqualifying them (especially Jack) in the forum of public opinion, its consequences were far greater and long reaching than likely any Kent or Davies realized.

No one would be in jail if he hadn't made an attempt to apologize to Coral because he'd thrown her in the river. Because he was to blame for her hearing loss.

Fault—and responsibility—lay at his mud-caked feet. He had to make reparations.

Gil and Dan murmured, nodded, and then broke apart.

"You can't keep us in here for three months," Gil argued. "School starts soon for the teeners. The Kents don't have enough workers, any more than we do, to bring in the harvest without us there to help. That financial loss would be greater than any fines." He pulled his brother Dan forward. "Dan's getting married in two months. He can't miss his wedding."

Swayze gave him a look of disdain. "You should have considered those things before you participated in a mud fight. Your own wife tried to stop you. Pride—arrogance—stupidity—they all go before a fall. Have the decency, Gil, to stop whining about why you can't stay in jail. You are in here on your own making."

Richard Davies's eyes flashed with anger. "Dr. Kent pushed our sister into the mud," he shot back. "The Kents started it. We just finished it. I will wear a misdemeanor conviction with pride."

The other Kent and Davies teeners agreed.

"With pride you say," began Swayze, brows raised. "You should know there are thousands of state and federal consequences to having a misdemeanor conviction on your record. It affects gun ownership, access to loans, adoption qualifications, university admissions, job applications, and even your ability to join the United States Armed Forces"—he gave Teddy a pointed look—"including the National Guard. What you think is a badge of honor is in reality a silent and continual punishment." He turned to the exit, and District Attorney Peters stepped out of the way to give him room to pass.

Jack stood.

"Wait!" Coral said before he did.

Swayze stopped a few feet from the threshold. He looked over his shoulder. "Yes, Miss Davies?"

She gripped the bars, her knuckles whitening. "I can't stay in here." She sounded panicked. "I—I—I have job responsibilities and plans."

"I cannot continue to employ you, should you be charged with a misdemeanor."

Despite the mud splatters on her face, Jack could see her skin paling. "We had an agreement," she said. "Your trip—shouldn't you be leaving in a couple hours?"

"I should." Swayze walked back to Coral's cell. His hand wrapped around hers. "You have become the closest I have to a child. The feud between your families ruined an anniversary dinner with my wife. Other people are being harmed now because of this inability of both families to let go of a grudge. One day someone is going to be seriously hurt"—for a second, his gaze settled on Jack—"if it hasn't already happened. I'm sorry, Coral." He released her hand. "Peters, file the charges."

"Wait," Jack said, "isn't there another solution?"

"Another solution?" Swayze repeated as if it was the most ridiculous thing he'd ever heard. He coughed a breath. "Short of a Kent marrying a Davies, I can't see one."

Chapter 3

If we could read the secret histories of our enemies, we should find in each man's life sorrow and suffering enough to disarm all hostility.
HENRY WADSWORTH LONGFELLOW

Until death do you part. Do you part. Do you part.

The words resounded as the steam engine chugged, iron wheels turned. With her mud-stained parasol overhead to block the bright sun, Coral watched the noon passenger train pull out of the station. The engine whistled again. Judge and Mrs. Swayze sat secure inside their rented Pullman car on this most pristine summer day. If either looked outside the gold-curtained windows to where she stood, in soiled garments, she didn't know.

Death do you part.

Just like your mother, you've made the Davies name the laughingstock of the town.

Coral's empty stomach lurched.

She'd rather her father had fled the jail after the wedding in tears like her mother had, wailing at the horrors of it all. No, he had to remind her of the gravitas of her action. He had to ensure she knew she was no longer a Davies. What she'd sacrificed for the family's benefit mattered not, because she'd married *one of them.* Gil's wife, Ann, had been the only family to give Coral and Jack hugs and wish them well.

Tears blurred her view.

Blinking them away, Coral straightened her shoulders, gripped her briefcase in one hand and parasol in the other. She glanced about the depot to spy him talking to a group of local businessmen. They wore smiles as broad as Jack's. If he was bothered by the mud he still wore, he showed it none. Even after a good cleaning, his Panama hat may never sit level on his head again. Things damaged were nothing, though, compared to lives—and futures—hurt. She shouldn't have been arrested. She hadn't been involved in the mud flinging. If she hadn't panicked when Hiram tried to grab her arm, she wouldn't have lost her balance. Of course, if she had better equilibrium she wouldn't have fallen. Jack hadn't been at fault, either. Yet the two people with the least blame were the ones paying the consequences for the guilty.

The men took turns shaking Jack's hand, actually looking like they were congratulating him. As they walked off, Jack strolled to her with the jubilant smile no longer on his face.

He stopped in front of her. "Where's the buggy?"

"I sent Byers on to the house so he would be spared the task of cleaning the dirt we would certainly leave behind on the seats." She released a weary sigh. "Why are you looking at me like I am a rash for which you must determine the degree of infectiousness?"

His lips twitched. "Something like that. After you," he said, motioning to the street.

She acquiesced.

He took the parasol and briefcase from her. Clearly lost in his own thoughts, he said nothing more as he held the parasol over her head. They left the depot and walked in the direction of the Swayze house. A wagon and two buggies rolled past at a snail's pace. Gossip traveled, it seemed, as fast as the afternoon breeze. The drivers and passengers gawked at the unusual sight of a Davies walking with a Kent. No, not just walking with a Kent. Walking with the one she'd agreed to marry despite her parents' and brothers' objections. Despite Jack's grandmother's objections. Despite Hiram's objections.

Despite her own.

Jack hadn't shown one inkling of an objection or doubt. Unlike her, he—in his blond-haired, blue-eyed, mud-splattered glory—had stood before the judge and recited his vows without hesitation. Not even a miniscule stumble over a syllable. Not the smallest bead of perspiration on his forehead. Was he not one to ever doubt a decision?

As they crossed the road, Jack steered her around muddy potholes.

Coral glanced at him out of the corner of her eye.

He nodded politely to anyone they passed by yet never held a gaze long enough to invite conversation. He didn't appear ashamed to be married to her. But every so often, she caught a flash of a guilty man fearful of people discovering his sins, and then the upstanding-citizen mask returned so quickly she was left doubting she'd ever seen anything.

They turned right onto a residential street, lined with trees, shrubs, and fragrant and colorful perennials. Jack shifted which hand held the parasol and briefcase as he moved around her to walk on the side near the road. Considering they'd exchanged minimal dialogue, despite living in a town with a grand population of almost fourteen hundred, it seemed strange that in the course of twenty-four hours, their relationship had evolved from adversarial to matrimonial.

She was married to Jack.

Married.

To. Him.

Yoked together. Husband and wife. And he was practically a stranger.

Oh dear.

Coral took a deep breath. "We need to talk."

"Are you sure?" He turned his head a fraction, enough to meet her gaze. His lips tugged upward at the corners. "I said that yesterday and we landed in jail."

If her mood wasn't so fretful, she would have chuckled at his attempt to amuse. How was their marriage going to work? Neither wanted this. Being metaphorically lassoed together had not changed their lives for the better.

She nipped her bottom lip. "A sackcloth-and-ashes, woe-is-us dirge is more fitting considering our circumstances," she said and noted how nervous she suddenly sounded talking to him. "But I believe looking for the good in a situation elevates one's mood." She sang, " 'Taint no use to sit and whine, when the fish ain't on your line. Bait your hook and keep on tryin'."

"Look for the good, huh?" He dipped under a low-hanging branch. "One: I'm pleased to not spend another night lying on a rickety cot that smelled of urine, sweat, and, strangely, bacon."

"My cot had no odor."

"And that's why you had nine hours of blissful slumber," he said, looking vaguely amused. "If I am ever arrested again, I will demand your cell."

Coral took a swift breath. "How do you know I slept for nine hours?"

"Two," he said and cleared his throat. "Neither orchard will be hindered by lack of workers during the harvest."

For a moment Coral stared. He was caked in as much mud as she was. He stood tall as he walked. His bright blue eyes glistened in the sun, yet he squinted like one did with eyes sensitive to the sun due to lack of sleep. "Jack, did you sleep at all?"

"Yes," he answered without pause.

She gave him her best *be honest* look.

He managed to grimace and smile at the same time, an adorable action, or at least she'd describe it as such if he weren't Jack Kent. "I would've slept longer had my cot been less malodorous."

Nothing in his expression or tone gave clue he was lying, yet something in her knew for certain he wasn't telling the *whole* truth. Why hadn't he been able to sleep? No one had been snoring—

Coral stumbled and quickly righted herself.

Jack gave her one of those *you are a rash and I must determine the degree of your infectiousness* looks. Oh! She looked away, mortified. He *was* diagnosing her. If anyone had been snoring, she wouldn't have heard it because she'd been sleeping on her right side. She'd been deaf to the world.

She had to tell him.

She needed to.

It was right, being that they were married and all.

"Three," she blurted with a bright grin. "Both families attended the wedding, the likes of which has never before been seen in Wathena."

He seemed to be contemplating his response. Then the right side of his mouth curved, a lazy boyish tilt of his lips that made her insides do a strange flip. "The grand spectacle of it all left them speechless."

"Save for my parents, who. . ." Coral's amusement died as her mind drew a blank. "Alas, there is no positive interpretation of their wails and barbs." The moment the words left her mouth she wished she could take them back. As cold and unloving as her parents were, that did not justify her vocalized complaint even to a man they considered their enemy. She would not be a person who returned evil for evil. "I shouldn't have said that about them. They mean well."

"Do they?" This time he gave her the *be honest* look.

Coral didn't answer. Jack had lived in Wathena all his life. He, like everyone in town, knew her parents, heard the gossip, and believed the worst because the worst was the truth. When it came to Coral, her parents didn't mean well.

Jack, to his credit, didn't press for a response.

They turned onto the wide shrub-lined brick path leading to the stately white two-story colonial where she'd been living for the last eleven months since Mrs. Swayze agreed to teach her what was expected in a social secretary. When they reached steps leading to the covered porch and terrace, Jack stopped. Coral did, too.

"Your parents," he said softly, "realized you loved others more than yourself, and that knowledge brought an outpouring of emotion. That is the perspective you should have on their reaction, because it is the truth."

Coral's throat tightened at the tenderness in his voice, in his eyes. Her chest ached. If only his words were as true as he tried to make her believe.

"Thank you," she whispered.

He nodded.

Jack closed the parasol, tucked it under his right arm, and then assisted her up the stairs. "Four: I can resume calling on my patients, while your employment with the Swayzes continues unabated." He reached for the door handle.

"Wait." She gave a tired smile. "Please."

"Yes?"

She gazed up at him for a long moment. A haphazard pattern of mud-colored polka dots covered the right side of his face, a few clumps matted in his ash-blond hair. Unlike the rest of the men in the fight, he had no bruises, no bloodied lip. His blue eyes, she noticed, had flecks of midnight and a dark ring. They were quite pretty. He was more handsome than Hiram. How had she not noticed before?

"Why did you marry me?"

"Someone had to," he said matter-of-factly.

She gave him a curious look. "Yes, but you hate me."

He blanched. His gaze shifted to the street and followed three cyclists as they rode down the street. "Coral, I don't hate you."

"I don't hate you, either," she admitted.

His stunned gaze met hers.

"I figured you were wondering," she added with a soft smile.

He shrugged. Was that to mean he didn't care, hadn't been wondering, or was pleased her feelings had changed?

"To be honest, I did hate you, for that first year." She frowned, thinking. "Actually the first two."

"What made you stop?" he asked with clear interest in his tone.

"I spoke to our preacher. He said a onetime prayer isn't always enough to forgive someone. I needed to replace the grudge with a positive, with what made me happy. Hating you made me miserable." She hadn't been able to figure out what made her happy until she figured out what didn't—the life her parents had. She loved them. She merely didn't want to become them.

He looked at her expectantly. "And?"

Coral gazed into his eyes. Either he was an exceptional actor or he truly wanted to hear more. He was interested in hearing more, in listening to her share her dreams. It gave her a queer feeling. Looking away from him, she said, "I realize what brought me joy was the thought of my children and my children's children not growing up hating another family for a reason no one can remember."

"Wathena is a *good* town," he argued.

She chose to ignore the defensiveness in his tone. "I know it is, but no Davies or Kent can live here and escape the feud."

"I have for the last four years."

Coral raised her brows at the incredulity of his statement.

He rolled his eyes. "All right, until yesterday."

"Until yesterday. Exactly." She punctuated her words with a smile. "I've worked dozens of jobs in the last two years, saving most of what I earned. All I need to leave Wathena is a letter of reference from the Swayzes. The irony is, even if they give me one, I'm married to a man who loves living here. Your gallant action—and I do not mean this maliciously, Jack, please know that—has doomed me to the life I yearn to escape."

He winced.

"You could have let Hiram volunteer," she reminded him.

"Do you wish I had?" he snapped.

"I would rather not be married to either of you, but at least he *wanted* to marry me."

He paused, but only for a moment. "It's my responsibility. Not his."

Coral nodded like she understood his reason. She didn't. While he was the oldest Kent grandson, he didn't own the orchard. Hiram became the owner the day his father died seventeen months ago, which made Hiram the male head of the household even though he was six years younger than Jack, even though Hiram's father had raised Jack like his son. And Hiram was the reason the mud fight began. Something, though, in Jack's eyes kept her from arguing with his reasoning. She might say it was guilt, but how was she to know? She didn't know him. Or at least he was proving she didn't. The Jack Kent she thought she knew wouldn't have shielded her from mud. He wouldn't have volunteered to marry her to keep her family—and his—from a misdemeanor conviction. He wouldn't have kissed her.

Her lips tingled as the memory returned, and she looked to the ground, finding it awkward to meet his gaze.

After Judge Swayze had pronounced them man and wife and told Jack he could kiss his bride, Jack could have brushed his lips against hers and been done with it. Should have. Instead, he'd cradled her cheek with one hand, pulled her against him, and kissed her well and good and long, far more than what she ever expected a first kiss would be. In front of his family and hers. Dozens of people. When he'd finished the kiss, her cheeks had burned, pulse raced, mind struggled to remember if she'd responded. No one applauded, as customary at a wedding. No one made a sound, until Mother began wailing. Hiram had looked as furious as Father.

Jack, though, had given her a sheepish look. An apology for the longer-than-necessary kiss? Or had he been feeling as befuddled as she'd been?

Coral looked up, only to find him regarding her, awaiting her response. A prickle started at her neck and descended down her spine. The last time she'd felt something like that was in high school when Hiram would give her a secret smile. True, she'd seen him toss the same sultry and flirtatious look at other girls, and had for years, but somehow that hadn't stopped her from believing the way he'd looked at her was different. Sincere. But she wasn't a besotted eighteen-year-old anymore. And Jack wasn't his roguish cousin.

Except, unlike Hiram, Jack *had* kissed her.

He was the only man in her whole life to have pressed his warm, full lips against hers. She'd liked every moment of it.

She didn't have to see her face to know her burning cheeks were red and splotchy.

He was watching her with an intensity that made her pulse leap. His gaze fell to her lips.

Coral held her breath in anticipation of a kiss she'd never in her life dreamed she'd want. He wanted it, too. She could see it in his eyes. She could feel it.

She swallowed nervously.

He shoved the parasol and briefcase into her arms then backed to the steps. "I need to pay house calls on Mrs. Zeizer and the McKinneys." He couldn't sound more eager to get away from her.

"I understand." She nodded in hopes the action would lessen any reddening of her cheeks. "Dinner will be at—"

"I could be gone all day."

"Oh." Coral gave a little smile to cover the odd ache in her chest. "Before you leave, I need you to know I'm truly sorry I wasted years hating you, blaming others, and complaining how life was unfair."

He moved his head slightly, acknowledging her words.

"I don't want to become that person again." She paused. Moistened her lips. Breathed deep. It was amazing how much better it made her feel to be honest with him. "Since we're married, can we agree to try and make the best of this?"

He nodded.

"We should arrive early for the parade, for everyone will want to congratulate you and wish me future happiness."

He nodded again.

"I'll see you later then." Feeling awkward at his silence, she turned the doorknob and took a step inside the shaded reception hall. She didn't know him well enough to know if he was angry at her or merely needed a nap.

Jack said something in a voice so low she couldn't make out the words.

She swiveled around. "Did you say something?"

He gripped his damaged hat with both hands, his posture stiff and angry. "I'm sorry," he ground out.

Coral stared at him in disbelief. The polite Jack, the gallant one who escorted her home, who helped find something good in the bad, who made her feel wanted. The Jack whom she could love. That Jack was gone.

"For what?" she asked.

"For everything I've done to ruin your life."

She couldn't speak. He hadn't ruined her life. Damaged yes, but not ruined.

"I'm going to fix this." His voice seemed a little strange, his eyes a little shiny. He slapped his hat atop his head and walked away, the back of his beige suit more mud-stained than the front.

"Jack?" she called out. "Dinner is at seven."

He kept walking.

Coral closed the door. She glanced at her wristwatch. Four minutes to one. She needed a bath. She also needed to explain events to Mr. and Mrs. Byers, who would not mind if Jack stayed here while the Swayzes were on holiday.

Or Coral could move in with him. His living quarters on the second floor of his office should be large enough for her, too.

No matter where she lived, she would make do.

In thirty days, she would leave Wathena. Until then, her job was to convince Jack that Cleveland, Ohio, needed another doctor.

Their marriage would work. She'd ensure it.

Chapter 4

It is easy to be brave from a safe distance.
AESOP

Word has it, Dr. Jackson Kent married Miss Coral Davies in a civil
ceremony this morning, attended by family and a few friends."

Jack removed his suit coat and draped it around the back of his
chair. He schooled a grin and accepted from Augustus McKinney the almost-black
pie pan heaping with beefy potato stew. He noted the darkened brown spots on the
farmer's leathered hand, more than what were there a week ago. Jack's gaze went
immediately to McKinney's face. Additional dark spots on the face, too. Redder
than usual nose. His breath had smelled bad. Could be a deficiency with his liver.
Eighty yet with the spryness—and hair—of a man decades younger did not mean
McKinney wasn't in need of an exam.

"Word has it, huh?" Jack said, sitting.

McKinney, with his own pie pan filled with stew, sat next to him at the two-
person table, two oil lamps providing the only light in the cabin now that the
sun had set. He tucked a red cloth napkin into the bib of his denim overalls. He
smoothed the bushy white hair around his mouth.

"I'm no priest, but"—McKinney's pale blue eyes narrowed with that *you'd better
listen to your elders* look—"confession is good for one's soul."

Jack picked up his fork and speared a potato chunk. It hadn't been ten
hours since the jail wedding, seven since he left Coral at the Swayze house.
"Who told you?"

"The Brazeltons, Drosselmeiers, and Sturgises separately when they stopped by
to see Eugenia and drop off food."

Jack took a bite. Good families all.

McKinney poked Jack's shoulder with his fork, leaving a streak of gravy on
Jack's clean white shirt. "Well, is it true?"

Jack motioned to his mouth full of stew.

"Humph." McKinney leaned back in his seat. "You tellin' me you married
the prettiest girl in all of Doniphan County, and you're here keeping an old man
company?"

"Something like that."

"Does she know you're skipping your wedding night?"

"She will understand."

"Almost thirty years old and not a lick of sense." Shaking his head, McKinney buttered one of Mrs. Sturgis's prized rolls. He handed it to Jack. "Sop up the gravy with that."

Jack did what he was told.

Forks scraped the pans as they ate.

He'd never believed in love at first sight. He had, in fact, known Coral since the day she was born, his mother acting as midwife when she and Jack had come across Mrs. Davies alone in her buggy on the road to town. He'd grown up hearing stories about the greedy, immoral Davies family, wealthy owners of the largest orchard in northeastern Kansas. A thousand acres. Two-thirds the size of the Kent orchard due to their thievery.

Something changed in him this morning after he'd made his vows.

In a jail.

While wearing mud-stained clothes.

After having little sleep and even less food.

A good lawyer could argue he hadn't been in his right mind, and still wasn't. As he'd listened to Coral stumble through her promise to love, cherish, and honor him until death did they part, he realized he wanted more than her forgiveness for the past. He wanted more than her not hating him anymore. He'd wanted more than to believe she'd silently begged *him* to rescue her when Hiram had tried to grab her arm. What he hadn't been sure of was what *more* he wanted until he kissed his bride.

Jack swallowed the stew despite the tightening of his throat.

He wanted Coral.

As his wife. Until death did they part.

He wanted her to want him, too.

Want didn't come near to describing how he felt about being with her tonight. Coral was his wife, married in the eyes of the law and God even though they hadn't married in a church or with a preacher. A license with both their names lay on the bed where he'd tossed it before taking a bath and changing clothes so he could pay calls on the Zeizers and McKinneys. He shouldn't feel guilty for the thoughts he'd struggled to not think since their kiss. She was his wife. He shouldn't feel guilty for wanting to—

"You're looking mighty peaked," McKinney said, leaning over the table. He touched Jack's forehead with the back of his cold hand. "Warm. You didn't catch something in jail, did you?"

"I think I did," Jack muttered.

It wasn't love, but it could become love. Strangely, it wasn't the condition of *her* heart that troubled him most.

She wanted to leave Wathena.

He didn't.

And he didn't want her to leave, either.

Jack laid his fork next to the empty pie plate. "I'm in a pickle."

"Go on." McKinney wiped his pan with the last of his bread.

"Coral and I didn't marry because we wanted to. We were under duress."

McKinney's bushy white brows rose. "Who was duressin' you?"

"Judge Swayze."

"Swayze?" he echoed, his voice tinged with skepticism. "Nah, there isn't a man in Kansas with more integrity. That'd be breaking the law."

Jack's shoulders slumped as he let out a long, tired exhale. He quickly summarized the events leading to the mud fight—Hiram's return, Coral falling into the mud, and the subsequent arrest and night spent in jail. He omitted his suspicions about her hearing loss.

"Well," Jack said, "now do you see?"

"Misdemeanor or marriage," muttered McKinney. He pushed back from the table and walked to the potbellied stove keeping a copper coffeepot warm. "That's duress, all right."

Jack gathered up the dirty dishes and carried them to the sink as McKinney filled two clay mugs. "There's more."

"Good or bad?"

"Depends on how you look at it." Jack took the proffered mug. "Before Swayze boarded the train, he pulled me aside. According to the law, duress at the time of consent voids a marriage, since one's consent must be voluntary. On that grounds, Coral and I can get an annulment. No harm, no foul."

"He forced you to marry then told you how to get"—McKinney looked incredulous—"unmarried?"

"Seems so. Why would he do that?"

McKinney shrugged.

It made no sense. Swayze was as forthright as they came. He wasn't the kind to manipulate, flatter, withhold information, or resort to any chicanery to get his way. If anything, the man had made a flippant remark in his frustration with the situation and wasn't sure how to backtrack once Coral and Jack agreed to marry.

McKinney leaned against the counter. Jack mimicked his action. They finished their coffee in silence, Mrs. McKinney's soft breathing the only noise in the two-room cabin.

Jack set his empty mug in the sink. "I'll go pump water and clean these up while you crack a few windows."

McKinney looked to the room where his wife had slept peacefully since Jack had given her medication for the pain. "Sixty-three years ago I took Eugenia as my wife. I pledged to comfort, honor, and keep her, in plenty and want, in joy and sorrow, in sickness and health until we are parted by death."

Which Jack expected would happen tonight.

"Vows are easy to make." McKinney's voice was rough. He patted Jack's back. "What's stinkin' hard is staying with the one you married when you're under duress."

"Coral doesn't want to be married to me."

"And in ten, twenty, thirty years she still may not want to be married to you."

"Meaning?" Jack asked impatiently.

McKinney refilled his mug. He placed the copper kettle back on the stove. After a long moment of silence, he said, "Not all marriages begin with love. Many don't end that way."

Jack said nothing. He could sense take-it-from-me advice coming along.

McKinney's eyes narrowed. "What you do every day after the wedding determines how the marriage will end. Women like it when we talk and share our feelings." He shrugged. "It's your choice to see this marriage as a blessing or blunder," McKinney added before sipping his coffee.

Blessing or blunder. As long as they shared a perspective, all was well. When their views differed—

Jack shook his head. "Even if this marriage could be a blessing to me, it's not to her," he retorted, his voice betraying his frustration. He shoved away from the sink and walked to the window, staring into the starry night. "Coral's hell-bent on leaving Wathena. An annulment is the best thing I can give her."

"Why don't you ask Coral what she wants?"

Jack let out an irritated little snort. She'd been quite clear in what she wanted. He headed outside to fill a bucket with water. He had to do the right thing, despite his feelings for Coral. And because of them, too.

⁓∞⁓

Coral jolted awake. She glanced around the living room, lit only by the moonlight streaming through the east windows. The lamps had been extinguished. Her teacup no longer on the coffee table. The book she'd been reading lay in the middle of the cream and burgundy couch. A quilt from her bedroom lay across the lap of her white lace dress. According to her wristwatch, it was twenty-three minutes after four.

If it'd been Jack who'd found her asleep, he would have woken her.

It had to have been Mrs. Byers. Maybe Mr. Byers, too. While she was as much an employee as they were, since the day she moved in with the Swayzes, the Byerses had treated her like she was an extension of the house. Another thing entrusted to their loving care.

When Jack hadn't returned for supper, they'd been the first to suggest he had a justifiable reason for being gone on their wedding night. If he wasn't with the McKinneys, he could be with the Zeizers. Mary's twins could have decided to arrive a month early. Or maybe he had to go on an emergency call. Thus was the life of a country doctor.

He had good reasons for not returning.

He wasn't shunning her.

No, that was for her parents to do, which infuriated Mr. Byers as much as his wife each time he brought it up. The Byerses were good people who wanted the best for her. God had blessed her with them, and with the Swayzes. She wanted to believe He'd blessed her with Jack, too.

"Oh, I'm such a hopeless optimist," she murmured to the empty room.

Coral blinked at the hot tears to keep them from falling. She stood, draping the quilt over her arm. She carried the book to the half-wall bookcase and laid it next to the parlor lamp. A doctor had to attend to his patients first.

He wasn't avoiding her.

No matter what her heart said.

Chapter 5

A wounded deer leaps highest.
EMILY DICKINSON

Labor Day ~ 6:23 p.m.

Jack ran a hand through his hair then replaced his hat as he waited at the Swayze front door. It'd been a long night and morning, with comforting McKinney and then assisting with the burial. Against his thigh, he tapped the manila envelope containing the annulment papers. With everyone in town for the parade, he hadn't been able to discreetly visit the district attorney until the floats and carnival were being dismantled.

The door opened.

The Swayzes' housekeeper, Mrs. Byers, looked over the wire spectacles perched on the tip of her pert nose. "Good afternoon, Dr. Kent. Where's your gift?"

"Gift?"

"You could've at least brought flowers after deserting her on her wedding night." She shook her head with a *tsk, tsk.*

Jack had no response. He'd been working. Coral understood.

Mrs. Byers reached across the threshold to pat his arm. "There, there. I know you had a rough night with Eugenia's passing. That you are here now is all that matters. Our poor girl's been overwhelmed all day. It's good you finally showed up. Ladies started arriving at nine, bringing gifts, offering well wishes, inquiring where the groom was."

"I thought it was proper not to call on a newly married couple until after the said couple sent wedding cards welcoming visitors."

"It's also proper for parents of the bride to host a reception following the wedding," she retorted, her disapproval evident, "which occurred in a jail. Etiquette must be adjusted in circumstances as this."

"Coral's best interests are my primary concern." His answer seemed to mollify her.

She stepped back to give him room to pass. Jack entered the reception hall and immediately removed his hat. The house smelled like a flower shop. Voices and sounds of clinking china came from the living room.

"This way," Mrs. Byers said, motioning him to follow.

Jack had taken two steps when he glanced into the dining room on the left. He did a double take. Ribbon-wrapped boxes covered the damask cloth draped over the table, as well as on two temporary tables near the front window. On the sideboard sat two folded quilts, a floral arrangement in a crystal vase, and a small crate that looked to hold four wine bottles, which he doubted. Doniphan was a dry county. Had to be cider vinegar. Another crate on the floor held rosebushes ready to be planted. Next to it were two rolled-up rugs. The number of gifts were beyond what anyone would give in celebration of an anniversary. They were more like ones for—

Dread settled like a rock in his stomach.

He and Coral had been married a day and a half. How had anyone had time to purchase or make a gift? He'd wager everyone had been watching or participating in the parade. Coral would have attended. If any altercation between a Kent and Davies had broken out, he would have heard about it by now.

"Dr. Kent," came Mrs. Byers's soft voice.

Jack gripped the manila envelope tightly and followed her to the living room. They stopped at the threshold. She took his hat and said something about crumpets and cucumber sandwiches. Jack absently nodded. Coral sat on the left side sofa, a prettier picture he'd never seen. On her head was a straw hat with an oversized red ribbon. Her red-orange hair lay in a fat curl over her shoulder looking more vibrant against the white of her shirtwaist. In the lap of her blue skirt was a sleeping white French bulldog pup oblivious to the dozen women wearing grandiose hats, giving marital advice, and taking tea. From where Coral was sitting, with the ladies in front or on her right, she was in the ideal spot to hear whoever spoke to her.

"You don't say," Coral said, her blue eyes sparkling with merriment. "I've never heard that story about Jack before."

Jack could see Coral smiling as she sipped tea. A genuine smile that reached her eyes. She'd known these women all her life. They seemed to genuinely care for her. And if the number of gifts were any indication, the town was supportive of their marriage. The real question was—

Were any of those gifts from a Kent or a Davies?

He'd wager not a one was.

Mrs. Sanderson, who wrote the social column for the *Weekly Republican*, was the first to notice him. "Speak of the devil."

Every lady turned his way, all voices fell silent.

Pink eased up Coral's neck and cheeks, making her porcelain skin glow. The way she looked at him, with an unveiled joy that he'd come back, literally stole his breath. It was the very look he wanted to see on his wife's face. Jack never wanted to tear his eyes away. He was fairly certain his heart stopped beating.

"Well then," Mrs. Sanderson said, "I'm satisfied. Let's go, ladies."

The women joined in paying salutations to Coral, who stood and accepted every hug, even with the sleepy-eyed pup cradled in her arms. Once they finished with Coral, they made their way to Jack with orders he take good care of his bride. Soon the living room had emptied of all but them.

"Cute pup," Jack said to break the silence.

Coral raised the pup to her shoulder. "Isn't she adorable? Mr. Byers found her this morning in a wicker basket along with a note of congratulations for the happy couple."

"We can't keep a dog."

"Why not?"

"Because our marriage is null," Jack said. He turned and caught the tea tray before it slid from Mrs. Byers's grasp.

⟋∞⟍

Coral sat silent on the end of the sofa. Null meant having no legal binding effect. If what he said was true, then they didn't need death to part them.

They only needed an official declaration of nullity from the court.

Jack carried the tray into the living room and sat it on the coffee table. He took a seat on the sofa while the Byerses sat in the two high-backed velvet chairs. As he ate the fruit salad, crumpets, and miniature cucumber sandwiches, he fielded Mr. and Mrs. Byers's questions about consent and duress, detailing the specifics of what the district attorney told him. While they had entered the marriage with good will, openness, honesty, maturity, and emotional stability, their action hadn't had full free will because of external pressure.

They'd been under duress.

Thus null.

Thus void.

Coral hadn't entered the marriage with openness and honesty, either. Though she was sure he had diagnosed her partial deafness, she had not informed him of her handicap. She should have. She'd had the time in the thirty minutes prior to the wedding. Her embarrassment had stopped her.

She didn't need to be embarrassed.

Her family knew. They were supposed to love and accept her, but after losing her hearing in one ear, her father had only increased his belittlement, treating her like she was stupid and less of a person when she didn't hear what was said. Meals with the whole family together often ended in hot tears—hers and her mother's—until Coral learned not to draw any attention to herself. When she moved in with the Swayzes, no Davies questioned her decision. No one begged her to come home.

No one cared.

Unable to bear the sudden warmth in the room, Coral stood. "Excuse me, I need to. . ."

She hurried out of the room, across the reception hall, and into the dining room before any tears could fall. She gripped the edge of the cloth-covered table. Breathed deep. Blinked. She looked to the left. Then the right.

Oh my.

Her mouth fell open. Eyes widened.

Good gracious, there had to be two hundred gifts. At the very least. When had the Byerses set up the tables? Coral didn't know. She'd been occupied with entertaining the constant stream of visitors. Had there been that many to call? Impossible. Half of the gifts had to have come from Wathenans who delivered them and left without saying a word. Had to.

But why?

The pup squirmed and whined. Coral placed it on the wooden floor, and it darted immediately to the living room, back into the wicker basket near the opened French doors. Coral returned her attention to the dining room table. Near the edge, in a basket, stuck between jars of preserves was an envelope with Inez Potter's elegant script.

Dr. and Mrs. Jack Kent

She reached for the card, only to draw back. Inez was too kindhearted to include a spiteful note, yet she couldn't bear to read Inez's words wishing them joy and happiness. Were things different, Inez could be the one looking at a card like this one—same inscription yet in Coral's penmanship. Inez should have married Jack instead. Inez had feelings for him. Inez loved living in Wathena as much as Jack did. Most of all, Inez wasn't a Davies who would have to force Jack to choose between his family and his wife.

Inez still had a chance for a future with Jack, once this unfortunate, not-of-their-full-free-will marriage was nullified.

Every gift in the room had to be returned. Even the pup.

An announcement would need to be placed in the papers. Coral drew in a sharp breath. Mrs. Sanderson! Tonight, before anything could go to press, the society columnist had to be notified. What if she'd already made telephone calls to other papers in the county? Coral would have to contact them, too.

Dishes clattered.

Coral looked into the hall. Mrs. Byers left the room with a tray full of teacups, while Mr. Byers carried out the four wooden folding chairs brought in for extra seating, the pup bounding along behind them. Jack leaned against the dining room's door frame, looking as dapper as ever in his charcoal pin-striped suit. He tapped a manila envelope against his thigh.

"I'll help you return the gifts tomorrow."

"Do you realize how much this community adores you?"

"The gifts are kind of them," he stated, "but—"

"What will they think when we give them back?"

His brow furrowed. "They will *think* we married to save everyone from a misdemeanor conviction—"

"Quite selfless of us," she murmured.

"—and they will *realize* they overstepped their bounds when they brought gifts without being invited," he finished in an irritated voice. "We aren't the ones at fault here." He pushed off the door frame and walked to the center table. He laid the manila envelope on Inez's basket of preserves. "There are three copies. I filled out everything. All you have to do is sign next to my signature. I will file the documents with the court in the morning."

Coral picked up the envelope, unwound the string, and withdrew the papers. She skimmed the document. "When the court nullifies our marriage, it will have officially never existed, and what we sacrificed to spare our families will be in vain."

"No, it won't," he said, his voice flat. "The DA recognized his culpability and agreed not to file charges."

A simple solution to an unwanted marriage.

Her parents would be pleased. Then again, even when she did something to earn their approval, they found fault.

Coral stared absently at the pages with his signature. During the last two years, her focus had been working to earn the funds to leave Wathena. When she wasn't working, she was sleeping. Once the court approved the annulment, she could leave without any encumbrance. She could resume her plans. No one in Cleveland would know about her utterly short marriage to Jack.

Coral would know.

Coral would remember standing before the judge and God and making—in free will—a vow to love, honor, and cherish Jack until death did they part.

How could a court decision null it away?

Her memory wasn't a chalkboard easily erased. Or muddy socks to be laundered clean.

Nor was her conscience.

She looked to Jack. "Yesterday when you promised me we would try and make this work, you knew what the judge had said about our marriage being voidable. You weren't under duress then. Why did you lie to me?"

His face reddened. "I didn't lie."

"You didn't?" she said with a bitter chuckle. She held up the papers. "Your signature—your action—contradicts you. Not telling the truth is a lie."

"I wanted to tell you yesterday!"

"Why didn't you?" she shouted back.

"At that time I didn't know what the right thing to do was."

"Didn't know?" That earned her a glare. Coral stared at him, shaking her head. His callousness hurt. "Jack, the right thing usually begins with a person doing what he said he would—" Her voice cracked. "In our case, it means honoring your vows."

"If I honor my vows," he said in crisp, angry words, "then you are doomed to a life you yearn to escape. You made that clear." He stopped next to her. "I am the reason we are in this mess. It's my responsibility to fix it."

She shook the papers in his face. "An annulment is the only *fix* you can think of?"

"What else is there?"

"Leave with me."

He slapped a present, indenting the box. "My patients are here!"

Now that was the Jack Kent she remembered, the one with the renowned temper. She'd been a fool thinking he'd changed.

If an annulment was what he wanted. . .

Papers in hand, she darted past him, through the hall, and to the secretary at the back of the living room. She found a pen. Signed her name. Dated the paper. Leaving the pen where she'd found it, she returned to Jack now standing in the reception hall with envelope in hand.

"Here you go."

He took the papers she offered.

She narrowed her eyes, unable to stop the consuming anger at him. And at herself for waking up this morning and praying God would grow love in her heart for her husband—the very man who wanted nothing to do with her. "It is not your job to make me happy, nor is it your responsibility to *fix* my problems. I can—and will—take care of myself."

"Coral—"

"Stop! I am finished with talking." She whirled around, lifted the front of her skirts, and ascended the stairs as gracefully as she could manage. She called over her shoulder, "Your patients need you more than I do."

Chapter 6

It is unworthy of God to unite himself to a wretched man, yet it is not unworthy of God to lift a man up out of his wretchedness.
BLAISE PASCAL

J ack didn't move, didn't even blink as Coral fled upstairs. He hadn't meant for this to end in an argument. He secured a way so she could have what she wanted. She should be thanking him, not yelling at him.

"Doc, you mucked that up well," came from the hallway.

Jack looked left of the staircase. Mr. Byers stood with his arm around his wife's shoulder, both looking at him as if he smelled of something foul. "You heard everything?"

"Enough," answered Mr. Byers.

Jack groaned. "What did I do wrong?"

"I can think of several things," Mr. Byers answered before his wife could. "The two most important: you didn't discuss this with Coral yesterday, and then you decided upon the solution today, again without discussing it with her."

Jack stuffed the papers in the envelope. Look where trying to discuss something with Coral led. She was too focused on always trying to find the good in a bad situation. Move to Cleveland? Wathena was where he worked. It was his home. His patients needed him. And Coral was quite clear that she didn't need him.

He looked around the hall for a hat rack. "Where's my hat?"

"You're leaving?" said Mrs. Byers.

"Yes," Jack snapped. "I have no reason to stay."

She stomped over to him. "Don't you dare step a foot out of this house!" She jerked the envelope from his hands. "Until the court nullifies your marriage, that girl is still your wife. I will not stand by and watch you abandon her again because of your own guilt."

He flinched. His guilt was why he had to walk away. This was for Coral's good.

"She made it clear she doesn't want to talk to me."

"Then you talk," Mr. Byers answered, and his wife added, "Give her time to hear your heart."

Jack looked from one to the other, shaking his head. If he went upstairs. . . If he stepped one foot in Coral's bedroom. . .

"I can't go up there." He drew his hand through his hair. "I can't."

"Would it be so torturous to talk to your wife?" Mrs. Byers said softly. "Tell her how you feel. She just may well feel the same." She laid the envelope on the bottom step. "Turn left at the top of the stairs. First door on your right after the bathroom."

Mr. Byers inclined his head toward the staircase. "Don't be as fool-stubborn as she is."

∽∾∾

Coral stepped out of the bathroom, hat in hand. The front door opened then slammed closed. She flinched. It was good he'd left. She didn't want to see—

Jack.

Reaching the top of the stairs, he turned the corner. He stopped. "I—" His gaze fell to her bodice where she'd unbuttoned the top three buttons of her shirtwaist, exposing a good deal of flesh. "We, uhh, I need to talk to you."

"Good night, Jack."

Holding her head high, she walked to her bedroom. When she turned to close the door, she started with surprise. Jack. Head cocked to the side, a lock of ash-blond hair across his forehead, he stared at her long enough to make her fidget. If he noticed her nervousness, noticed how she tried not to breathe deep and inhale his familiar leather and soap scent, he didn't smile. He had the look of someone who'd been ordered to apologize and wasn't the least bit pleased about it.

"Say what you came to say," Coral rushed out, "and be gone."

His eyes closed, lips pursed tight. After a deep breath, he looked at her with an odd expression. "You meant nothing to me. For years if your name was mentioned or I noticed you in town, I felt nothing. When I threw you in the river, I felt nothing. You weren't a person. You were a Davies. Inconsequential."

Tears welled in Coral's eyes. He didn't have to tell her what she knew. He didn't care about people who didn't matter to him.

"I was fine with being inconsequential to you, too," he added.

He had been—she wouldn't argue that. Vowing to love, honor, and cherish him changed how she felt.

"I wanted to be a doctor for as long as I can remember." His voice held no emotion. "I wanted to heal people. With all my training, all my skill, I couldn't keep my uncle from dying." The wrinkles in his forehead deepened; he looked so utterly broken. "I told God I wanted nothing to do with Him or with being a doctor. I took down my shingle and locked my door."

She didn't remember any of this. What had she been doing seventeen months ago? Working. Saving money. Ignoring Jack and everyone else named Kent.

He cleared his throat. "I decided if I died, no one would miss me."

"You didn't try to kill yourself?" she said, mortified.

He gave her a bland look. "No."

She opened her mouth then thought better of it and said nothing.

For the longest time, she thought he wasn't going to continue, and just when she figured he was waiting for her to speak, he said, "I looked in the mirror and saw an angry, bitter man." He shifted his stance, leaning his back against the door frame, gaze on the floor. "I blamed God. I railed at Him, at me, and I broke a good number of things. And then I tried to fix them. I did everything I knew how, everything, and nothing worked. Nothing I could do would repair what I'd broken. That's when it hit me: a broken table can't fix itself. I couldn't fix myself. I couldn't make myself a better man. Only God could change me."

She'd never broken anything, but of the rest she was guilty.

He still didn't look back at her when he said, "I resumed seeing patients. Life was better than it'd ever been. I'd forgotten what it was like to be overwhelmed with guilt and shame until I saw you at the library benefit. Mrs. Sanderson asked you a question. You didn't respond until she touched your arm. You hadn't heard her."

Coral tensed. With the crowd and the band playing, it'd been hard to hear unless the person was speaking beside her good ear. "Have you been diagnosing me for a month?"

His jaw tightened. His head turned, gaze found hers with startling directness, eyes glistening. He reached out and gently cupped her left ear. A tear ran slowly down his cheek. "This is my fault," he choked out.

Coral's breath caught. She'd never seen a man cry, not her father when either of his parents passed, not Whit when he had to put down his dog, not Gil when his broken arm was set. She ached for his pain, and for the added guilt that wasn't his to bear but what he bore because he was a good man. Because he had a tender heart.

Because he cared.

"Oh, Jack." She drew his hand from her face and held it against her heart. "Tossing me in the river ruptured my eardrum. The subsequent infection caused the hearing loss." She offered a tiny smile. "It took time, but I adapted."

"I never meant to hurt you."

"I know."

She released her hold on his hand. She leaned on the opposite side of the door frame. The side of her boot touched his, yet he didn't move. He was looking at her with the most gentle of expressions. If they'd grown up in a different town, he could have asked to court her. She would have been delighted to accept. They could have fallen in love. They could have had babies and laughter and decades being each other's friend.

If their families hadn't hated each other.

She felt wretched.

He looked wretched.

"Coral," he whispered. "An annul—" He groaned. "I can't tell if it's you who smells like roses, or if it's the house."

Her cheeks warmed. "Both," she murmured.

He rubbed the back of his neck, as if he was uneasy about what to say next. "An annulment never crossed my mind until the judge mentioned it."

"Then—"

He raised a hand. "Let me finish. Please."

She nodded.

"Of my own free will I made my vows, and I would love, honor, and cherish you every day for the rest of our lives if you'd allow me. Yesterday I didn't tell you we could annul our marriage because I feared you'd agree."

"I would have," she absently replied as her heart soaked up what he'd confessed. He didn't want an annulment any more than she did.

He smiled just a bit. It was the saddest thing.

"I should go," he said, his voice flat.

"Wait," she blurted as he took a step toward the stairs.

His brows drew close.

They stood there looking at each other.

He nodded, a silent *go on*.

Her pulse pounded between her ears. She moistened her lips. "Before yesterday I didn't know."

"Didn't know what?" he whispered.

Her chest felt like someone was squeezing her heart. Tears formed in her eyes. Not from pain. From hope. "I didn't know how alone I was." She wrapped her fingers around his warm hand. "I don't want to annul this marriage. I want to know your fears, dreams, and hopes, as well as you know mine. I want to laugh with you, and cry. I want to love, honor, and cherish you, too. Tonight, and until death do we part. I believe our marriage will be beautiful. I choose to believe God brought us together for a purpose."

She paused, smiled, and waited for him to return the romantic sentiment.

"Tonight?" he said, his voice rough.

Coral chuckled. A one-word response was nothing close to what she'd been expecting. She nodded before her nervousness could change her mind.

"We barely know each other."

"You've known me since I was born."

He tipped his head a bit as if to acknowledge that as true. "We signed annulment papers."

"Those papers mean nothing until they're filed with the court, right? In the eyes of God, the court, and every person in Wathena, that means we're still married." She released his hand. Gave him a flirtatious grin. "But if you don't want to—"

He was kissing her and chasing away all thoughts of what else she'd intended on saying. He lifted her into his arms.

Coral managed, at the last moment, to kick the door closed.

Chapter 7

Life is made up of marble and mud.
NATHANIEL HAWTHORNE

A month later

O h Jack, she's beautiful, isn't she?"
Jack stopped a step inside the spare-bedroom-turned-parlor. Coral sat in the same spot he saw her last since he left this morning to deliver the Zeizer twins. Her gaze, though, languished on an abstract spot on the north wall. She tapped the mahogany edge of her quill against her bottom lip. He knew her well enough now to know when her questions were rhetorical. Since moving Coral from the Swayze house and into the second floor of his house, he was still getting used to the strangeness of having a female sharing his food, his bathroom, his bed.

His lips twitched. Not so much the latter.

He loved waking up to a cascade of red-orange hair on his pillow. He loved how her porcelain skin pinked when she blushed. He loved that his house and office now smelled of roses because *she* smelled of roses. He loved the overwhelming rush of feelings he had every time her blue eyes met his.

A flirtatious glance. The trailing of her fingers along his arm. A kiss.

Love. It could be nothing else but love.

He loved Coral.

Even when she moved his razor to a different shelf so she could put her toothbrush and paste there. Even when her cooking skills paled next to his. Even when she insisted they discuss the pros and cons of which church they would attend and they ended up choosing his. Even when she didn't tell him the reason she wanted him to accompany her weekly visit to the Soldiers' Orphans' Home in Atchison until after she introduced him to five-year-old Gracelyn Rhodes.

"I know Gracie likes you," Coral said in a dreamy tone. "I could see it in her eyes."

The little girl's feelings had been in her eyes, laughter, and death-grip hug she'd given them before they left the orphanage yesterday afternoon. Gracie and Coral adored each other. Until yesterday, he hadn't realize how many children lived at the state orphanage—hundreds of sad-eyed girls all looking like Gracie with their close-cropped hair, gray knee-length dresses, and black stockings.

Orphans. Neglected. Abused.

All needing parents to love them.

Jack walked to the oak desk now positioned behind the couch. "Coral, we talked about why we can't adopt Gracie," he reminded, "or any of them."

She laid her quill down and looked his way. "You talked. I listened."

"Coral—"

"No one could love Gracie like we can."

She could be right, but they'd been married a month. Thirty-one glorious days and nights of being husband and wife. They needed more time alone before they invited another into their family. That's why Mr. and Mrs. Byers offered to train the pup for them.

Jack wasn't any more ready to be a parent than Coral was.

He slid the plate of sliced apples on the desk that held more of Coral's things than his. Typewriter. Three quill pens. Blue and black ink bottles. Waxes and seals, which he still couldn't figure out why she had because he hadn't seen her use them. Boxes of pens, pencils, stationery, and gummed envelopes. Four social calendar books, the leather outer covers of each dyed a different shade and with the embossed name of each of her employers.

"Have a snack," he said, perching on the edge of his desk.

She took a wedge of apple. "How was the delivery?" she asked before eating the slice.

"Quicker than expected. I left the twins sleeping contently in their father's arms."

"And Mary?"

"Exhausted." When Coral's eyes narrowed, he added, "And looking more beautiful than ever. Speaking of beauty. . ."

He leaned forward and kissed her cheek then ear before moving to her neck, pulling her to her feet and into his arms. He drew back and studied her face, the desire in her eyes reflecting what he felt. His heart quit beating quite so properly. She gripped the lapels of his coat. His hands slid down the gentle slope of her spine and held her against him.

Her gaze shifted to where sunlight streamed in through the window sheers he'd helped her hang the day after she—and their wedding gifts—invaded his home.

"Jack, it's the middle of the afternoon. Don't you have patients to see?"

He smiled. "I'd rather examine you."

She smiled back, and looked deliciously devious. "I imagine you would."

She gave him an apple-flavored kiss that left him breathless and thankful for a wife who enjoyed flirting with him. Just when he was about to carry her to the other room, she pushed him back and smoothed his hair and the front of his gray suit coat.

"Go to work, Dr. Kent," she ordered yet was still smiling.

He groaned. "You're torturing me."

"I could say the same."

Jack picked up an apple slice and took a bite, glancing at the covered desktop. "Is any of this new mail?"

Her eyes sparkled. "Yes, several things came for you." She handed him two manila envelopes, a folder, and a white, already opened envelope with a Wathena postmark. "Two hospitals in Cleveland have already responded to your employment request, exactly the two I've been praying would answer, and they are both interested. The third item is a folder containing adoption forms. I've filled out everything. It only needs your signature. Dr. Becker included a letter detailing how he believes surgery could open Gracie's ear canal and possibly enable her to hear. I haven't found a surgeon yet. Finally, Hiram invited us to Saturday's apple picking and pig roast, and I will post our regrets in the morning." She drew in a breath. "You look angry. Did you want to go see your family?"

Jack closed his eyes for a moment, pinching the bridge of his nose. What did she expect from him? He loved her kindness to others, determination to find the good in any situation, generosity, and how she talked about their future. She was also stubborn to the bone.

Once Coral latched on to an idea, she wouldn't let go.

This was one idea she needed to let go.

Two ideas, actually. They weren't adopting Gracie. Not this year. Not next. Children were their future, not their present. He'd had a free hour in which he'd wanted to spend with her, and now *this*? They'd agreed not to make any major decisions without talking to the other. He let out an aggravated breath.

"Coral, I didn't contact any hospitals in Cleveland."

She smiled, patted his hand. "Of course not, I did," she said, clearly unperturbed by his tone.

"If I'd wanted to contact any hospitals in Cleveland, I would have."

"You didn't have the time."

Jack gritted his teeth. "I could have *made* the time if it was something I wanted."

Again, she did not take the hint.

She touched his face, her skin soft and warm along his jaw. "Dear husband, sometimes we don't realize we want something until we learn of that something's existence. You will love Cleveland. It has electricity, streetcars, and a nine-story shopping mall. The Arcade sells things we've never dreamed of. Clevelanders need doctors, too."

"For heaven's sake, Coral, will you let things alone?" he said irritably.

She gave him a peeved look. "This is for our future. It's the only way we can be free of the feud."

"We are free of it."

"Until something happens again, and you know something *will* happen because the adults keep feeding hostility to the children. Generation to generation."

"Be optimistic," he told her.

"I have three facts for you." She held up a pointer finger. "Rain falls from the sky"—two fingers—"roosters crow"—three—"and our families will always hate each other."

He dropped the mail onto the desk. "Four: we are not moving to Cleveland."

"But—"

"No."

She looked at him with such disappointment, it was almost too much to bear. "Won't you at least look at what the hospitals sent?"

"No."

"But—"

"No."

"Can't you say anything besides no?"

Jack released a ragged breath. "Yes, I can." He cradled her face in his palms. "Be the one to end the hate."

Her chin trembled. "How?" she said, her voice sounding like it might crack.

Jack brushed his lips across hers, lingering, relishing how blessed he was to be the man responsible for cherishing her. "Love me, Coral, and let me love you. When our families see what we have, they will realize what they're missing." He rested his forehead against hers. "I will take you to Cleveland at Christmas so we can see this behemoth shopping mall you speak of and the mighty and mystifying wonders therein."

Her eyes shone bright with tears. He hoped from joy, not heartbreak.

"Next year," he said softly, "we can add a child to our family."

Her head tipped in acknowledgment of his words.

"I love you," he whispered.

Her lips parted. His mouth found hers, and he kissed her until they were both breathless. She was his. More importantly, he was hers to do with as she wished.

Jack chuckled.

Coral drew back. "What was that for?"

"I was doing my own planning for future." He winked. "Tonight."

She blushed.

"Until later, Mrs. Kent."

Jack snatched another apple slice off the plate. He chewed as he descended the staircase. He strolled into his office. Leaving the door open, he sank into his chair. She hadn't declared her love, but he didn't mind. When she did, the words would come from her heart, not out of an obligatory response.

He stared at the front door.

Waited for his afternoon appointment.

No sound could be heard, save for the ticking of the wall clock.

He tapped the top of his desk. That Coral hadn't found an ear surgeon yet meant she was looking. Even if she found a listing of surgeons, she wouldn't know what to ask when interviewing. His gaze fell on the wall of textbooks and medical journals. If a surgery was all it would take to help Gracie hear, it may be possible Coral could be helped, too. Jack grabbed the most recent *American Medical Directory*. Flipped the pages until he came to a list of eye, ear, nose, and throat hospitals.

New Jersey. Buffalo. Bronx. Baltimore. Maine.

Fort Dodge, Iowa, was so far the closest.

No, there was one in Cincinnati. . .but it specialized in ophthalmology.

Philadelphia. Pittsburgh.

"Wait, what's this?" he murmured. "New Orleans. The institution was established not alone for the treatment of indigent patients but also for the education of practitioners of medicine. The hospital's *new* building latterly erected and embodying the *latest* improvements. . .H. D. Bruns, MD, surgeon-in-charge. . . W. DeRoaldes, MD, surgeon-in-chief." He slapped the book. "That's who I need to contact."

Chapter 8

While there is life, there is hope.
JULES VERNE

The following Saturday

A tree-lined horizon. Crisp Kansas breeze. Not a cloud in the blue sky.

Coral kicked the leg she'd crossed over the other as she rocked on the porch, enjoying the beautiful autumn afternoon, the floorboards under the rocker squeaking. She'd smile if her cheeks didn't already ache from a day of smiling, even though no one but Jack smiled in return. Or talked to her. That she was a Kent in name didn't atone for being a Davies by birth. She hadn't expected the Kents to give up decades of hostility after a month of a Davies married to one of theirs.

Change never came easy.

She would change.

For Jack, she was going to overcome her doubts, fears, and desire to move to Cleveland. She was going to do her part to end the feud. Because he loved her. Because she loved him. Love was much like horticulture. Begin with a single seed. Gently plant. Then prune, cultivate, and feed.

After twenty years of watching her father cultivate over a thousand varieties of apple, peach, and pear trees at the Davies orchard, she now knew why the Kents struggled to produce an abundant crop. They weren't good horticulturists. Jack's uncle (Hiram's father) either hadn't known enough about spraying or pruning or hadn't cared to read up on it in the *Kansas Farmer*. Or maybe Mr. Kent hadn't been able to read. If that had been the case, someone in the family could have read it to him. Why hadn't his wife? Could be she didn't know how to read, either.

But Jack did. So did Hiram. Enough of their kin had to know, too.

From what little she could remember of Howsley Kent, the man never took "charity" from anyone. Advice given without being requested amounted to charity. Even without listening to others, he'd been able to see farms where hedges had been planted as a fence to hinder farm stock from plundering the trees. He could've figured out what apple varieties produced best in summer, fall, and winter. He could've planted other fruit-bearing trees besides apples.

Yet he hadn't.

Coral released a sad sigh. She wasn't a horticulturist. She'd never read a paragraph in the *Kansas Farmer* or any of the pamphlets her father'd brought home from State Horticultural Society meetings. If she could figure out these things by giving halfhearted attention, then Howsley Kent should have, too. Now that Hiram had taken over from Jack in managing the orchard since he earned a degree in—

How strange.

She had no idea what degree he earned from the University of Missouri, or if he earned a degree at all. She'd have to ask Jack.

From her spot on the covered porch, she leaned forward in her rocker and looked to where Hiram stood pointing at the packed barrels that were to be loaded on wagons and shipped north. The past was the past, and if Hiram wanted the farm to prosper, someone needed to tell him that no amount of spraying would make a tree produce fruit, if those trees haven't already produced fruit.

She breathed deep. From the smell of it, the pig roasting over a pit was ready to be served. She probably ought to go find Jack.

She glanced around the yard filled with Kents of all ages. Jack held two glasses of lemonade and politely nodded as he listened to one of his cousins. Gerald. No. . .George. George had three boys and was married to. . .Where was she? There. With the other Kent women clustered near the food tables. None looked her way. Oh, what was her name? She was one of the Losees from Troy. Lyla. That's it. Lyla Losee.

"You can try to hide, but that hair will always give you away."

The spite-filled voice sent a chill up Coral's spine. The first—and last—conversation she'd ever had with Jack's grandmother after accidentally bumping into her at the post office had been enough for Coral to vow *never again*. Thankfully at the wedding, the woman had limited herself to fiery glares and a cold shoulder.

"No response, girl?" the icy voice continued. "I was rather shocked it took a wedding to a Kent before Lou Davies finally disowned ya."

Coral gripped the rocker's arm rests. *Don't respond. Look at Jack.*

"All that money and he couldn't keep his wife faithful. Everyone knows ya can't trust a Davies to be faithful."

Coral grit her teeth.

The woman cackled. "Five children and only three of them his."

She waited a minute in hopes Jack would intervene before she had to speak to his vitriolic grandmother. As if he could feel her staring at him, he turned and smiled, every bit of his love clear.

"Fool boy," Mrs. Kent spat along with a few other denigrations. Her slurs truly knew no bounds.

Be the one to end the hate.

Coral forced a smile and stood. "Mrs. Kent, you are blessed to have such an honorable grandson. He is a fine doctor."

Marsella Kent's thin lips pursed tightly, almost vanishing. Unlike the other ladies in attendance, with hair pinned up and covered with a hat, the haughty elder Kent wore her white hair in two shoulder-length braids. Rumor was she had Potawatomi blood. In her younger years, she must have been a striking woman. Over the years, sun and age bore some responsibility for the heavy lines in her skin, but the ones about her lips, which drew her mouth into a perpetual frown, those came from bitterness, from jealousy, from grief.

What had made her so angry?

She couldn't have been born with it. No one was born with that much fury.

It had to have come from loss and wounds and grief. From the lack of love to give and to receive. From having no one to share the burden.

From feeling alone.

Coral thought that rather sad, and accurate. She tried to speak, but her words tangled in her throat.

"Don't look at me like that!" Mrs. Kent drew air in through her nose and blinked several times in rapid succession. "I know what you're doing."

"I don't understand," Coral said softly. "What am I doing?"

"Pitying me," she seethed.

Coral couldn't look away from the rage in the petite woman's eyes. Of course she pitied her. Two sons, three stillborn daughters, and a husband buried not fifty feet from the kitchen window. Every day she washed dishes she saw the graves. Daily reminders of her loss. Daily reminders she was alone. One widowed daughter-in-law, Jack's mother, leaving her fifteen-year-old son for Marsella to raise. The other daughter-in-law, Hiram's mother, dying in childbirth.

How could any woman bear such loss? Such responsibility?

"I am so sorry for this feud between—" Coral flinched the moment Mrs. Kent's hand struck her cheek. Coral blinked.

Be the one to end the hate.

She raised her chin and held her hands together, clasped before her, to keep from touching the stinging skin. "Between our families," she finished. "I pray we can be—"

❧

Jack grabbed his grandmother's palm before it connected with Coral's reddened cheek a second time. Coral looked shocked. She looked terrified. It was his fault for agreeing to attend.

"Don't touch her again," he warned.

339

Marsella jerked free. "Get that filth off my land."

"She's my wife."

"Only because you didn't have the courage to stand up to the judge."

"I volunteered!"

She snorted. "She has done a devil of a number on you."

Jack could feel his blood boiling. He'd seen little of his family since the wedding. He'd missed them. This Marsella—the one who was quick to unleash her vindictive hands and words in punishment—he did not miss.

Coral touched his arm, and Jack immediately sought her eyes, her soft and inviting gaze. She loved him. He knew it, though she hadn't yet said the words. She loved him. She calmed him. She strengthened and believed in him. She trusted him to do the right thing. He could see it there in her bright eyes. He needed her to believe in him as much as she needed him to cherish her. To be one. Until death did they part.

Her lips curved.

Jack felt his own curving as well.

She gave him an encouraging nod.

Jack winked at Coral then looked at Marsella. "It doesn't have to be like this."

Her lips were parted in surprise.

"We don't have to keep hating each other," he said gently. "What we perceive to be the truth isn't always the truth. We have wronged the Davies family as often as they have wronged us."

"We never stole from them!" Marsella bit off.

Jack didn't have to look behind him to know Kents surrounded all sides of the porch. Coral's warm palm slid against his. He held tight. Together they could end the feud. It wouldn't be easy, but they could do it. They could return love for hate, kindness for selfishness.

He breathed deep then spoke loud, clear, and calm. "I examined all the acreage titles after Uncle's death. I looked at bills of sales and anything I could think of to prove ownership. No Kent ever owned a square inch of Davies—"

Marsella slapped him hard. "You think they didn't destroy the originals?"

Jack's cheek stung, yet he tempered his emotions to say, "The past cannot be rewritten."

Several Kents gasped at his retort.

Marsella studied his face, looking intently, looking at him as if she didn't recognize him. She cackled. "You think she cares for you." Her mocking laughter stopped. "You're fool-stupid not to see what she's doing. She's been twisting your thoughts, Jack. Making you forget the truth. You"—she poked his chest—"you're weak. Hiram isn't. She tried to seduce him, but he got away because he's strong. She's after him again. I saw her watching him. Once she's buried you, she'll go after your cousin."

Jack stared speechless. Had she gone mad?

"Do you actually believe that?" came Coral's girlish voice, her tone numbingly calm.

"Yes," Marsella snapped.

"But why would I do this?" Coral asked.

Marsella's eyes flashed. "The land!"

"She's trying to steal it back," someone yelled.

Coral flinched. "Ow."

Jack turned in time to see two rocks pelt her skirt. The fourth hit her back. She screamed.

"Stop," he roared. He swung around and shoved Coral behind his back, shielding her from any other attacks. "Put the rocks down."

Seven-year-old Samuel dropped the stone he held. Two others hid behind their mother's skirt. Teddy and another teen stood defiant. Coral was right—the adults were feeding hostility to the children. Generation to generation.

"It's bad enough children are throwing stones." He raked his hand through his hair. "The rest of you, you're adults. You know better, and yet you stood by and did nothing as your children attacked my wife. Shame on you. Shame on us all."

Jack clenched Coral's hand.

The crowd parted as he led her to the buggy. Jack lifted her onto the bench. Coral slid over and he pulled up next to her. With a flick of his wrist, Jack clicked his tongue. The horse started down the dirt lane, hooves clopping on the hardened road framed by apple trees.

They traveled in silence.

He should have listened to her. He should not have agreed to visit the orchard today. His wife was hurt because he hadn't protected her. Because he naively believed she would be safe among his kin. He was to blame for refusing to see the feud for what it was—children repeating what they'd been taught.

Kindness—love—could overcome hate. He believed this to the core of his soul.

It could. It didn't always.

His uncle carried his bitterness to the grave. His grandmother, he feared, would as well. And Hiram. . . Jack wasn't sure. Hiram had a chance to lead the Kents on a different course, if he chose it. Today, when they talked, he'd seemed open to it. He'd even congratulated Jack on the wedding. Hiram, he knew, was a schemer. Time would prove his words true or false. Time would also reveal bruises caused by thrown stones.

Jack kicked the floorboard. He should have known better than to take Coral onto Kent land.

Coral rested her head on his shoulder. "Jack, I'm all right."

"I'm not," he said, his pulse still pounding.

She wrapped her arms around his right arm. "I am sorry I accepted Hiram's invitation. I shouldn't have pressured you into attending."

He kissed the top of her head. "I'm sorry, too. It won't happen again."

"But—" She straightened on the bench, turned to face him. "Are you giving up that quickly?"

He pulled the reins, stopping the buggy. "They threw rocks at you."

She stared at him blankly for a second. "Well, yes," she said, shifting to face him. "Years of hate can't be unlearned in one day."

He shook his head. He didn't have her optimism.

"Let's think about this." She removed the reins from his hold, rested them on the side hook, and then took both his hands in hers. "A minor skirmish, only a few harsh words, and no one tossed in jail. I'd say that's a grand improvement over the last Kent-Davies altercation." She smiled.

Jack didn't.

She leaned forward and gave him a quick peck on the lips. "We're together. That's what counts."

Jack didn't say anything. His grandmother—and likely most Kent and Davies kin—believed he and Coral were married only because they'd been forced into it. They had been. The judge admitted they'd made the decision under duress. Love was a choice. Marriage was a choice, too. His heart leaped. It was a perfect idea.

"Marry me," he blurted. The startled look on her face made him chuckle. "I'm serious, Coral."

She raised an eyebrow. "Really? Why? We're already married."

Jack did not take his eyes off her beautiful face. "Marry me again."

She gave him a *have you lost your mind?* look.

"I am serious."

"Jack. . ."

"Coral. . ." he said in the same *I'm trying to placate you, but you're pestering me* tone. "We'll send invitations to everyone who gave us gifts. Seems only right. We don't need a host of attendants or an ice sculpture. You, me, a preacher, two- or three-hundred witnesses, and plenty of food is all we need."

"Why?" she asked, her tone still wary.

He looked at her as if it were obvious.

"Why?" she repeated.

"We were married in a jail, in muddy clothes, after a night of no sleep—"

"I slept," she put in.

"—on empty stomachs, and while we were under duress." Jack grinned, never feeling surer of a spontaneous idea. "I want you to look back at our wedding and have a good memory, not one you have to find something good in. Marry me, Coral. Let's show everyone in our families we are together because we want to be."

Her head slowly shook, but she was thinking about it. Jack could tell she was considering the idea. The time she would need to address the invitations. What food to serve. What dress she would wear. He said nothing. He was far too happy to watch the play of emotions on her face as she considered the pros and cons and added together time and cost.

She opened her mouth, and he blurted, "Even a simple wedding will be costly, which is why I will sell Hiram my share of the orchard. He's been pestering me about it for weeks."

She eyed him. "Why didn't you tell me?"

"I didn't want to sell."

"Why not?"

"I didn't need the money. Until now." Jack pulled her onto his lap, and she immediately wrapped her arms around his shoulders. "You, my love, are a worthwhile investment."

She placed a gentle kiss on his cheek. "*We* are. I love you, Jack, and I believe I will love you forever."

"Mrs. Coral Davies Kent, will you marry me again?"

She looked thoughtful. "I daresay, this is the strangest marriage proposal I've ever received." Her lips tipped up at the edge. She then held up a bare left hand. "Will I get a ring this time?"

"Absolutely. Take note we are in a doctor's buggy, surrounded by apple trees, on a dirt road where no one can be seen for miles. Miles," Jack emphasized, taking note of the close proximity of her lips to his. "Miles. Just you and me."

"And the horse."

The gelding's ears flickered, yet he never stopped eating the grass on the side of the road.

Jack tossed his hat and hers onto the buggy's hood. "Trust me, he never tells anything he sees."

She leaned close, touching her nose to his. "Are you planning on compromising me before our second wedding?" she asked and then gave him no time to respond.

He could live with that.

Epilogue

There is no remedy for love but to love more.
HENRY DAVID THOREAU

August 20, 1905

The train's whistle blew. The last of the passengers boarded the car.

Coral nervously smoothed the skirt of her blue traveling suit as Jack placed his hat on the upper shelf. "I've never been farther from Wathena than St. Joseph."

He slid next to her. "Are you nervous?"

He obviously read her expression. "I may be a tad nervous." Coral sighed and noted how ragged her breath sounded. Her stomach churned, hands trembled. She'd been waiting for this day for years. "Anxious. Nervous. Excited. I'm a bundle of emotions."

Jack looked over his shoulder and scrunched his face in a funny expression. Giggles came from the seat behind them. He then draped his arm over Coral's shoulder. Kissed her cheek.

"Why are you so calm?" she asked him.

"Because I am leaving with what I hold most dear," he whispered. "You will like New Orleans."

She thought about it. Last night she'd even made a list of the pros and cons. She expected she would like living in Louisiana, yet couldn't help ask, "And if I don't?"

"It's only two years."

Coral sighed again. He was right, as always. Two years didn't seem enough time for Jack to learn all he needed to know about eardrums and surgical repair, but he was confident, and thus Coral would be confident, too.

The whistle blew again.

The conductor walked down the aisle, checking tickets. He then left their car and moved to the one behind theirs.

Coral looked out the window. She waved at the Swayzes as they stood next to Whit, Gil, Ann, and Hiram. All waved back. No other kin came to the station to see them off. Three Davieses. One Kent. The rest of their family continued to nurse their grudges.

More giggles came from the seat behind them.

Coral looked over her shoulder.

Four-year-old Sophie sat on Gracelyn's lap, looking out the window as Gracelyn wedged a pencil into Sophie's left braid. The child's blond hair now stuck out like five-inch horns on the side of her head. Yet both girls looked even happier than they'd been the day Jack and Coral walked them out of the orphanage for good.

Jack snorted.

Coral elbowed him in the side. "Did you give her the idea?"

The right side of his mouth hitched into an enchanting grin. "Isn't that what fathers are for?" he said all innocent, and all guilty.

"Jackson Kent, you are the most. . ." Her words trailed off as the train jerked into motion.

His lips grazed her ear. "Devoted husband you will ever have."

Coral looked at him out of the corner of her eye. A smile teetered on her lips. Devoted he certainly was. . .to her, to their daughters, to being kind to all.

Marriage suited Jack Kent quite well.

Coral Davies Kent Applesauce

The best time to make applesauce is in the fall, when the apples have just ripened on the trees. Visit a local orchard and pick your own.

Gather one pound of apples for every cup of applesauce. Peel apples, and cut each into four pieces, removing core and seeds. Put the pieces into a kettle or Dutch oven. Cook the apples over medium heat, stirring from time to time, until they are soft. (If the mixture seems too dry or the apples start to stick, add a little water.) Mash the apples. Add honey or sugar to taste. Sprinkle on a bit of cinnamon and nutmeg. Enjoy warm or cooled!

Author's Note

The United States, at the beginning of the twentieth century, enjoyed the distinction of being the greatest fruit-producing nation of the world. The largest and most profitable apple orchards were located in the central part of the United States—on the most fertile lands of Missouri, Kansas, Iowa, and Nebraska. According to the report of the State Horticultural Society for 1909, Kansas had over seven million apple trees, five million pear trees, five million peach trees, one million cherry trees, and almost one million combined plum, quince, and apricot trees.

One of the first commercial orchards was planted in the spring of 1876, in the southern part of Leavenworth County in Kansas by Frederick Wellhouse, who became the largest apple grower in the world. He owned at one time 1,600 acres in orchards in Leavenworth, Miami, and Osage Counties. In the late 1870s, Doniphan County reported 140,000 apple trees, mostly located around Wathena. Tree fruit acreage expanded to where an Apple Grower's Association was formed in 1905.

Visit kansasfruitgrowers.org to learn more about Kansas orchards.

ECPA-bestselling author **Gina Welborn** wrote public service announcements until she fell in love with writing romances. A moderately obsessive fan of *Community* and *Once Upon a Time*, Gina lives in Oklahoma with her pastor husband, their five Okie-Hokie children, two rabbits, four guinea pigs, and a dog that doesn't realize rabbits and pigs are edible. Find Gina online at www. ginawelborn.com

The Colorado Coincidence

by Kathleen Y'Barbo

Dedication
To my agent Wendy Lawton. Here's to ten more years!

*For thou wilt light my candle: the L*ORD *my God will enlighten my darkness.*
PSALM 18:28

Chapter 1

San Francisco
April 1878

Mack McCoy slipped the envelopes into his vest pocket and willed himself to remain calm. To smile at the three pretty girls who were vying for his attention on the sidewalk outside the San Francisco Post Office. To walk back toward his hotel room as if it were any normal day.

Once inside, he gathered up what he could shove into his saddlebag to wait until darkness descended. A glance around the elegantly appointed room should have caused him to consider all he would miss in leaving San Francisco.

He'd been wealthy before, and he'd been poor as well. Neither suited him for long before his old friend wanderlust came along and sent him off on the next adventure.

Mack pressed his palms against the desk and stared at the envelopes stacked in front of him. Two letters.

One had been expected. The envelope plain but sturdy and embossed with the seal of his father the Duke of Crenwright, came regular as clockwork. Inside was the remittance paid to ensure he never returned to his homeland, a remittance Mack would place in a new envelope and mail to his mother for her care.

The other letter was no less noble in origin, no less elegant in the materials used to carry the message from London to this distant city. And yet this envelope and its contents, a simple emerald stickpin, carried the strongest warning.

For unlike Father, who paid Mack to stay away, his half brother Colin, younger by some five years, used a more persuasive means.

Colin's promise that if Mack set foot on English soil, his mother would surely die held much more meaning than any amount of money. Until today, Mack had no proof that his half brother had found the home tucked away in a quiet part of the English countryside far from Crenwright lands.

Until today.

Colin or someone in his employ had not only found her but had the gall to steal from her. If his mother was hurt, he'd kill Colin. Of this, Mack was certain. There was no need to involve her. Colin was heir even though he was the younger son. For only Colin carried the pure blood of the duke and his legitimate wife the duchess.

Mack held the emerald stickpin up to the light, allowed a moment's perusal to be certain of its ownership. Yes, it was his mother's. Of this there was no mistaking.

"You're my hero, Mack," he could almost hear his mother say.

Her hero. Mack snorted. He was no one's hero, and he knew it.

He wrapped the pin in his fist and willed himself to think rationally, calmly, as he walked to the window and gazed out over the city he had grown to love and the Pacific Ocean beyond. Any number of the vessels bobbing at anchor might take him away from here, though their destinations would prove far too difficult to discern. Much as he wished to slip from his father's grasp, not allowing the remittances to reach him meant that they also did not reach his mother.

So Mack was in a fine fix. The only solution was to keep moving. To provide a change of address for his father and to beg the elder man's indulgence that Colin not be told of his whereabouts.

For all that the duke loved both his sons—as much as he could love anyone—Mack knew he was his father's favorite. Sending Mack away had been the duchess's doing, an act meant to ensure that her son was named the rightful heir upon their father's death.

So he would keep his promise and would keep providing for his mother. Though she had once been a simple maid to the nobility, Mother had settled into the life of country gentlewoman with a happiness that Mack intended to see continued.

Carefully, he slipped the pin into his lapel and then rose to begin the process of packing his saddlebags. His final act before closing the door to his life in San Francisco was to deliver a forwarding address to the postmaster.

"So you'll be moving to Denver?" the elderly man said as he duly noted the information in his ledger. "Nice place, Colorado. Thought many a time of heading that direction. Good for the lungs, you know."

Mack responded with a nod and a tip of his hat. It didn't matter whether Denver was nice or not. It was merely a stop on a journey that was unlikely to end.

Not as long as Colin drew a breath.

∞

May 1878
Callyville, Colorado

Gloree Lowe tossed a clod of wet dirt toward the three graves and wondered again why she wasn't in one of them. "Oh, that I had wings like a dove, for then would I fly away, and be at rest." More than once on the trail up from Texas she had whispered those words, usually during the labored breathing that came with the illness that sent them to the rarified healing of Colorado.

As if by suggestion, she inhaled a long breath of clear, cold morning and let it out slowly. Pitt always told her God heard every prayer, even the ones we sent forth in tortured groanings. Her husband was the smartest man she knew; he'd been right about this.

He also told her to marry again if something happened to him—which she agreed to without meaning a word of it—and never to go anywhere without the Springfield in her hand, and she'd forgotten. Not that she could imagine anything worse that could happen to her than the things she'd already endured.

Besides, she hadn't touched the rifle except to move it to the porch since the sheriff brought it back from the fields still strapped to Pitt's lifeless body. A sob threatened and she doubled over, ready to spill the contents of her meager breakfast. Again.

Gloree lifted her face to a cloudless cornflower sky. Heat rose from skin nearly frozen by the Colorado morning. An odd thought, that tears would warm you like that. She leaned back on her heels, beyond caring about the muddy mess she'd made of her apron and skirt or the splotches that must be staining her checks.

The cross had slipped out of place again. Gloree made another attempt to right it then gave up. It would just have to stay crooked until the frozen ground thawed and proved more cooperative.

The ache in her heart intensified. With the need to curl up between her babies so strong it startled her into rising, Gloree fisted her icy fingers and felt the grit rub into her palms. A glance at the largest of the three graves proved impossible, so she turned her back.

Odd, how the Lord went about His business.

She lifted her gaze and then her fist to the majestic Rockies, rising gray-blue and dusted with sugar-white peaks against the cornflower-blue spring sky. Dirt from her palms dusted her face and most likely turned the tracks of her tears into muddy rivers.

Had she known the trek from Texas to Colorado would end this way, she'd have refused to go. But it would have done her no good. With her husband, there was no refusing to do anything. Once that man set his cap on something, he did it and that was that. That was his way, and what first drew her to the handsome rancher.

"Colorado's gonna heal ya, Gloree, I just know it."

Even now Gloree could hear the determination in his voice, see the crease on his brow that appeared only when he thought on a subject real hard. Thomas had that same crease and the same determined voice. Had she not been the weak one, the sickly one, her husband and children would be alive today.

His last words echoed in her ears even now. "Just hold on, Gloree. Help's comin'."

Again she focused upward at the deep-blue sky. "Well, Pitt Lowe, I sure could use some of that help right now."

"Miz Lowe?"

Gloree jumped at the gruff voice. A rider approached flanked by two others.

A gasp escaped her lips as she used her apron to smear the grime from her face. Was she so far gone that she'd missed hearing three men on horseback galloping toward her?

Evidently, yes.

The rider reined in his mare, a lovely paint, and allowed the two men riding matching bays to catch up. The trio, well-armed and obviously trail weary, approached with a boldness that set Gloree's heart thumping. These were obviously no circuit riders. More likely, a band of outlaws had come to visit.

Strange, but the thought of dying today didn't appeal as much as she expected it would now that the opportunity might be presenting itself. Gloree dropped the corner of her apron and set her hands firmly on her hips. As an afterthought, she pasted on a look of defiance.

The man called her name once more, and this time she responded. Surely an outlaw wouldn't stand on formality before he picked her place clean and put her in a grave beside the rest of the Lowe family. However unexpected, these men must be coming as friend rather than foe.

Relief shot through her. She let her scowl slip.

Horse hooves on mud mixed with snow made the oddest sound. Odder still that Gloree would notice, and yet she did. As the trio neared, she focused on those hooves instead of the faces of the riders. Only when slush nearly splattered her shoes did Gloree take a step backward and look up.

Shadowed by the brim of his hat, the fellow leading the trio looked to be the eldest, possibly even father to the pair who lagged behind. The horse whinnied, no doubt protesting her presence. Its rider seemed to be of a similar mind as he swung his leg over and dropped into a relatively dry spot.

Pushing back his hat, the man revealed a pair of narrow-set eyes and a thatch of gray hair that hung low over his brow. "Miz Lowe," he said slowly, "you and me's got business to discuss."

He must be looking for silver; most were nowadays. Maybe she ought to tell him now that the creek had nothing of value in it besides the water itself.

"I don't reckon I know you, mister," she decided on instead.

Gloree spoke with more bravado than she felt, and the expression on the man's face showed he knew it. Searching for something else to say, she landed on one that was only slightly leaning toward untruth.

"What with my husband inconvenienced at the moment you might ought to get back on that horse and come back when he's able to speak to you." *Like never.*

The statement brought guffaws from the trio.

"Oh, he's inconvenienced, all right." This from a skinny man not much bigger than Gloree. Probably not much older, either.

"Inconvenienced all the way to a hole in the ground, oh about two months ago. Or was it three?"

It was almost four, but she kept her silence rather than correct the ruffian. Instead, she tried another tack.

"Gentlemen, I'd be obliged if you'd go on back the way you came. You're obviously not here on a polite social call."

Trembling fingers balled into fists as she forced herself to turn her back on the threesome and walk toward the house and the Springfield that leaned against the wall behind the butter churn.

To her surprise, they didn't try to stop her when she picked up her pace and stepped across the sodden prairie like it was a city sidewalk. They followed at a distance, this much she knew by the sound of the horses. Her pride, or maybe it was self-preservation, refused to let her turn and look. It also refused to let her run.

Her stomach began to churn and her breaths shortened. Unlike her years spent as a consumptive, her lungs were clear here in Colorado, but their capacity for taking in the thin mountain air was poor. Still, she pressed on, even when she began to see spots in front of her eyes.

By the time she reached the porch steps, however, she'd begun to breathe easier. The Lord had taken almost everything she held dear. The last thing she intended was to let three strangers steal the rest of it.

Gloree turned slowly, forcing herself to act as if she hadn't a care in the world. The older fellow stood not ten paces away, already off his horse and seemingly ready to charge the house.

Or her.

Swallowing hard, she pressed her palm to her stomach and pulled herself to her full height. "Sir, I'm going to ask you again to leave my home."

"She's a pretty one, Pa. Can't I have her?" This from Skinny.

Gloree glared at him, daring the coward to climb off his horse and willing him to stay put all at the same time. To her surprise, his father shot him a look that would have curdled milk. The third member of the group, a plain-faced man of middle years, seemed to ignore the scene entirely.

"I'm sorry, Miz Lowe," the man on foot said. "My son's strong as an ox but not quite as smart." He punctuated the comment with another look at Junior before turning his attention back to Gloree. "Tell the lady you're sorry, Del Junior."

"I'm sorry, lady." As soon as the words were out, Del Junior gave Gloree a leering look that let her know an apology was the last thing on his mind.

"That ain't funny, Delbert."

Gloree turned to stare at the one who'd remained silent. Until now. He gave her a look devoid of expression then studied the knife at his belt. Another glance at Del, then he smiled.

Something in that smile held a much stronger threat than anything the other two might say. Maybe it was his lack of teeth and abundance of scars. More likely, it was the way he kept looking from the knife to Gloree as if he might draw amusement from one of them at any moment. From her vantage point it was hard to know which was more likely.

She had to do something. Anything.

Another move backward and she'd reach the wall. Then it was four sidesteps to the left and she'd be at the churn. If her stomach would just calm a bit she might make it without being pounced on.

She was thankful she'd paid attention when Pitt taught Thomas how to shoot. Still, there were three of them.

Delbert Senior set a booted foot on the first step then placed the other beside it. Stomping hard, he left mud and snow all over the bottom stair. "Sorry about that, Miz Lowe. Sometimes I have a hard time controllin' my sons." He shrugged as if this were not of much concern to him. "But that ain't why I'm here."

"Nah," Del Junior echoed. "That ain't why we're here."

Scarface just studied his knife blade then ran it across his thumb. Lifting the blood to his lips, he met her gaze with a steely stare.

Forgetting pretenses, Gloree collided with the wall then scrambled toward the churn. She'd almost reached the spot where the gun was hidden when Delbert Senior caught up to her.

"It ain't there."

She threw the churn aside and stared in horror at the empty place behind it. Just as the stranger said, the rifle was gone.

Gloree's attention followed the sound of laughter to where Delbert Junior sat atop his bay. "It ain't there," he echoed.

"Wonder where it is?" Scarface patted the bedroll behind his saddle. "Can't imagine."

Delbert Senior shot them both a look. "Shut up, Francis."

"Francis?" Gloree chuckled then clamped her lips shut. Had she said that out loud?

The man in question leaped from his horse and yanked a rifle from his bedroll. *Her* rifle. The click of the Springfield broke the silence.

"I'm named after my *mama*," he said through gritted teeth as he aimed the weapon at her. "You wanna make somethin' of it?"

Fear colder than last week's blizzard danced around Gloree's field of vision. *"I will lift up mine eyes unto the hills, from whence cometh my help."* Gloree stared past the trio to the Rockies. No help in sight.

No, nothing but prairie and purple mountains dotted with snow and spikes of green. Odd how much a person noticed in the last moments of life.

I wonder if this is what Pitt and the babies felt. The thought stung worse than the realization she was about to join them.

And she'd been worried about Pitt sending for his cousin to come marry her. Not worried. Plumb riled up. She'd had one husband. Didn't need another. But Pitt, oh, he was stubborn. Said he couldn't rest until he knew she'd be taken care of after he was gone.

Yesterday she was glad Pitt's cousin hadn't arrived like his letter said he would. Today, she wasn't so sure.

"We ain't here t' kill her. Give me that gun, son."

Del Senior yanked the rifle away from Francis and stalked toward Gloree. Ignoring the relief his statement gave, she stood her ground and prayed.

The man stopped just shy of colliding with her and held the gun in the slight space between them. "I'm gonna make you a deal, Miz Lowe." He craned his neck to see inside the cabin. "I know you're out here all by yourself. That ain't safe, dear."

Never had she heard the word *dear* used in such a threatening manner. She opened her mouth to retort and found she'd lost her voice.

"And I know about your troubles with the bank." She must have let her surprise show, for he grinned. "Didn't think that was common knowledge, did ya?" He shrugged. "You'd be surprised what a man can learn when he asks the right questions. This is a fine piece of property."

"It's not for sale," she somehow managed.

"I figure anything's for sale if a man's willin' to pay the right price." He walked to his horse and pulled a roll of bills from his saddlebag. Peeling off a few, he set them on the icy porch rail between them. "That there's the down payment. I'll bring the rest come Friday when you're cleared out."

"Friday?" came out more like a squeak than a word.

Off in the distance she thought she saw something. A rider, perhaps? Could be the husband Pitt had ordered. Or maybe it was the circuit rider who'd promised to stop by sometime this week and do the deed of marrying them legal.

Whoever it was, Delbert Senior saw him, too.

"We best be headin' home, boys," he said. "Looks like Miz Lowe's 'bout to have some comp'ny." He gave Gloree a hard look. "I can see how Friday might be a bit too soon to expect a little thing like you t' vacate the premises. Despite what you might think, I'm not an unreasonable man, and I'm gonna prove it by givin' you a full two weeks. I'll be back the first of the month."

The rider pressed forward. He looked to be in a hurry. Gloree let out a breath she didn't realize she'd been holding. *Thank You, Lord.*

She squared her shoulders and braved a direct look at Delbert Senior. "This land is *not* for sale. It belongs to my husband and me."

He leaned closer, and Gloree could smell his rank breath. "You misunderstand. I didn't *ask* you, I *told* you. Now you put on your purtiest smile and you tell whoever that is comin' that the boys'n me was just transactin' a little business with you. Tell 'em we're the new owners come the first of the month." He peeled off another bill and sat it atop the pile on the rail. "That's for movin' expenses."

Gloree yanked the money off the ledge and threw it back at the intruder. Del Junior slid off his horse and gathered up the money then handed it to Delbert Senior.

Delbert Senior took great pains to check for bullets and then laughed and thrust the Springfield toward her before returning to his horse. "Might want to see it's loaded and hide it in a better place next time. Better yet, take it with you when you leave."

"I'm not going."

"Miz Lowe," Delbert Senior said as he shook his head, "you don't have any say ' in the matter."

He glanced over his shoulder then grasped the reins. "Way I see it, there's one of him and three of us. I like them odds. Let's go and pack our Sunday go t' meetin' duds, boys. Looks like we'll be movin' soon."

Out of the corner of her eye she saw the horse picking its way across the muddy plain. Another few minutes and the rider would be at her doorstep.

Delbert Senior took off in the opposite direction at a lope, the other two on his heels. As the stranger reined in his mount, the trio reached the tree line. She set the Springfield against the rail and waited.

Chapter 2

Mack had seen the woman and her companions well before she spied him. Though everything in him said turn and go the opposite direction, something drew him toward her. It was almost as if he had no choice in the matter.

He'd shown himself when he guessed she might be in distress, so an argument could be made for checking to be certain she was not in peril. Yes, that's what spurred him forward.

It had to be.

The home was ramshackle at best, the sort of two-story wooden structure erected by carpenters with good intentions and few skills. Though the lace curtains hinted at some level of domestication inside, nothing on the exterior could be called welcoming in the least.

A lone horse grazed in the side yard, and a half-dozen meager-looking goats roamed in a fenced enclosure. Snow lay in spare patches, likely where the shadow from the mountain darkened the land, and chickens fussed along the fence line, their squawking clearly audible across the expanse of prairie.

Just beyond the homestead there was a barn, but the structure was so poorly made that he could see right through it to the empty wagon inside. If anyone hid in wait there, they would be easily seen. Thus, he discounted the threat from that direction.

He glanced down at the Winchester strapped to his pack and then scanned the horizon once more before returning his attention to the woman. Hair like yellow sunshine curled in tendrils around her face and teased shoulders clad in a frock of blue gingham.

Though he couldn't see them from astride the horse, Mack guessed the woman's eyes to be a bonny blue. As he moved closer, he saw they were indeed as green as the English countryside in spring.

If he'd met her anywhere but in this barren stretch of Colorado, he would have thought her worthy of a second look. Truth be told, he thought that now.

"Ma'am," he said as he lifted his hat in a courtly greeting worthy of the time he was introduced to the Queen and Princess Royal at Ascot. "A fine day, is it not?"

She glanced over to where a Remington rifle leaned against the porch rail and then back at him. "I reckon it's fine enough. Unless you're with one of them."

"If they were the men you just parted ways with, then no, I am not."

"Then you're late."

To be sure. Pitt's choice for her husband was handsome in that way that some men have of being pleasing to the eye and yet offering just enough hint of danger to make a woman wonder. And he was nice and tall like Pitt, almost a foot above her own height with shoulders broad enough to hint at his ability to work hard even if his clothing told another tale.

He removed his hat, revealing a thick shock of ink-black hair that he tamed at the back of his neck with a length of leather. Though Pitt swore that his cousin was a farmer by trade, this man wore the clothes of a man who appeared to spend more time indoors than out.

Then there was the matter of his English accent.

She thought about the glittery stone in his lapel, an emerald if it was real, and couldn't help but think it cost more than she owed to the bank for the house and land where she now stood. The gold signet ring on his left hand would pay for her trip home to Texas and provide a nice place for the child she carried to grow up. All she had to do was. . .

Steal them? Oh. *Forgive me, Lord.*

"Come on, then. I didn't have any say in you being here, but I won't be accused of not showing you the proper welcome." Without a backward glance to see if the man would follow, she set off toward the porch at a brisk pace. "Don't think I agree with what Pittman Lowe did, but he always was a stubborn man. I'll abide by his wishes."

"I did sense that you were disagreeable about something."

"I'd say I've got good reason."

The man shook his head. "And I've got good reason to be completely confused."

Gloree spied a lone rider coming over the ridge. *Francis.* She sighed.

"You know who that is?" her companion said.

"I expect so."

"Friend or foe?" he demanded.

"Foe."

"And there's no one here but you? No one inside the house?"

"No," she said softly. "Not anymore."

"Go inside and lock the door," he commanded as he rushed the mare into the side yard, removed his rifle and pack, and penned her up with the other horse.

Instead, Gloree grabbed for the Springfield and gave aim. She might not be able to shoot anyone, but she could give the impression it was possible.

Then came the first shot as the remainder of the group appeared in the distance. The stranger stood between her and the riders and fired three times, knocking one of the riders off his horse and causing a second one to veer off course.

The rider got up then fell back down. From where she stood, it looked to be Delbert Senior. That meant Francis and Junior were left. And armed.

Her companion aimed and attempted to fire, but nothing happened. "It's jammed," he said as he reached down for the rifle at his feet.

Fire the Springfield. The thought made no sense because she hadn't put any bullets in it.

Fire it.

Gloree steadied the Springfield against her shoulder and took aim. "I'm a blame fool for not listening to you, Pitt. I should have kept this thing loaded." Pressing the trigger, she closed her eyes.

Gloree's bottom hit the porch and the rifle went spinning past the stranger across the uneven boards. She scrambled after it, ears ringing.

By the time she fought her skirts and crawled over to where the rifle landed, Pitt's man stared down at her. "That was some fancy shootin', ma'am."

"Fancy shooting?" She let the Springfield drop and allowed the fellow to pull her to her feet. "But it wasn't loaded."

"I beg to differ. Those two were down before I lifted my Winchester to take aim."

He pointed to a spot some forty yards away where a man lay. The darkened pool he lay in told Gloree someone had shot him dead. His companion lay nearby in a similar condition.

"Oh, no. I didn't. . .that is, I couldn't have. . ."

But apparently she had.

Gloree set the rifle against the house and sank into the porch rocker she'd hauled in the wagon all the way from Texas. "Wasn't me," she whispered under her breath as she watched the stranger make tracks to remove the weapons from the corpses.

He came back to the porch with three rifles, a pistol, and the knife Francis had threatened her with. Depositing the weapons on the wooden boards at Gloree's feet, the stranger took a step backward and looked toward the horizon.

Heaving herself to her shaky legs, Gloree joined him. "At least we got them all."

"Maybe."

Gloree jerked her attention from the horizon. "We got all three," she insisted.

"Ma'am," he said slowly, "are you certain these three were working alone? Might it be possible there are others? Maybe womenfolk or other kin who will want to bury their dead?"

She hadn't thought of that. "I suppose it's possible, but I'll not have another member of this family step foot on my property, no matter the reason." She nodded to the barn. "You're welcome to water your horse at the stream behind the barn, but I'm afraid I can't offer any hospitality behind sending you on your way with a biscuit and some bacon."

"Not necessary," he said. "But I must ask what you plan to do with these three."

"I plan to hitch up the wagon and deposit them at the undertakers in Calleyville. Their womenfolk or kin can call for them there."

"Then I'm going with you."

"That isn't necessary."

"Go on and get yourself ready. I'm not worried about what's necessary," he said simply before turning toward his work.

Oh. She ran her knuckles across her cheek and felt the grit of the graves crumbling away at her touch. Maybe she could run a comb through her hair and wash her face. She stumbled inside, the reality of what she'd done chasing her through the door.

By the time she'd made herself presentable, the stranger had the wagon hitched and filled with three bodies wrapped in horse blankets from the barn. He'd tied his horse to the back of the wagon.

"Best I could do on short notice," he said as he gestured to the contents of the wagon. "I'll see that the blankets are returned to you."

"Thank you, but I'll not be needing them."

The stranger helped her up into the wagon and then climbed up beside her to set the wagon in motion. "What did those men want?"

She slid him a sideways look. "My land. They made an offer, but I declined to accept it."

They rode for a while in silence. Her senses dulled by the slow pace of the wagon and the warmth of the sunshine on her back, drowsiness quickly set in. By the time she roused, Calleyville was clearly in view up ahead. Unfortunately, she'd chosen the stranger's broad shoulder for a pillow.

Gloree jerked back into a sitting position and straightened her bonnet. "I'm sorry," she said as she met his amused gaze.

"You earned the rest," was his companionable response.

∽∞∾

"I don't know what I'd have done without your help."

It had been a long time since he'd felt like anyone's hero, but the way she looked at him made Mack feel proper good. "You did all the fancy shooting. I just happened to be there to do the lifting."

He cringed at his poor attempt at a joke. Thankfully, the woman seemed oblivious.

Next thing he realized, the woman was reaching over in his direction. "Gloree," she said as she shook his hand. "Gloree Lowe."

Her hand was small, her grip firm. "The pleasure is mine, Miss Lowe." He shook her hand and then turned his attention back on the road ahead. "Mack McCoy at your service."

"You're not from around here, Mr. McCoy," she said. "And you're sure not a Texas farmer."

"An astute observation," he responded as he guided the clumsy wagon around a narrow turn. "England," he said simply. Though the true response was much more complicated, this generally worked to assuage the curiosity of the Yanks he encountered.

"You're a long way from home," she said. "I am, too, though not like you are."

He nodded. "I tend to make my home wherever my boots land. It's a policy that has served me well." He slid her a sideways glance. "What about you? Where's home?"

"That ranch where I buried my kin," she said with more force than he expected. "Before that, Oyster Creek, Texas."

"Ah, the Texas coast. I have fond memories of Galveston."

She smiled. "So do I. Pitt and I were married there."

His memories were less romantic, though they did involve a lovely week in the springtime four years ago. Or was it five?

A few card games and a well-timed toss of a coin over a bet regarding whose horse was the swiftest had landed money in his account to send him off to San Francisco in style. He still missed that horse, though.

"I'm sorry for your loss," he managed as he spied a shimmer of tears threatening.

"Mama used to say that the Lord would never give us more than we can manage." She shrugged as a tear traced a path down her cheek and landed with a plop on her skirt.

Mack dug into his pocket and handed the woman beside him a handkerchief embroidered with double *M*s. The emerald green of his mother's needlework matched the woman's weeping eyes, he noticed, as she seemed reluctant to accept his offer.

"It's clean," he said. "I promise."

The smile she offered, though fleeting, lit her face. She dabbed at her cheeks and then clutched the handkerchief and stared straight ahead. "Thank you," she said after a while. "I figure if Mama's right then God sure must trust me a lot."

This talk about God made him antsy. His mother said much the same thing, only with a wee bit of an Irish accent to sweeten the words. The idea was the same, though. Trust an invisible heavenly being and all would be well.

Lately he'd given that more thought than was comfortable. It was almost as if this invisible heavenly being was trying to tell him something.

He caught her watching him and decided he'd better respond, even if the truth rang hollow. "Mothers are always right, don't you know?"

She smiled again. "I suppose so."

Ahead Mack spied the first buildings of Calleyville, Colorado. He'd had a good bit of success at the card tables here last night, and it was possible a few of the town's less stellar citizens might want to have a chat with him regarding their losses.

The road ahead was thick with wagons, horses, and people, making for slow going as he made a wide circle around the saloon to pull the wagon up in front of the undertaker's office.

"What do we have here?" the proprietor said as he ambled outside, his spectacles balanced on the end of a rather longish nose. Mack suppressed a groan as he got out of the wagon and then helped Mrs. Lowe down. He recognized the fellow from among those at his table last night.

The undertaker, Ben Tucker if the sign behind him was to be believed, must have recognized Mack, too, because he suddenly whirled around on him. "Did one of these fellows take exception to how you play cards? Not that I'd blame them."

Mrs. Lowe stepped between them. "They were shot by me on my land, sir. I was defending my property."

"And her person," Mack added as he reached out to shake the undertaker's hand. "Mack McCoy," he offered by way of introduction. "I saw the whole thing."

The undertaker declined his handshake to walk around to the back of the wagon and lift the corner of one of the blankets. His gray brows rose then quickly fell.

"Looks like two Jones boys and their pa." His gaze found Mrs. Lowe. "I don't doubt your story, ma'am, but you'll need to go and tell it to Sheriff Drummond."

"I expected I would need to do that." She nodded toward the wagon. "Mr. Tucker, I wonder if I could trouble you to have those men removed before I return."

"Of course," he said. "You go on, and my boy and I will handle this." He whistled twice and a gangly lad responded. "Fetch these fellows inside."

Mack watched Mrs. Lowe turn her back just in time to miss the lad shouldering a corpse and hauling him inside. "We will just be going down to speak to the sheriff." He slipped the undertaker a few coins. "Would you have the boy clean Mrs. Lowe's wagon once you've got the bodies removed."

The undertaker looked over at the woman, who appeared ready to faint dead away. "I'll do it for her," he said quietly as he tucked the coins into his pocket.

"Thank you." Mack walked over to Mrs. Lowe and grasped her by the elbow. "I'll handle the sheriff. Why don't I find you a place to sit in the shade while you wait?"

She gave him a look that pinned him in place. Before he recovered, she had stalked off and left him behind. He caught up to her at the door to the sheriff's office.

"I've been expecting someone to drag you in here," the sheriff said when Mack stepped inside. "But not you," he said to Mrs. Lowe.

The little lady stepped around him to shake hands with the sheriff. "Mr. McCoy was passing by my ranch and was nice enough to help me deliver the Jones boys to the undertaker." She nodded to the chair next to his desk. "Now, how about I give you my statement so I can get back home?"

Sheriff Tucker looked confused. "What was this card shark doing out at your place, Gloree?"

Mrs. Lowe didn't bat an eye. "He was coming to my rescue, Sheriff," she said as she sat down. "Now you might want to write it all down, though."

It had been a long time since he'd felt like anyone's hero. But this woman, with her dress so recently smeared with mud and her eyes filled with fear, would likely have been grateful with just about anyone who would come to her assistance at that point.

Or maybe she'd gone beyond the point of caring by the time he rode up. He never could tell the difference, especially with women.

The sheriff grudgingly took his seat and pulled out pencil and paper from his desk drawer. While Mrs. Lowe dictated her statement, Mack stood back and watched. When she was done, she swiveled to find him. "Do you have anything to add?"

"Just that I don't intend to make you mad, ma'am. You're quite a good shot."

His attempt at humor was lost on Sheriff Drummond, although Mrs. Lowe did manage a smile. Mack offered his hand to assist her as she rose.

"Just a minute, McCoy," the sheriff said. "I need a word with you." He turned his attention to Mrs. Lowe. "Just him and me," he told her.

Mrs. Lowe gave him a tentative look. Likely she had noticed the sheriff's tone was less than welcoming.

"It will be fine," Mack told her, though he wasn't at all certain that was the truth.

She appeared ready to respond then settled for a nod and a quick escape, leaving Mack alone with Sheriff Drummond.

"You sure have good luck with the cards," the sheriff said as he studied Mack. "Wonder how that is."

Mack let out a long breath and affected the expression he used in situations like this. "Guess it was just my night."

The sheriff rose and leaned one hip against his desk, burly arms crossed over his chest. "Interesting that your run of good luck happened the same night my son lost a month's rent and the ownership of a good horse." He stared down at Mack. "Looks a lot like that horse Miz Lowe has tied to her wagon."

Mack rose. "I'm sorry for your son's misfortune, but I—"

The punch came so fast, Mack hardly realized what hit him until he landed on the floor a few inches from Drummond's boots. Experience told him to take his time standing up. Men whose naive sons were fleeced at cards generally weren't satisfied with just one punch.

The sheriff reached down and jerked him to his feet. Though Mack could have taken him, he allowed the older man the advantage and awaited the next fist to his face.

"The only thing that's saving you from the beating you deserve and a long stay in that jail cell for a laundry list of charges I'm still adding to is the fact you came in here with Gloree Lowe," he said as he held Mack by his collar. "Pittman Lowe was a good man. A man I was privileged to call a friend."

He paused as if to allow that statement to sink in. Meanwhile, Mack was calculating his options and figuring how fast he could get out of this town in one piece.

"If you're the man he chose, then so be it." He let go of Mack's shirt. "Just understand one thing. If you hurt that woman, you will find yourself hurting, too. I'll see to it myself."

The sheriff leaned close enough to make Mack decide not to ask what in the world he was talking about. "I assure you she's in no danger from me."

"Oh, but you're in plenty of danger from me." The sheriff nodded toward the door. "Now, go take care of your woman."

Mack shook his head and then winced. "Wait just a minute. She's not my woman."

Sheriff Drummond didn't move, nor did he look pleased. Slowly his right hand gravitated to the pistol holstered at his waist.

"Pitt led me to believe he was sending a man to marry up with Gloree so she wouldn't be alone out there at the ranch. Gloree herself just sat here in my office and told me a story about you coming to her rescue. If you're not Pitt's man. . ."

Pitt's man.

Mack edged toward the door as he kept his eyes on the sheriff. He'd leave, but he'd not leave a like coward.

"You're not toying with her affections, are you?"

Mack froze. "Of course not! The idea is absurd. In fact, all of this is absurd."

What he was toying with was a way out, not a pretty widow woman. Just as soon as he deposited Mrs. Lowe back at her farmhouse, he'd be off to greener pastures. To safer towns where the men across the card table weren't related to the town sheriff.

But Drummond seemed to want a response, so Mack thought carefully before speaking. "From my brief observation, Mrs. Lowe appears to be a remarkable woman. The loss of her family is unfortunate, and I have been happy to assist her, even in this small way."

"So the circuit rider hasn't come to Gloree's place yet?" Drummond asked, cutting through Mack's thoughts.

He was happy to give an honest answer to the question, even if the question made no sense. "I have seen no circuit rider since I arrived."

"Well, good news, boy," the lawman said. "I spied him having his breakfast over at the boardinghouse this morning. I'll have one of my boys fetch him over and let him do the deed right here in my office."

Mack swallowed hard. "Do the deed?"

"Marry you and Gloree Lowe," he said. "I'd be happy to stand up as witness. Or were you just saying what you thought I'd want to hear to save your neck?"

Chapter 3

Mack found Gloree Lowe waiting for him in the wagon. True to his word, Undertaker Tucker had not only cleared the wagon of its grisly contents, but his boy had done a brilliant job of removing any evidence of the Jones boys last ride.

"The wife is doing her best to get those blankets cleaned," he said as he eyed Mack warily. "You can pick them up next time you're in town, Miz Lowe."

"Burn them," Gloree Lowe said without looking up from the papers in her hand.

"As the lady wishes," Mack said to the scowling undertaker as he climbed up to join her. "Mrs. Lowe," he said when Ben Tucker had slipped back inside, "you and I need to have a conversation."

She looked up sharply, and Mack could see she was fighting tears again. "What about?"

"I have been asked if I was Pitt's man." He swiveled to face her. "I want to know what that means."

Her brief laughter held no humor. "I didn't realize anyone but me knew what my husband was up to."

"Apparently he told his friend the sheriff."

"Who then had a conversation with you privately. Wonderful." Mrs. Lowe waved at the air as if clearing away the response. "Look, Pittman Lowe moved me and our two young'uns to Colorado because the doctor in Texas said I'd die if we stayed there. True, I breathed better once I got here, but the trip did in both the little ones and made him sick, too. He told me he'd promised the Lord to take care of me, and his last act of protection was going to be to send someone else to take over for him after he was gone."

Those emerald eyes met his. Her look, so direct and yet so vulnerable, took his breath.

Then it hit him.

He'd been mistaken for a man sent to be another man's last act of protection. Someone had thought that he, Mack McCoy, was a hero.

He cleared his throat and let out a long breath. "I'm sorry," he said. "I don't know how to respond except to say that it sounds as if you had a good man. I applaud his desire to protect you."

The blond beauty shook her head. "I'm sorry, I know you meant those words kindly, but the problem is when Pitt put his mind to something, no amount of talking could convince him otherwise." She shook the papers in the air. "So, yes, Pittman Lowe decided to send for a man to come save me. The problem is, he used just about every last penny in our bank account to pay for that man's way here to Calleyville. Far as I can tell, the man hasn't shown up, and neither has the money this fellow was supposed to be bringing."

He glanced over at the topmost paper in her hand, decidedly a letter, and easily spied the words "Bank of Calleyville." "How much was he bringing to you, Mrs. Lowe?"

"Doesn't matter," she said. "It won't be enough. My cattle started disappearing about the time Pitt got sick. Sheriff Drummond did some investigating but never did figure out who was taking them." She shrugged. "Not much of a ranch without cattle."

Mack snatched the letter from her hand and jumped down from the wagon. There were few things he could repair about her situation, but this one thing he could.

"Where are you going?" she demanded.

Ignoring the question, he pointed his boots toward the Bank of Calleyville. Before Gloree Lowe could catch up to him, Mack was standing in front of the president of the bank himself.

"This is quite unusual," the banker, a fellow named Wainwright, said as he swept his hand in the direction of a pair of leather chairs that could have easily come out of Mack's father's home in London.

"I think not," Mack said calmly. "I am merely offering to pay a debt." He lifted his hand to show the older man the letter he'd snatched from Mrs. Lowe. "By the words on this page, a widow woman is being told her lands will belong to the bank if her husband's debt is not paid. I wish to pay that debt. It is a simple transaction."

Wainwright removed his spectacles and swiped them against the fine fabric of his sleeve. "I rarely have a stranger offering money to a pretty lady out of the supposed goodness of his heart." He returned his spectacles to his nose. "And from what I understand, the goodness—and the integrity—of your heart was notably absent last evening at the card tables."

Was there anyone in this town who hadn't heard about his winnings?

He turned to see Mrs. Lowe step inside. "What in the world is going on here?"

"Hello, Mrs. Lowe," Wainwright said. "This gentleman and I were just having a discussion about your delinquent account. I was explaining to him that I am unable to fulfill his request to pay your debt."

"That might be his request, but it isn't mine," she said as her gaze went from the banker to Mack. "I never asked you to do this."

"Nor did I ask your permission." Mack turned back to the banker. "Now, I see the amount here and am willing to pay it in full plus add a sum equal to any taxes that might come due. I understand there is a man due to arrive in this city who will add to what I have put on account."

"Goodness, Mrs. Lowe," the banker said with a chuckle. "Widowhood does suit you."

Mack stood. "I'm sorry," he said in his most polite tone. "Exactly what were you attempting to say, Mr. Wainwright? Is it peculiar to you that a gentleman might wish to assist a lady without expecting anything in return? And were you insinuating something in complimenting Mrs. Lowe in such a way?"

Wainwright adjusted the lily-white collar that contrasted sharply with the scarlet flush traveling up his neck, and stood. "I am saying those sorts of arrangements are generally left to the other side of town and handled in Miss Callie's Cathouse, and this great institution will have no part in them." He looked over at the shocked widow. "However, I stand by my statement that this woman is well suited to her current situation and quite lovely."

That's when Mack hit him. Twice. The first blow landed just under the chin and the second sent him sprawling to the floor behind his desk.

The commotion caught the attention of the banker's associates, who swarmed into the room with gasps. "Get the sheriff," someone called.

"Yes," Mack echoed. "Get the sheriff. I think he'd be interested in hearing what Mr. Wainwright said about his best friend's widow."

The banker stumbled to his feet and cleared the office of his employees. Closing the door behind him, he pointed at Mack. "You will pay for this," he said. "Now, before I press charges against you for assaulting me, I want you to understand that my bank will not be party to any transaction that is used for illicit purposes. So if you are not this lady's husband, your money is no good here." He pointed to Mrs. Lowe. "As for you, madame, if I am wrong about the nature of this situation, please accept my apologies. However, I cannot let the reputation of this establishment be besmirched in any way."

Mrs. Lowe marched over to the banker and pointed her finger at him. "Mr. Wainwright, there are plenty of things I would like to say to you right now, but contrary to what your opinion of me might be, my mama raised a lady, and I intend to act like one. I might not have known that my husband mortgaged our place to the point where only a miracle would save it, but I will never let it be said that he wasn't a good man and I'm not a good woman."

"Now, don't go putting words into my mouth."

"I'd like to put my fist there like Mr. McCoy did," she snapped, "but as I said, I won't. I will raise that money fair and square and bring you every penny I owe. You mark my words. Now, Mr. McCoy, if you'll come fetch your horse, I will take my wagon and go home."

With that, she turned around and walked out, her backbone straight and her head held high. Mack watched her go, smiling.

"Pretty words for a pretty lady," the banker said. "But that place is already in foreclosure. It's not hers anymore."

"Then I will buy it," Mack said. "Name your price."

"I'm sorry," Wainwright said. "It's not for sale. Not yet, anyway. It is still listed as belonging to the Lowes, though that is just a technicality. There are details to be handled, paperwork to be filed." He shrugged. "Who knows how long this could take?"

Mack moved just close enough to cause the banker to cease his talking. "Show me the papers that woman's husband signed." When Wainwright didn't immediately take action, Mack added a single word as a warning. "Now."

That sent the older fellow scurrying to his filing cabinet where after a few moments of searching, he retrieved a file and set it on the desk in front of him. Mack picked up the file and opened it.

Though he did his best work at a card table, there had been a time when Mack studied the law. Some of what he learned came back to him as he sorted through the multitude of statements on the documents in the file. Satisfied, he closed the file and pushed it across the desk into the banker's hands.

"Mrs. Lowe still has one option for keeping her land," he said. "And she will be exercising it."

Wainwright clutched the file and then opened it to search through the papers. "I see no options for her, sir," he finally said.

Mack grinned. "That's where you're wrong. Page seven, paragraph four."

Wainwright shuffled through the pages until he located the correct one. "In the event of the death of Pittman Lowe, all rights shall pass to the man who becomes the husband of Mrs. Glorietta Lowe." He paused to look up at Mack.

"Keep reading."

"Included in those rights of said husband are the right of sale, transfer, or rescue from foreclosure." He looked up. "Yes, I remember adding that line to the contract. Thought it an odd request, but Pittman Lowe insisted."

"And that line means what?"

The banker adjusted his spectacles and held the contract up to read it again. "Well, it means just what it says. Any subsequent husband of Mrs. Lowe has the same legal rights to her property and its upkeep as the current one."

"Exactly," Mack said as he headed for the door. He found Gloree back at the wagon, this time offering Mack's horse an apple.

"I got hungry," she said with a shrug as she scratched the horse's ear. "Figured he'd be hungry, too." She nodded toward the bank. "Thank you for standing up for me in there. I never liked that man, but Pitt said he could be trusted. I'm beginning to see that Pitt wasn't exactly a good judge of character."

Mack shook his head. "Maybe not, but he was a good judge of what to put into a real estate contract." He reached for her arm. "Come with me."

She allowed the Englishman to lead her down the sidewalk, doing her best to ignore the astonished stares of those she passed. "Afternoon, Miz Miller," she said to the blacksmith's wife. "Nice day, isn't it?" she commented to the proprietor of Calleyville Mercantile as she hurried to keep pace with the man whose iron grasp held her wrist.

Finally he stopped in front of Sheriff Drummond's office. He paused only a moment to remove his hat before opening the door and marching inside. "Come on," he called as once again he grasped her wrist.

She tumbled inside, and Mr. McCoy caught her and set her upright. "Sorry," she mumbled. "I've gotten clumsy since. . ."

No, she'd not let on about her condition. Not in front of these men. For there stood Sheriff Drummond and a stranger. The pair spoke amicably like old friends, though their laughter and conversation had stopped short when they spied her and Mack.

"I sure didn't expect to see you back here," Sheriff Drummond said to Mr. McCoy. "Or you, Gloree." He nodded to his companion. "This here's Reverend Clanton, the circuit rider. Don't reckon you've met him before."

The reverend reached out to shake her hand, and she instantly liked his kind face and quick smile. "No, I don't believe I have."

"It's been some time since the church has had a man riding circuit in these parts." He nodded to the sheriff. "I was just telling Sheriff Drummond that I've been given permission to look for a permanent church location here in Callyville. I'm looking forward to holding regular services here."

"Yes, that's wonderful," Mr. McCoy said, "but there's a more pressing service you need to hold right now." He glanced over at Gloree then back at Reverend Clanton. "Mrs. Lowe and I are in need of being wed."

"What?" She shook her head. "Have you lost your mind?"

The Englishman shrugged. "Looks as if the bride's nerves have gotten the better of her. Sheriff, is there someplace she and I can speak privately?"

Sheriff Drummond nodded toward a door behind him. "No place to run, though. I use it to exercise prisoners, but the wife thinks it's for growing her garden. Either way, it works."

"I assure you neither of us wishes to run."

Speak for yourself.

"Just give me a chance to explain," he whispered as he wrapped his arm around Gloree's waist and escorted her out the side entrance and into the sunshine of the enclosed back alley.

"I can't imagine what you have to say to me that would make me walk back in there and agree to marry you," she said, her heart racing.

"The only way to keep your property from being sold to someone else by the bank is to get married, Mrs. Lowe. It doesn't have to be to me, but it needs to be to someone." He paused. "And soon. You heard Mr. Wainwright say the property is already in foreclosure."

She nodded. That was one of the few things she'd heard in the banker's office that *had* stuck with her. "All right," she said slowly, "you've got my attention."

"Thanks to specific wording that your husband insisted on, the property rights he held transfer directly to the next man you marry. Without that clause in the loan, you would have no hope of keeping your land."

"But with it?" she asked, knowing the answer.

"With it, your husband can pay off the mortgage and the property no longer belongs to the bank." He leaned against the wall and seemed to be watching her for a reaction. "I assume he had that clause in mind when he sent for this fellow from Texas to come and wed you. Seeing as he hasn't arrived, I am offering to be Pitt's man, Mrs. Lowe. Will you let me help you?"

She shook her head and turned away. "I don't even know you. And why?" She turned around again. "Why would you do this for me?"

"Because I can," he told her.

"But what if Pitt's man. . ." She paused to choose her words carefully. "That is, what if the man Pitt sent for shows up? Then what?"

"Then you will have him if you choose."

"Thank you," she said sarcastically, "but I'm old-fashioned. I prefer one husband at a time."

"And one husband is all you'll have." He moved closer then looked around before returning his attention to Gloree. "I will marry you in name only. Give the bank time to process the papers and give you the deed free and clear, and then you can get yourself an annulment."

"How is that possible?"

"The law allows recourse for a spouse when the marriage has not been. . ." He gave her a look that completed the sentence for her.

"I see."

And she did. It helped that Pitt had written the clause into the loan papers. Surely he wouldn't be opposed to the notion.

"I can see you're considering it," he said. "Look, I don't have a decent reputation in this town, and for good reason. For that matter, there are few places other than my own mother's home where I'm thought well of."

"You are not helping your case, Mr. McCoy," she said.

"I am being honest, Mrs. Lowe." His look was both direct and intense. "I'm far from a decent man, but I will do the decent thing today if you'll let me."

"I won't take your money permanently," she said, "even if I am signing up to take your name."

He looked surprised, and she wondered which of those statements was the cause. "Fair enough," he said.

"Soon as the ranch is back up and running and we're making a profit, you'll be paid back every penny you've put into it."

At Mr. McCoy's nod, Gloree inhaled deeply of the sun-scented air and then let it out slowly. "Then we have a deal?" she said as she reached out to shake his hand.

If the Englishman thought it odd that a woman would make such a gesture, his expression did not show it. Instead he gripped her hand firmly and looked her in the eyes. "We do."

Ten minutes later, she walked out of Sheriff Drummond's office as Mrs. McCoy. She couldn't help but notice that though the sheriff easily agreed to act as witness, he wasn't nearly as free with congratulations afterward as his wife was. In fact, he appeared not to like her new husband at all.

No matter. She didn't have to like him, either, for he wouldn't be around much longer. She would always respect his decision, though, and would never forget the man who made it possible for her to keep her land.

Gloree touched the slight beginning of a swell just below the ribbons of her dress. Now to decide how to tell Mr. McCoy he would be a father. If he stayed married to her, that is. Which he wouldn't. So why bother with such personal information?

Her decision made, Gloree kept her mouth shut as she and her new husband walked over to the bank to have their second meeting of the day with Mr. Wainwright. This time Sheriff Drummond and the preacher came along to verify a wedding had taken place and to sign papers as witnesses that the Pittman Lowe property, now known as the Lowe-McCoy property, was owned free and clear by Mack and Gloree McCoy.

"Once the papers are in order, the bank will officially remove the foreclosure proceedings from the property," Mr. Wainwright said when the last page was signed. He met her gaze. "Congratulations, Mrs. McCoy, on your very recent wedding."

Ignoring his obviously sarcastic statement, Gloree watched the banker deposit the signed papers into a folder and then place that folder into a cabinet behind him. "How long will it take until the land is officially is mine? Ours," she corrected.

The banker closed the cabinet with a thud and shrugged. "I will do my best to get this situation handled with all the expediency it deserves."

Though the pastor and sheriff probably did not understand the meaning behind those words, Gloree did. Likely her new husband did, too.

Gloree turned her attention to the lawman. "But the bank can't take the property as long as it's paid for and they've given you a receipt for the money. Isn't that right, Sheriff?"

Sheriff Drummond laughed and nudged the pastor. "Well, that's true, but what possible reason would Mr. Wainwright have for delaying a payment your husband made fair and square?"

The lump rising beneath the banker's right eye was one. The fresh bruise on his chin, another.

Gloree exchanged a look with her new husband and then affected her sweetest smile. "I'm sure I can't think of a thing."

"All right, dear," Mr. McCoy said as he patted her arm. "Now that we have taken care of things with the preacher and the banker, what do you say to a trip to the mercantile before we go home? I sure would like some of your biscuits and gravy tomorrow for breakfast, and our flour is running low."

❧

"Biscuits and gravy, Mr. McCoy?" Gloree said when they were back in the wagon headed for home. "You're assuming a lot for a man who agreed to a temporary marriage in name only."

He slid a grin across the space between them. "It was all I could think of at the time, and I was afraid if I didn't get you out of the banker's office, you'd hit him harder than I did."

She matched his smile. "I was tempted, that's for sure."

"However," he said, "I feel I ought to point out that even a temporary husband has to eat. So if you can't cook biscuits and gravy—"

"Oh, I can make it just fine. And I do owe you for getting the ranch out of hock and filling the pantry with the things you bought at the mercantile." She paused to count her blessings even as she bit back the fear that came along with them. "And the livestock you managed to buy off Mr. Quentin are going to bring this place back to being profitable again.

"Fancy running into the man whose cattle are considered the best in three counties while waiting for our order to be filled at the mercantile. That's quite a coincidence."

"There are no coincidences." She brushed a strand of hair from her face and focused her attention on the road ahead. "I know the Lord arranged it all." At his scowl, she shook her head. "What?"

"I'd rather not argue with you." He paused. "Not on our honeymoon."

Gloree nudged him. "I'm serious. Why do you make that face when I talk about God?"

"Because it has been my experience that the ones who talk about God the most are the ones who appear to know Him the least. If He indeed exists at all."

"Oh, He exists all right. If He didn't, how would you explain everything that has happened since sunup this morning? Can't you look at all of what's transpired and say there is a God and I see Him everywhere I look?"

He shrugged. "I assure you that statement has never crossed my mind."

"Well then, I'm going to challenge you to ask Him to show you He's here."

"You mean you want me to speak to an invisible being and demand he become visible?" The sarcasm in his voice was impossible to miss.

"No, Mr. McCoy, that's not what I mean at all. Yes, He may be invisible to our eyes, but sometimes that's just because we don't know where to look. Why don't you just ask Him where to look?"

"That's all?" At her nod, he continued. "I'll do that. Now one more thing. As long as you're cooking my breakfast and advising me on spiritual matters, I wonder if we ought to dispense with the formalities and call each other by our first names." He shrugged. "Of course, if you prefer to refer to me as Mr. McCoy, then I will be forced to call you Mrs. McCoy. For accuracy's sake, of course."

"No," she quickly said. "Gloree is fine."

"Gloree it is," he said, "though I couldn't help but notice the mortgage papers called you Glorietta. That's a pretty name."

"Mama always said that was too much name for me. It was her mama's, and she was obligated to pass it on, but she never did call me by it." She smiled at the memory. "I was always Gloree ever since I was a little baby girl, or at least that's what I was told."

"Then you'll continue to be Gloree."

She shifted positions and regarded him curiously. "Tell me about yourself, Mack. I know you're just my husband temporarily, but I'm curious how a man from practically the other side of the world ended up in Colorado."

"By boat and by horseback with at least two trains," he said mischievously then looked her way, grinning.

"Stop it," she said. "If you don't want to tell me, just say so."

"It's not that I don't want to tell you," he admitted. "I just don't know *what* to tell you."

She settled back against the seat and stretched her legs. Exhaustion, her constant companion in her other two pregnancies, tugged at her now.

"Tell me about your mama," Gloree said.

"Oh, that's a story for another day," was his cryptic response as he pulled the wagon to a stop. "Right now I'm torn between concentrating on the road and worrying if you run out of words, you're going to fall asleep and tumble out of the wagon." He gestured behind him. "There's a pile of blankets that'd make a fine place for a new bride to take a nap."

"And while I'm sleeping, you and the Lord can have a nice chat," she said with a grin as she climbed into the back of the wagon and settled into a comfortable spot.

Though she intended to lightly doze, Gloree closed her eyes and did not open them again until the sunlight blinded her. Shielding her face, she sat up and looked around to find she was home.

In her own bed.

But how?

She sat up and stretched. It all looked the same. Same whitewashed walls. Same white iron bedstead on the other side of the room where the children used to sleep. Same view of the barn and the pasture beyond from the window opposite her.

Indeed she was home.

And then she smelled it. Biscuits and gravy.

Chapter 4

His bride was radiant in her rumpled yellow dress and blond curls tumbling down her back and around her shoulders. Sleep had softened her expression and given her a peaceful look she hadn't worn yesterday.

Mack had dispensed with the fancy clothes he'd worn yesterday and put on a simple pair of workingman's trousers and shirt. He'd borrowed an apron from the peg beside the stove, something Gloree seemed to find amusing.

"I've set out the jelly I found in the larder," he said as he set the plate of biscuits on the table then reached for the pan of gravy. "I've also got a few fresh eggs I collected from the yard if you want something to go along with the biscuits."

"Thank you, but no. This'll be plenty." She reached for a biscuit. "I guess I was sleeping pretty hard."

"Hard enough," he said. "I hated to wake you."

"Where'd you. . .?"

"Sleep?" He nodded to the bedroll stowed in the corner. "Suits me."

"I hadn't thought about offering a place for you. What with the house only having the one room upstairs for beds, it just didn't occur to me that you'd need a place, too." She set the biscuit down. "The barn'd fall down around your head in a decent breeze, so that's not an option."

Mack nodded. "Actually, my first act as ranch owner. . ." At her scowl, he shook his head. "That is, as temporary husband to the ranch owner, is to see what I can do to fortify that structure. I've found enough boards stacked behind it to do some patching. I think there are sufficient nails to do the job, but I may have to make a trip back into Calleyville if there isn't."

Gloree reached for the ladle and scooped up some gravy. "I still don't think it'll be sufficient to house you, though."

"Nor do I," Mack said. "That's why I'm going to move in upstairs with you."

The ladle landed in the pan of gravy with a plop. "You'll do no such thing."

"Was my guess correct in putting you in the bed across from the window?"

"Yes," she said tersely as she swiped at the splashes of gravy on her sleeve.

"Then the other is mine." He rose and turned away as if that was the end of the subject.

"I won't allow it," she declared.

Mack swiveled around, his expression turned dangerous, or as dangerous as a man could look while wearing a flowered apron with ruffles and bows. "That was a statement, not a question, Gloree."

A ruckus rose outside as the horses began to protest. Mack tossed the apron over his head and let it fall to the floor as they hurried to the window investigate. A cloud of dust materialized at the horizon along with several riders.

"Looks like a cattle drive," she remarked.

"My guess is it's our cattle." Mack hurried to his horse and headed out to meet them while Gloree watched from the window. And though she knew she'd be sparring with the man again before bedtime, she couldn't help but smile as she watched him now.

The remainder of the day was taken up with getting the cattle settled, mending the fences, and feeding the men Mr. Quentin had sent over to deliver the animals. By the time the last plate was washed and the kitchen set to rights, the sun had gone down behind the mountains.

Mack remained outside well past the time the shadows gathered and the sky darkened to black. She heard him speaking in low tones with Quentin's men on the porch until the sound of hoof beats told her they had gone.

Still he didn't come inside.

Gloree tended the fire and lit a lamp beside her chair then reached for the book she'd started weeks ago. She jumped when she heard an owl's call. Jumped again when a coyote barked off in the distance.

Finally she'd had enough. She set her book aside and extinguished the lamp then went to the window. Her husband sat at the edge of the porch, seemingly staring up into the night sky. Though she was tempted to latch the door, she turned away.

She'd managed through near death in Texas and real death here in Colorado. What was one stubborn man? She'd manage him, too.

She headed upstairs, shaking her head at the squeaking noise the first riser had made since a few weeks before Pitt's death. Odd that even the staircase marked the time since she'd been left alone.

Oh, but it did. But then, so did she.

Removing the pins from her hair, she sat on the edge of the bed to brush it. If she stretched her toes, she could reach the other bed. Though the room filled the length of the house, she had clustered the beds together to make caring for her sick family easier. She hadn't been able to keep Pitt in bed—he'd been determined to get the crop in the ground before the illness took him. But her babies had been just an arm's length away from her throughout those long, anxious nights.

Now, however, it just meant that the man she'd married solely for convenience was going to attempt to sleep a most inconvenient distance away.

Mack closed the door behind him and waited until his eyes adjusted to the murky darkness of the farmhouse's interior. It had been far too long since he'd spent the day outdoors doing real, satisfying work. He smiled as he slipped off his boots and then stepped away from the door to move toward the staircase.

The first riser squeaked beneath his feet, though the remainder of them did not. A quirk of the old house, he decided. Eventually he would have to repair it. For now, the item would go at the bottom of an ever-lengthening list.

At the top of the stairs he stopped to place his hand on the doorknob. Locked. Of course.

He reached into his pocket for a tool from one of his former not-so-legal trades: a small metal pick that made short work of his bride's locked door. Bowing to her sense of propriety, he tiptoed past his sleeping wife with the intention of climbing into the bed he'd claimed.

But the sight of the moonlight slanting over Gloree's features captured his attention and held it. She'd woven her hair into a braid and donned a white gown with a ruffle that teased her neck.

A chill breeze puffed up the curtains and caused her to shift positions. Mack tiptoed over to the window to close it.

"Leave it open."

He froze and then turned around slowly to find his bride siting up in bed with the covers drawn up to her chin. "Leave the window open," she repeated. "And then leave."

He chuckled at the threat in her tone. "I'll do one of the two," Mack said. "But I won't be doing the other."

He stalked over to the empty bed and reached down to fluff the pillow. The lamp came on, and he glared over at Gloree.

"Go sleep wherever you slept last night," she demanded.

"Last night I laid my bedroll on the kitchen floor because that parlor set of yours is the most uncomfortable furniture I've had the unfortunate experience of trying to sleep on. And I have slept in some uncomfortable places."

"I do not care where you've slept before," she snapped. "I only care where you think you will be sleeping here."

The fact that this woman—his wife—was even prettier when she was riled wasn't lost on Mack. Neither was the fact that theirs was a marriage in name only.

"I can sleep with or without that lamp, but if you're worried about your modesty or what you might see when I drop these trousers, you probably ought to shut it off."

"You wouldn't," she said, her eyes wide.

Exhaustion had worn down his patience just enough to cause him to reach for the tail of his shirt and slip it over his head. Before an inch of his chest could be exposed, darkness flooded the room.

Though he was sorely tempted to leave his dusty trousers on the floor with his shirt, he lay down on top of the blankets and fitted the pillow beneath his head. Out of the corner of his eye, he saw Gloree turn her back on him and pull the covers over her head.

She was still in that position when Mack donned his shirt and headed downstairs to find his boots and start his day. Gloree met him in the barn just after sunrise.

"Good morning, wife," he said as cheerily as he could manage. "What have you got there?"

"Breakfast," she said as she left the cloth-wrapped bundle on a stack of lumber and walked away without a backward glance.

He considered letting Gloree know how pretty she looked when she was mad then wisely decided against it. He stood and admired her until she disappeared inside.

If she'd been his wife—his real wife—he might have followed her inside. Instead, he went back to the massive job of trying to piece together the patchwork that was the barn's walls.

Before he realized the time had gone by, Mack was startled from his work by Gloree delivering lunch. "Thank you," he said to her retreating back.

Again, he allowed a moment to watch her walk away. Indeed, Gloree could have easily held her own among women of distinction and wealth. And the spunk she showed? Mack grinned as he tore off a piece of bread. His mother would have heartily approved.

As the shadows lengthened across the pasture, Mack straightened from his work on the barn and decided he'd start again tomorrow. One quick round of the fences on horseback, and he was ready to call his day complete.

Then he spied a calf, new by his measure, caught in the brush some distance away from the herd. Mack jumped off his horse and hurried to free the baby from its trap, expecting it would rejoin the herd. Instead, the calf stumbled and fell at his feet. Now what?

He picked up the calf and felt it go limp in his arms. He'd need to get this one to its mama soon, or it would be in trouble.

Approaching the herd slowly, he set the little one on its feet and then stepped away to watch and see what happened. The calf began raising a ruckus that showed it had a healthy set of lungs.

Just when Mack was ready to give up and bring the little one back to the barn, a cow broke from the herd and moved toward it. Mack stood stock-still as the heifer nudged the baby and then allowed it to nurse.

He waited until he was sure the calf wouldn't be rejected or wander away again, and then he headed back. Gloree met him at the door, worry etching her face.

"Where have you been?" she demanded. "Supper's cold." She gave him an imperious, sweeping glance. "You're a mess!"

He told her about the calf, and her expression immediately softened. "Oh that sweet baby," she said. "You're sure his mama isn't going to let him get lost again?"

"Well," he said slowly, "I suppose it could happen again, but I doubt it."

Her eyes misted. "I just can't imagine not being able to find my little one. How awful."

"It's just a cow, Gloree," he said. "And don't worry about heating up supper. I'll have whatever you made cold. I'm that hungry."

A few minutes later she set a plate of beans and leftover chicken on the table and nodded for him to sit down. Gloree was a good cook, but it wouldn't have mattered if she hadn't been tonight. He barely finished his meal before he felt his eyes wanting to fall shut.

Only when he removed his boots and stepped on the first squeaky riser did he recall the bedroom battle of last night. Too tired to repeat the exchange, Mack decided he'd fall asleep wherever he landed and ignore the consequences.

What he did not expect was that while he'd been patching up the barn and saving a calf, his wife had been rearranging the bedroom and making a few other changes. The beds that had once been situated close together were now on opposite ends of the room. To further delineate the ownership of the space, Gloree had strung a clothesline across the center of the room. Hanging from it were what appeared to be every mismatched sheet and blanket the woman owed except for what was on the beds.

While she'd retained ownership of the lamp, she had provided him with another along with a washstand, a pitcher of water, and a length of toweling. Exactly what he needed before falling into bed.

Mack slipped through the curtain and removed his shirt. Then off came his trousers. Once clean, he pulled back the blankets to find a nightshirt folded under the pillow.

Tired as he was, Mack managed a smile. He'd put the nightshirt on tomorrow night. When he could raise his arms high enough to slip them into the sleeves.

For tonight, all he could do was fall into bed and close his eyes.

⁓∞⸱

Gloree stared at the closed curtain and waited for Mack to turn off his lamp. The minutes ticked away, witnessed by the sound of the mantel clock's chime. Still the lamp burned on the other side of the room.

She'd been quite proud of herself to come up with such an ingenious solution to a problem completely caused by the stubborn Englishman. Until she realized the one flaw in the plan lay in the fact that she had no control over when his side of the room went dark.

So she lay there very still and tried to be patient. Mama had once warned her not to pray for patience, because that was one prayer the Lord loved to answer. It felt as if He was answering it now.

Finally, she decided to take action. "Mack," she called timidly.

Nothing.

She tried again.

Still nothing.

"This is silly," she decided. "I'll just sleep with that light on."

Gloree turned over and closed her eyes, willing herself to fall asleep. Unfortunately, the harder she tried to force sleep to come, the more awake she felt. Finally, she'd had enough.

Throwing back the blankets, she stalked over to the makeshift wall and called her temporary husband's name again. Once again, nothing happened.

"Mack," she said louder. "Turn. Off. The. Light."

The snorts began immediately, settling quickly into a resonant and very male snore.

"Great."

Then she realized that if he was asleep, she could easily slip over to his side of the room and turn off his lamp. As a measure of protection of her decency, she went back to her bed and wrapped a blanket around her shoulders.

Retracing her path to the wall of blankets, she paused only a moment before moving a blanket aside and stepping into the golden glow of the lamp she intended to douse. And, apparently, into a room where her sleeping husband had not bothered to don the nightshirt she had so generously offered.

Horrified, she ran back toward her bed. The blankets that tangled around her as she attempted to escape slowed her progress only slightly. They did, however, cause her to tumble to the floor and slide against the wall.

"Blast it for polishing the floors today," she muttered as she stumbled to her feet.

Only then did she realize the snoring had ceased. In its place was soft but audible laughter.

"It's not funny," she called as she stalked back to bed.

The laughter continued.

"Turn off your lamp," she demanded. A moment later, darkness descended on the room. "Thank you," she snapped as she punched at her pillow until she feared feathers would fly.

More laughter.

"Oh stop it," she demanded. "Just go back to sleep."

Finally the laughter ceased. "Good night, Mrs. McCoy," her temporary husband said from the other side of the room.

She ignored him.

Chapter 5

Denver, Colorado
July 1878

As spring turned to summer, their lives settled into a predictable rhythm. Though Mack hadn't told Gloree the full reason, he intended to inquire about the status of their ranch while he was in Denver. He also planned to call at the post office to see if he'd received any letters from home.

His inquiry told him that Wainwright had not yet turned in the papers needed to transfer the ranch from foreclosure to paid in full. This news would require a trip to Calleyville, which he would have to take on another day. His trip to the post office yielded two envelopes, both of which he stuffed into his pocket until he was safely on the trail back toward home.

A few hours out of Denver, Mack stopped to water the horse. Pulling one of the letters out, he saw it contained his remittance, as expected. What he didn't expect was a letter from his father asking him to come home and take up his place in the household.

Though Colin has protested—and for good reason, I suppose—I have initiated a search for you. When my men find you, and they will, please allow them to bring you home to me. My health is not as it should be, and I wish to see my family united while I still can. To that end, the remittance contained here is your last.

Mack crumpled the letter and tossed it into the creek, watching the ink blur as the rushing water whisked it away. He tore into the second letter and recognized Colin's handwriting immediately.

The letter was full of insights on life at their father's house, chatty comments that his brother would never have made in person but that were likely designed to make any reader other than Mack think it was merely an innocent letter sent from one brother to the to the other. And then he read this:

No doubt you've received the gift I sent. Know there are others of a similar nature still to come. I hope you continue to enjoy your prolonged visit to America. It is my wish that you travel extensively and only return home when you think it advisable.

Mack disposed of this letter in the same way as the first and then climbed into the saddle and headed for home. As the miles fell behind him, he contemplated his dilemma. The money in his pocket was the last of what he would be receiving from his father. Thus, it was the last of what his mother would be receiving from him, at least until such a time as he could find another way to earn an income outside of the ranch. Every penny he'd saved before coming to Colorado had been spent on its salvation and upkeep.

There was always cards. He'd certainly made a good living playing at the tables. Perhaps he could collect enough to send for his mother.

Mack let out a long breath as he considered the idea. He thought of the life he was building with Gloree. He'd forgotten the satisfaction and sense of self-respect that came with earning an honest living. But what about his mother's safety? It certainly held considerable appeal to have her here where she could be protected from Colin and the greed that came with being associated with that family.

By the time he reached the fork in the road that would either take him home or to Calleyville, Mack had made up his mind. He turned the horse toward the little town where he hoped enough time had passed since the last time he'd sat at the card tables. Just a few rolls of the dice, a few rounds of cards, and he'd have the money to send for her. Then he'd go back to being a fine, upstanding citizen and model husband.

He'd ridden a few miles down the road when he spied someone coming toward him. As the rider neared, he saw it was the pastor who married him and Gloree.

"Afternoon," Reverend Clanton called. "How's married life?"

"I married a good woman," was the best and most true response Mack could manage.

"You did at that," the pastor said. "Say, do you have a minute?"

"I do," Mack said as he followed the reverend's lead and climbed down from his horse. "Something bothering you?"

"It is, actually." The pastor nodded toward a rocky outcrop on the banks of the creek. "Join me?"

Mack sat near him and waited for the man to speak. The rock, warmed by the sun, had almost lulled him to sleep, when Pastor Clanton cleared his throat.

"So, I've got an unusual assignment. I was told to come and fetch you to this very spot, so it seems quite the coincidence that you're here without any coercion on my part."

"There are no coincidences." Mack smiled at Gloree's words.

"Something funny?"

"No, sir. It's just that my wife likes to remind me there are no coincidences. I wonder if you agree."

"Yes, I suppose I do." He shrugged. "But whatever the reason, I'm here to answer your question. That's the purpose of our meeting here."

"My question?"

Reverend Clanton nodded. "I was told you had a question. Something about where to look?"

"Where to look?" More pieces of the memory rose, of the conversation held with Gloree on the first day of their marriage.

"Can't you look at all of what's transpired and say there is a God and I see Him everywhere I look? Well then, I'm going to challenge you to ask Him to show you He's here."

Was that the question?

"I see you know what I'm referring to now," the reverend said.

"Maybe so," Mack agreed. "I'm thinking of a conversation I had with my wife. Seems silly now."

"I assure you there are no silly conversations to be had when it comes to the Lord."

"All right," Mack said. "We were talking about coincidences and how God shows Himself through things we pass off as accidental. She challenged me to ask Him to show me He's here. That He's real, I suppose."

The preacher grinned. "Well, it looks like your question has already been answered."

"How so?"

"Look where we are, and look at what we've said to each other since we arrived at this place. You said that Gloree believes there are no coincidences, am I correct?"

Mack shrugged. "That's the theory."

"When you decide it's the truth, you let me know, because it is then that your question will have been answered."

"You're talking in riddles, Pastor."

"If you agree there are no coincidences, then our meeting here today wasn't an accident. It was God showing Himself just as you asked." He paused. "Or perhaps before you even knew to ask it."

Mack allowed that idea to take hold. To sink deep inside.

"Where were you going, son?" the pastor asked him.

"Calleyville." Suddenly he felt ashamed of his intentions. "Post office and bank," he added.

"Then I won't keep you." Pastor Clanton laid a hand on Mack's shoulder. "I wonder how married life is going for you, son."

"Well," Mack said as he looked away, "it's going just fine, I guess."

Pastor Clanton gave him a look that told Mack he wasn't sure he believed him.

"I wonder about something," he said slowly. "Did you marry that girl to help her out of her predicament, or did I get that wrong?"

"You did not get that wrong," he admitted.

"And is this a marriage you two intend to honor?"

"I don't follow."

"You said vows, son," Reverend Clanton said. "I'm asking if you're going to keep those vows." He waved his hands in the air as if clearing the question from the space between them. "Forget I asked. It's enough to know that you know the answer to that. You don't have to tell me what it is."

The pastor said his good-bye and turned back toward Calleyville. Mack watched him go and then headed for home. Along the way, he found plenty of time to wrestle with the Lord about Clanton's timely interception of his backsliding intentions and about the questions the reverend had asked, especially the last one. By the time he arrived at the ranch, he knew the answer.

He took a vow when he married Gloree, and he was honor bound to keep it. Now to convince her of that.

He'd have to be honest with her, starting with who he really was—how his last name wasn't really McCoy—and ending with a promise he'd be the man she needed. The husband God wanted him to be.

Mack took the steps up to the porch two at a time, and when he stepped inside he could easily find Gloree by following the smell of supper. She'd made chicken again, and it waited on the sideboard along with heaping helpings of some of his favorite dishes. She was pulling corn bread out of the oven when he walked into the kitchen.

"Welcome home," Gloree said. "Did you get what you needed in Denver?"

"I got more than what I needed," he said with a grin as he waited until she set the corn bread down to cool and then pulled her into his arms.

⟳

"What's this?" Gloree said as she tried to wriggle from his grasp. Too late, from the expression on his face.

"I could ask the same question, Gloree." He held her at arm's length and then placed his palm beneath her waist. "What's this?"

The last I have of Pitt Lowe, she wanted to say. *The baby that I cannot lose*, came to mind. Instead, she remained mute.

He looked angry. She didn't blame him. "When were you going to tell me you were with child?"

"Eventually," she managed.

"Eventually?" He shook his head. "I suppose something like that would be difficult to hide after a while."

When she didn't respond, he took a step back and leaned against the door frame. She realized once again how handsome he was. How tall and broad shouldered.

Macks's humorless laugh surprised her. "You know what's funny, Gloree? I came home to tell you I didn't want to hide anything from you anymore. I had decided I wanted to be your husband, and not in name only." His gaze swept the length of her. "How far gone are you?"

"Five months, near as I can tell," she admitted.

"So you and Pitt are having a baby."

Her head snapped up as she met his stare. "Yes, it appears so."

"When were you really going to tell me?" He paused. "The truth, Gloree."

The truth was she didn't know the answer. "I hadn't decided," she finally said. "I just tried not to think about it. Because thinking about it was too. . ."

Too much like admitting Pitt was gone.

Like admitting he'd never see this baby.

Things she thought but couldn't say. Her eyes clouded and the image of her husband—this husband—swam before her. Hot tears rolled down her cheeks, and words became impossible.

Rather than remain in the close quarters of the kitchen, Gloree pressed past Mack to step outside onto the front porch. The stars glittered overhead pinpoints of light in a sky of deepest purple and black.

Back in Oyster Creek, she'd stood many a night on their porch looking out over the water and watching for what Pitt called shooting stars. There were always plenty, especially around her birthday in the middle of August.

She hadn't seen one yet in Colorado, but she always looked for them. Even now, with her angry husband standing behind her, she was looking up. At the stars.

She heard the porch boards creak behind her and felt Mack drawing near. His arms wrapped around her and held her against him as he rested his chin on the top of her head. How long they stood that way without speaking, Gloree couldn't say. Slowly, Mack turned her around to face him.

Though she expected a scowl, she saw that he was looking at her with a tender expression. "Did you think I'd leave you alone to raise this child, Gloree? I know I'm just your temporary husband, but we said vows, and I mean to keep them."

Gloree buried her face in his chest and cried. When she'd spent all her tears, she looked up at her husband and saw that he was watching the sky. "Look there," he said as he pointed upward. "It's a shooting star."

If she blinked, she would have missed it. Instead, Gloree saw the flash of light streak across the sky and disappear behind the mountain. "Oh," she said on an exhale of breath. "My first here."

"Mine, too," Mack said.

"What do you think it means?" she whispered.

"Well," he said softly, "I can tell you my opinion, for what it's worth."

She leaned back against him. Allowed herself to feel comfortable in his arms, at least for this moment. "Yes, please do."

"If you read up on what a shooting star is, the mechanics behind them are pretty unspectacular. A meteor falls out of orbit and the dust it leaves behind causes streaks of light. So a shooting star isn't a star at all."

"Hmm," was all she said.

"And yet, if you think about how rare it is to see this happen, well, I just think maybe the Lord allows certain people to see certain things that might be invisible to others."

"Do you now?" Gloree smiled. "And does that extend beyond shooting stars?" She paused. "To other invisible things?"

"Enough digging for information," he said. "I will admit you were right. I asked, and He answered."

Her smile broadened. "Well, good."

"Other people say when a shooting star falls from the sky it's God lighting a candle and enlightening our darkness."

She thought of Pitt's favorite verse from Psalms. "For thou wilt light my candle: the LORD my God will enlighten my darkness."

"Yes," he said. "That's probably where the saying comes from." He turned her around again, and this time he held her at arm's length. "I don't think that you and I getting married was an accident, Gloree. I think it was part of a plan, just like I believe this child of yours. . ." He shook his head. "Of ours," he corrected, "was not an accident. He's going to do great things someday. I know it."

"Or she," Gloree amended.

"Or she," he said with a chuckle. "And if the Lord is willing, I want to be here to see those things."

"I guess we'll just have to see about that, then."

Later that night, when Gloree was supposed to be sleeping, she lay very still and felt the first fluttering movements of her little one. She wasn't sure how she felt about knowing Mack was willing to stay and help raise this child, but the fact he'd offered was enough for her tonight.

Shifting positions, she looked out the window and watched for another shooting star. "Maybe the Lord does allow certain people to see certain things that might be invisible to others," she whispered.

"Gloree," Mack said from the other side of the wall of blankets. "Everything okay over there?"

"I'm fine," she said as she stared up at the ceiling. "I just can't sleep."

"Want some warm milk?" he asked.

"Does that work?" she asked with a giggle.

She heard the bedsprings squeak and imagined him moving to sit up. "Never has for me, but I'm willing to test it on you if you'd like."

"Thank you, but it's not necessary, really." She closed her eyes and willed the sleep to come. Just as she was dozing off, she heard Mack call her name.

She thought of not responding then changed her mind. "What is it?"

"Something you said tonight has me thinking."

Silence stretched between them until Gloree thought Mack might have fallen asleep. She closed her eyes only to hear his bedsprings squeak again.

"Yes, you did owe me an apology for hiding that baby from me, but I owe you an apology, too, Gloree."

"Why?" She rolled to face the blanket wall and waited.

"I'm not who I said I was, but I'll be who I said I'll be." He paused. "Will you accept my apology?"

"Of course," she said as she waited for him to tell her more. When snores rose from his side of the room, she knew she'd have to wait until morning to find out the rest of his story.

⁓◦⦵◦⁓

Feigning sleep was the coward's way out of the conversation, but Mack knew he needed to be face-to-face with Gloree to tell her who he was. When he heard Gloree's soft breathing even out, he knew she'd finally succumbed to sleep.

He slipped on his pants and tucked his nightshirt into them then tiptoed out of the bedroom and down the stairs. The bottom stair creaked under his weight, reminding him he had not yet repaired it.

Someday soon, he decided. After he finished the other things clamoring for his attention that were more important. He stuck his feet into his boots and walked outside onto the porch for some fresh air.

It sure felt good holding Gloree in his arms. He'd been furious with her for hiding her pregnancy, mostly because she hadn't trusted him enough to be honest. Then again, he'd done the same thing to her.

Tomorrow he'd sit her down and tell her who he really was. About his father the Duke of Crenwright and his mother, the Scottish maid who gave the duke a son even when the duke would not give her his name. He would warn her about Colin, the half brother who could never believe Mack did not want the dukedom and all that went with it.

He would tell her all the reasons he couldn't go home and why he wanted to use the last money he'd received from his father to bring his mother here to Colorado so he could keep her safe.

But most of all, he wanted to tell her the reason why he wanted to live up to the vows he had spoken and make a home with her.

The chickens began to squawk, alerting Mack to a likely predator in the henhouse. He grabbed the Winchester and went in search of the source of the trouble.

Three steps off the porch, something hit him hard on the back of the head. With the second blow, everything went black.

Chapter 6

Mack woke up on the floor of a carriage, or maybe it was a wagon. Whatever it was, the springs were poor, and the road was worse. He'd been rolled into a blanket, just as he'd done with the Jones boys, leaving him unable to move or cry out. Unlike the Jones boys, however, at least he was alive.

By the time the ride was over, his head ached and he was surely black and blue from head to toe. He heard the rumble of what had to be a train. His hands and feet were bound, and a foul-tasting gag kept him from calling out as someone hauled him up and then tossed him down again.

His thought as he lay there waiting for the next thing to happen was that his father's men had finally found him. Or, perhaps, Colin had.

The last thing he expected when the blanket was peeled away was to see Sheriff Drummond standing over him. The sheriff's boot lifted and moved toward him, and the world went black once more.

⤬

He'd lied. He said sweet words but didn't mean any of them.

Those were the thoughts that kept taunting Gloree as she paced the front porch and kept watch for her husband. He'd told her he would stay and help her raise this child. Said he wanted to keep the vows they'd made.

"Well, you've got a strange way of showing it," she muttered as she turned back toward the door and then walked past it to stare over in the direction of the barn.

He'd been doing a fine job of bringing the ranch back to what it once had been. The barn now stood straight and fine, and no longer could a person stand on one side and see all the way through to someone standing on the other.

"He's just gone into town," she decided after she'd searched every inch of the ranch on horseback twice. "Or maybe he's gone off to help a neighbor."

Yes, of course. She turned the horse toward the east and the nearest ranch, where she was told he hadn't been seen there. The result was the same at the other places she tried—all of them neighbors who looked at her with pity when she begged for any help to find him.

Finally, she rode into Callyville to alert the sheriff that her husband was missing. She found him deep in conversation with an elderly man whose accent sounded familiar.

393

"You're English, aren't you?"

The fellow rose with care and waved away help from a younger fellow, who must have been his assistant. "Nicholas Crenwright, at your service, Miss. . .?"

"Mrs.," she corrected. "Mrs. McCoy."

At the name McCoy, the man's silver brows rose. He cast a glance at the younger fellow and then returned his attention to the sheriff. "It appears this young lady has business with you. Perhaps I shall allow her to converse with you alone." He nodded to the assistant. "Come, and let's leave these two."

Sheriff Drummond remained mute until the older man was gone. Then he nodded toward the chair the Englishman had recently vacated. "What can I do for you, Gloree?"

"Who was that man?"

The sheriff shook his head. "Private business," he stated firmly. "Now tell me what brings you to Calleyville."

"My husband," she said as she collected her thoughts. "It appears he's missing."

He nodded. "Go on."

"Well, you see, that's all I know. When I woke up this morning, he was gone. I've looked all over the ranch and spent the better part of the morning going to the neighbors to see if anyone has seen him, and they haven't."

"That's most unfortunate." The sheriff rested his palms on the desk. "I'm sorry to be so blunt, Gloree, but it sounds like your husband has run off. Now the good news, which I was going to have to find a way to tell you, is that Pitt's man has finally arrived. He's staying at the hotel until I can escort him to the ranch that's properly his."

She shook her head. "I don't understand. Mack and I were legally married. He paid to remove my property from foreclosure. You were there. You witnessed it."

"And so I did," he said. "But unfortunately, another document has turned up. A will that Pitt sent along with his payment to his cousin." He shrugged. "I hate to be the one to tell you, but Pitt was so sure his cousin was coming out here to marry you that he gave everything he owned, including the ranch, to him."

"But that's not possible," she managed as she gasped for a breath. "Pitt wouldn't do that. He just. . ." She shook her head. "He just wouldn't."

"But he did." The sheriff rose and came around his desk to help Gloree to her feet. "You're looking poorly, Miz Lowe. Why don't I—"

"McCoy," she corrected with all the force she could manage. "It's McCoy. Gloree McCoy, and I'll thank you to remember that." She shrugged out of his grasp and stumbled toward the door.

"I'm truly sorry, Gloree," Sheriff Drummond said. "But I've seen the will myself."

She stopped just short of the door and turned to face him. "I don't need a will to know that Pitt would never bypass me to give our property to someone else, and I certainly don't need to hear it from you or some fellow who manages to show up two months late."

"Suit yourself," he said as he leaned back in his chair. "But if I were you I'd take a trip over to the hotel and see for yourself. Meanwhile, I'll get to work on that missing-person report. Where do you figure it is that a card shark like Mack McCoy would be going?"

Gloree let the door slam on the question as she stumbled out into the afternoon sunshine. To her surprise, the elderly Englishman was waiting on the sidewalk. His companion was nowhere to be seen, although she guessed he was probably nearby. Men of this man's caliber rarely traveled alone. Or at least that was what she guessed.

"Might I have a word with you?" The Englishman nodded toward the hotel. "I've a private railcar at the station. We will not be disturbed there."

She must have looked doubtful, for the man's eyes softened. "You have my word as a gentleman that I merely wish to discuss family business in private."

Private business. That's what Sheriff Drummond said, too.

He leaned close, his right hand clutching a cane with a silver crest. "It is about Mack."

❧

Gloree needed no more convincing. "Where is he?" she demanded as soon as she stepped into the sumptuous surroundings of the railcar.

"That is what I had hoped you could tell me." The elderly man took a seat on a massive velvet chair and motioned for her to sit in the one nearest to him.

"Who are you?" she said as she complied.

"Haven't you figured it out?" He gestured around the room and then returned his attention to her.

The crest hung on the wall above his head declared him to be the Duke of Crenwright. When she repeated that to the older man, he grinned.

Something in that smile looked very familiar.

"Indeed, that is my title," he said. "But that isn't who I am." He paused as a fit of coughing took over him. Gloree rose to offer him the handkerchief she always kept close.

The duke held the folded cloth in his hand and studied it closely. Tracing the double *M*s with his forefinger, his eyes misted.

"She always did the best needlework." He met Gloree's gaze. "I miss that woman," he said as he dissolved into tears.

Instinctively, Gloree placed her hand over his. When that simple touch did not console the elderly gentleman, she rose to wrap one arm around his shoulder. He leaned against her and cried. Then he dabbed at his eyes with the handkerchief and shook his head.

"I'm an old man. Forgive me for my emotion." He reached to grasp her hand again. "You're Mack's wife, aren't you?"

Gloree came around to stand in front of him. "I am," she said. "He married me some two months ago. Almost three, actually."

His eyes went to her belly where the evidence of her child was likely showing. "No," she said. "The child is not his. You see, I was widowed, newly so. When Mack heard I was about to lose the land where Pitt and my children are buried, he stepped in to help."

He clutched her hand tighter. "Yes, he would do that." He paused to dab the handkerchief against his eyes once more. "Tell me what you know about Mack."

She smiled. "I know all I need to know about him, sir," she said. "I know he's a good man who sacrificed all he had to keep me from losing my home. I know he's worked hard to make the ranch something to be proud of." She paused. "And I know that even though we started out thinking we were making a temporary marriage, he didn't run when he could have."

"Yes," he said. "He didn't run."

"Do you know where he is, sir?"

The duke looked away. "I know where he was. I've known for some time." When he returned his attention to Gloree, he was smiling. "You see, I planned to bring him home. I even warned him of it. I told him I had men coming after him. What I didn't tell him is that it was I who was coming. See, he and I, well, we haven't gotten along well for some time."

"Oh?"

"It's all my fault," he admitted. "I'm rather stubborn. I'm afraid it runs in the family." He met her gaze. "He's my son, you see."

"Your son?" She shook her head. "How is that possible? You're a duke and he's a. . ."

"Gambler and a card shark?" The duke shrugged. "I've been accused of worse but generally from another member of the House of Lords." His expression sobered. "He believes I paid him to stay away because I was ashamed of him. You see, his mother and I weren't married. She was a maid, and well, it just wasn't done." He swiped his hand through the air. "Yes, I know how it sounds, but I was young and stupid. I married the woman I was told to marry. From that marriage came his brother Colin."

"Mack has a brother?"

"A half brother," he said, "and not a man I'm proud to call my son. I have recently become aware of what Colin has been up to, and I felt it was time to show myself to Mack. To let him know the truth about some things that he does not know." He shook his head. "His mother is dead, you see. Has been for almost two years."

"Oh," she said softly. "Does he know?"

He shook his head. "Nor does he know that before she died, we were married. She's buried in the family plot. And Colin? While I would like to have had him arrested, suffice it to say he will not trouble your husband again."

"My husband," she said. "Where is he?"

The duke checked the clock on the mantel and smiled. "We're due to meet him in Denver in an hour's time. Would you consent to coming along?"

"Just try and keep me from it," she said.

"I've just one matter to attend to before we're off. Might I offer you some refreshment in my absence?"

"Of course," she said as his assistant entered the room to assist the duke's exit. A short while later, both men returned and the train soon left the station.

During the trip to Denver, the duke entertained Gloree with stories of Mack's childhood. The older man seemed to delight in telling the tales of the young man's misadventures. "Oh, but he was stubborn," he told her.

"He still is," she said with a laugh as the train began to slow, indicating they were approaching Denver.

"You wait here," he said when the train stopped moving. "They'll bring him to us."

A few minutes later, two men in suits arrived, and the duke went outside on the platform to speak to them. When one of them turned, she spied the badge pinned to his lapel.

The pair shook hands with the duke and then went off to disappear into the crowd milling about on the platform. She stood to pace the railcar's elegant parlor. It seemed as though hours were passing when the clock only ticked away a few minutes.

Finally the door opened and Mack stepped inside. She hurried across the room to fall into his arms.

"Well now," he said with his familiar laugh. "That's a nice welcome, wife."

"Mack, I was so afraid I wouldn't see you again. Then when the sheriff said. . ." She held him at arm's length and studied the bruise that darkened his right cheek. "What happened to you?"

"Someone took exception to the fact that I married you," he said. "Or at least that's how I understand it."

"Yes," the duke said. "You certainly ruined what was a well-thought-out plan."

He shrugged. "They just didn't count on an old man's persistence and a young man's thick head."

Mack winced. "Not thick enough."

"I don't understand," Gloree said.

Mack and his father exchanged matching glances. How had she missed the fact these two were related?

"It all starts with my younger son, Colin," the duke said. "He decided his chances of inheriting were increased if he was the only son. Mack here isn't keen on taking over for me, so it was a simple matter to send him off on an adventure where he'd be safe from Colin and his schemes. It took some time, but I finally managed to catch Colin in the act of intercepting mail sent to Mack's mother and banish him." He shrugged. "Not that it's a terrible banishment. He is in charge of my holdings in the Caribbean."

Mack chuckled. "Colin detests the heat. For him, it's a terrible banishment."

"Your mother," Gloree said.

"Yes, I know." His voice was rough, his expression soft. "But they married and were happy. A much better fate than I expected."

She nodded and then leaned into him again. "I have news," she said. "We may no longer own the ranch. A will has been produced. Pitt's man finally arrived in Calleyville."

The duke snorted. "That will is as fake as the man who delivered it. Both hired by Colin and supported by the sheriff himself. You'd be surprised what money will buy, including a sheriff's loyalty."

"It was the sheriff who hauled me out of the ranch and threw me on a train. I don't know where they thought they were taking me, but they didn't get any farther than Denver." Mack glanced over at the older man. "Thanks to my father, they were caught."

The duke smiled and clasped his hand on Mack's shoulder. Neither spoke.

Finally, Gloree's curiosity got the better of her. "So, you're the son of a duke and not a card shark?"

"Yes, I'm sorry to disappoint you, but that's true," he said with a grin.

"That makes me. . ."

"The wife of the next duke, I suppose," the elderly man said. "Though he's going to accept the title with much argument, I'm sure."

Mack shrugged. "I'm learning to like the idea," he said. "Though my wife will wish us to split our time, won't you, dear?"

"Split our time?" She shook her head. "You mean. . ."

"The title will be ours someday," he said gently, "but for now Father presides over the family home and lands. However, we'll never be far from the ranch, I promise."

She grasped his hand and held on until she could manage to speak. "I just have one more question, then."

"What's that?"

"If your name isn't Mack McCoy, what is it?"

Both men laughed. "McCoy was his mother's family name," his father said. "The man you married was christened Maximillian Alexander Claudius Kennedy Crenwright."

He shrugged. "I never knew if Mack was an abbreviation for my mother's last name or just created from the first letter of my many names."

The duke shrugged. "Could be either."

Epilogue

The letter tumbled out of the Bible that Mack had found when he finally got around to fixing the loose board on the stairs. He had kept up with his repairs of the ranch because, much as Gloree loved England and Crenwright House, her home was here in Colorado with the man folks here knew simply as Mack.

Someday he would take his place as the next duke, but with his father's restored health thanks to the clear air of the Colorado mountains, that day was likely many years in the future.

Gloree smiled as the child in her belly stirred. Funny how the Lord worked things. This time last year she thought her life was over. Now she had a husband who loved her and two sons.

Yes, she knew this child she carried would be a boy just as she knew the son she held sleeping against her shoulder would be as much loved by Mack and his family as his brother.

She slid the letter out of its place marking the sixteenth Psalm but hesitated before opening it. When she was ready, she unfolded the page.

Dear Gloree,

If you're reading this, then I know you've found my hiding place. I'm sorry I never did find the right man for you. I tried, the Lord knows I did. Just seemed like every time I sent a letter to someone, it came back unopened. I reckon I lost track of just about everyone I knew who might be worthy of you. Not that anyone is, Gloree, because they aren't.

Still, I prayed for a hero for you, for a man who would take my place and love you like I do. God keeps telling me he is out there and I shouldn't worry. I'll try not to, but you know me. I worry about you. So if you're reading this, I figure that whoever took the time to fix the step I broke on purpose has given this letter to you. I sure hope I didn't put my trust in a God who wouldn't come through. I can't imagine that I did.

With all my love,
Pitt

"Oh Pitt," she whispered as she kissed the head of their sleeping son. "He did come through."

Gloree tucked the letter back into the Bible and returned it to its hiding place. Someday she would tell the whole story to their son, a story that began with the loss of a good man and ended with the love of another.

Someday, but not tonight. Tonight the tale was too fresh, the boy too young to understand that sometimes great love comes from great loss.

And that sometimes true love means setting aside what seems to be for what is. That's what faith looked like to Gloree Lowe McCoy, or rather Gloree, future Duchess of Crenwright, as the shadows of the fire danced across the floor and her husband slept beneath a quilt that once hung on a rope in the middle of the room.

Gloree went to the window to watch the stars. The sky looked as if God had tossed diamonds into the darkness and allowed them to stick in place.

A movement caught her eye. A shooting star!

She smiled as she settled her son in his cradle and climbed into bed, nestling herself against her husband. He turned and wrapped her in an embrace as he drifted back to sleep.

The words Pitt had underlined in his Bible drifted through her mind as she fell asleep.

"For thou wilt light my candle: the LORD my God will enlighten my darkness."

"Oh yes," she whispered. "He certainly has."

Bestselling author **Kathleen Y'Barbo** is a Romantic Times Book of the Year winner as well as a multiple Carol Award and RITA nominee of more than fifty novels with almost two million copies in print in the United States and abroad. A tenth-generation Texan, she has been nominated for a Career Achievement Award as well a Reader's Choice Award and Book of the Year by *Romantic Times* magazine.

Kathleen is a paralegal, a proud military wife, and an expatriate Texan cheering on her beloved Texas Aggies from north of the Red River. Connect with her through social media at www.kathleenybarbo.com.

Railroaded into Love

by Rose Ross Zediker

Chapter 1

Montana
1895

S he can't stay here." Noah Manning gave his brother, Seth, a hard stare. His raised voice echoed off the walnut-paneled walls of the railroad chapel car *Emmanuel.*

"Why not? There are living quarters back there." Seth flashed Noah a lopsided grin and pointed to the door behind the pulpit.

Noah paced in front of the first row of pews trying to ease his building anger. He chanced a glance at Pastor Glass, who sat on the deacon's bench. The pastor, who'd just turned the pulpit of the church on wheels over to Noah, raised his bushy brows. His pursed lips pulled into a frown, which seemed to elongate his already long face, and reminded Noah of the proprieties for a man serving God.

Clearing the angry words he longed to shout at Seth from his throat, Noah aimed his gaze at the two-seat pew where Seth and the young woman handcuffed to his brother's wrist sat.

"I'm sorry. A chapel railroad car is not a hideout for an. . ."

"Outlaw?" The word snapped from the young woman's lips. "I'm not an outlaw. You of all people know I was raised to honor God's commandments." She jerked her arm, leaving his brother's hand dangling in midair. Narrow eyed, she glared at Noah.

Me of all people. What did she mean? Was she referring to his pastoral position? Noah rubbed his temples with his fingertips hoping to quell his tension and confusion over this entire situation.

"Tell your brother to release me."

How did she know Seth was his brother? Had Seth babbled on to the poor young thing while traveling to the train station?

Noah's eyes met the young woman's. "I can't do that unless I know why he took you into custody. Perhaps you could enlighten me?" Noah's voice slipped into the even tone he used to comfort the sick.

"I have no idea why the marshal arrested me." Her gaze dropped to the floor. The corners of her mouth drooped, and sadness veiled her pretty face.

A thread of compassion wove through Noah's heart at the girl's distress. He turned to his younger brother. "Why did you arrest her?"

"Because she wouldn't come here peaceably." Seth rubbed his jaw and grinned.

Noah didn't have time for games. He wanted to grab Seth by the lapel that proudly displayed his marshal star and give him a good hard shake. Knowing his actions would deepen Pastor Glass's frown and possibly cost him his first missionary assignment, he quirked a brow at Seth instead.

"You do know the train pulls out in thirty minutes and the chapel car goes with it."

Seth nodded while he reached into his shirt pocket and pulled out a small key. "I know the train schedule. I also know the next town where the chapel car is scheduled to sit on the spur track for a month, which is why she needs to stay with you."

Noah watched Seth insert the key into the handcuffs and release the young woman from her capture. "She is telling the truth. She is not an outlaw; however, her brother is. He's wanted for rustling."

"That's not true!" The young woman stopped rubbing her wrist and jumped to her feet. Her pretty blue eyes rounded. She fisted a hand on her hips.

Her expression and pose struck Noah with familiarity. He wrinkled his brow while he took his first good look at the young woman. Auburn ringlets, which had escaped the thick braid knotted at the nape of her neck, framed her heart-shaped face. Her hair color and the rosy glow on her high cheekbones reminded him of Mrs. Callahan, his Sunday school teacher and best friend's mother.

The memory of Mrs. Callahan brought a smile to his lips. She was the woman who instilled the love of God and His law in Noah. There wasn't a more Christian family in all of Rosebud County, Montana. Sorrow pushed the happy memory aside and tugged away his smile. Mr. and Mrs. Callahan passed away from an influenza outbreak shortly after he left his small hometown in 1890 to attend seminary school.

"Boy, you should see your face. It took you long enough." Seth's guffaws rolled through the chapel car pulling Noah back to the present situation.

Noah looked at his brother and shook his head. The only thing that kept him from throwing up his hands in exasperation was Pastor Glass's presence. When Seth had entered the chapel car with the lovely young woman, he thought one member of his family had come to support his vocation and first pastoral position. Or as cozy as Seth and the young woman seemed, sitting shoulder to shoulder, maybe they needed to be pronounced man and wife. Never had he dreamed Seth planned to dump this young woman into his lap. "What took me long enough?"

Seth kept laughing.

The young woman's hands flew into the air. "He thought you finally recognized me. I'm Molly Callahan."

"Little Molly Callahan?" Noah lifted his hand chest high. He blinked his eyes several times. This petite young women with her womanly curves couldn't be his best friend's lanky younger sister. "I can't believe it. You're all grown up." Noah stepped toward Molly, arms outstretched.

Molly held out a halting hand. "Five years does turn a thirteen-year-old girl into a woman. I always thought you were smarter than this brute of a brother of yours, but I guess not." Her eyes narrowed. "You do realize Seth is accusing *my* brother and *your* best friend, Cass, of being a rustler."

Noah's arms turned to lead, dropping to his side.

Pastor Glass cleared his throat. Noah drew a deep breath and held in a frustrated sigh. No doubt the good pastor would wire the supervisor of Christian Missionaries about this incident. His missionary service on the railroad line would be over before it'd begun.

"Why do you want Molly to stay with me?"

"Cass keeps rustling the rancher's cattle. He is holed up somewhere near the next town. We need to smoke him out before a war is started over the fence lines going up across Montana like happened in Wyoming a few years back."

Molly turned hate-filled eyes on Seth. "He is not a cattle rustler. He's a businessman."

"Yeah, he's in the business of stealing cattle and selling them for profit." Seth snorted and stood. "And he's getting all the wealthy ranchers riled up."

Molly fisted both hands to her hips and glared at Seth. "He is not."

Noah stepped between the two of them, finding it hard to believe Cass rustled cattle for a living. "Are you sure about Cass?"

Seth reached into his pocket and handed Noah a folded piece of paper. Noah didn't have to open it. Even backward, he could read the silhouette of the large black letters—WANTED. Cassidy Callahan and Noah had shared all the boyhood rites of passage and turned into fine, honest men. This just couldn't be true.

"Could this be a mistake?" The thin paper rattled when Noah shook it toward Seth.

Seth's lips drew into a grim line. His eyes conveyed his regret while he gave his head a discreet shake.

Noah preached God's laws, but he couldn't ignore man's laws. He turned and surveyed Molly. She oozed defiance from her stance to her expression. If he agreed to this, it would be trouble. Something he didn't need on his first church assignment.

"Can't you just watch their home place?"

Molly's shoulder's sagged. She slowly slid down until she sat on the pew. "There is no home place. Cass lost it when Pa and Ma died."

Noah heard the shame in her voice. He stepped to the edge of the wooden seat and knelt down beside Molly. "I'm sorry. Where have you been living?"

Moisture pooled in Molly's blue eyes. She bit the corner of her lip before dropping her gaze.

"She lives at a saloon."

"What?" Noah failed to keep his shock out of his voice. Molly buried her face in her hands. Noah chanced a glance at Pastor Glass, whose repulsed expression cinched Noah's fears. He'd be wiring the supervisor.

"You heard me. Cass dumped her there to live and work."

Molly's hands flew from her face. She glared at Seth. "I don't work there."

"Yes, you do."

"Not in the way you are implying." Molly's pleading eyes roved Noah's face. "I play the piano and sing for the customer's. That. Is. All."

Standing, Noah drew in a deep breath. He couldn't believe Cass would take his sister to live in a saloon where anything could happen—especially to a pretty young woman like Molly. What had happened after Noah left their hometown? He needed more details. He pulled his pocket watch from his jacket. Fifteen minutes until the train pulled out of the depot. He looked at Pastor Glass. His stern expression sent Noah a message. He needed to send his brother and Molly away.

Noah knew what he had to do. He squared his shoulders, cleared his throat, and looked at Molly. His mind flashed back to the spunky little girl who tagged after her brother and helped her mother bake bread and hang clothes on the line. They were such a happy family. How could things have taken such a horrible turn? Sadness squeezed his heart.

He didn't like how Seth was using Molly as bait. However, in good conscience Noah couldn't let Mrs. Callahan's daughter go back to living and working in a saloon.

"She can stay here."

∞

"No she can't."

Molly had half breathed a sigh of relief when the older pastor bellowed his protest. The cool spring air thickened inside the tight confines of the church car.

"Miss Callahan living with Pastor Manning would be very inappropriate." The elderly gentleman strode around the pulpit and stood before Noah. "Such behavior should not be tolerated in society and is never allowed for a man of the cloth."

The rapid patter of Molly's heart made her breathing shallow and her head light. She couldn't abide the life she'd lived for the last five years one moment longer. The saloon owner had kept her locked in her room except for the time he expected her to entertain. Molly shuddered at the bawdy songs he'd forced her to sing and play.

If Cass was alive, why hadn't he come back for her? Years of hurt burned her eyes.

She needed to find Cass. She needed to warn him he was the target of a manhunt. She needed answers. She couldn't get what she needed locked in a small bedroom.

She'd witnessed Noah solving many school-yard squabbles in her youth. Surely, he could convince the pastor she could stay. She looked at Noah. He stood stupefied. His mouth agape, moving in a wordless protest.

The sight before her doused her small flame of hope like coffee on a campfire. She had to do something. Molly surveyed the chapel car. The last time she'd stepped foot in a church was her parents' funeral. The small country church paled in comparison to the opulence of this chapel.

Although compact, the chapel housed a small coat closet, deacon's bench, altar, and pump organ along with a magnificent brass lectern and chandelier. Small panels of stained glass lined the ceiling above the windows. Who knew what lay behind the wooden door with the etched portrait of a man in the glass door window?

Molly stood. All the wood, brass, and glass would need a woman's attention. Many bachelors employed housekeepers. "I can be his housekeeper and assist during services by playing the organ and leading the singing."

When Molly stopped looking around the railcar sanctuary, she realized all the men's eyes bored into her.

A lopsided grin took residence on Seth's rugged features. Although he had the same dark hair and eyes as Noah, he wasn't nearly as handsome. "Why didn't I think of that?"

Molly didn't fight her satisfied smile. She'd found a way to gain freedom.

"Calling Molly a housekeeper doesn't solve the problem." Noah looked to the pastor. They shook their heads in unison.

"True." Seth rubbed his chin before his lips curled into a cocksure smile. "Making Molly your wife will, though."

Chapter 2

Nah, nah, no." Noah stretched out his arms and waved his palms at his brother.

The sly smile slipped from Molly's lips. She swallowed hard. She understood Noah's sputtering and hand gestures. The last thing she wanted to do was marry Noah Manning, yet his response tugged at her heart.

Hurt moistened her eyes. She'd clung to her Christian upbringing but had realized long ago no God-fearing man, the only kind she'd be yoked to, would ask for her hand in marriage. Entertaining in the saloon had soiled her reputation. Spinsterhood was her future.

Drawing a deep breath, Molly tried to conquer her emotions enough to speak. "I believe Noah is trying to say we both believe in the sanctity of marriage. It's not to be entered into lightly." Molly dragged her gaze from Noah's relieved face to Seth's bemused features. "Or forced."

Seth shrugged. "Suit yourself." He reached for the handcuffs he'd thrown down onto the pew.

"No." Noah's loud protest echoed off the paneled ceilings, drawing all eyes to him. He glared at Seth. "You said she wasn't an outlaw."

Molly stepped backward when Noah forced his lanky frame in the small space separating her and Seth. His broad shoulders, that she barely came to, hid her completely and blocked her view. Standing behind him she felt safe—a feeling she hadn't experienced in a very long time.

Another round of moisture sheened her eyes. Relief urged her to take a step, lean against him, and let his protection envelope her.

"That's true." Seth wiggled his wrist, jingling the handcuffs.

Molly leaned sideways to look past Noah.

Seth's eyes, twinkling with merriment, locked to hers. "Molly has no home unless she wants to go back to the saloon."

Molly hitched a brow in reply. She knew Seth was using his school-yard antics to goad her and Noah in an attempt to get his way. If she had anything to do with it, he wouldn't. Cass would never steal. Their parents had raised them to abide by the Ten Commandments.

Pastor Glass clicked his tongue, drawing Noah and Molly's attention to him. He gave his head a small shake.

Noah turned back to Seth. "I know even you aren't heartless enough to send

Molly back to a life of slavery."

Seth shrugged. "If I don't take her back to the saloon, she has no home. This county has laws. Vagrants are locked up."

Molly gasped. The gravity of her situation hit her full force. She had nowhere to go nor anyone to flee to unless she could find Cass. Her knees wobbled. She eased closer to the pew. When the hard wooden seat edge brushed her leg, she sank down on it. Tears burned her eyes, and her bottom lip trembled. Her situation was hopeless.

She needed help. She needed to find Cass. If Seth was right and Cass's whereabouts were close to the next town, she needed to stay on this train.

⌒∞⌒

The instant a tear trickled down Molly's ivory cheek, something moved in Noah's heart. The urge to protect Molly overtook him. He turned to Seth. "This isn't a school-yard game."

His brother sobered. "I know. She only has three choices, return to the saloon, go to jail, or stay here."

"Which requires marriage."

Noah's jaw dropped as he looked from Seth to Pastor Glass. Molly's movement caught his eye. She held her head high and swiped at the tears trickling down her cheeks. She blinked several times before she looked directly into his eyes.

He caught his breath. He thought he'd see pleading. Instead Molly's eyes emitted strength. She knew her future lay in his choice. She was ready to face her fate. She gave him a weak smile and stood.

Shoulders erect, Molly jutted out her chin. Her eyes were directed on something past Seth's shoulder. She was clinging to her pride, which he guessed was all she had, with all of her might. Noah's heart twisted. Molly should be giggling with school chums, not facing a grim future. What was wrong with Cass? Why would he do such a thing to his little sister?

Molly held her wrists out to Seth. "I prefer jail to the saloon."

"No." His firm protest drew all of their attention to him. He inserted two fingers into the neckline of his shirt and pulled to ease the constriction in his throat, knowing full well his clothing had nothing to do with the strangling feeling. He wanted to preach God's Word more than anything, but out of respect to Mrs. Callahan he couldn't let Molly go to jail, even if it meant being relieved of his chapel car appointment.

Noah drew a deep breath and looked Molly square in the eye. "We have no choice."

For a brief second her eyes searched his, then she lowered her gaze and gave a short nod of confirmation.

"Pastor Glass, I know it isn't customary for the pastor of a chapel car to be married. . . ."

The pastor held up a halting hand. "Under these circumstances, I'll allow it and explain it to the Christian Council."

Slipping a small book from his jacket pocket, Pastor Glass nodded toward Noah. "Take your bride's hand and join me at the altar. Your brother will bear witness."

Molly fixed her eyes to his. Did he see a trace of fear? He reached out his hand. Her lips trembled into a hesitant smile. Sadness veiled her lovely eyes. Slowly, she raised her hand and rested it in his. He closed his fingers around her silky skin. "It will be all right."

Doubt etched her face. He wished his words held more conviction. How could they when he believed in his heart nothing was right about this situation?

Turning, Noah led them to the railing in front of the pulpit.

Seth's boot heels scuffed behind. "Better make this quick. The train leaves in five minutes."

Noah stepped to Molly's right. Pastor Glass cleared his throat. "We are gathered together today to join Noah Manning and Molly Callahan in holy matrimony." He continued by reciting scripture. Noah stole a glance a Molly. Her eyes were fixed to Pastor Glass's face. Her full lips mouthing each word of the scripture being read.

How proud Mrs. Callahan would be of her little Molly knowing her scriptures by heart. Sadness tugged at Noah's heart. Mrs. Callahan wouldn't be proud of Cass if what Seth said was true. What had turned Cass to the wrong side of the law? Grief? Greed?

"Noah."

His name started him back into the moment. He looked at the pastor.

"Please take your bride's hands in yours."

Noah clasped Molly's long fingers in his hands, once again, amazed at the silkiness of her skin.

"Noah, do you take Molly as your lawfully wedded wife?"

"I do." He cringed at the reluctance in his voice. Molly didn't seem to notice.

"Molly, do you take Noah as your lawfully wedded husband?"

"I do." Molly's affirmation clipped out. She glared at Seth instead of looking lovingly into her groom's eyes.

"I pronounce you man and wife."

The pages of the pastor's book thumped together.

"Congratulations." Seth wacked Noah on the back. His grin stretched from ear to ear. Once again, he'd managed to get his way. "I didn't think you had it in you."

Anger swelled in Noah's chest at Seth's implication of his cowardice. His family would never understand his choice to lay aside his gun belt.

The train whistle blew.

"We'd best go, Preacher. Molly." Seth tipped his hat, turned, and walked down the aisle. When he reached the door, he paused. "I'm sure I'll see you at the next stop."

"Good luck with your appointment and your marriage." Pastor Glass shook Noah's hand and hurried out of the *Emmanuel*.

Noah raked his fingers through his hair and blew out a deep breath. The air remained thick with tension, even with Seth and Pastor Glass's departure. What should he do now? He looked around. "Did you have a bag?"

Molly pursed her lips and shook her head.

"So all you have. . ."

"Yes. All I have is the dress on my back and the shoes on my feet." Molly spat out the words and fisted her hands to her hips. Defiance shone from her pretty blue eyes.

"I'm sorry." Noah looked around. *Lord, I need some help here.*

A sudden jerk of the chapel railcar knocked them off balance. Noah grasped the altar banister to steady himself just before Molly thumped against his chest. Instinctively he wrapped his free arm around her to keep her steady. Her small frame snug against his warmed him with comfort.

The emotion reeled him. He squeezed the altar rail harder. He'd always found his comfort in God's Word, not the human touch.

His gaze captured Molly's when he felt a soft pressure on his chest.

"You can let go of me now." Molly quirked a brow but never broke eye contact.

Noah released his hold. Molly righted herself and moved away, taking her warmth with her.

She smoothed down her dress and looked around the chapel. "Where are the living quarters?"

Of course, he needed to show Molly her new home.

"Behind this door." Noah released his grip on the altar and stepped toward the etched-glass door.

The train chugged with an even rhythm, making it easier to walk. Noah opened the door, stepping aside to allow Molly to enter.

The efficient design of the living quarters provided all the necessities for daily living. He walked into the rectangular kitchen. Molly stood between the wooden table and the small cast-iron cookstove, both bolted to the floor. Her gaze roamed every inch of the area.

"There is a small sink behind you." Noah moved to the opposite side of the table while Molly turned around. "The cupboards have a latch." Noah pressed the latch edge down and opened a cupboard. "And a built-in ledge to keep items in place."

Molly nodded her head, eyes wide.

"As you can see, this cupboard was built for the dishes. The one in the corner beside you is the pantry."

Molly turned to see where his finger pointed and looked back at him, her face as blank as a new school slate.

"You may change it to suit your needs."

Molly nodded so he knew she'd heard him. She seemed to have lost her voice.

Her gaze continued to dart around the room, always lingering on something past his shoulder. Noah allowed her to familiarize herself with her new home. It was compact and surely better than her past living conditions. Finally her eyes met his.

"Where are the sleeping quarters?"

Noah heard the trepidation in her whispered question.

She thought he expected her to be his wife in every way. Noah's heart thundered in his chest. They might be married in God's eyes, but they held no love for each other in their hearts. Noah believed coupling involved love.

Thankfully, this chapel car was designed for a single preacher. Noah stepped to a curtain-drawn door and slid the brocade drape to the side, revealing two bunk-style beds. "You don't have to worry, Molly. I don't have that wifely expectation of you."

Chapter 3

Absently, Molly glided her fingers over the smooth wood of the pulpit while her eyes remained fixed on the organ. Once she reached it, she caressed the outer plains of the intricately carved instrument with her palms. Slipping onto the bolted-down bench in front of it, Molly rested her fingers on the ivory keys. She sighed and pushed down on the keys, reveling in the melodic note. She hadn't played an organ since Cass removed her from their home.

Her finger missed a key. A sour note mourned through the chapel, and her heart twisted. Why had he left her at the saloon for all of those years when he was still alive?

She opened a hymnbook to a random page. Could she remember how to play the organ after plunking out bawdy songs on the upright piano? She shivered, remembering the hungry looks of the men when she sang the suggestive words.

Closing her eyes, she thanked her Lord those days were behind her and that He'd led her to Noah, an honorable man who didn't take advantage of a woman. A fair man, unlike Seth, who knew a Callahan couldn't be an outlaw. Had bad men kidnapped Cass and forced him into a life of crime? Is that why he never came back to get her?

Molly opened her eyes, studied the music, and poised her fingers. Taking a deep breath, she began to play "Amazing Grace." The tone of the instrument soothed her frazzled nerves and chased her unanswered questions from her mind.

This was the first time since Seth and two of his deputies stormed the saloon and threatened to arrest the owner if he didn't release her into their custody, that she could catch her breath. Two days ago, she thought she'd been freed. Then Seth handcuffed her and headed out to find Noah. Now, she was married. A fact that should have filled her heart with joy instead of sorrow. Would her loveless marriage prove to be another type of prison?

Her finger hit a wrong key, souring the song's tune the same way her thoughts were affecting her heart's disposition.

She was married to a man who didn't love her, didn't want her because of her past. Shame engulfed every fiber of her being until it stung her eyes. How fitting she'd chosen to practice "Amazing Grace." Sucking in a ragged breath, Molly played the chorus before adding her voice to the music.

She sang low so she didn't disturb Noah, who retreated to his desk to work on a sermon after a lunch of bread slathered with jelly and a tall glass of milk. When she finished the song hope filtered into her heart like sunbeams through a stained-glass window, lifting it with joy.

Opening her eyes, she gasped. Heat burned her cheeks. Noah sat in the pew in front of the organ. His brown eyes held a faraway look.

Flustered, Molly fisted her hands and rested them in her lap. "I'm sorry if I interrupted your sermon time."

"Don't be sorry. That was wonderful. You sound like your mother when you sing."

Molly smiled. The memory of her mother's voice comforted her during many a long night.

"Do you remember her favorite?"

" 'In the Sweet By and By.'" Molly sang the title. "I don't remember how to play the music, though."

"It's in the hymnal. You can practice." Noah smiled, a genuine smile that created gentle crinkles in the corners of his eyes. Her brother's cute friend had grown into a handsome man. Her heart fluttered and her cheeks warmed.

"Forgive me. I wasn't criticizing."

Relief settled Molly's pattering heart at Noah's mistake of her blush.

Noah ran his fingers through his hair before leaning forward and resting his elbows on his knees. "I'm at quite a loss here, Molly. A lot has happened today. Things I don't understand."

Molly nodded.

The *click-clack* of the train rolling along the track filled the silent tension. Molly hadn't understood anything that had happened since her parents died.

"I know you have questions, too. I'm assured in my heart God will reveal the answer in His own good time." Noah's eyes locked to hers.

She saw his confusion over their current circumstances, but she also saw compassion. "May I tell you something?"

"Of course." Noah nodded for her to continue.

Molly rose, rounded the altar, and sat down a seat away from Noah. She turned so she faced him. "I remember Mama's favorite hymn and her voice because I hear it when I sing."

Noah's gentle smile returned.

Allowing her gaze to roam Noah's face, Molly wondered if he'd think less of her with her admission. Her stomach clenched. "I have trouble remembering Mama and Daddy's faces." Even though her voice shook, she continued. "And their touch." She closed her eyes. "Scents, though, like lilacs and peppermint. . ." She stopped, inhaled, and opened her eyes. "They bring me comfort."

"I'm not surprised." Noah reached out and clasped her hands. "Your mama wore lilac water and your father enjoyed peppermint sticks." Noah chuckled. "Your mama couldn't control her fiery red curls, any more than you can."

Noah released her hand and twirled a stray wisp of her hair around his finger. "You used to help her bake bread and hang clothes on the line." Noah freed his finger from her ringlet. He raised his brows in question.

She shook her head.

"Your daddy had the heartiest laugh of anyone in Rosebud County."

Molly wanted to remember. Noah was trying so hard to help her remember. It was no use. "I'm afraid my memories have faded."

"Well, you have been in a trying situation. Perhaps that is why you are having trouble recollecting your loved ones."

Cass was one of her loved ones, too. Him she could still picture, young, slender, and reckless. He inherited her daddy's coloring, light hair.

Smiling, she squeezed Noah's hand. "Talking to you is good medicine for me. I was thinking about Cass and remembered people said I favored Mama and Cass favored Daddy."

"That's right." Noah didn't return her smile.

She didn't let it stop her joy of voicing her memories. "The last time I saw Cass he was a boy. I supposed he's a grown man like you now."

⟜✧⟊

Noah clenched his teeth. He didn't want to tarnish Molly's image of her brother. Yet, if what Seth said was true, Cass wasn't the person Molly recollected.

He'd planned to ask Molly if she had any notion as to why Cass abandoned her at a saloon. Had Cass befriended someone who led him away from God's narrow path?

Pulling his hand free of Molly's, frustration forced him to his feet. He stepped past Molly and paced down the center aisle. It'd do him no good to question Molly if she couldn't remember her happier times. Yet it was information Noah needed in order to defend his pulpit appointment on the chapel car, *Emmanuel*. What would the council think when Pastor Glass reported the situation back to them? Although the seasoned pastor seemed unbothered by the fact he performed a sacred marriage ceremony to a loveless couple.

Noah turned to pace back toward the altar. Molly stood at the end of the pew, hands fisted to her hips.

"You're unhappy with me because I think fondly of my brother? Let me tell you, Noah Manning, I don't believe Seth. Cass was raised better. He'd never steal."

Molly's feistiness hitched Noah's heart, urging him to tell her how pretty she looked riled up. The corner of his mouth twitched, threatening to release joyous laughter. He managed to tamp his bemusement down to a chuckle but couldn't stop his wide smile.

His merriment was met with a hard stare. "I find none of this amusing. Your brother is trying to besmirch my brother's good name."

Noah sobered. He walked to Molly and grasped her shoulders. *Draw her close.* He shook the thought from his mind. "Neither of us can know what is true. I've been out of touch with Rosebud County for a long time, and so have you."

Molly drew a deep breath. With its release, her features softened. Her blue eyes searched his face. "You are right."

"We need to turn our situation over to God. He will provide the answers to us." Noah smoothed his hands down Molly's arms and clasped her hands. She bowed her head, and Noah began to pray.

Echoing his "Amen," Molly pulled her hands free.

"You say a nice prayer, Pastor Manning. I look forward to your sermons."

His heart somersaulted at her compliment, which forced a wide smile to his lips.

A flush jumped to Molly's cheeks, and her full lips turned up in a shy smile before she cast her gaze downward. She brushed her hands against the front of her threadbare dress.

It was apparent Molly had altered the dress to fit the best she could. What had Cass been thinking leaving her there? Did he have any idea the trials she'd face?

Noah planned to do right by Molly. Although the marriage was of convenience, he'd provide for her.

"As soon as the train stops and the chapel car is secured to the spur track, we'll walk into town and purchase you a new dress and other necessary clothing. Tonight you'll have to use one of my shirts as a nightgown."

Molly lifted her eyes and opened her mouth. Noah set his lips in a firm line and shook his head. He didn't want to hear her protest.

"You are my wife and will dress accordingly. Besides, I want you to assist me with services. You'll play the organ and lead the singing. As I'm sure you remember, I can't carry a tune."

A sparkle of merriment danced through her eyes before she giggled. "Will you mouth the words with the congregation the way the schoolmarm taught you so you didn't ruin our school program?"

Finally, the joy-filled girl he remembered from his past. He'd take all of her teasing if it meant that pretty look stayed fixed to her face.

Chapter 4

The fragrance of frying bacon woke Molly. For a moment her heart raced in panic until she realized her surroundings. Pushing aside the drape that covered the sleeping quarter's door, Molly peeked into the kitchen area. Noah stood beside the stove poking a fork into a fry pan.

The fabric swished as she pushed it aside and jumped from the lower bunk. "That is my job." Hands fisted on her hips, she waited for Noah to turn.

When he did, his bright expression changed. Tenderness edged the planes of his face. His brown eyes smoldered with emotion. Molly gasped. She crossed her arms over her body. She'd forgotten she was wearing one of Noah's shirts. Although it fell past her knees, her ankles and bare feet were exposed.

She backed into the sleeping area. Eyes locked to Noah's, drinking in the appreciation he emoted as she drew the curtain closed.

Stop that. Molly chided herself. She had always liked Noah, but she shouldn't like the admiration in his eyes. No, couldn't like it. He'd told her they'd never consummate their marriage. Sadness tugged at her heart. She must be happy with his friendship.

Once dressed, Molly made a less spectacular entrance to the kitchen, only to find Noah finishing his breakfast.

"I left bacon and eggs in the skillet on the warming shelf." The chairs legs scraped against the wooden floor when Noah stood. His eyes riveted to the empty plate on the table.

"The train should pull into town within the hour. I'll need to work with the conductor to get the chapel car safely on the spur track. You were sleeping soundly, so I didn't wake you."

Noah stepped over to his desk area and removed a hat from a wall peg. His choice surprised Molly, a black cowboy hat similar to the brown one Seth wore as marshal. Noah hesitated by the door. He studied the brim on his hat.

"From this point on, the kitchen duties are your responsibilities. When the train pulls into the depot, you need to disembark so the chapel car can be moved. It's too rough of a ride to stay inside. Please make sure the cupboards are secured."

Thumping the hat on his head, he nodded curtly in her direction and exited the kitchen.

Molly stared at the man's face etched in the glass of the door for a few minutes after Noah left. Had she embarrassed Noah when she'd burst into the kitchen? It'd been so long since she'd lived as a family.

After a quick breakfast, Molly washed and dried the dishes. She slid them onto the cupboard shelf, making sure the latch was secured. She surveyed the kitchen. *Her kitchen.*

Her heart plummeted. What had she done? She didn't remember how to cook. The saloon owner's wife did the cooking so Molly didn't get splattered with grease or burned, which might tarnish their entertainer and they'd lose business.

Yesterday, Noah had mentioned her helping her mother cook. Molly rubbed her temples. Helping and cooking were two different things. Why hadn't she kept quiet? Noah obviously knew how to cook. The bacon and eggs tasted delicious.

The train jerked to a stop. Molly stumbled against the table. She hadn't noticed the train slowing. After regaining her balance, she stepped into the chapel and hurried down the aisle and out the door.

She'd worry about cooking later. Right now she wanted to be out among the people at the depot. Perhaps she'd see Cass.

Disappointment filled her heart when she stepped onto the wooden depot platform. A scarce few stood around the building.

Noah spoke to the engineer whose head poked out of a window. When he was finished, he turned and strode over to her.

"You can wait on a bench in the depot. It doesn't take long to park the chapel car on the spur track. Then we can walk into town."

Molly started when Noah clasped her hand and looped it through the crook of his arm.

"This is how a gentleman treats a lady." Noah's gentle smile held no condescension. He was simply providing information.

He took a step. Molly followed, glad that of all places Seth could have taken her he'd chosen Noah. She felt safe with Noah. He'd always been kind and brave like Cass.

Pausing in front of a wooden bench by a window, Noah removed her hand from his arm. "This shouldn't take long."

"I'll be here." Molly sat on the bench and watched Noah exit the same door they'd entered. Her gaze roamed the oblong room. Each wall facing the railroad tracks had a window with a bench beneath it. A framed map hung on the opposite wall. One man worked behind a caged-in counter where passengers purchased tickets.

A hinge creaked and echoed through the silent depot. A young boy about eight, Molly guessed, stepped into the building. He wore tattered clothes close to becoming too small. The unbuttoned cuffs of his sleeves hit above his wrists. His pants hem skimmed the tops of his worn boots.

"Got any passengers who need help?" The boy stood on his tiptoes to peer into the caged office.

"Not this stop." The ticket man answered without looking up from his work.

The boy turned around and noticed Molly. "Got any bags that need carryin'?"

"No."

Disappointment sagged the boy's shoulders. "You waitin' for someone?"

"Yes, Noah."

The boy walked over to the bench. "Noah your brother?"

"My husband." It was the first time Molly called Noah her husband. The words sounded strange.

The boy stood in front of her, eyes narrowed. "Are you stayin' or passin' through?"

"We are staying. . .for a short time." Molly stumbled over the end of her sentence. She wasn't certain how long the chapel car would be parked on the spur track.

"Got kin here?"

She hoped so. She hoped Seth was right about Cass's whereabouts and wrong about his occupation. "Maybe. I'm not sure."

Her laughter rang through the depot at the face the boy pulled. He crossed his arms over his chest. "You're not hurtin' me by laughin' at me. People do it all the time."

Molly sobered. "I beg your pardon. I was laughing at the funny face you made at my answer because it was confusing. I'd never laugh at you or anyone."

The boy's features gentled. He slipped onto the bench beside her.

"I've heard my brother might live near here. I haven't seen him in five years."

"I know 'most everyone in town, even if they pretend not to know me."

Molly's heart went out to the boy. It was obvious by his dress and attitude his family was poor, but that was not a reason to mistreat a child. "I can't see why anyone would treat you badly."

The boy shrugged. "It's 'cause of my parents."

The matter-of-fact way he admitted this shame told Molly he'd accepted his lot in life. Something she'd yet learned to do.

"What's your name?" Molly yearned to reach out and ruffle the young boy's blond hair, a shade darker than Cass's.

"Tom."

"I'm Molly. Molly Calla—" Molly stopped and cleared her throat. "Manning. I'm Molly Manning. What's your last name?"

"Don't have one."

Molly's eyes widened. She turned her head so Tom couldn't see her surprise.

"I've heard about a marshal named Manning. He don't live here, if he's your brother."

"Marshal Manning is my brother-in-law." Molly looked back at the boy. "My maiden name is Callahan."

"Is Cass Callahan your brother?"

Happiness shot through Molly. Could this child lead her to her brother?

"Tom!"

The ticket agent hollered from behind the wrought-iron bars. "I've told you not to badger my customers. Ma'am, I hope the boy hasn't swindled you out of any money. He's a little beggar. Go on, get." The man waved his hand at the door.

"I was only visitin'. I didn't ask for no money." The defense in Tom's voice matched the expression on his face but didn't mask the loneliness in his brown eyes. He stood.

So did Molly. "Sir, the young man was doing no harm." Molly needed to keep the boy here. If he knew Cass, he'd know where to find him.

"Right now." The ticket agent clicked his tongue while his eyes roved her from head to toe. "I haven't seen you around before. You say you know this boy?"

Molly realized the man was judging her based on her threadbare clothes.

She cleared her throat and strode over to the counter. "Yes, I know this young man. He is my first friend in this town. I'm Mrs. Manning. Pastor Manning is overseeing our home, the chapel car *Emmanuel*, while it's being parked on a spur track."

"Begging your pardon, ma'am. I understand now, but the boy needs to leave."

"All right." Molly grasped Tom's shoulders and guided him toward the screen door.

When they were outside, Tom stopped and raised his arm to his forehead to shade his eyes from the noonday sun. "You didn't have to do that."

An image flashed in Molly's mind. Another young man shading his eyes from the sun while taking a break hoeing the garden. She smiled. Tom reminded her of Cass. They had the same hair and eye coloring. "It was my pleasure. Besides, I didn't have a chance to answer your question. Cass Callahan is my brother. Do you know where I can find him?"

The boy shrugged.

"Have you seen my wife?"

Molly turned and peered through the screen door. "We're out here, Noah." When she turned back to talk to Tom, he was gone.

⌒∞⌒

Noah thanked God one thing went right on his new appointment. The chapel car was secured on the track with no mishaps. The first service would take place tomorrow night, then nightly thereafter.

Rubbing his chin, he watched Molly. She seemed to be looking for something or someone. Noah doubted Cass Callahan lived in this town. It was quite bustling. Wouldn't an outlaw hide out somewhere secluded?

"Are you looking for someone?" Noah cupped Molly's hand in the crook of his arm and patted it.

"No."

Noah stole a glance at his wife. Guilt etched her pretty features. "Then what are you looking for?"

Molly stopped and pulled her hand free of his arm. By the time he stopped and turned, her fists rested on her hips. "I haven't been in a town this big before, Noah Manning. Can I help it if this is all new to me?"

He arched a brow. He hadn't considered that. "Forgive me. It seemed like you were looking for someone. Molly, I don't think Cass lives here." Even if he was hiding out in this town, he'd never show his face in the light of the day, would he?

Dropping her hands to her side, Molly sighed. "I met a young boy in the depot. He took off in a hurry. I was hoping to see him."

Noah smiled. All the guilt left her face at her admission. "Thank you for telling me. Husbands and wives shouldn't keep secrets from each other." He offered his elbow.

Molly looped her hand through, and they continued toward town. The depot sat a half mile from the actual main street of town, which from this distance appeared to be four blocks long with side streets and houses spreading out on each side.

The scent of the blacksmith's shop welcomed them long before they walked past. Finally, they reached the boardwalk. Noah searched the buildings for a dress shop or general store.

"Do you know how to sew?"

"Yes, I mended the...um...other girls' clothes at the saloon."

Anger surged through Noah at the embarrassment flushing Molly's face. How could Cass put his sister through that type of life? A small part of Noah hoped Cass did live in or near this town. He'd like some answers. He planned to make a quick visit to the sheriff's office to verify Seth's story. He hadn't wanted to ask in front of Molly yesterday, but he wondered if this was an isolated case of rustling. People who fell on hard times sometimes took drastic measures. Or was this Cass's occupation?

Noah scanned the street locating the sheriff's office, a dressmaker's shop, and a general store. "You're in immediate need of a new frock. Let's go to the dress shop first. After that I'll let you browse the fabric at the general store. You should have two house dresses and a Sunday dress in addition to an apron and well. . ." Heat burned Noah's cheeks that had nothing to do with the summer sun. He leaned toward Molly's ear. "Other ladies items."

"I can't accept all of that." Molly's eyes searched his face.

"You are my wife and I am pastor of the chapel car *Emmanuel*. You need to dress appropriately." A girl as pretty as Molly should have been dressed in many fine dresses by this age.

Noah marched them toward the dressmaker's shop and stopped in the doorway. He hesitated. Nothing in his training prepared him for entering a dress shop. He reached into his jacket pocket and withdrew some money. "This should take care of a dress. I have an errand to run. I will meet you in the general store."

He didn't give Molly time to argue before he strode off.

Chapter 5

Molly admired her new Sunday dress in the plate-glass windows of the stores as she passed by. She smoothed a hand down the soft blue calico with lace overlay on the long sleeves, cuffs, and bodice.

Clutching the brown paper parcel that held her tattered dress, Molly looked up and down the street. There was no sign of Noah. Although the general store was two buildings away from where she stood, the sherriff's office across the street called to her. She longed to check the wanted posters. Seth could have easily printed up a false poster with Cass's name, couldn't he?

Lifting her skirt so it didn't drag in the dusty street, Molly quickly crossed to the opposite boardwalk. Her eyes focused on the large board papered with wanted posters that hung to the right of the jail entry.

Molly glanced over both shoulders. No one seemed to notice her standing in front of the board. She started at the top and scanned each picture and name. One-third of the way down, her gaze froze to a sheet of paper. Her heartbeat rivaled the pace of a hummingbird's wings. There was a poster with Cass's name and the word *rustler*.

The picture didn't look right. She rose to her tiptoes and squinted at the faded notice. A scar marred the man's cheek, and stringy hair poked out from under his hat like a scarecrow's hay hair. This couldn't be Cass. Someone was posing as her brother. Was that why he left her? To protect her?

"What ya lookin' at?"

"Oh!" Molly had been so engrossed in the picture, she'd forgotten to keep her wits about her. Looking down, she saw Tom.

Tom's eyes rose to the board. "Oh, I see. You're lookin' at your brother."

"Hush," Molly scolded. She twisted her neck both ways to make sure no one in town had heard. Once satisfied that bystanders hadn't heard, she reached down and grabbed Tom's hand. Their footsteps thumped along the boardwalk until she spotted an opening between buildings. She pulled Tom into the narrow space.

She looked down to find his lips trembling.

"I thought you was my friend."

Molly sucked in a deep breath in hopes it'd steady her racing heart. "I am. Tom, I'm sorry I was gruff on the street. I'm trying to find my brother, but it's kind of a secret."

"You don't want nobody to know he's your brother?"

Molly was taken aback. "It's not that at all. I think there's been a mistake. I'm not sure the picture of the man on the wanted poster is my brother."

"Well, if your brother is Cass Callahan, it is."

The earnest expression on Tom's face caused her hopes to plummet. She pursed her lips, blinked rapidly, and willed the hurt not to pool in her eyes. She cleared her throat to remove the tightness. "How do you know that for sure?"

"I work for him." Tom shrugged. "Sort of."

"What do you mean?"

"He comes to town, gives me money, and a list of supplies. I do his trading over a couple of days. He comes back and picks up the stuff."

"Where does he pick up the supplies?"

Tom lowered his eyes and twisted the marred toe of his boot into the powdered dirt. "I oughtn't to tell you, but since he's your brother." He heaved a sigh. "I live in a lean-to behind the livery. He leaves me some food and money to tide me over to the next time."

Molly crossed her arms over her chest and studied Tom. He didn't appear to be lying. She pulled a penny from her pocket. "I'd like you to work for me, too." She pressed the penny into his palm. "The next time Cass comes to town, tell him where I am."

Noah swallowed, hard, and prayed his stomach didn't revolt. He plastered a smile to his face. He looked across the table at an anxious Molly waiting for approval that her attempt at cooking breakfast fared better than last night's fried chicken. It didn't.

He forked a clump of brown eggs. Bacon grease dripped from the bite onto his plate. His stomach lurched. He took the bite. Pretended to chew before he drank a big swig of coffee and swallowed it like a bitter pill.

The shine of pride on Molly's face was worth the agony on his tongue.

"I'm sorry about burning the chicken and scorching the potatoes last night. I need to get used to the stove. I so wanted to do something nice for you, since you purchased me a dress and fabric."

"You're welcome. It is a husband's duty to provide for his wife." Noah hoped Molly sewed better than she cooked. He flashed her a smile. Her heart was in the right place, and she was trying. He picked up a piece of charred bacon and snapped it in two. How could someone manage to burn a quarter-inch-thick slice of meat?

"And a wife's duty to take care of her husband."

Molly scooped a bite of eggs in her mouth. Her pretty pink lips puckered. Her brows drew together. She dropped her fork and reached for her coffee cup to wash down the grease-soaked eggs. "That is awful. Why didn't you tell me?"

Her shoulder's drooped.

"You wanted to run the kitchen. Your mother was a wonderful cook, and you used to cook with her."

Molly pushed her plate away. "That was a long time ago." She fixed him with her gaze. Her blue eyes held apology. "I'm sorry I've ruined two meals and wasted food."

She arose and went to the cupboard. She returned with a loaf of bread and strawberry jelly. "It seems this is the only food I can prepare and not burn."

Noah accepted the jelly-slathered slice she offered him and wondered if she remembered how to bake bread. His monthly stipend would be stretched tight between the two of them. They couldn't afford to waste food.

After finishing his meager breakfast, Noah excused himself and retreated to the chapel car for prayer time. He never needed to commune with God more. Worry burdened his spirit. While Molly was in the dress shop, Noah paid the sheriff a visit. The sheriff verified Seth was right. Cass was a cattle rustler.

He paced the length of the aisle. What had happened? Cass had been closer to Noah than any of his brothers. Their opinions and morals mirrored each other's. Could Molly be right? Had someone forced Cass to rustle and leave Molly at a saloon?

Anger surged through Noah at the thought of Molly being held prisoner and forced to use her God-given talent for illicit purposes. Noah stopped mid-pace. He drew a deep breath. He needed to stop his wandering thoughts and talk to God.

Cass had ruined enough lives: his own, his sister's, and all the ranchers he'd stolen from. Noah wouldn't let Cass's actions ruin his ministry. His first pulpit post would dictate the rest of his career. He already had a mark against him with his unexpected marriage to Molly.

Tonight at his first service, he needed a clear head and a strong spirit to deliver his sermon with the conviction necessary to lead sinners to God and strengthen the believers' faith.

He dropped to his knees at the altar. When he lifted his head sometime later, Molly, dressed in her old frock, polished the organ's brass music holder.

The brass pieces on the pulpit and the light fixtures on the opposite wall gleamed in the sunbeams streaming in the windows.

"How long have you been working out here?" Noah stood.

Molly rubbed the fixture base. "An hour."

"I didn't even hear you. You are as quiet as a church mouse." Noah stepped over to the organ and admired her work. "The fixture is beautiful."

"Thank you." Molly smiled at him. "I tried to be quiet and respectful of your prayer time, but I want the chapel car sparkling for your first service tonight."

Pride expanded Noah's heart.

"I'll wash the windows, pews, and floors, too." Molly stopped polishing and pushed a stray tendril out of her eyes. "This place needed a woman's touch."

"It certainly did. I never even noticed." Noah yearned to tuck the errant curl behind Molly's delicate ear. He stuffed his hands in his pockets.

Molly's eyes, darkened with emotion, met his. Had she read his mind?

"It's not in a man's nature to notice dust and smudges." Molly returned to her work.

Noah immediately missed the intimacy.

The door hinges creaked. Noah turned. A young boy, obviously poor judging by the condition of his clothing and appearance, took apprehensive steps up the aisle. His eyes rounded as his gaze roved the chapel car's furnishings.

"Hello, young man. I'm Pastor Manning. How may I help you today?"

"I'm here to see Molly."

"Tom."

The boy's face lit up. "I ain't never seen a place as fine as this."

The boy continued to survey his surroundings.

"Me, either." Molly sighed. "It's very beautiful."

"Does that piano play?" Tom nodded toward the instrument. "I've heard fine music coming out of the saloon door."

Noah cringed. What was a child doing near a saloon at night? He studied Molly's reaction to the boy's question. Would the memory of her performing make her cross with the boy?

"This is an organ not a piano. It plays fine music, better than any you'll hear coming out of a saloon." Noah kept his voice light. "The music played on this instrument honors God."

The boy's brows drew together. "I don't know much about God, so I don't know what kind of music He likes."

Noah was appalled by the boy's admission, but when Molly giggled Noah's heart jumped with happiness, and he saw the humor in the young boy's words.

"May I ask how you know each other?"

"We met in the depot yesterday." Molly smiled at Noah. "This is my friend Tom."

"Nice to meet you, Tom." Noah held out his hand.

Fright filled Tom's features. He stared at Noah's outstretched hand and stepped toward Molly.

"It's okay. You can shake Noah's hand. That's what young gentlemen do."

A shy smile broke out on Tom's face. "I ain't no gentleman. I'm an orphan. No one wants to shake hands with me."

"Well, I do." Noah stretched his arm closer to the boy. This is what his job was all about. Making sure all of God's children felt welcomed and loved.

Finally, a tiny hand touched his. The skin, rough and weatherworn, told the story of a hard life. "It's nice to meet you, Tom."

Noah eyed Molly. The loving way she looked at the boy made his heart lurch with longing for something other than his pastoral duties. A family.

Chapter 6

The chapel car entry door opened and closed while Molly scraped most of their breakfast into a slop bucket. Noah kept the door separating the living quarters from the chapel car sanctuary propped open during the day hours to ensure any visitor or wayward soul was greeted and welcomed.

The only visitor who came this early in the day was Tom. Aggravation swirled through Molly. If Tom didn't stay in town, he'd miss Cass, and her message would go undelivered.

Molly placed a plate in the dishwater. She closed her eyes while she swirled the dishcloth over the greasy china, envisioning her and Cass's reunion. His light brown eyes shining with happiness as he'd clasp her waist, lift and twirl her through the air the way he had when they were growing up.

She dunked the plate in a bucket of rinse water and released a contented sigh.

"Morning, Molly."

Molly turned and looked into Tom's shining eyes, almost the same color as Cass's. "Good morning."

"I brought you something." His face beamed. He held out a handkerchief with the ends tied into a knot at the top. The contents bulged the cloth.

Drying her hands, Molly took the red paisley package and set it carefully on the table. The package didn't move. She sent up a silent prayer of thanks, since sometimes little boys thought frogs, toads, or snakes were priceless gifts.

Noah entered the room as she untied the first set of knotted ends. "What's this?"

"I brought you somethin'."

"I'm glad I didn't miss the surprise." Noah patted Tom's shoulder and earned a wide smile from the boy.

Molly's heart melted. Over the past couple of days she'd watched Noah and Tom together. Noah would make a good father. Disappointment blanketed her heart. That would never be. Noah made it clear intimacy and love went hand in hand, and he didn't love Molly.

Diverting her eyes to the handkerchief, she loosened the second knot. Large, plump raspberries spilled out onto the table. "Oh my. They look delicious."

"I picked 'em myself." Pride shone on Tom's face; then he sobered. "Off a bush down by the creek, not outta anyone's yard."

Noah raised his brows at Molly. "We believe you, Tom."

"I'll wash them and make a pie for supper." Molly turned to the cupboard to get a bowl.

"No." Noah's voice boomed through the tight kitchen area.

Molly spun around.

"You wash them up now." Noah stepped past her and removed three bowls from the cupboard. "I believe we have a little cream in the icebox. We'll have berries and cream for breakfast."

Fisting her hands to her hips, Molly stared Noah down for a few seconds. "We just ate breakfast." She'd seen his disappointment this morning when she told him the bread, boiled eggs, and ham that congregants had brought as their tithes were gone. She looked at the slop bucket and dropped her arms to her sides. "I'm sorry I'm not a better cook."

"What you lack in kitchen abilities, I gain in service assistance and cleaning."

Noah's earnest expression told Molly he meant every word he just uttered. Her face flushed from his praise.

"I'll get fresh water out of the reservoir so you can wash the berries." Noah grabbed the bucket she'd been using to rinse the dishes. "I'll be right back."

"Tom, wash your hands in my dishpan. Your face, too." Molly handed him a soft towel.

"Yes, ma'am." Tom smiled up at her.

"You didn't forget our agreement?" Molly lowered her voice. Noah had never said if he fully believed Seth about Cass. She didn't want to take any chances.

"No." Tom rolled the lye soap over and over in his hands.

"You've been spending a lot of time here." Molly's aggravation intoned her statement. Tom had spent most of his waking hours with her. She worried Cass had come to town and left again in the two weeks that had passed since the railroad parked *Emmanuel*.

Tom stopped scrubbing his hands. "I like it here. I feel safe. I thought we was friends." His bottom lip trembled.

In an instant, Molly regretted her tone. She wrapped an arm around his shoulders. "We are friends. I just don't want you to miss giving Cass my message when he comes to town."

"I won't. He only comes to town at night."

∽∾

Noah smiled out at the gathering of family and friends who'd come to witness a marriage ceremony of two of the residents. His first wedding officiating, and he'd worked hard marking the pages of the marriage ceremony book and special verses in the Bible. He wanted this couple off to a good start.

His heart sank a few inches in his chest. It took effort to keep his smile on his face. Didn't he and Molly deserve a good start, too, loveless marriage or not? Pastor Glass only had time to recite a Bible verse and administer their vows.

Molly's solid soprano hit the hymn's ending note, the wholeness rang through the sparkling chapel car. What she lacked in cooking, she made up for in cleanliness and worship assistance.

The happy couple repeated after Noah, and he pronounced them man and wife. The groom lovingly embraced the bride. They shared their public kiss. Noah chanced a glance at Molly. Her lips were drawn into a soft smile. Her fingers brushed the skin below her eyes.

His heart sank as low as it could go. She deserved better. She deserved a husband who loved her. She deserved to live a life of her own choosing.

"Pastor Manning."

His name drew him from his thoughts. He returned the mother of the bride's smile.

"We are having a dinner at our home. We'd be pleased if you and your wife could join us."

The thought of succulent food made Noah's mouth water. He motioned for Molly to approach them. "We have been invited to the wedding dinner. Shall we accept?"

"Yes." Molly's smile faded. "I'm sorry." She looked from Noah to the woman. "What about Tom? He's waiting in our living quarters. Would you mind if he joined us?"

Noah studied Molly while she conversed with the parishioner and marveled at her manners. She'd held on to her upbringing under difficult circumstances. How had Cass not? There was no doubt in Noah's mind Cass rode on the wrong side of the law, man's and God's.

When Molly's smile fell and concern veiled her blue eyes, Noah turned his attention to the woman. Her smile thinned into a grim line. She wrung her hands. "I know it's our Christian duty to feed the poor. He may eat in the kitchen with our servants, and I'll have Cook keep an eye on him. You do realize"—the woman leaned closer to Molly and Noah—"he's an outlaw's son."

❧

"We have a surprise for you." Molly had purposely chosen plain fabric for her two everyday dresses. She'd been frugal with the cloth and managed to pattern a shirt out of the green and breeches out of the brown. The sturdy cotton should serve Tom well until his next growth spurt.

Tom stood before Molly and Noah in the kitchen of the chapel car. Molly handed him a parcel wrapped in plain brown paper tied with a string. She suspected he'd never received a gift before after listening to the endless innuendos during the wedding dinner. It was the consensus of the dinner guests that Tom's mother was a soiled dove and his father an outlaw.

Molly studied Tom's features as he tugged on the string to open the package. A thought niggled at the back of her mind, a knowing really. He did resemble Cass in many ways. Yet if Molly believed Tom was her nephew, that meant she believed Cass was an outlaw. She shook her head. It couldn't be true. Their parents taught them to live by the Ten Commandments.

"New clothes." Tom grabbed the clothing. The paper dropped to the floor. He held the shirt to his shoulders. The olive green complemented his brown eyes. Tucking the shirt under his chin, he held the pants to his waist. "Look, they go clear to my ankles."

Noah clapped Tom's back. "You can put them on after you take a bath." Noah pointed at the filled tub sitting beside the cookstove.

Tom wrinkled his nose then looked down at his new clothes. "Okay."

Noah shooed Molly out of the kitchen and closed the door behind her. She seized the opportunity to practice her hymns.

A short time later, a door creaked open. Molly stopped playing and turned on the organ bench. Tom ran toward her, arms out. "Thank you." His little arms wrapped around her neck.

Molly returned his embrace. She'd forgotten how wonderful a hug felt.

Too soon Tom's arms released his hold. "What do you think?"

"You look handsome." Molly rolled the cuffs of his shirt to adjust them to the length of his arms.

"Noah said you made these." Tom pulled on the loose legs of his new britches. "I did."

"Why are you so nice to me when other people aren't?"

Molly's breath hitched in her throat. Her gasp echoed through the silent chapel car. "Because my parents taught me the Lord wants us to serve others."

"Why?"

"It's the right thing to do. God gave us ten commandments to follow. One of them is to love your neighbor as you love yourself."

Tom's face scrunched. "Even when people are mean to you?"

Molly drew a deep breath. "Yes. Before I became Noah's wife, I lived with people who made me sing songs I didn't like because they weren't very nice. Whenever I faced difficulties there, I remembered my favorite Bible verse from Romans 7:22. " 'For I delight in the law of God after the inward man.' It always made me feel better."

Tom repeated the verse. "I'll try to remember it. I'm going to the train depot so people can see my new clothes."

Molly watched Tom run down the aisle. When he was out of sight, she glanced up at Noah. Tenderness shone from his eyes.

"Molly, that is my favorite Bible verse, too." He stepped toward her. "It's the Bible verse that convinced me to follow my heart and teach God's laws rather than enforce man's like the rest of the Manning men."

Sliding from the organ bench, Molly walked over to Noah. "I might not remember much about my parents, but I do remember how proud my mother was of your choice. She couldn't understand why your family rebuked the idea of their kin being a man of the cloth."

Happiness shone from Noah's eyes before a wide smile creased his face. "Thank you for telling me that, Molly."

Noah reached out and drew her to him. Caught off guard, she stumbled into his arms. Placing her palms on his chest to steady herself, she looked up to find Noah's eyes filled with emotion. "You don't know how much it means to me to know other people don't think I'm a coward for preaching God's Word."

Molly planned to respond, but Noah's lips captured her voice. Her heart beat a rapid tempo in her ears when Noah deepened the kiss and pulled her closer to him. Happiness swirled through Molly.

Noah ended the kiss and looked into her eyes. Something deep inside of her stirred. Was it love, and did Noah feel it, too?

Chapter 7

Molly walked on air for days after their kiss, although their daily routine returned to normal. She'd pondered what the kiss meant to Noah. Shyness overtook her, and she couldn't muster up the nerve to ask him.

She stopped sweeping the chapel's aisle and closed her eyes, savoring the memory of the light that sparkled in his eyes after the kiss. He'd held her gaze for only a moment before he'd released her, cleared his throat, and left the chapel car, but even in her surprise, she'd seen the swirl of emotion his dark eyes emitted. Noah hadn't said so, but surely, it was love. Hope filled every inch of her soul.

The outer door to the chapel car opened and Noah entered carrying a small gunnysack.

"How is Mrs. Mount?" Molly stepped aside to allow Noah to pass.

He stopped in front of her. "Not well. I believe she is close to meeting the Lord. Her daughter sent us some canned beef and pickled vegetables. I'll put them in the pantry."

Thank You, Lord. Married a month and still Molly's cooking skills hadn't improved.

In minutes Noah returned. "I need to talk to you, Molly."

His deep frown concerned her. Had she done something to displease him? Her gaze roamed the chapel car searching for dust particles or smudges a congregant may have complained about. Or was he going to profess his love and he was afraid she didn't return his feelings? Or worse yet was he going to tell her the kiss was a mistake?

Her heart skittered through her chest.

"Please sit." Noah folded his lanky frame onto the seat of the pew, linking his fingers together and twiddling his thumbs.

The silent anticipation frazzled Molly's nerves.

Finally, Noah drew and released a deep breath. He stared directly into Molly's eyes. "I've wired Seth. He'll be here by tomorrow evening."

"What?" Flabbergasted at the reality of the conversation, Molly couldn't quite grasp what Noah was trying to say.

"I've alerted Seth about Cass."

A cloud of anger covered Molly's heart. "How could you?"

"Because it's the right thing to do. I've spoken with enough town folks to know. Cass's hideout is somewhere in the mountains around this town."

"Hideout? You make Cass sound like an outlaw." Molly's voice rose with her growing ire.

"Molly." Noah reached for her hand.

She pulled it away. "Cass isn't an outlaw."

"I wish that were true. Everyone in town knows Cass is a rustler."

"I don't believe it. If only Cass would come to town and clear up this confusion." Her heart dipped at her words. Was she the one who was confused?

"Search your heart, Molly. You'll find the evidence weighs against your brother. I know you love him, but with what he's done to you and. . ."

Noah's voice trailed off. He swallowed hard. "The entire town suspects Tom helps Cass because Tom is his son."

"I don't believe you or them. It's just gossip and can't be true." Molly wanted to jump up and run away. Yet where would she go, and what would happen to Tom if she did?

◦◦◦◦◦◦

Noah hated delivering bad news, especially to Molly. She'd had such a tough life. It didn't seem fair to add to it. She'd avoided him since their argument. He knew they shouldn't let the sun go down on their anger, but duty called him to Mrs. Mount's sickbed.

He focused on the bright full moon that seemed suspended over the blacksmith's shop. His footsteps sounded like thunder on the boardwalks in the midnight hour. Mrs. Mount had passed away a short while ago.

Although he knew glory awaited her soul, the loss added to his sullen mood. At least he'd experienced a wedding and death during what he was certain would be a short pastoral appointment once the Christian Committee learned of Molly's shameful family, none of which was her doing.

A small ball of anger formed in his gut at the thought of anyone thinking less of Molly. Everything about her was wonderful. Well, maybe not her cooking. Noah smiled for a moment before he allowed it to fade. He shouldn't have kissed her. He'd yielded to his temptation. It couldn't happen again. Molly had been forced into an unwanted life, he couldn't do that to her again. Once Seth apprehended Cass, Noah would figure out a way for their marriage to be dissolved so Molly could begin to live the life God intended for her.

Noah paused and leaned against the corner of a store. He needed to pray these burdens be lifted from him.

A shadow moved in the alley between the store and blacksmith's shop. A dim light from an upstairs window threw the silhouette of a man and child against the building.

Worry niggled at Noah's mind. Molly had mentioned that Tom lived in a lean-to somewhere back there. He stepped carefully down the wooden steps. With his back to the side of the building, Noah inched along the wall, staying in the shadows.

He stopped before he reached the end of the building's outer wall so he could remain in the shadows. Tom faced his way. He didn't appear scared or worried. The man's head was bent. He held something in his hand. Noah wished their positions were reversed. Then the man spoke. Noah didn't need to see his face.

Noah knew.

It was Cass.

Cass reached into his pocket, drew out a pencil, and scratched on the paper he held. "I'll be back in three days for those supplies. Give this to Molly."

Tom nodded and retreated to his shanty.

All of this time Molly knew Tom had contact with Cass. She'd sent him a message. Of warning, no doubt. Could she be in on this scheme? Had she really been captive and forced to sing those songs?

There was one way to find out. Noah stepped from the shadows while Cass mounted his horse.

"If it isn't the happy groom."

The venom in Cass's tone raised the hair on the back of Noah's neck.

"My sister needs to go back to the saloon owner. That is her life now."

"No, it's not. She has a better life with me in a loveless marriage than what she's lived the past five years." The moment the words left his lips, Noah's heart rebelled. He'd lied. Their marriage wasn't loveless. He loved Molly.

The evil lilt in Cass's laughter sent a shiver up Noah's spine. Confirming the friend he'd once known was gone. "Send her back." Cass pulled his gun and cocked it. "And tell your brother to stop trailing me or you're gonna be performing a funeral."

Froze in place, Noah watched Cass ride away.

❧

The next morning as Noah watched Molly bustle around the kitchen, he wrestled with his inaction. Should he have done something to stop Cass from leaving town? No matter what scenario he played in his head, the answer always came around to yes.

Maybe he was a coward hiding behind the pulpit. Shame shuddered through him. He hung his head. He imagined the ridicule he'd hear when Seth arrived today.

The door to the living quarters squeaked.

"'Morning."

"Good morning, Tom. You are just in time for breakfast."

No footsteps scuffed across the hardwood kitchen floor.

Noah raised his head. Tom wore a somber expression and stayed planted on the threshold.

"I need to talk to you, Molly." His gaze darted to Noah. "By ourselves."

Molly's brows knitted together. She sat a bowl of lumpy oatmeal in front of Noah.

"Wait in the chapel. I'll be right there."

Noah opened his mouth to tell Molly husbands and wives had no secrets, but since they were husband and wife in name only, did he have a right? Besides he knew why Tom wanted to see Molly alone. The little scamp needed to give her Cass's note. Had Cass been using him for more than supplies? Did Tom help Cass to avoid the law?

After their conversation last night, Noah had a good idea what the note said. His heart clenched at the thought of Molly being disappointed by Cass. Cass had shown Molly the stark realities of life at a young age. Tom, too, for that matter.

The need to protect the two he'd grown to love grew so strong in Noah, he pushed back from the table and strode to the door separating the living quarters from the chapel car. No more being a coward, he needed to tell Molly the truth. He'd fallen in love with her.

Noah planned to burst through the door until he saw Molly embracing Tom through the cracked opening. Tears smattered both of their cheeks.

"Please, don't go away." Tom's plea sent a shiver of fear down Noah's spine. He'd never considered Molly wouldn't stay here with him.

Molly pulled Tom to arm's length. "I don't want to." She swiped at her tears with the back of her hand. "But I can't let Cass hurt Noah or Seth."

"Don't you love us?"

"That is the reason I have to leave, because I love you both very much." Happiness lurched inside of Noah. He needed to proclaim his love to Molly. He opened the door wider and stepped into the chapel car at the same time Seth entered the outer door and scuffed up the aisle. While Molly and Tom looked Seth's way, Noah closed the door making his presence known.

"You must have ridden all night." Noah greeted his brother.

"I did." Seth glanced around the room, slightly frowning when his gaze settled on Tom. "You need to run along now."

Tom gave Seth a wide berth, like he was diseased, and scurried down the aisle.

Molly narrowed her eyes and glared at Seth.

Noah hated the tone Seth used to send the boy away, too. Yet he didn't know if Tom was an innocent pawn or if his loyalty lay with Cass. Noah couldn't take a chance on the latter.

Chapter 8

Molly huffed from the train's sanctuary with Tom's dismissal.

Seth shot Noah a lopsided smile and rubbed his chin. "I chafe against your wife's grain."

"Yes, you do. Try being nice to her."

Seth's brows arched. "Well, fancy that. I made a good match after all."

He had, not that Noah would ever admit it to Seth. "You could have taken your time. I saw Cass last night. He won't be back in town for three days." Noah paused, placing his hand on Seth's shoulder. "He plans to kill you."

"Comes with wearing the star, but thank you for your concern."

For once, Seth didn't look at him with contempt in his eyes. Noah gave Seth's shoulder a small squeeze before he dropped his hand.

"Do you have a gun?"

Noah shook his head.

Seth pulled a six-shooter from a holster on his hip and stuck the pearled handle out.

After a moment of hesitation, Noah drew a deep breath and took the gun.

"I have a room at the hotel with a window facing *Emmanuel's* entry door, so I can watch the comings and goings. You won't see me again until Cass comes to town."

"Okay." Noah stuck the gun barrel in the waist of his breeches. He'd stash it under his bunk when Molly wasn't around.

৩৩

Molly's emotions had rolled like train wheels for the past two days. Noah acted like he had something important to say. Every time he looked at her, a new appreciation shone in his eyes. Her heart soared, thinking he returned her love, until her head reasoned a good man like Noah would never love her because of her past and her family. Cass's note confirmed in her mind that Seth was right. Her brother was an outlaw.

She wanted to run away. The only thing that stopped her was Tom. She couldn't leave him behind, and she had no way to support him without Noah. So she stayed put, failing at cooking, and assisting with service, which was almost over for tonight.

At Noah's "Amen," she started playing the last hymn of the evening. The congregation stood and raised their voices. Molly's gaze roved the sea of faces in the chapel car; her eyes locked with those of a cowboy leaning against the back wall

440

who still wore his hat in church.

Molly's fingers continued to press the organ keys, but her voice faltered as the familiar eyes narrowed, sending a threatening shiver up her spine. *Cass.* She knew by his stance and his eyes; nothing else about him looked like the brother she once knew.

Scraggly blond hair hung to his shoulders. A scar ripped across his cheek. She should alert Noah, yet she couldn't break their stare, and as usual Noah had walked down the aisle to the back of the chapel car.

She held the last chord until it faded. Noah gave the benediction, and the congregation started to file out of their seats. Cass didn't move. With her gaze still fixed to him, Molly rose from the organ bench and made her way around the pulpit to the aisle.

Tom started to rise from a seat in the second row. The movement pulled her gaze away from Cass. "Stay there."

Warning threaded her command. Tom's eyes grew wide. He turned around.

Cass let the last congregant pass then stepped into the aisle to block Molly's path.

"You're going back to the saloon." He grabbed her arm. His tight grip pinched her skin. She bit her lip to keep from crying out as he started to drag her toward the back of the chapel car.

"Leave her alone, Cass." Tom ran toward them and pulled at Cass's grip.

Cass shoved him hard, sending him reeling into the nearest pew. His soft whimper when he hit the hard wooden seat broke Molly's heart and raised her ire. She flailed and twisted her arm in an effort to escape. Where was Noah?

Cass's grip tightened.

"Let go of me!"

"No."

"Let her go." Noah's voice was soft but authoritative. He'd come back into the chapel car after shaking the last congregant's hand. Surely Cass would respect a man of the cloth, who was once his best friend.

"Can't." Cass pulled a gun.

Noah raised his hands.

"Get over there with the boy." Cass jerked his head in Tom's direction.

Slowly, Noah walked around them.

"Help me." Molly reached her free hand out to him. Noah kept backing away. The pinch of her heart was ten times worse than the pinching on her arm where Cass held her. She'd been wrong. Noah didn't care for her. He'd married her out of respect to her mother and nothing more.

"Help her, Noah," Tom pleaded.

But Noah kept backing away from them until his boot thudded against the raised altar; then he turned and quickly entered the living quarters, slamming the door behind him.

A sob caught in Molly's throat. She'd have to save herself. She beat a fist against her brother's hold until the cold barrel of his pistol poked into her side. He pushed her through the outer door and down the wrought-iron step. Fear's chill goose-fleshed her skin.

"Leave her be. She's my friend. I'm not gonna help you anymore." Tom jerked on Cass's sleeve, causing him to stumble as he stepped from the train stair.

Molly jerked her arm hard to free herself. It didn't work. Cass's grip tightened. He dragged her around the side of the train car to where his horse was tied. Tom ran along behind them.

A clear image of her parents' faces popped into her mind, bringing her comfort and strength. "Cass, what's happened to you? Don't you remember our loving family? What our parents taught us about God? Why are you being so hateful to me?"

Cass paused a moment. His face remained hard. "Are you going to get up on the horse, or do I have to throw you up there?"

"You're not going anywhere." Seth stepped from the shadows, rifle aimed at Cass.

In a swift move, Cass pulled Molly and Tom in front of him. "I'm not afraid of you, Seth. Especially now. Your aim isn't sure enough to miss Molly and Tom. If it was Noah holding that rifle, I'd take pause. I saw him shoot a wolf off the back of a deer it was attacking without harming a hair on the deer."

A click behind them silenced Cass.

"I'm glad you remember something about your past."

Cass turned, bringing Molly and Tom with him.

Noah. Hope filled Molly. Yet he didn't seem to see her or Tom as he walked closer to the trio.

"Remember your upbringing. Let them go. You don't want to harm your family. Surrender to Seth."

Noah's words snapped something inside of Molly. "I'm not his family. I haven't been since he dropped me off at the saloon. Why did you do it, Cass? Why did you abandon me?"

A guttural laugh burst from her brother. "I didn't abandon you. I lost you in a poker game the same way I lost our farm." Cass shook Tom's shoulder. "I'm not claiming this one, either."

∞

The hurt on Molly's face at Seth's confession broke Noah's heart. All he wanted to do was drop the gun, wrap her in his arms, and love her for the rest of his life.

He couldn't though, not yet. Seth had been creeping up behind Cass while Noah distracted him.

Seth was in arm's reach when he kicked a rock and startled Cass. Molly saw an opportunity. Instead of saving herself, she shoved Tom out of harm's way. Cass wrapped his arm across her chest while Molly struggled to free herself and turned toward Seth. The barrel of Cass's pistol pointed at Molly's head.

Noah set his jaw. He knew he could shoot Cass and not harm Molly. At this moment that was all he wanted to do. However, his vocation was preaching God's Word not upholding man's law. He couldn't shoot Cass. Noah turned his gun, took two quick steps, and rapped Cass's head with the six-shooter handle.

Cass dropped to the ground. Noah caught Molly in his arms so she didn't fall. Shivering, she nestled close to him and buried her face in his shoulder. Tom ran over and hugged Noah.

He'd done it. He'd protected the family he loved.

Seth kneeled down, handcuffed Cass's still body, and rolled him over faceup. When he stood, he smiled at Noah. "Good job, brother. You'd have made a good lawman."

Noah drew a deep breath and braced for his brother's criticism.

"But you make a better preacher. You're a brave man going against family tradition."

Emotion clogged Noah's throat. He swallowed hard before he smiled at Seth. "Thank you."

"I owe you and Molly an apology."

Molly lifted her head and looked at Cass.

"I knew Molly's presence would lure Cass out of hiding, but I also wanted her protected. I knew you were the perfect person to keep her safe. I didn't mean to force you into marriage. I can talk to a judge."

Molly's gasp echoed through the silent night. Noah's heart dipped. He'd never be happy without her, even if it meant he had to change his occupation.

"No."

Molly turned and searched his face at his firm refusal.

When her pretty blue eyes locked to his, he saw a flicker of hope and knew it was time to reveal his heart.

"I love you, Molly. I want to be married to you."

"You don't care about my past and the reputation it brings?"

Noah pursed his lips and shook his head.

A sheen of moisture covered Molly's eyes. "We'll be husband and wife in *every* way?"

"Yes." Noah pulled her closer to him. "Will you continue to be my wife?"

"I'd be honored to stay married to the man I love."

∞

One month later, Molly and Tom stood outside the entry door of the chapel car *Emmanuel*.

"Stop being so antsy." Molly placed a hand on Tom's shoulder.

"The suit's scratchy." Tom started wiggling again.

"Well, you look handsome." Molly smiled at the nephew that she and Noah would raise as their son.

"You look pretty, too."

Molly looked down at the white lace wedding gown that Noah insisted on buying for her to wear when he told her she deserved a proper wedding.

"There's the music." Tom opened the door and allowed Molly to step inside. Once inside, Tom slipped his small hand into hers. She couldn't have been happier to have her nephew escort her down the aisle and become part of their family.

She paused in the entry while the small congregation stood.

Pastor Glass sat behind the organ with a welcoming smile that erased all of his sternness. He'd been pleased to officiate their wedding, again. Although it was hard, they'd lived chaste while waiting for Pastor Glass. Noah and Molly only recited their vows the first time. This time they'd mean their pledge.

Upon his arrival, Pastor Glass praised Noah for the fine job of spreading God's message in the first stop of his railroad ministry, and also credited Molly's assistance as part of the success. He planned to put Noah's name in for a transfer to a railroad car with bigger living quarters to better house his growing family.

Noah waited in front of the altar railing looking handsome in his new brown suit. Emotion formed a lump in Molly's throat when her eyes found Noah's. The tender love that emanated from his brown eyes assured her she was loved and erased all the pain and shame of her past.

Molly longed to race down the aisle and into Noah's arms but took deliberate, slow steps for propriety's sake. She'd never do anything to besmirch Noah's vocation. The world needed more brave men, like her intended.

Once they reached the altar, Tom placed Molly's hand in Noah's. Pastor Glass finished playing and came to stand before the lectern. Tom sat beside Seth in the first pew to bear witness to their vows along with the town congregants. Molly listened close and took to heart the Bible verse the pastor chose. It wasn't her and Noah's favorite, but a very appropriate scripture for two people joining their hearts and lives. When he asked them to take their vows, Molly stared deeply into Noah's brown eyes and allowed herself to revel in the love she saw there and hoped her love for him shone in her own.

When Pastor Glass instructed Noah to kiss the bride, he tenderly gathered

Molly in his arms. His soft lips found hers. Powerful emotions swirled through Molly, weakening her knees and making her glad Noah's strong arms held her close. The congregation clapped when Noah ended the kiss.

"That was the first of many kisses I plan to give you, Mrs. Manning," Noah whispered.

"I will accept them all." Molly smiled through happy tears.

Feeling safe and loved, Molly sent a silent thank-you to God for blessing her with a husband who knew His laws and upheld them in the same way she did.

Multi-published author and RITA finalist, **Rose Ross Zediker** writes contemporary and historical inspirational romances and has over eighty publishing credits in the Christian magazine genre for children and adults. Rose works full-time at the University of South Dakota and writes during the evening or weekends. She is a member of American Christian Fiction Writers and Romance Writers of America.

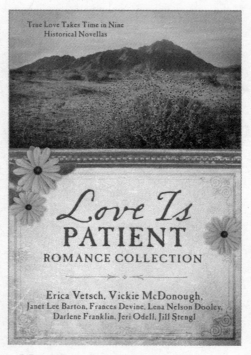